ALSO BY HARLAN COBEN

HARLAN COBEN

FOOL ME ONCE

DUTTON

An imprint of Penguin Random House LLC
penguinrandomhouse.com

Previously published as a Dutton hardcover.

First premium mass market printing, August 2016
First movie tie-in mass market paperback edition: December 2023

Dutton mass market movie tie-in paperback ISBN 9780593475355

Printed in the United States of America
10 9 8 7 6 5 4 3 2 1

For Charlotte:
Doesn't matter how old you get,
you're still my little girl

Chapter 1

They buried Joe three days after his murder. Maya wore black, as befitted a grieving widow. The sun pounded down with an unflagging fury that reminded her of her months in the desert. The family pastor spouted the clichés, but Maya wasn't listening. Her eyes drifted to the schoolyard across the street.

Yes, the cemetery overlooked an elementary school.

Maya had driven past here countless times, the graveyard on the left, the elementary school on her right, and yet the strangeness, if not obscenity, of the placement had never really registered with her before. Which came first, she wondered, the schoolyard or the cemetery? Who'd been the one to decide to build a school next to a cemetery—or vice versa? Did it even matter, this life-ending and life-beginning juxtaposition, or was it, in fact, somewhat poignant? Death is so close, always, a breath away, so perhaps it was wise to introduce children to that concept at an early age.

Maya filled her head with inanities like this as she watched Joe's casket disappear into the earth. Distract yourself. That was the key. Get through it.

The black dress itched. Over the past decade, Maya had been to a hundred-plus funerals, but this was the first time she'd been obligated to wear black. She hated it.

To her right, Joe's immediate family—his mother, Judith; his brother Neil; his sister, Caroline—wilted from the combination of high temperatures and deep sorrow. To her left, getting antsy and starting to use Maya's arm as a rope swing, was her (and Joe's) two-year-old daughter, Lily. The parenting cliché states that children do not come with instruction manuals. That never seemed more true than today. What, Maya had wondered, was the proper etiquette for a situation like this? Do you leave your two-year-old daughter at home—or do you take her to her father's funeral? That was an issue that they didn't cover on those know-it-all, one-size-fits-all mommy websites. In a fit of pity-anger, Maya had almost posted that question online: "Hi, Everyone! My husband was recently murdered. Should I bring my two-year-old daughter to the graveyard or leave her home? Oh, and clothing suggestions? Thanks!"

There were hundreds of people at the funeral, and in some dimly lit corner of her brain, she realized that this would have pleased Joe. Joe liked people. People liked Joe. But of course, popularity alone wouldn't explain the crowd. Mourners had been drawn in by the horrible lure of being near the tragic: a young man gunned down in cold blood, the charming scion of the wealthy Burkett family—and the husband of a woman mired in an international scandal.

Lily wrapped both arms around her mother's leg. Maya bent down and whispered, "Not much longer, sweetheart, okay?"

Lily nodded but held on even tighter.

Maya stood back at attention, smoothing the itchy black dress she'd borrowed from Eileen with both hands. Joe would not have wanted her in black. He'd always preferred her in the military formals she'd worn back in the days when she'd been Army Captain Maya Stern. When they'd first met at a Burkett family charity gala, Joe had walked straight up to her in his tails, given her the rakish smile (Maya hadn't understood the term "rakish" until she saw that smile), and said, "Wow, I thought the turn-on was supposed to be *men* in uniform."

It was a lame pickup line, just lame enough to make her laugh, which was all the opening a guy like Joe needed. Man, he was so damn handsome. The memory, even now, even standing in this stifling humidity with his dead body feet away, made her smile. A year later, Maya and Joe were married. Lily came not long after that. And now, as though someone had fast-forwarded a life-together tape, here she was, burying her husband and the father of her only child.

"All love stories," Maya's father had told her many years ago, "end in tragedy."

Maya had shaken her head and said, "God, Dad, that's grim."

"Yes, but think about it: You either fall out of love, or, if you're really one of the lucky ones, you live long enough to watch your soul mate die."

Maya could still see her father sitting across from her at the kitchen table of yellowing Formica laminate in their Brooklyn town house. Dad wore his customary cardigan sweater (all professions, not just those in the military, wear uniforms of some kind or another), surrounded by the college essays he'd have to grade. He and Mom had died years ago, within months of each other, but in truth, it was still hard for Maya to know which category of tragedy their love story fell into.

As the pastor prattled on, Judith Burkett, Joe's mother, took hold of Maya's hand in the death grip of the grieving.

"This," the old woman mumbled, "is even worse."

Maya didn't ask for clarification. She didn't have to. This was the second time Judith Burkett had been forced to bury a child, two of her three sons now gone, one supposedly by tragic accident, one by murder. Maya glanced down at her own child, at the top of Lily's head, and wondered how a mother could live with such pain.

As if she knew what Maya was thinking, the old woman whispered, "It'll never be okay," her simple words cutting through the air like a reaper's scythe. "Never."

"It's my fault," Maya said.

She hadn't meant to say it. Judith looked up at her.

"I should have . . ."

"There was nothing you could have done," Judith said. But there was still something off in the tone. Maya understood, because others were probably thinking the same thing. Maya Stern had saved so many in the past. Why couldn't she have saved her own husband?

"Ashes to ashes . . ."

Wow, did the pastor really trot out that hackneyed chestnut or had Maya imagined it? She hadn't been paying attention. She never did at funerals. She had been around death too many times not to understand the secret to getting through them: Go numb. Don't focus on anything. Let all sounds and sights blur to the point of being unrecognizable.

Joe's casket reached bottom with a thud that echoed too long in the still air. Judith swayed against Maya and let out a low groan. Maya maintained her military bearing—head high, spine straight, shoulders back. She recently had read one of those self-help articles people always emailed around about "power poses" and how they were supposed to improve performance. The military understood that tidbit of pop psychology way before its time. As a soldier, you don't stand at attention because it looks nice. You stand at attention because, on some level, it either gives you strength or, just as important, makes you appear stronger to both your comrades and enemies.

For a moment, Maya flashed back to the park—the glint of metal, the sound of gunshots, Joe falling, Maya's shirt covered in blood, stumbling through the dark, distant streetlights giving off hazy halos of illumination . . .

"Help . . . please . . . someone . . . my husband's . . ."

She closed her eyes and pushed it away.

Hang on, she told herself now. *Just get through it.*

And she did.

Then there was the receiving line.

The only two places you stand on receiving lines are funerals and weddings. There was probably something poignant in that fact, but Maya couldn't imagine what it could be.

She had no idea how many people walked past her, but it took hours. Mourners shuffled forward like a scene in some zombie movie where you slay one but more just keep coming at you.

Just keep it moving.

Most offered a low "Sorry for your loss," which was pretty much the perfect thing to say. Others talked too much. They started in about how tragic it all was, what a waste, how the city was going to hell, how they were almost robbed at gunpoint once (rule one: never make it about yourself on a receiving line), how they hoped the police fried the animals who did it, how fortunate Maya was, how God must have been looking out for her (the implication being, she guessed, that God hadn't cared as much about Joe), how there is always a plan, how there is a reason for everything (a wonder she didn't punch those people straight in the face).

Joe's family grew exhausted and had to sit midway through. Not Maya. She stood throughout, maintained direct eye contact, and greeted each mourner with a firm handshake. She used subtle and not-so-subtle body language to rebuff those who wanted to be more expressive in their grief via hugs or kisses. Inane as their words might have been, Maya listened attentively, nodded, said, "Thank you for coming" in the same sincere-ish tone, and then greeted the next person in line.

Other hard-and-fast rules of the receiving line at a funeral: Don't talk too much. Short platitudes work well because innocuous is far better than offensive. If you feel the need to say more, make it a nice, quick memory of the dead. Never do, for example, what Joe's aunt Edith did. Never cry hysterically and become the most theatrical "look at me, I'm suffering" of mourners—and never say something chillingly stupid to the grieving widow like: "You poor girl, first your sister, now your husband."

The world stopped for a moment when Aunt Edith voiced what so many others were thinking, especially when Maya's young nephew, Daniel, and younger niece, Alexa, were within earshot. The blood in Maya's veins thrummed, and it took everything she had not to reach out, grab Aunt Edith's throat, and rip her vocal cords out.

Instead, Maya said in a sincere-ish tone: "Thank you for coming."

Six of Maya's former platoon mates, including Shane, hung back, keeping a watchful eye on her. That was what they did, like it or not. Guard duty seemed to never end when they were together. They didn't get in line. They knew better. They were her silent sentinels, always, their presence offering the only true comfort on this horrible day.

Every once in a while, Maya thought that she could hear her daughter's distant giggle—her oldest friend, Eileen Finn, had taken Lily to the playground at the elementary school across the street—but maybe that was just her imagination. The sound of laughing children felt both obscene and life affirming in such a setting: She longed for it and couldn't bear it.

Daniel and Alexa, Claire's kids, were the last two in line. Maya swept them into her arms, wanting, as always, to protect them from anything else bad happening to them. Eddie, her brother-in-law . . . Is that what he was? What do you call the man who was married to your sister before she was murdered? "Ex-brother-in-law" seemed like something more for a divorce. Do you say "*former* brother-in-law"? Do you just stick with "brother-in-law"?

More inanity designed to distract.

Eddie approached more tentatively. There were tufts of hair on his face where he'd missed with the razor. Eddie kissed Maya's cheek. The smell of mouthwash and mints was strong enough to drown out whatever else might be there, but then again, wasn't that the point?

"I'm going to miss Joe," Eddie mumbled.

"I know you will. He liked you a lot, Eddie."

"If there's anything we can do . . ."

You can take better care of your kids, Maya thought, but her normal anger with him was gone now, leaked away like a raft with a pinhole.

"We're fine, thanks."

Eddie went silent, as if he too could read her mind, which in this case he probably could.

"Sorry I missed your last game," Maya said to Alexa, "but I'll be there tomorrow."

All three of them suddenly looked uneasy.

"Oh, you don't have to do that," Eddie said.

"It's okay. It'll be a nice distraction."

Eddie nodded, gathered up Daniel and Alexa, and headed to the car. Alexa looked back at her as she walked away. Maya gave her the reassuring smile. *Nothing has changed,* the smile said. *I will still always be there for you, just as I promised your mother.*

Maya watched Claire's family get into the car. Daniel, the outgoing fourteen-year-old, took the front seat. Alexa, who was only twelve, sat alone in the back. Since her mother's death, she seemed to always be wincing as though preparing for the next blow. Eddie waved, gave Maya a tired smile, and slipped into the driver's seat.

Maya waited, watching the car drive slowly away. When it did, she noticed NYPD homicide detective Roger Kierce standing in the distance, leaning against a tree. Even today. Even now. She was tempted to walk over and confront him, demand some answers, but Judith took her hand again.

"I'd like you and Lily to come back to Farnwood with us."

The Burketts always referred to their house by its name. That probably should have been clue one of what would become of her if she married into such a family.

"Thank you," Maya said, "but I think Lily needs to be home."

"She needs to be with family. You both do."

"I appreciate that."

"I mean it. Lily will always be our granddaughter. And you'll always be our daughter."

Judith gave her hand an extra squeeze to emphasize the sentiment. It was sweet of Judith to say, like something she was reading off a teleprompter at one of her charity galas, but it was also untrue—at least the part about Maya. No one who married a Burkett was anything but a tolerated outsider.

"Another time," Maya said. "I'm sure you understand."

Judith nodded and gave her a perfunctory hug. So

did Joe's brother and sister. She watched their devastated faces as they stumbled toward the stretch limos that would take them to the Burkett estate.

Her former platoon mates were still there. She met Shane's eyes and gave him a small nod. They got it. They didn't so much "fall out" as quietly fade away, being sure not to disturb anything in their wake. Most of them were still enlisted. After what happened near the Syrian-Iraqi border, Maya had been "encouraged" to take an honorable discharge. Seeing no other real option, she did. So now, instead of commanding or at least teaching the new recruits, retired Captain Maya Stern, for a short time the face of the new Army, gave flying lessons at Teterboro Airport in northern New Jersey. Some days it was okay. Most days she missed the service more than she'd have ever imagined.

Maya finally stood alone by the mound of dirt that would soon cover her husband.

"Ah, Joe," she said out loud.

She tried to feel a presence. She had tried this before, in countless mourning situations, seeing if she could sense any sort of life force after death, but there was always nothing. Some believed that there had to be at least a small life force—that energy and motion never die completely, that the soul is eternal, that you can't destroy matter permanently, all that. Perhaps that was true, but the more of the dead Maya hung around, the more it felt as though nothing, absolutely nothing, was left behind.

She stayed by the gravesite until Eileen came back from the playground with Lily.

"Ready?" Eileen asked.

Maya took another look at the hole in the ground. She wanted to say something profound to Joe, something that might give them both—ugh—closure, but no words came to her.

Eileen drove them home. Lily fell asleep in a car seat that looked like something designed by NASA. Maya sat in the front passenger seat and stared out the window. When they got to the house—Joe had actually wanted to name it too, but Maya had put her foot down—Maya somehow managed to release the complicated strapping mechanism and eased Lily out of the backseat. She cradled Lily's head so as not to wake her.

"Thanks for the ride," Maya whispered.

Eileen turned off the car. "Do you mind if I come in for a second?"

"We'll be fine."

"No doubt." Eileen unbuckled her seat belt. "But I've been meaning to give you something. It'll just take two minutes."

Maya held it in her hand. "A digital picture frame?"

Eileen was a strawberry blonde with freckles and a wide smile. She had the kind of face that lit up a room when she entered, which made it a great mask for the torment beneath.

"No, it's a nanny cam disguised as a digital picture frame."

"Say again?"

"Now that you're working full-time, you've got to keep a better eye on things, right?"

"I guess so."

"Where does Isabella play with Lily most of the time?"

Maya gestured to her right. "In the den."

"Come on, I'll show you."

"Eileen . . ."

She took the frame from Maya's hand. "Just follow me."

The den was right off the kitchen. It had a cathedral ceiling and plenty of blond wood. A big-screen television hung on the wall. There were two baskets filled to the brim with educational toys for Lily. A Pack 'n Play stood in front of the couch where there used to be a beautiful mahogany coffee table. The coffee table, alas, hadn't been child friendly, so it had to go.

Eileen moved toward the bookshelf. She found a spot for the frame and plugged the cord into a nearby outlet. "I already preloaded some pictures of your family. The digital frame will just shuffle through and display them. Do Isabella and Lily normally play by that couch?"

"Yes."

"Good." Eileen shifted the frame in that direction. "The camera built inside this thing is wide-angle, so you can see the whole room."

"Eileen—"

"I saw her at the funeral."

"Who?"

"Your nanny."

"Isabella's family goes way back with Joe's. Her mother was Joe's nanny. Her brother is the family gardener."

"For real?"

Maya shrugged. "The rich."

"They're different."

"They are."

"So do you trust her?"

"Who, Isabella?"

"Yes."

Maya shrugged. "You know me."

"I do." Eileen had originally been Claire's friend— the two had been assigned as freshman roommates at Vassar—but all three women quickly grew close. "You trust no one, Maya."

"I wouldn't put it that way."

"Fine. When it comes to your child?"

"When it comes to my child," Maya said, "yeah, okay, no one."

Eileen smiled. "That's why I'm giving you this.

Look, I don't think you'll find anything. Isabella seems great."

"But better safe than sorry?"

"Exactly. I can't tell you how much comfort it gave me when I left Kyle and Missy with the nanny."

Maya wondered about that—whether Eileen had just used it with the nanny or whether she had built a case against someone else—but she kept the thought to herself for now.

"Do you have an SD card port on your computer?" Eileen asked.

"I'm not sure."

"Doesn't matter. I got you an SD reader that connects into any USB port. Just plug it into your laptop or computer. Really, it doesn't get easier than this. You take the SD card out of the frame at the end of the day—it's back here, see?"

Maya nodded.

"Then you stick the card into the reader. The video pops up on your screen. The SD is thirty-two gigs, so it should last days easily. There's also a motion detector, so it's not recording when the room is empty or anything like that."

Maya couldn't help but smile. "Look at you."

"What? The role reversal bothering you?"

"A little. I should have thought of doing this myself."

"I'm surprised you didn't."

Maya looked down and met her friend's eye. Eileen was maybe five two, Maya nearly six feet tall, but with the ramrod posture, she looked even taller. "Did you ever see anything on your nanny cam?"

"You mean, something I shouldn't have?"

"Yeah."

"No," Eileen said. "And I know what you're thinking. He hasn't been back. And I haven't seen him."

"I'm not judging."

"Not even a little?"

"What kind of friend would I be if I didn't judge a little?"

Eileen came over and wrapped her arms around Maya. Maya hugged her back. Eileen wasn't a quasi-stranger paying her respects. Maya ended up going to Vassar a year after Claire. The three women had lived together in those halcyon days before Maya had started Army Aviation School at Fort Rucker in Alabama. Eileen was still, along with Shane, her closest friend.

"I love you, you know."

Maya nodded. "Yeah, I know."

"You sure you don't want me to stay?"

"You have your own family to take care of."

"It's okay," Eileen said, pointing at the digital frame with her thumb. "I'm still watching."

"Funny."

"Not really. But I know you need downtime. Call if you need anything. Oh, and don't worry about dinner.

I already ordered you Chinese from Look See. It'll be here in twenty minutes."

"I love you, you know."

"Yeah," Eileen said, heading to the door. "I know." She stopped. "Whoa."

"What is it?"

"You have company."

Chapter 2

The company was in the short, hirsute form of NYPD homicide detective Roger Kierce. Kierce entered the house with his best attempt at swagger, glancing all around the way cops do and saying, "Nice place."

Maya frowned, not bothering to hide her annoyance.

Kierce had something of a caveman thing going on. He was stocky and broad, and his arms seemed too short for his body. He had the kind of face that looked unshaven even immediately after a shave. His bushy eyebrows resembled a late stage of caterpillar metamorphosis, and the hair on the back of his hands could have been the work of a curling iron.

"Hope it's okay I stopped by."

"Why wouldn't it be okay?" Maya said. "Oh, right, that whole just-buried-my-husband thing."

Kierce feigned contrite. "I realize my timing could be better."

"You think?"

"But tomorrow you go back to work and, really, when is a good time?"

"Great point. What can I do for you, Detective?"

"Do you mind if I sit?"

Maya gestured toward the couch in the den. A spooky thought came to her: This encounter—in fact, every encounter in this room—would now be recorded by the hidden nanny cam. What an odd thing to think about. She could, of course, manually turn it on and off, but who would remember or want to go through that hassle every day? She wondered whether the camera recorded sound too. She would have to ask Eileen, or she could wait and see when she checked its content.

"Nice place," Kierce said.

"Yeah, you said that on the way in."

"What year was it built?"

"Sometime in the nineteen twenties."

"Your late husband's family. They own the house, right?"

"Yes."

Kierce sat. She stayed standing.

"So what can I do for you, Detective?"

"Just some follow-up, that kind of thing."

"Follow-up?"

"Bear with me, okay?" Kierce gave her what he must imagine was a disarming smile. Maya wasn't buying it. "Where is it . . . ?" He dug into his inside jacket pocket and pulled out a frayed notepad. "Do you mind if we go through it one more time?"

Maya wasn't sure what to make of him, which was probably what Kierce wanted. "What would you like to know?"

"Let's start at the beginning, okay?"

She sat and spread her hands as if to say, *Go ahead*.

"Why did you and Joe meet up in Central Park?"

"He asked me to."

"On the phone, right?"

"Yes."

"Was this normal?"

"We had met up there before, yes."

"When?"

"I don't know. A bunch of times. I told you. It's a nice area of the park. We used to spread out a blanket and then we'd have lunch at the Boathouse . . ." She caught herself, stopped, swallowed. "It was just a nice place, that's all."

"During the day, yes. But it's a little secluded at night, don't you think?"

"We always felt safe there."

He smiled at her. "I bet you feel safe most places."

"Meaning?"

"When you've been where you've been, I mean, in terms of dangerous places, I guess a park must rank pretty low." Kierce coughed into his fist. "Anyway, so your husband called you and said, 'Let's meet there,' and so you did."

"That's right."

"Except"—Kierce checked his notepad, licked his fingers, started paging through it—"he didn't call you."

He looked up at her.

"Excuse me?"

"You said Joe called you and said to meet you there."

"No, you said that. I said he suggested we meet there on the phone."

"But then I followed up with 'He called you' and you said, 'That's right.'"

"You're playing semantics with me, Detective. You have the phone records for that night, am I correct?"

"I do, yes."

"And it shows a phone call between my husband and me?"

"It does."

"I don't remember if I called him or he called me. But he suggested that we meet at our favorite spot in the park. I could have suggested it—I don't see the relevance—and in fact, I might have, had he not suggested it first."

"Can anyone verify that you and Joe used to meet up there?"

"I don't think so, but I don't see the relevance."

Kierce gave her an insincere smile. "Neither do I, so let's move on, shall we?"

She crossed her legs and waited.

"You describe two men approaching you from the west. Is that correct?"

"Yes."

"They wore ski masks?"

She had been through this dozens of times already. "Yes."

"Black ski masks, am I right?"

"You are."

"And you said that one was about six feet tall—how tall are you, Mrs. Burkett?"

She almost snapped that he should call her captain—she hated being called missus—but that rank wasn't apropos anymore. "Please call me Maya. And I'm right about six feet tall."

"So one man was your height."

She tried not to roll her eyes. "Uh, yes."

"You were pretty precise in your description of the assailants." Kierce started reading from his notepad. "One man was six feet tall. The other you estimated to be about five eight. One wore a black hoodie, jeans, and red Converse sneakers. The other wore a light blue T-shirt with no logo, beige backpack, and black running shoes, though you couldn't tell the brand."

"That's correct."

"The man with the red Cons—he was the one who shot your husband."

"Yes."

"And then you ran."

Maya said nothing.

"According to your statement, they wanted to rob you. You said that Joe was slow to give up his wallet. Your husband also wore a very expensive watch. A Hublot, I believe."

Her throat was dry. "Yes, that's correct."

"Why didn't he just hand it over?"

"I think . . . I think he would have."

"But?"

She shook her head.

"Maya?"

"Have you ever had a gun jammed into your face, Detective?"

"No."

"Then maybe you don't understand."

"Understand what?"

"The muzzle. The opening. When someone is pointing it at you, when someone is threatening to pull the trigger, that black hole grows impossibly large, like it's going to swallow you whole. Some people, when they see that, they freeze."

Kierce's voice was soft now. "And Joe . . . he was one of those people?"

"For a second."

"And that was too long?"

"In this case, yes."

They sat in silence for a few long moments.

"Could the gun have gone off by accident?" Kierce asked.

"I doubt it."

"Why do you say that?"

"Two reasons. One, it was a revolver. Do you know anything about them?"

"Not a ton."

"Because of the action, you either have to cock it back or squeeze very hard. You don't accidentally fire."

"I see. And the second reason?"

"More obvious," she said. "The gunman fired two more times. You don't 'accidentally' fire three bullets."

Kierce nodded and checked the notes again. "The first bullet hit your husband's left shoulder. The second hit landed in the right tangent of his clavicle."

Maya closed her eyes.

"How far away was the gunman when he fired?"

"Ten feet."

"Our ME said neither one of these shots was fatal."

"Yes, you told me," she said.

"So what happened then?"

"I tried to hold him up . . ."

"Joe?"

"Yes, Joe," she snapped. "Who else?"

"Sorry. Then what happened?"

"I . . . Joe dropped to his knees."

"And that was when the gunman fired the third shot?"

Maya said nothing.

"The third shot," Kierce repeated. "The one that killed him."

"I already told you."

"Told me what?"

Maya raised her eyes and met his. "I didn't see the third shot."

Kierce nodded. "That's right," he said too slowly. "Because you were running away by then."

"Help . . . please . . . someone . . . my husband's . . ."

Her chest started to hitch. The sounds—gunfire, the whir of helicopter rotors, the screams of agony—rushed her all at once. She shut her eyes, took a few deep breaths, kept her face composed.

"Maya?"

"Yes, I ran. Okay? Two men had guns. I ran. I ran and left my husband behind, and then somewhere, I don't know, maybe five, ten seconds later, I heard the blast coming from behind me and yes, now, based on what you told me, I know that after I left, the same gunman put the gun against my husband's head while he was still on his knees, pulled the trigger . . ."

She stopped.

"No one is blaming you, Maya."

"I didn't ask if anyone was, Detective," she said through gritted teeth. "What do you want?"

Kierce started paging through the notes. "Besides very detailed descriptions of the perpetrators, you were able to tell us that the one with the red Cons carried a Smith and Wesson 686 while his partner was armed with a Beretta M9." Kierce looked up. "That's pretty impressive. Identifying the weaponry like that."

"Part of the training."

"That would be your military training, am I correct?"

"Let's just say I'm observant."

"Oh, I think you're being modest, Maya. We all know that about your heroics overseas."

And my downfall, she almost added.

"The lighting in that part of the park isn't great. Just a few distant streetlights."

"It's enough."

"Enough to know specific gun makes?"

"I know firearms."

"Right, of course. You are, in fact, an expert marksman, is that correct?"

"Markswoman."

The correction came automatically. So did his patronizing smile.

"My bad. Still it was dark—"

"The Smith and Wesson was stainless steel, as opposed to black. Easy to see in the dark. I could also hear him pull back the hammer. You do that on a revolver, not a semiautomatic."

"And the Beretta?"

"I can't be sure of the exact make, but it had a floating barrel in the style of Beretta."

"As you know, we recovered three bullets from your husband's body. Thirty-eight calibers, consistent with the Smith and Wesson." He rubbed his face as if in deep thought. "You own guns, don't you, Maya?"

"I do."

"Would one of them happen to be a Smith and Wesson 686?"

"You know the answer," she said.

"How would I know that?"

"New Jersey law requires that I register all weapons purchased in state. So you know all this. Unless you're a complete incompetent, Detective Kierce, which you are definitely not, you checked my gun records immediately. So can we stop playing games and get to it?"

"How far would you say it is from where your husband fell to Bethesda Fountain?"

The subject change threw her. "I'm sure you did the measurements."

"We did, yes. It's approximately three hundred yards with all the twists and turns. I ran it. I'm not in as good a shape as you, but it took me about a minute."

"Okay."

"Well, here's the thing. Several witnesses said they heard the gunshot but then you emerged at least a minute or two later. How do you explain that?"

"Why would I need to explain it?"

"It's a fair question."

She didn't so much as blink. "Do you think I shot my husband, Detective?"

"Did you?"

"No. And you know how I can prove it?"

"How?"

"Come to the range with me."

"Meaning?"

"Like you said, I'm an expert markswoman."

"So we've been told."

"Then you know."

"Know what?"

Maya leaned forward and met his eye. "It wouldn't have taken me three shots to kill a man from that distance if I was blindfolded."

Kierce actually smiled at that. "Touché. And I'm sorry for the line of inquiry because no, I don't think you shot your husband. In fact, I can pretty much prove you didn't."

"What do you mean?"

Kierce stood. "Do you keep your guns here?"

"Yes."

"Do you mind showing me?"

First, she took him to the gun safe in the basement.

"I guess you're a big fan of the Second Amendment," Kierce said.

"I don't get into politics."

"But you like guns." He looked at the safe. "I don't see a combination wheel. Does it open with a key?"

"Nope. You can only access it with your thumbprint."

"Ah, I see. So it's set that only you can open it."

Maya swallowed. "It is now."

"Oh," Kierce said, realizing his mistake. "Your husband?"

She nodded.

"Anyone else besides you two have access?"

"No one." She placed her thumb on the opening. The door opened with an audible pop. She stepped aside.

Kierce looked inside and whistled low. "What do you need all these for?"

"I don't need any of them. I enjoy shooting. It's my hobby. Most people don't like it or get it. That's fine with me."

"So where is your Smith and Wesson 686?"

She pointed into the safe. "Here."

His eyes narrowed. "May I take it with me?"

"The Smith and Wesson?"

"Yes, if it isn't an issue."

"I thought you didn't think I did it."

"I don't. But we might as well eliminate not only you but your gun, don't you think?"

Maya took out the Smith and Wesson. She was, like most good shooters, OCD when it came to cleaning and loading/unloading her weaponry, which just meant you always check again to make sure it is unloaded. It was.

"I'll give you a receipt for it," he said.

"I, of course, could ask for a court order."

"And I'd probably be able to get it," he said.

True enough. She gave him the weapon.

"Detective?"

"What?"

"You're not telling me something."

Kierce smiled. "I'll be in touch."

Chapter 3

Isabella, Lily's nanny, arrived at seven the next morning.

At the funeral, Isabella's family had been among the most animated of the mourners. Her mother, Rosa, Joe's childhood nanny, had been especially distraught, clutching a handkerchief and continually collapsing on her own children, Isabella and Hector. Even now, Maya could still see the tinge of red in Isabella's eyes from yesterday's tears.

"I'm so sorry, Mrs. Burkett."

Maya had asked her several times to call her by her first name, not Mrs. Burkett, but Isabella would just nod and continue to call her Mrs. Burkett, so Maya let it go. If Isabella was more comfortable with formality in her work environment, who was Maya to force it?

"Thank you, Isabella."

Lily hopped out of her kitchen chair, the cereal still in her mouth, and ran toward them. "Isabella!"

Isabella's face lit up as she swooped the little girl into her arms and gave her a big hug. Maya felt the quick pang of the working mother: grateful that her daughter liked her nanny so much while ungrateful that her daughter liked her nanny so much.

Did she trust Isabella?

The answer was, as she had said yesterday, yes—as much as she would trust any "stranger" in this situation. Joe had hired Isabella, of course. Maya hadn't been sure about it. There was this new day care center on Porter Street called Growin' Up, which Maya read as a small homage to the old Bruce Springsteen song. A pretty, young smiley thing named Kitty Shum ("Call me Miss Kitty!") had given Maya a tour of the clean, sleek, multihued rooms of overstimulation, with all kinds of cameras and security procedures and other young smiley things and, of course, other children for Lily to play with, but Joe had been insistent on a nanny. He reminded Maya that Isabella's mother had "practically raised me," and Maya had jokingly countered, "Are you sure that's a résumé enhancer?" But since Maya had been heading overseas for a six-month deployment at the time, she really had little say in the choice—and no reason not to embrace it.

Maya kissed Lily on the top of her head and headed off to work. She could have taken a few more days and stayed at home with her daughter. She certainly didn't need the money—even with the prenup, she would be a very wealthy widow—but classically doting mother-hood was simply not for her. Maya had tried to dive into the whole "mommy world," the coffee klatches with her fellow moms where they discussed toilet train-ing, top preschools, stroller safety ratings, and slow-bragged with genuine interest about their own children's mundane development. Maya would sit there and smile, but behind her eyes, she would be flashing back to Iraq, to a specific blood-filled memory—usually Jake Evans, a nineteen-year-old from Fayetteville, Ar-kansas, getting the entire lower part of his body blown off yet somehow surviving—and trying to somehow come to terms with the unfathomable fact that this gos-sipy coffee klatch existed on the same planet as that blood-soaked battleground.

Sometimes, when she was with the other moms, the sounds of the rotors more than the gruesome visuals would come roaring back. Ironic, she thought, that this in-your-face, never-back-off parenting was nicknamed "helicoptering."

They all just didn't have a clue.

Maya assessed her surroundings as she headed to the car in her own driveway, looking for places where the enemy could hide or spring an attack. The reason for doing this was simple: Old habits die hard. Once a sol-dier, always a soldier.

No sign of the enemy, imaginary or not.

Maya knew that she suffered some textbook mental malady from being over there, but the truth is, no one comes back without scars. To her, that malady felt more like enlightenment. She got the world now. Others didn't.

In the Army, Maya had flown combat helicopters, often providing cover and clearing for advancing ground troops. She'd started by flying UH-60 Black Hawks at Fort Campbell before logging enough miles to apply for the prestigious 160th Special Operations Aviation Regiment (SOAR) in the Middle East. Soldiers routinely called helicopters "birds," which was fine, but there were few things more grating than when a civilian did the same. It had been her plan to stay in the service, probably for life, but after that video had been released on the CoreyTheWhistle site, that particular plan was blown up as though it too, like Jake Evans, had stepped on an IED.

The flight lessons today would take place aboard a Cessna 172, a single-engine four-seater that just so happened to be the most successful aircraft in history. Teaching ends up being about hours in the air for the student. Maya's job was often more "watch and see" than active instructions.

Flying, or just being in a cockpit when the plane was up in the air, was the equivalent of meditation for Maya. She could feel the bunched muscles in her shoulders loosen. No, it didn't offer the rev or, let's be honest, thrill of flying a UH-60 Black Hawk over Baghdad or being one of the first women to pilot a Boeing MH-6 Little Bird helicopter gunship. No one wanted to admit that awful high of combat, the adrenaline boost that some compared to narcotics. It was unseemly to "enjoy" combat, to feel that tingle, to realize that nothing else in your life would ever really approach it. That was the terrible secret you could never voice. Yes, war was horrible and no human being should ever have to experience it. Maya would have laid down her own life to make sure that it never came close to Lily. But the unspoken truth was a part of you jonesed for the danger. You didn't want that. You didn't like what it said about you. Liking it means you are prenatally violent or lack empathy or some such nonsense. But there was an addictive element to fear. At home, you live relatively calm, placid, mundane lives. You go over there and live in mortal fear, and then you're supposed to come back home and be calm, placid, and mundane again. Human beings don't work that way.

When she was in the air with a student, Maya always left her phone in her locker because she wanted no distractions. If there was an emergency, someone could radio up. But when she checked her messages during her lunch break, she saw a strange text from her nephew, Daniel.

Alexa doesn't want you to go to her soccer game.

Maya dialed the number. Daniel answered on the first ring.

"Hello?" he said.

"What's wrong?"

When Maya tapped Alexa's soccer coach on the shoulder, the big man turned so quickly the whistle around his neck nearly slapped her across the face.

"What?" he shouted.

The coach—his name was Phil, and his daughter was an obnoxious bully named Patty—had been shouting and pacing and throwing tantrums pretty much non-stop the entire game. Maya had known drill sergeants who'd have considered his behavior over the top for hardened recruits, let alone twelve-year-old girls.

"I'm Maya Stern."

"Oh, I know who you are, but"—Coach Phil gestured theatrically toward the field—"I'm in the middle of a game here. You should respect that, soldier."

Soldier? "I have a quick question."

"I got no time for questions now. See me after the game. All spectators need to be on the other side of the field."

"League rules?"

"Exactly."

Coach Phil dismissed Maya by turning so that his expansive back was now facing her. Maya didn't move.

"It's the second half," Maya said.

"What?"

"League rules specify that you're supposed to play

each girl half the game," Maya said. "It's the second half. Three girls haven't gotten in yet. Even if you put them in now for the rest of the game, it wouldn't total half a game."

Coach Phil's shorts probably fit him okay twenty, thirty pounds ago. His red polo shirt with the word "Coach" stitched in script across the left breast was also snug enough to double as sausage casing. He had the look of an ex-jock gone to seed, which, Maya surmised, he probably was. He was big and intimidating, and his size probably scared people.

Keeping his back to her, Coach Phil said out of the corner of his mouth, "For your information, this is the semifinals of the league championship."

"I know."

"We're only up by one goal."

"I checked the league rules," Maya said. "I don't see an exception to the half-game rule. You also didn't play all your players in the quarterfinals."

He turned toward her and again faced her full-on. He adjusted the brim of his cap and moved into Maya's personal space. She didn't step back. During the first half, sitting with the parents and watching the guy's constant tirades at both the girls and the refs, Maya had seen him slam-dunk that stupid cap onto the ground twice. He'd looked like a two-year-old midparoxysm.

"We wouldn't even be in the semis," Coach Phil said as though spitting glass, "if I played those girls last game."

"Meaning you'd have lost because you followed the rules?"

Patty, Coach's daughter, chuckled at that one. "Meaning they suck."

"Okay, Patty, that's enough. Go in for Amanda."

Patty smirked her way toward the scorer's table.

"Your daughter," Maya said.

"What about her?"

"She picks on the other girls."

He made a face of disgust. "Is that what your Alice told you?"

"Alexa," she corrected. "And no."

Daniel had told her.

He leaned in close enough for her to get a whiff of tuna salad. "Look, soldier—"

"Soldier?"

"You're a soldier, right? Or you were?" He grinned. "Rumor has it you were a bit of a rule breaker yourself, no?"

Her fingers flexed and relaxed, flexed and relaxed.

"As a former soldier," he continued, "you should get this, plain and simple."

"How so?"

Coach Phil hoisted up his shorts. "This"—he gestured to the field—"is my battlefield. I'm the general, these are my soldiers. You wouldn't put some dumb grunt behind the wheel of an F-16 or whatever, would you?"

Maya could actually feel the blood in her veins start

to warm. "Just to be clear," she said, somehow managing to keep her tone even, "are you equating this soccer game to the wars our soldiers fight in Afghanistan and Iraq?"

"You don't see it?"

Flex, relax, flex, relax, flex, relax. Take nice even breaths.

"This is sports," Coach Phil said, gesturing toward the field again. "Serious, competitive sports—and yes, that's a bit like war. I don't coddle these girls. I mean, this isn't fifth grade anymore where everything is rainbows and sweetness. It's sixth grade now. It's the real world. You get my meaning?"

"The league rules on the website—"

He leaned in so that the brim of his cap touched the top of her head. "I don't give a damn about what's on the website. If you have a complaint, file an official grievance with the soccer board."

"Of which you are president."

Coach Phil gave her a big smile. "I have to coach my girls now. So buh-bye." He gave her a toodle-oo finger wave and slowly turned back toward the field.

"You shouldn't turn your back on me," Maya said.

"What are you going to do about it?"

She shouldn't. She knew that. She should just leave it alone. She should not make the situation worse for Alexa.

Flex, release, flex . . .

But even as such lofty ambitions swam through Maya's mind, her hands had other ideas. Moving with lightning speed, Maya bent down, grabbed hold of his shorts, and—praying that he hadn't gone commando—pulled them all the way to his ankles.

Several things happened in pretty short order.

There was a collective gasp from the crowd. The coach, sporting tighty-whities, also moved at lightning speed, bending down to pull his shorts up but tripping in the process. He tumbled to the ground.

Then came the laughter.

Maya waited.

Coach Phil quickly regained his balance. He jumped to a standing position, pulling up his shorts, and charged toward her. The red of both rage and embarrassment came off his face like a call girl's beacon.

"You bitch."

Maya quietly prepared herself, but she didn't move.

Coach Phil cocked his fist.

"Go ahead," Maya said. "Give me the excuse to put you down."

The coach stopped, looked into Maya's eyes, saw something there, and lowered his hand. "Ah, you ain't worth it."

Enough, Maya thought.

Maya was already semiregretting her actions, what with teaching her niece the wrong lesson about violence being an answer. She, of all people, should know better. But when she glanced over at Alexa, expecting her quiet niece to look scared or mortified, Maya instead saw a small smile on the little girl's face. It wasn't a smile of satisfaction or even pleasure at the coach's humiliation. The smile said something else.

She knows now, Maya thought.

Maya had learned it in the military, but of course, it applied to real life. Your fellow soldiers had to know that you had their back. That was rule one, lesson one, and above all else. If the enemy goes after you, he goes after me too.

Maybe Maya had overreacted, maybe not, but either way, now Alexa knew that no matter what, her aunt would be there and fight for her.

Daniel had started toward her when the commotion began, looking in his own way to somehow help out. He too nodded at Maya. He too got it.

Their mother was dead. Their father was a drunk.

But Maya had their back.

Maya spotted the tail.

She was driving Daniel and Alexa home, again doing that surveillance thing that just came to her naturally, scanning her surroundings, looking for anything out of place, when she saw the red Buick Verano in the rearview mirror.

There was nothing suspicious about the Buick yet. She had been driving only a mile, but she'd noticed the same car when she'd pulled out of the soccer field lot. Could be nothing. Probably was nothing. Shane talked about the sixth sense of being a soldier, that sometimes, somehow, you just knew. That was bullshit. Maya had bought into that mumbo jumbo until they'd all been proven wrong in a horrific way.

"Aunt Maya?"

It was Alexa.

"What's up, honey?"

"Thanks for coming to the game."

"It was fun. I thought you played great."

"Nah, Patty's right. I suck."

Daniel laughed. So did Alexa.

"Stop that. You like soccer, right?"

"Yeah, but this will be my last year."

"Why?"

"I won't be good enough to play next year."

Maya shook her head. "It's not about that."

"Huh?"

"Sports are supposed to be about having fun and getting exercise."

"You believe that?" Alexa asked.

"I do."

"Aunt Maya?"

"Yes, Daniel."

"Do you believe in the Easter Bunny too?"

Daniel and Alexa laughed again. Maya shook her head and smiled. She glanced in the rearview mirror.

The red Buick Verano was still there.

She wondered whether it was Coach Phil looking for round two. The car color was right—red—but no, the big guy would drive a penis-envy sports car or a Hummer or something like that.

When she pulled up to Claire's house—even this long after the murder, Maya still thought of the house as her sister's—the red Buick passed them without hesitating. So maybe it wasn't a tail. Maybe it was just another family at the soccer game that lived in the neighborhood. That would make sense.

Maya flashed back to the first time Claire had shown this house to her and Eileen. It had looked something like it did now—grass overgrown, paint chipping, cracks in the pavement, drooping flowers.

"What do you think of it?" Claire had asked her then.

"It's a dump."

Claire had smiled. "Exactly, thank you. Just watch."

Maya had no creativity for such things. She could not see the potential. Claire could. She had that kind of touch. Soon the two words that came to mind when you pulled up to the home were "cheerful" and "homey." The whole place ended up looking like a happy kid's crayon drawing somehow, with the sun always shining and the flowers taller than the front door.

That was all gone now.

Eddie met them at the door. He too was a reflection of the house—one thing before Claire's death, something faded and gray since. "How did it go?" he asked his daughter.

"We lost," Alexa said.

"Oh, sorry."

She kissed her father's cheek as she and Daniel hurried inside. Eddie looked wary, but he stepped aside and let Maya in. He wore a red flannel shirt and jeans, and once again Maya got a whiff of too much mouthwash.

"I would have picked them up," he said defensively.

"No," Maya said, "you wouldn't have."

"I didn't mean . . . I had a drink after I knew you were taking them."

She said nothing. The boxes were still piled in the corner. Claire's stuff. Eddie hadn't yet moved them into the basement or garage. They just sat in the living room like the work of a mad hoarder.

"I mean it," he said. "I don't drink and drive."

"You're a prince, Eddie."

"So superior."

"Hardly."

"Maya?"

"What?"

The tufts of stubble still dotted his chin and right cheek—spots he'd missed shaving. Claire would have seen them and told him and made sure that he didn't leave the house looking so disheveled.

His voice was soft. "I didn't drink when she was alive."

Maya didn't know what to say to that, so she kept quiet.

"I mean, I had a drink every once in a while, but—"

"I know what you mean," Maya interrupted. "Anyway, I better go. Take care of them."

"I got a call from the town soccer association."

"Right."

"Seems you made quite a scene today."

Maya shrugged. "I just discussed the rules with the coach."

"What gave you the right?"

"Your son, Eddie. He called me to help your daughter."

"And you think you helped?"

Maya said nothing.

"You think an asshole like Phil forgets something like this? You think he won't find a way to take it out on Alexa?"

"He better not."

"Or what?" Eddie snapped. "You'll handle it some more?"

"Yeah, Eddie. If that's what it takes. I'll stand up for her until she can stand up for herself."

"By pulling down a coach's pants?"

"By doing what it takes."

"Do you even hear what you're saying?"

"Loud and clear. I said I'll stand up for her. You know why? Because no one else will."

He recoiled as though he'd been slapped. "Get the hell out of my house."

"Fine." Maya started for the door, stopped, faced

him. "Your house, by the way, is a toilet. Straighten it out."

"I said, get out. And maybe you shouldn't come by for a while."

She stopped. "Pardon me?"

"I don't want you around my children."

"Your . . . ?" Maya moved closer to him. "Do you want to explain?"

Whatever anger had been in his eyes seemed to dissipate. Eddie swallowed, looked off, and said, "You don't get it."

"Don't get what?"

"You were the one who did battle so the rest of us didn't have to. You used to make us feel safe."

"Used to?"

"Yes."

"I don't understand," she said.

He finally met her eye. "Death follows you, Maya."

She just stood there. In the distance, someone turned on a television. She could hear muffled cheers.

Eddie started counting on his fingers. "The war. Claire. Now Joe."

"You're blaming me?"

He opened his mouth, closed it, tried again. "Maybe, I don't know, maybe death found you in some shithole in the desert. Or maybe he's just always been inside of you and somehow you let him out or he followed you home."

"You're not making any sense, Eddie."

"Maybe not. Man, I liked Joe. Joe was good people. And now he's gone too." Eddie looked up at her. "I don't want anyone else I love to be next."

"You know I would never let anyone harm Daniel or Alexa."

"You think you have that power, Maya?"

She didn't reply.

"You wouldn't let anyone harm Claire or Joe either. How did that work out for you?"

Flex, relax.

"You're talking nonsense, Eddie."

"Get out of my house. Get out of my house and don't come back."

Chapter 4

A week later, the red Buick Verano was back.

Maya had been coming home from too long a day of flight lessons. She was tired and hungry and just wanted to get home and relieve Isabella. But now that damn red Buick was back.

How should she play it?

Just as she started going through her possible options, the Buick veered off again. Another coincidence, or had the driver figured that she was just heading home? Maya was willing to bet on the latter.

Isabella's brother, Hector, was waiting by his pickup truck when she pulled up. He usually gave Isabella a ride home when he finished gardening.

"Hello, Mrs. Burkett."

"Hi, Hector."

"I just finished the flower beds." He zipped his hoodie, an odd fashion choice in this heat, to the neck. "You like?"

"They look great. Can I ask you a favor?"

"Of course."

"My sister's house could use a little work. If I paid you extra, do you think you could cut the grass and maybe do a cleanup?"

Hector looked a little uncomfortable with the suggestion. The family worked for the Burketts exclusively. They paid his salary.

"I'll clear it with Judith first," Maya said.

"Then sure, I'd be happy to do it."

As Maya headed toward the house, her phone dinged. It was a text from Alexa.

Soccer Day is Saturday. You coming?

She had made her excuses not to stop by since the incident with Coach Phil last week. Much as she knew that he was wrong, Eddie's accusation haunted her. She knew that he was being irrational with that "death follows you" gobbledygook. But perhaps a father had the right to be irrational when it came to his own children—for a short period of time, anyway.

Years ago, when Daniel was born, Claire and Eddie had made Maya the guardian for first Daniel, then both their children, in the unlikely event that something happened to Claire and Eddie. But even back then, even back before Claire had a clue how wrong it would all go, she had pulled Maya aside and said, "If something happens to just me, Eddie won't be able to cope."

"What makes you say that?"

"He's a good man. But he's not a strong man. You need to be there, no matter what."

She didn't have to add "Promise me" or any of that. Claire knew. Maya knew. Maya took the responsibility and her sister's concerns seriously, and while she might obey Eddie's wants for a short period of time, even he knew that it wouldn't be forever.

She replied to the text: **Dang, can't. Work is crazy. See you soon? XO.**

As Maya continued her way to the back door, she flashed back to that day at Camp Arifjan in Kuwait. It had been noon on the base, 5:00 A.M. at home, when the call came in.

"It's me," Joe said, his voice cracking. "I have some bad news."

Odd, she had thought in that brief lull before her world was destroyed, to be on the other end of the line, so to speak. These terrible calls had always gone the other way for her—the bad news emanating from the Middle East and traveling west toward the United States. Of course, she never made the calls herself. There was a protocol involved. A "death notification officer"— yes, there was such a thing—told the family in person. What a task. No one volunteered for it—they were "voluntold," to use a military term. The death notification officer donned his dress blues, got in a car with a pastor, knocked on your door, had the death script memorized.

"What is it?" she had asked Joe.

Silence. The worst silence she had ever known.

"Joe?"

"It's Claire," he said, and Maya felt something inside her crumble to dust.

She opened her back door. On the couch, Lily drew with a green crayon. She didn't look up when her mother entered, but that was okay. Lily was the kind of kid who had amazing concentration. All of it right now was focused on the drawing. Isabella got up slowly, as though afraid to wake her, and crossed the room.

"Thanks for staying late," Maya said.

"It's no problem."

Lily looked up and smiled at them. They both smiled and waved back.

"How was she today?"

"A joy." Isabella looked at Lily with a forlorn face. "She has no idea."

Isabella said this or something similar every day.

"I'll see you in the morning," Maya said.

"Yes, Mrs. Burkett."

Maya sat next to her daughter as she heard Hector's truck pull away. She saw the pictures go by on the digital frame/nanny cam, always cognizant of the fact that everything she did was recorded. She checked it most days, just to make sure that Isabella wasn't . . . well, what exactly? Whatever, the video was always pretty un-eventful. Maya never watched herself playing with her own child. It felt strange. Then again, it felt strange just having a surveillance camera in the room, as though you had to behave differently because of it. Did the camera in part dictate Maya's own interactions with Lily? Yeah, probably.

"What are you drawing?" Maya asked.

"You can't tell?"

It looked like squiggly lines. "No."

Lily looked hurt.

Maya shrugged. "Can you tell me?"

"Two cows and a caterpillar."

"The cow is green?"

"That's the caterpillar."

Mercifully, Maya's phone rang. She checked her phone and saw it was Shane.

"How are you holding up?" Shane asked her.

"Good."

Silence. Three seconds passed before Shane spoke.

"I'm digging this awkward silence," Shane said. "You?"

"It's awesome. So what's up?"

They were too close for this "how are you holding up" stuff. It just wasn't something that was a part of their relationship.

"We need to talk," he said.

"So talk."

"I'll come over. Are you hungry?"

"Not really."

"I can pick up a buffalo chicken pizza from Best of Everything."

"Hurry, dammit."

She hung up. Camp Arifjan had served pizza as a choice at almost every meal, but the sauce tasted like turned ketchup and the dough had the consistency of toothpaste. Since she'd been home, she craved only thin-crust pizza and nobody did that better than Best of Everything.

When Shane arrived, they all sat at the kitchen table and wolfed down the pizza. Lily loved Shane. Kids, in general, loved Shane. It was adults he didn't do quite as well with. There was an awkwardness to him, a stoicism that most people, with their need for appearances and fake smiles, found off-putting. Shane couldn't handle small talk or the excess bullshittery of modern society.

When they finished the pizza, Lily insisted that Shane, not Maya, get her ready for bed.

Shane pouted. "But reading to you is so boring."

That cracked Lily up. She grabbed his hand and started dragging him toward the stairs. "No, please!" Shane cried, falling to the ground. Lily laughed harder and kept pulling. Shane protested the entire way. It took ten minutes for Lily to get him up the stairs.

When they reached the bedroom, Shane read her a story and Lily conked out so fast Maya wondered whether he had slipped her an Ambien.

"That was fast," she said when he came back down.

"Part of my plan."

"What was?"

"Having her drag me up the stairs. It tired her out."

"Clever."

"Yeah, well."

They both grabbed cold beers from the fridge and headed into the backyard. Night had fallen. The humidity weighed them down, but after you experienced desert heat wearing forty pounds of gear on your back, nothing else in the hot family really bothered you.

"Nice night," Shane said.

They sat by the swimming pool and started to drink. There was something there, some sort of chasm, and Maya didn't like it.

"Stop it," she said.

"Stop what?"

"You're treating me like . . ."

"Like?"

"Like a widow. Cut it out."

Shane nodded. "Yeah, okay, my bad."

"So what did you want to talk to me about?" she asked.

He took a swig of beer. "It may be nothing."

"But?"

"There's an intelligence report floating around." Shane was still in the military, heading up the local branch of the military police. "Seems Corey Rudzinski may be back in the United States."

Shane waited for her reaction. Maya took a deep, long sip of the beer and said nothing.

"We think he came across the Canadian border two weeks ago."

"Is there an arrest warrant out on him?"

"Technically, no."

Corey Rudzinski was the founder of CoreyTheWhistle, a website where whistle-blowers could safely post information in a confidential manner. The idea was to disclose illegal activities by government and big business. Remember that story about the South American government official who had been taking kickbacks from the oil companies? A leak to CoreyTheWhistle. That police corruption case with the racist emails? CoreyTheWhistle. The abusive prisoner treatment in Idaho, the covered-up nuclear accident in Asia, the security forces hiring escort services? CoreyTheWhistle.

And, of course, the civilian deaths due to an overzealous female Army helicopter pilot?

Yep, you guessed it.

All those "scoops" were courtesy of Corey's confidential whistle-blowers.

"Maya?"

"He can't hurt me anymore."

Shane tilted his head.

"What?"

"Nothing."

"He can't hurt me," she said. "He already released that tape."

"Not all of it."

She took a slug of beer. "I don't care, Shane."

He leaned back. "Okay." Then: "Why do you think he didn't?"

"Didn't what?"

"Release the audio."

It was a question that haunted her more than Shane would ever know.

"He's a whistle-blower," Shane said. "So why didn't he air it?"

"Don't know."

Shane looked out. Maya knew that look.

"I assume you have a theory?" she said.

"I do."

"Let's hear it."

"Corey has been saving it for the right time," Shane said.

Maya frowned.

"First he gets the big press hit off the initial release. Then, when he needs fresh publicity, he releases the rest of it."

She shook her head.

"He's a shark," Shane said. "You have to constantly feed a shark."

"Meaning?"

"For his operation to be a success, Corey Rudzinski needs to not only take down those he believes are corrupt, but he has to do it in a way that will maximize publicity."

"Shane?"

"Yeah."

"I don't really care. I'm out of the military. I'm even—gasp—a widow. Let him do his worst."

She wondered whether Shane would buy the bravado, but then again, he didn't know the full truth, did he?

"Okeydokey." Shane finished the beer. "So are you going to tell me what's really going on?"

"What do you mean?"

"I ran that test for you, no questions asked."

She nodded. "Thank you."

"I'm not here for gratitude, you know that."

She did.

"Running that test was a violation of my oath. It was, not to put too fine a point on it, against the law. You know that, right?"

"Let it go, Shane."

"Did you know Joe was in danger?"

"Shane—"

"Or were you the real target?"

Maya closed her eyes for a moment. The sounds were raging toward her.

"Maya?"

She opened her eyes and turned toward him slowly. "Do you trust me?"

"Don't insult me like that. You saved my life. You're the best and bravest soldier I've ever known."

She shook her head. "The best and bravest came home in a box."

"No, Maya, they didn't. They paid the biggest price, yes. Mostly, they were the unluckiest. We both know that. They were just standing in the wrong spot at the wrong time."

It was true. It isn't as though the more competent warriors had a better chance of surviving. It was a crap-shoot. War is never a meritocracy for the casualties.

Shane's voice was soft in the darkness. "You're going to try to do this on your own, aren't you?"

She didn't reply.

"You're going to take down Joe's killers by yourself."

It wasn't a question. The silence hung there for a while, just like the humidity.

"I'm here if you need help. You know that, right?"

"I do." Then: "Do you trust me, Shane?"

"With my life."

"Then leave it alone."

Shane finished his beer and headed for the door.

"I need one more thing," Maya said.

She handed him a piece of paper.

"What's this?"

"A license plate for a red Buick Verano. I need to know who the car belongs to."

Shane made a face. "I won't insult either of us by asking why you want this," he said. "But this is the last freebie."

He kissed her on the top of the head, fatherlike, and left.

Maya looked in on her sleeping daughter. Then she

padded down the corridor to the high-tech workout room Joe had built when they first moved in. She did some light weights—squats, bench, curls—and then hit the treadmill. The house had always felt too big for her, too fancy. Her family hadn't been poor by any stretch, but this kind of wealth didn't sit well with her. Maya didn't feel comfortable here, hadn't ever, but that was the way the Burketts were. No one really left the family's environs—their compound just spread out.

She worked up a good sweat. Exercising always made her feel better. When she was done, Maya threw a towel around her neck and grabbed a frosty Bud. She pressed the bottle against her forehead. Nice and cold.

She moved the mouse, waking up the computer, and jumped on the web. She typed in the URL for the CoreyTheWhistle website and waited for it to load. Other similar sites like WikiLeaks had no-nonsense layouts— very cookie-cutter, monochromatic, informational. Corey had gone for a far more stimulating visual. The motto, written in alternating fonts across the top, was simple and crude: "We Provide The Whistle, But You Provide The, Uh, Blow."

There were bursts of color. There were thumbnails of videos. And while rival sites downplayed any hyperbole, Corey's had brought all the best and cheesiest click-bait terminology: "Top Ten Ways The Government Is Watching—Number 7 Will Blow Your Mind!" "Wall Street Goes For Your Green . . . and You Won't Believe What Happens Next." "Think the Cops Are

There to Protect You? Think Again." "We Kill Civilians. Why the Four-Star Generals Hate Us." "Twenty Signs You're Being Robbed By Your Bank." "The Wealthiest Men in the World Pay No Taxes—How You Can Too." "Which Despot Are You Most Like? Take Our Test."

She hit the archive and found the old video. She wasn't sure why she went to Corey's site to get it. You-Tube had a dozen variations of it up. She could have easily just gone there, but somehow it felt right to go to the source.

Someone had leaked to Corey Rudzinski what had started off as a rescue mission. Four soldiers, including three Maya knew and loved, had been killed in an ambush in Al Qa'im, not far from the Syrian-Iraqi border. Two were still alive but pinned down by enemy fire. A black SUV was moving in for the kill. Maya and Shane, flying at full speed in a Boeing MH-6 Little Bird light helicopter gunship, had heard the terrified calls for help from the two surviving soldiers. They both sounded so young, so damned young, and she knew the four already dead would have sounded exactly the same.

Once they had the target in view, they waited for confirmation, but while everyone thinks military gear is infallible, the radio signal from Joint Operations Command at Al Asad kept coming in and out. Not so with the two soldiers who were begging to be saved. Maya and Shane waited. Both were cursing through the radio, demanding a reply from JOC, when they heard the two survivors scream.

That was when Maya's MH-6 took out the black SUV with an AGM-114 Hellfire Missile. The SUV blew up high into the air. The infantry moved in and rescued the soldiers. Both had been hit, but both survived.

At the time, it had all seemed pretty righteous.

Maya's cell phone rang. She closed the web browser quickly, as though she'd been caught watching porn. She saw the caller ID read "FARNWOOD," the name of the Burkett family estate.

"Hello?"

"Maya, it's Judith."

Joe's mom. It had been more than a week since Joe's death, but the tone still had that same heaviness, as though every word was a task, a struggle, painful.

"Oh, hi, Judith."

"I wanted to know how you and Lily are faring."

"That was thoughtful. We're as well as can be expected."

"I'm glad to hear it," Judith said. "I'm also calling to remind you that tomorrow Heather Howell will read Joe's will in Farnwood Library at nine A.M. sharp."

The rich even name their rooms.

"I'll be there, thank you."

"Would you like us to send a car?"

"No, I'll be okay."

"Why not bring Lily? We would love to see her."

"Let's play that by ear, okay?"

"Of course. I . . . I really miss seeing her. She looks so much like . . . Well, we'll see you tomorrow."

Judith held back the tears long enough to hang up.

Maya sat there for a moment. Maybe she would bring Lily. Isabella too. That reminded her that she should check the nanny cam's SD card. Maya hadn't watched it in two days, but then again, so what? She was feeling tired. It could wait for the morning.

Maya washed up. There was a big chair in the bedroom—Joe's chair—and she sat in it now and opened her book. It was a new Wright brothers biography. She tried to focus, but her mind wouldn't settle.

Corey Rudzinski was back in the United States. Was that a coincidence?

"You're going to try to do this on your own, aren't you?"

She felt the warning signs coming on. Maya closed the book and quickly slipped into bed. She turned off the lights and waited.

First came the sweats, then the visions—but it was the sounds that always battered her. The sounds. The ceaseless noises, the constant cacophony of the helicopter rotors, the static voices on the radio, the gunfire— and, of course, the human sounds, the laughter, the ridicule, the panic, the screams.

Maya pulled her pillow tight around her ears, but that just made it worse. All those sounds didn't just surround her. They didn't just echo and reverberate. They tore through her head. They ripped through her brain tissue, shredding her dreams and thoughts and wants like hot shrapnel.

Maya bit back a scream. Tonight would be bad. She would need help.

Maya opened the drawer in her night table. She pulled out the bottle and downed two Klonopins.

The pills didn't stop the sounds, but eventually, after she rode it out a little longer, they muffled the noise enough to let her sleep.

Chapter 5

First thought when Maya woke up: Check out the nanny cam video.

Maya always woke up at exactly 4:58 A.M. Some claimed that she had one of those internal alarm clocks, but if she did, it could only be set for 4:58 A.M. and it couldn't be turned off, even on nights she stayed up late and craved a few extra minutes of sleep, and if she tried to "set" the internal alarm even a few minutes earlier or later, it switched back to the default setting of 4:58 A.M.

This had started during basic training. Her drill sergeant had a wake-up time of 5:00 A.M., and while most of her fellow recruits would groan or struggle, Maya had already been awake a full two minutes and was ready for the drill sergeant's imminent and rarely pleasant arrival.

Once Maya had fallen asleep (read: passed out) the night before, she had slept soundly. Oddly enough, whatever demons possessed her, they rarely came out in her sleep—no nightmares, no twisting of the sheets, no waking up in a cold sweat. Maya never remembered her dreams, which could mean that she slept peacefully or that whatever happened in those dreams, her unconscious was merciful enough to let her forget them.

She grabbed her hair band from the night table and pulled her hair back into a ponytail. Joe had liked the ponytail. "I love your bone structure," he would say. "I want to see as much of your face as possible." He also liked to play with the ponytail and even, on some occasions, gently pull it, but that was another matter altogether.

Her face flushed at the memory.

Maya checked her phone for messages. Nothing important. She swung her legs out of bed and padded down the hallway. Lily was still sleeping. No surprise there. In the genetic internal alarm department, Lily was more like her father: Sleep until you absolutely have to rise.

It was still dark outside. The kitchen smelled of baking, obviously the handiwork of Isabella. Maya didn't cook, bake, or otherwise engage in culinary activities unless forced to. Many of her friends were big-time into cooking, which Maya found amusing, since for generations, and indeed throughout pretty much the entire existence of mankind, cooking was considered a tedious and grueling chore one tried to avoid. In history books, you rarely read about monarchs or lords or anyone the slightest bit elite enjoying spending time in the kitchen. Eating? Sure. Fine dining and wine? Of course. But preparing the meals? That was a menial task given to lowly servants.

Maya debated scrambling herself some eggs with a side of bacon, but the act of merely pouring milk atop cold cereal called out to her. She sat at the table and tried not to think about the reading of Joe's will that day. She didn't think that there would be any surprises. Maya had signed a prenup (Joe: "It's a family thing—if any of us Burketts don't sign, we get disinherited"), and once Lily was born, Joe had set it up so that, in the event of his death, all his holdings would go into a trust for their daughter. Maya was happy enough with that.

There was no cold cereal in the cabinet. Dang. Isabella had been complaining about the sugar content in them, but had she gone so far as to toss them? Maya headed to the fridge and then stopped.

Isabella.

The nanny cam.

She had woken up thinking about it, which was odd. Sure, she checked it most days, but not all. It never felt urgent to her. Nothing even the slightest bit questionable ever occurred. Maya normally kept the fast-forward button pressed down. On camera, Isabella was always sunny and happy, which was a bit troubling because that wasn't Isabella's default state. She did light up around Lily, but Isabella had a face like a totem pole. She wasn't big on smiling.

Yet she always smiled on the nanny cam. She was the perfect nanny all the time, and let's face it, no one is that. No one. We all have our moments, don't we?

Did Isabella know the nanny cam was there?

Maya's laptop and the SD card reader Eileen had given her were in her backpack. For a while she had used her military-issue backpack—a beige nylon thing of many pockets—but too many military wannabes ordered the same thing online and something about it felt too showy. Joe had bought her a Kevlar laptop backpack from Tumi. She thought that it was overpriced until she saw what those military wannabes paid for their backpacks online.

She picked up the picture frame, pressed the button on the side, and took hold of the SD card. Suppose Isabella had figured it out. First off, would that be such a stretch? Not really. If you were at all perceptive—and Isabella was—you might wonder why your employer would suddenly buy a new picture frame. If you were at all perceptive—and again, Isabella was—you might wonder why this new picture frame would show up for the first time on the day after your employer buried her murdered husband.

Or if you were at all perceptive, you might not. Who knew?

Maya slid the SD card into the reader and then plugged the reader into the USB port. Why was she feeling anxious about this? If her suspicions were correct, if Isabella had figured out that the new picture frame held more than a potpourri of family photographs, then, of course, all Maya would see would be Isabella on her best behavior. She wouldn't be dumb enough to do something suspicious. The whole idea of a hidden nanny cam was that it was *hidden*. Once a nanny knew about it, the whole enterprise became at best moot.

She hit the play button. The video worked on a motion detector, so it started up when Isabella walked by carrying a cup of coffee in, of course, a mug with a protective lid. No chance any hot liquid would spill on a little girl's skin. Isabella picked Lily's stuffed giraffe off the floor and started to walk back to the kitchen and out of the frame.

"Mommy."

There was no audio with this camera, so Maya turned away and looked up the stairs at her daughter. The familiar warmth flowed through her. She might be cynical about so much of the parenting process, but that feeling when you look at your child, when the rest of the world fades away, when everything but that little face becomes just scenery in the deep background— that Maya understood.

"Hey, precious."

Maya had read somewhere that the average two-year-old has a vocabulary of about fifty words. That seemed about right. "More" was a big one on the little-kid list. Maya hurried up the stairs and reached over the kid gate and lifted Lily into her arms. Lily clutched one of those indestructible cardboard books in both hands, this one an abridged version of Dr. Seuss's classic *One Fish Two Fish Red Fish Blue Fish*. Lately she'd been carrying the book around the way some kids carry a teddy bear. A book rather than a stuffed animal—this pleased Maya to no end.

"You want Mommy to read you the book?"

Lily nodded.

Maya brought her downstairs and sat her at the kitchen table. The video was still running. One thing Maya had learned: Little kids love repetition. They didn't want new experiences quite yet. Lily had a whole collection of board books. Maya loved the narrative drive of the P. D. Eastman books like *Are You My Mother?* or *A Fish Out of Water*, both featuring scary moments and twist endings. Lily would listen—any book was better than no book—but she always returned to the rhymes and artwork of Dr. Seuss, and really, who could blame her?

Maya glanced at the computer monitor as the nanny cam video played on. On the screen, Lily and Isabella were both on the couch. Isabella fed Lily one Goldfish cracker at a time, like they were smelts awarded to a performing seal. Taking a cue from the feed, Maya grabbed the Goldfish down from the pantry and spread some out on the table. Lily started to eat them one at a time.

"You want something else?"

Lily shook her head and pointed to the book. "Read."

"Not 'Read.' Say, 'Please, Mommy, will you read . . .'"

Maya stopped. Enough. She picked up the book, turned to page one, started with the one fish, two fish, turned the page. She was just reaching the fat fish with the yellow hat when something on the computer monitor snagged her gaze.

Maya stopped reading.

"More," Lily demanded.

Maya leaned toward the screen.

The camera had turned itself on again, but the view was completely blocked. But how . . . ? Maya guessed that she was staring at Isabella's back. Isabella was standing directly in front of the picture frame and that was the reason Maya couldn't see anything.

No.

Isabella was too short. Her head might block it. But her back? No way. Plus, Maya could now make out color. Isabella had been wearing a red blouse yesterday. This shirt was green.

Forest green.

"Mommy?"

"One second, honey."

Whoever it was moved away from the picture frame and out of view. Now Maya could get a look at the couch. Lily sat on it alone. She held that very book in her hands, paging through it on her own, pretending to read it.

Maya waited.

From the left—the kitchen—someone stepped into view. Not Isabella.

It was a man.

At least it appeared to be a man. He was still standing close to the camera and at an angle that made it impossible to see his face. For a moment Maya figured that it might have been Hector, coming inside for a break maybe, grabbing a glass of water or something, but Hector had been wearing overalls and a sweatshirt. This guy was wearing blue jeans and a green—

—forest green—

shirt . . .

On the screen, Lily looked up from the couch toward the maybe-man. When she smiled widely at him, Maya felt a rock take form in her chest. Lily wasn't good with strangers. So whoever this was, whoever was wearing that familiar forest green shirt . . .

The man started toward the couch. His back was to the camera now, blocking Maya's view of her daughter. Maya felt panic when her daughter was out of sight, actually leaning to the left and right as though she could see around this man and make sure that her daughter was still there, on the couch, safe with that same Dr. Seuss book. It felt as though her daughter was in danger and that danger would last until, at the very least, Maya could once again see her and keep an eye on her. The danger was, of course, nonsense. Maya knew that. She was watching something that had already happened, not a live feed, and her daughter was sitting next to her, healthy and seemingly happy, or at least she had been happy until her mom had gone silent and started staring at the computer screen.

"Mommy?"

"One second, honey, okay?"

The man in the familiar blue jeans and forest green shirt—that was how he'd always described the shirt, not green or dark green or bright green but forest green—had obviously not harmed or snatched her daughter or anything like that, so the anxiety Maya was now experiencing seemed uncalled for and more than overblown.

On the screen, the man moved to the side.

Maya could see Lily again. She figured that the fear would subside now. But that wasn't what happened. The man turned and sat on the couch right next to Lily. He faced the camera and smiled.

Somehow Maya didn't scream.

Flex, relax, flex . . .

Maya, always cool in battle, always managing to find someplace inside of her that made her pulse stay even and kept the adrenaline spikes from paralyzing her, tried to find that place now. The familiar clothes, the blue jeans, and especially the forest green shirt should have set her up for the possibility—and by "possibility," she meant "impossibility"—of what she was now seeing. So she didn't scream out loud. She didn't gasp.

There was instead a steady spreading across her chest that made it hard to breathe. There was a chilling in her veins. There was a small quiver in her lips.

There, on the computer monitor, Maya watched Lily crawl onto the lap of her dead husband.

Chapter 6

The video didn't last long.

Lily was barely on "Joe's" lap when he stood with her and carried her out of camera range. The recording stopped thirty seconds later when the motion detector turned the nanny cam off.

That was it.

The next time the cam was activated, Isabella and Lily entered from the kitchen and started to play, just as they had many times before. Maya fast-forwarded it ahead, but the rest of the day was pretty much the same as every other. Isabella and Lily. No dead husbands or anyone else.

She rewound and played the video a second time, then a third.

"Book!"

It was Lily, who was growing impatient. Maya turned to her daughter and wondered how to ask this. "Honey," she said slowly, "did you see Daddy?"

"Daddy?"

"Yes, Lily. Did you see Daddy?"

Lily looked suddenly sad. "Where Daddy?"

Maya didn't want to upset her daughter, but then again, this was a pretty huge turn of events. How to play this? Maya saw no way around it. She put the video on one more time and showed it to Lily. Lily watched, entranced. When Joe came on, she squealed with delight: "Daddy!"

"Yes," Maya said, pushing the pang away at her child's enthusiasm. "Did you see Daddy?"

She pointed to the screen. "Daddy!"

"Yes, that's Daddy. Was he here yesterday?"

Lily just stared at her.

"Yesterday," Maya said. She got up and moved to the couch. She sat in the exact same spot "Joe"—she could only think of his name with air quotes—had. "Was Daddy here yesterday?"

Lily wasn't getting it. Maya tried to stay upbeat, tried to make it more like a game or something happy rather than desperate, but either her body language was wrong or her little girl was more intuitive than Maya imagined.

"Mommy, stop."

You're upsetting her.

Maya plastered a big phony smile on her face and swooped up her daughter. She brought Lily upstairs, giggling and dancing the whole way, until Lily's face seemed to clear of the downstairs' unpleasantness. She placed her on the bed and flipped on the television. Nick Jr. was playing *Bubble Guppies*, one of Lily's favorites, and yes, Maya had sworn not to use the television as a babysitter—all parents swear this and fail—but maybe it would be okay as a baby distractor for a few minutes.

Maya hurried over to Joe's closet and hesitated at the door. She had not so much as opened it since his death. It was too soon. But now, of course, there was no time for that kind of thing. With Lily's eyes glued to the screen, Maya opened the closet door and turned on the light.

Joe loved clothes, and he took good care of them the same way that, well, Maya took care of her guns. His suits were hung neatly with each hanger exactly three inches from the next. His dress shirts were laid out by their colors. The pants always had those hangers that pinched the cuffs and hung straight down, never the kind that would fold over and maybe cause a crease.

Joe liked to shop for himself. He almost always detested whatever Maya tried to gift him in terms of clothing. There had been one exception—a forest green "brush twill" button-down shirt she'd ordered from a company called Moods of Norway. That shirt, unless her eyes were lying to her, which seemed a pretty strong possibility, was the one "Joe" had been wearing in that video. She knew exactly where he kept it.

And it wasn't there.

Again no scream, no gasp. But now she knew for certain.

Someone had been in the house. Someone had gone through Joe's closet.

Ten minutes later, Maya watched the one person who could provide immediate answers arrive.

Isabella.

Isabella had been here yesterday, purportedly watching Lily, and so, at least in theory, she should have noticed anything unusual like, say, Maya's dead husband rummaging through his closet or playing with her daughter.

From the bedroom window, Maya watched Isabella heading up the walk. She tried to assess the approaching nanny as she might any enemy. She didn't appear armed with anything other than her handbag, though that could certainly contain a weapon. She held on to the handbag tightly, as though she feared someone might try to snatch it, but that was how Isabella always held it. Isabella was not a particularly warm person, except, of course, where it mattered most. With Lily. She had loved Joe, the way loyal employees love a benefactor, and only tolerated Maya as an interloper. You see this sometimes in loyal employees. They are more protective and snootier toward outsiders than their wealthy employers.

Did Isabella look a little warier than usual today?

Hard to say. Isabella always looked wary, what with the shifting eyes, the fixed expression, the closed body language. But was there more of it today, or was that Maya's imagination, already on overdrive, clouding her judgment?

Isabella used her key to open the back door. Maya stayed upstairs and waited.

"Mrs. Burkett?"

Silence.

"Mrs. Burkett?"

"We'll be down in a second."

Maya picked up the remote control and snapped off the television. She expected Lily to protest, but that didn't happen. Lily had heard Isabella's voice and was eager now to go down. Maya scooped Lily in her arms and started down the stairs.

Isabella was at the sink washing out a coffee cup. She turned when she heard the footsteps. Her eyes found Lily's, only Lily's, and the fixed, wary expression broke into a smile. It was a nice smile, Maya thought, but did it perhaps lack some of its customary luster?

Enough.

Lily started to stretch her arms toward Isabella. Isabella turned off the water, dried her hands on a towel, and started toward them. Isabella too stretched out her arms, made a cooing noise, and wiggled her fingers in a "give me, give me" gesture.

"How are you, Isabella?" Maya asked.

"Fine, Mrs. Burkett, thank you."

Isabella again reached for Lily, and for a moment Maya almost pulled the child away. Eileen had asked her if she trusted this woman. As much as she could trust anyone with her child, she'd replied. But now, after what she had just seen on the nanny cam . . .

Isabella snatched Lily from her hands. Maya let her. Without another word, Isabella moved into the den with Lily. They sat together on the couch.

"Isabella?"

Isabella looked up as though startled. A smile was frozen on her face. "Yes, Mrs. Burkett?"

"May I have a word with you?"

Lily was on her lap.

"Now?"

"Yes, please," Maya said. Her own voice suddenly sounded funny to her. "I would like to show you something."

Isabella gently placed Lily on the couch cushion next to her. She handed Lily a cardboard book, rose, and smoothed down her skirt. She moved slowly toward Maya, almost as if she were expecting a blow.

"Yes, Mrs. Burkett?"

"Was anyone here yesterday?"

"I'm not sure what you mean."

"I mean," Maya said, keeping her tone even, "was there anybody inside this house yesterday besides you and Lily?"

"No, Mrs. Burkett." The fixed expression was back. "Who do you mean?"

"I mean, anyone. Did Hector come inside, for example?"

"No, Mrs. Burkett."

"So no one was here?"

"No one."

Maya glanced toward the computer, then back at Isabella. "Did you leave at all?"

"Leave the house?"

"Yes."

"Lily and I went to the playground. We do that every day."

"Did you leave the house any other time?"

Isabella looked up as though trying to remember. "No, Mrs. Burkett."

"And did you leave the house at all by yourself?"

"Without Lily?!" She said it with a sharp intake, as though this were the most offensive thing she could imagine. "No, Mrs. Burkett, of course not."

"Did you leave her alone at all?"

"I don't understand."

"It's a simple question, Isabella."

"I don't understand any of this," Isabella said. "Why are you asking me these questions? You don't like the job I'm doing?"

"I didn't say that."

"I never leave Lily alone. Never. Maybe when she takes a nap upstairs, I come downstairs and clean up a little—"

"That's not what I mean."

Isabella studied Maya's face now. "Then what do you mean?"

There was no reason to delay this any longer. "I want to show you something."

The laptop was on the kitchen island. Maya reached for it as Isabella moved in closer. "I keep a camera in the family room," she began.

Isabella looked puzzled.

"A friend gave it to me," Maya said in a way of explanation, though really, did she need to explain herself? "It records what goes on when I'm not here."

"A camera?"

"Yes."

"But I never saw a camera, Mrs. Burkett."

"You're not supposed to. It's hidden."

Isabella's gaze slid back toward the family room.

"A nanny cam," Maya continued. "You know that new picture frame we have on the shelf?"

She watched Isabella's eyes land on the bookshelf. "Yes, Mrs. Burkett."

"That's a camera."

Isabella looked back at her. "So you were spying on me?"

"I was monitoring my child," Maya said.

"But you didn't let me know."

"No, I didn't."

"Why not?"

"There's no reason to get defensive."

"No?" Isabella's tone spiked up. "You didn't trust me."

"Would you?"

"What?"

"It wasn't a question of you, Isabella. Lily is my child. I am responsible for her well-being."

"And you think spying on me is best for her?"

Maya maximized the screen setting and cued up the video. "Before this morning, I figured that it couldn't hurt."

"And now?"

Maya flipped the screen around so Isabella could see it. "Watch."

Maya didn't bother to watch the video again. She had seen it enough times for now. Instead, she focused on Isabella's face and looked for signs of stress or deception.

"What am I supposed to be looking for?"

Maya glanced at the screen. The fake Joe had just exited the screen after blocking the camera. "Just watch."

Isabella narrowed her eyes. Maya tried to keep her breath even. They say you never know how someone will react when the grenade is thrown. That was always the hypothetical: You are standing with your comrades in arms and a grenade is thrown at your feet. Who flees? Who ducks? Who jumps on the grenade and sacrifices themselves? You can try to predict, but until the grenade is actually thrown, you don't have a clue.

Maya had proven herself to her fellow soldiers repeatedly. They knew that under the pressure of combat, she could be cool, calm, collected. She was a leader who had displayed those qualities time and time again.

The odd thing was, this leadership and coolheadedness had not transferred to her real life. Eileen had told her about her little son, Kyle, who was so organized and tidy at his Montessori preschool—and such a mess at home. Something similar happened with Maya.

So as she stood over Isabella, as "Joe" entered the screen and put Lily on his lap, as Isabella's facial expression didn't change, Maya could feel something inside of her give way.

"Well?" Maya said.

Isabella looked at her. "Well, what?"

Something behind Maya's eyes snapped. "What do you mean, well, what?"

Isabella cringed.

"How do you explain that?"

"I don't know what you mean."

"Stop playing games with me, Isabella."

Isabella took a step back. "I don't understand what you mean."

"Did you watch the video?"

"Of course."

"So you saw that man, right?"

Isabella said nothing.

"You saw the man, right?"

Isabella still said nothing.

"I asked you a question, Isabella."

"I don't know what you want from me."

"You saw him, right?"

"Who?"

"What do you mean, who? Joe!" Maya reached out and grabbed Isabella by the lapels. "How the hell did he get into this house?"

"Please, Mrs. Burkett! You're scaring me!"

Maya pulled Isabella toward her. "You didn't see Joe?"

Isabella met her eyes. "Did you?" Her voice was soft, barely a whisper. "Are you telling me you saw Joe on that video?"

"You . . . you didn't?"

"Please, Mrs. Burkett," Isabella said. "You're hurting me."

"Wait, are you saying—"

"Let go of me!"

"Mommy . . ."

It was Lily. Maya looked toward her daughter. Isabella used the distraction to push back and put her hand against her throat as though she'd been choked.

"It's okay, honey," Maya said to Lily. "It's all okay."

Isabella, acting as though she were catching her breath, said, "Mommy and I were just playing, Lily."

Lily watched them both.

Isabella's right hand was still on her own neck, rubbing it far too dramatically. Maya turned toward her. Isabella quickly raised her left palm toward Maya to signal for her to stop.

"I want answers," Maya said.

Isabella managed a nod. "Okay," she said, "but I need some water first."

Maya hesitated and then turned toward the sink. She turned on the water, opened a cabinet, grabbed down a cup. A thought flashed across her brain.

Eileen had been the one to give her the nanny cam.

Maya considered that as she placed the glass under the faucet. She filled it halfway, turned toward Isabella, and then heard the strange hissing.

Maya screamed as the pain—white-hot pain—consumed her.

It felt as though someone were jamming tiny shards of broken glass directly into her eyeballs. Maya's knee buckled. She dropped to the floor.

The hissing.

Somewhere in the clouds past the burning, past the agony, the answer came to her.

Isabella had sprayed something into her face.

Pepper spray.

Pepper spray not only burned the eyes but also inflamed the mucous membranes in the nose, mouth, and lungs. Maya tried to hold her breath so that it wouldn't enter her lungs, tried to blink fast and hard and let her tears wash it away. But for now there was no relief, no escape.

Maya couldn't move.

She heard the sound of someone running, then a door closing.

Isabella was gone.

*   *   *

"Mommy?"

Maya had managed to make her way to the bathroom.

"Mommy's fine, honey. Draw me a picture, okay? I'll be there in minute."

"Isabella?"

"Isabella's fine too. She'll be back soon."

It took longer to get over the effect than she'd originally thought. Rage burned like her eyes. For the first ten minutes, she had been completely incapacitated, helpless to mount even the most minimal defense against an enemy. Eventually the pain and dry heaving subsided. Maya caught her breath. She rinsed out her eyes and washed her skin with dishwashing detergent. Then she scolded herself.

Turning her back on the enemy. Amateur hour.

How could she have been so stupid?

She was furious, mostly with herself. She had even started buying Isabella's act, thinking maybe she really didn't know anything about it. So she let her guard down. Just for a second. And look at the results.

Hadn't she seen enough times when a slipup, a second of lost concentration, had cost lives? Hadn't she learned this most obvious of lessons?

It wouldn't happen again.

Okay, enough self-flagellation. Time to remember, learn, and move ahead.

So what next?

The answer was fairly obvious. Take another few minutes. Recuperate to full strength. Then track down Isabella and make her talk.

The doorbell rang.

Maya rinsed her eyes one more time and headed to the door. She debated getting a gun first—no more chances—but she could see right away it was Detective Kierce.

He stared at her when she opened the door. "What the hell happened to you?"

"I got hit with pepper spray."

"Come again?"

"Isabella. My nanny."

"Are you serious?"

"No, I'm a gifted comedian. Nothing warms up a crowd like jokes about pepper-spraying nannies."

Roger Kierce's eyes wandered around the room before returning to Maya. "Why?"

"I saw something on my nanny cam."

"You have a nanny cam?"

"I do." Again she thought about Eileen giving it to her, even telling her exactly where to put it. "It's hidden in a picture frame."

"My God. Did you . . . did you see Isabella do something to . . . ?"

"What?" But of course it was natural that a cop's mind would go right there. "No, that's not it."

"Then I'm not sure I follow."

Maya debated what route to take here, but she knew that the most direct one would be the only one that would protect her in the long run. "It'll be easier to show you."

She headed toward the laptop on the kitchen island. Kierce followed her. He looked confused. Well, she thought, that look was about to be raised to the tenth power.

Maya spun the screen toward him. She moved the cursor arrow, clicked on the play button, and waited.

Nothing.

She checked the USB port.

The SD card was gone.

She checked the island and the floor around it. But she knew.

"What?" Kierce asked.

Maya took deep even breaths. She needed to stay calm. She looked two or three steps ahead now, again like on a mission. You can't just think about firing rounds downrange at the black SUV. You need to consider your response. You need to have the best intel before making any sudden, life-altering moves.

She knew what this would sound like. If she blurted out what she had seen on the nanny cam, Kierce would think that she was a lunatic. Hell, it sounded crazy replaying it now in her own mind. There were still strands of cobwebs from the pepper spray. What exactly had happened here? Was she, for certain, thinking straight?

Take it slow.

"Mrs. Burkett?"

"I told you to call me Maya."

The evidence for her crazy assertion—the SD card—was gone. Isabella had taken it. It would probably be wisest for Maya to handle that on her own. But at the same time, if she did that, if she didn't tell him now and it came back . . .

"Isabella must have taken it."

"Taken what?"

"The SD card."

"After, what, she hit you with the pepper spray?"

"Yes," Maya said, trying like hell to sound authoritative.

"So she sprays you, she grabs the video card, and then, what, she runs off?"

"Yes."

Kierce nodded. "So what was on it?"

Maya glanced toward the den. Lily was happily engrossed in a giant four-piece zoo puzzle. "I saw a man."

"A man?"

"Yes. On the video. Lily sat on his lap."

"Whoa," Kierce said. "I assume the man was a stranger?"

"No."

"You knew him?"

She nodded.

"So who was it?"

"You won't believe me. You'll understandably think I'm delusional."

"Try me."

"It was Joe."

To his credit, Kierce didn't make a face or gasp or look at her as though she were the craziest person in the history of the world.

"I see," he said, as though he too were trying to maintain his composure. "So it was an old tape?"

"Pardon?"

"It was something you taped when Joe was still alive and maybe, I don't know, you thought you taped over it or—"

"I only got the nanny cam after the murder."

Kierce just stood there.

"The date stamp said it was recorded yesterday," Maya continued.

"But . . ."

Silence.

Then: "You know that can't be."

"I do," Maya said.

They stared at each other. There was no point in trying to convince him. Instead, Maya changed the subject. "Why are you here?"

"I need you to come to the station."

"Why?"

"I can't tell you. But it's really important."

Chapter 7

The same young smiley thing was on duty at the Growin' Up Day Care Center.

"Oh, I remember you," she said. She bent down toward Lily. "And I remember you too. Hi, Lily!"

Lily said nothing. The two women left her with blocks and moved into the office.

"I'm ready to sign her up," Maya said.

"Terrific! When would you like to start?"

"Now."

"Um, that's a little unusual. We usually need two weeks to process an application."

"My nanny quit unexpectedly."

"I'm sorry to hear that, but—"

"Miss . . . I'm sorry, I forget your name."

"Kitty Shum."

"Right, Miss Kitty, sorry. Kitty, do you see that green car out there?"

Kitty looked out the window. Her eyes narrowed. "Is that person bothering you? Do we need to call the police?"

"No, see, that's an unmarked police car. My husband was murdered recently."

"I read about that," Kitty said. "I'm sorry for your loss."

"Thank you. The thing is, that police officer needs to take me to his precinct. I'm not sure why. He just stopped by. So I have a choice. I can bring Lily with me while they ask me about her father's murder . . ."

"Mrs. Burkett?"

"Maya."

"Maya." Kitty still had her eyes on Kierce's car. "You know how to download our phone app?"

"I do."

Kitty nodded. "It's best for your child if you don't have a big emotional good-bye."

"Thank you."

When they reached the Central Park Precinct, Maya asked, "So can you tell me now why we are here?"

Kierce had barely spoken a word the entire ride over. That was okay with Maya. She needed the time to think everything through—the nanny cam, the video, Isa-bella, the forest green shirt.

"I need you to do two lineups for me."

"Lineups of what?"

"I don't want to prejudice your answers."

"It can't be the shooters. I told you. They wore ski masks."

"Black ones, you said. Just eye and mouth holes?"

"Yes."

"Okay, good. Come with me."

"I don't understand."

"You'll see."

As they walked, Maya checked out the Growin' Up Day Care's app. The app allowed you to pay your bill, sign up for hours, review your child's "curriculum of activities," get bios on all the caregivers. But the best part of the app—the reason she'd been drawn to Growin' Up in the first place—was one specific feature. She clicked on it now. There were three choices: the red room, the green room, the yellow room. Lily's age group was in the yellow room. She clicked on the yellow icon.

Kierce opened the door. "Maya?"

"One second."

The screen on her phone came alive, giving her a live feed of the yellow room. You would think Maya would have had enough with the surveillance videos for one day. But no. She turned her phone on the side to make the picture bigger. Lily was there. Safe. A caregiver—

later Maya could look her up and read her bio—was stacking blocks with her and a boy about Lily's age.

Maya felt relief course through her. She almost smiled. She should have insisted on putting Lily in a place like this months ago. Having a nanny left you dependent on one unsupervised person with few checks and balances. Here, there were witnesses and security cameras and socialization. It had to be safer, right?

"Maya?"

It was Kierce again. She closed the app and put the phone in her pocket. They both stepped inside. There were two other people in the room—a female DA assigned to the case and a male defense attorney. Maya tried to focus, but her mind was still swirling from the nanny cam and Isabella. The lingering effects of the pepper spray were still playing havoc with her lungs and nasal membranes. She sniffed like a coke addict.

"I wish to once again put my protest on the record," the male defense attorney said. He had a ponytail halfway down his back. "This witness has admitted she never saw their faces."

"So noted," Kierce said. "And we agree."

Ponytail spread his hands. "So what's the point?"

Maya was wondering that too.

Kierce pulled the cord and the shade came up. Kierce leaned into a microphone and said, "Bring in the first group."

Six people walked into the room. They all wore ski masks.

"This is silly," Ponytail said.

Maya had not expected this.

"Mrs. Burkett," Kierce said, speaking up as though he was being recorded, which, she figured, he probably was, "do you recognize anyone in this room?"

He looked at her and waited.

"Number four," Maya said.

"This is bullshit," Ponytail said.

"And how do you recognize number four?"

"'Recognize' might be too strong a word," Maya said. "But he is the same build and same height as the man who shot my husband. He is also wearing the same clothes."

"Several other men in there are wearing the exact same clothes," Ponytail said. "How can you be sure?"

"Like I said, they're the wrong build or height."

"You're sure?"

"Yes. Number two matches the closest, but he's wearing blue sneakers. The man who shot my husband was wearing red."

"But just to be clear," Ponytail continued, "you can't say for certain that number four is the man who shot your husband. You can say you recollect that he's relatively the same size and build and is wearing similar clothing—"

"Not similar," Maya interjected. "The same clothing."

Ponytail tilted his head. "Really?"

"Yes."

"You can't possibly know that, Mrs. Burkett. There must be more than one set of red Cons out there, am I right? I mean, if I put four red Cons out there, are you going to be able to tell me for certain which ones the assailant was wearing that night?"

"No."

"Thank you."

"But the clothing isn't 'similar.' It isn't as though he's wearing white Cons instead of red. Number four is wearing the exact same outfit as the shooter."

"Which brings me to another point," Ponytail said. "You don't know for certain it's the shooter, do you? That man in the ski mask could be wearing the same clothing and be the same size as the shooter. Isn't that correct?"

Maya nodded. "That's correct."

"Thank you."

Ponytail was done for now. Kierce leaned into the microphone. "You can leave. Send in the second group."

Six more men came in wearing ski masks. Maya studied them. "It's most likely number five."

"Most likely?"

"Number two is wearing the same clothing and is nearly the same height and build. My recollection would be that it's number five, but they are close enough that I couldn't swear to it."

"Thank you," Kierce said. Again he leaned into the microphone. "That's all, thank you."

She followed Kierce out.

"What's going on?"

"We picked up two suspects."

"How did you find them?"

"Your description."

"Can you show me?"

Kierce hesitated, but not for long. "Okay, come on." He brought her to a table with a large-screen monitor, probably thirty inches, maybe more. They sat down. Kierce started typing. "We searched through all nearby CCTV cameras the night of the murder, looking for two men who fit your description. As you can imagine, it took some time. Anyway, there's a condo building on Seventy-Fourth and Fifth Avenue. Take a look."

The CCTV shot the two men from above.

"Is that them?"

"Yes," Maya said. "Or do you want me to give the legalese about just matching the build and clothes?"

"No, this isn't on the record. As you can see, they aren't wearing ski masks. We wouldn't think they would on the street. That would draw attention."

"Still," Maya said, "I don't see how you got an ID from that angle."

"I know. The camera is so damned high. It's so annoying. I can't tell you how many times we get this. The camera is set ridiculously high, and the perps just keep their chins tucked or wear a cap and we can't see their faces. But anyway, once we had this, we knew that they were in the area. So we kept looking."

"You spotted them again?"

Kierce nodded and started typing again. "Yep. At a Duane Reade half an hour later."

He brought up the video. This one was in color. It was shot from the side of the cash register. The two guys' faces were clear now. One was black. The other looked lighter-skinned, maybe Latino. They paid in cash.

"Cold," Kierce said.

"What?"

"Look at the time stamp. This is fifteen minutes after they shot your husband. And here they are, maybe half a mile away, buying Red Bulls and Doritos."

Maya just stared.

"Like I said, cold."

She turned to him. "Or I got it wrong."

"Not likely." Kierce stopped the video, freezing the two men. Yes, men. They were young men, no question about it, but Maya had served with too many men that age to call them boys. "Take a look at this."

He hit an arrow button on the keyboard. The camera zoomed in, blowing up the picture. Kierce focused in on the Latino. "That's the other guy, right? The one who wasn't the shooter?"

"Yes."

"Notice anything?"

"Not really."

He zoomed in closer now, with the camera focused squarely on the guy's waist. "Look again."

Maya nodded. "He's packing."

"Right. He's carrying a gun. You can see the handle if you zoom close enough."

"Not very subtle," she said.

"Nope. Hey, I wonder how all your open-carry patriot buddies would react to these two guys strolling down their street strapped like that."

"I doubt it's a legally purchased gun," Maya said.

"It's not."

"You found the gun?"

"You know it." He sighed and stood. "Meet Emilio Rodrigo. Got an impressive rap sheet for a young punk. They both do. Mr. Rodrigo had the Beretta M9 on him when we arrested him. Illegally owned. He'll serve time for it."

He stopped.

Maya said, "I hear a 'but.'"

"We got a warrant and searched both of their residences. That's where we found the clothes you described and identified today."

"Will that stick in court?"

"Doubtful. Like our ponytailed pal in there said: They're red Cons. Lots of people own them. There was also no sign of ski masks, which I found odd. I mean, they kept the clothes. Why throw out the ski masks?"

"Don't know."

"They probably dumped them in a garbage can. You know. Right away. They shoot, they run, they rip off the masks, they dump them somewhere."

"That makes sense."

"Yeah, except we searched all the nearby garbage cans. Still, they could have found a place, maybe a sewer or something." Kierce hesitated.

"What?"

"Thing is, we located the Beretta, like I said. But we didn't find the murder weapon. The thirty-eight."

Maya sat back. "I'd be surprised if they kept it, wouldn't you?"

"I guess. Except . . ."

"Except what?"

"Punks like these guys don't always dump the gun. They should. But they don't. It has value. So they reuse it. Or they sell it to a buddy. Whatever."

"But this was a pretty big case, right? High profile, lots of media?"

"True."

Maya watched him. "But you don't buy that, do you? You have another theory."

"I do." Kierce looked away. "But it makes no sense."

"What doesn't?"

He started scratching his arm. A nervous tic of some kind. "The thirty-eights we took from your husband's body. We ran them through ballistics. You know. To see if the bullets matched any other cases in our database."

Maya looked up at him. Kierce kept scratching. "I'm guessing from your expression," she said, "that you found a match."

"We did, yeah."

"So these guys. They've killed before."

"I don't think so."

"But you just said . . ."

"Same gun. Doesn't mean the same guys. In fact, Fred Katen, the one you identified as the shooter, had a stone-cold alibi for the first murder. He was serving time. He couldn't have done it."

"When?"

"When what?"

"When was the first murder?"

"Four months ago."

The room chilled. Kierce didn't have to say it. He knew. She knew. Kierce couldn't meet her eye. He looked away, nodded, and said, "The same gun that killed your husband also killed your sister."

Chapter 8

"Are you okay?" Kierce asked.

"Fine."

"I know this is a lot to take in."

"Don't patronize me, Detective."

"I'm sorry. You're right. Let's go through this again, okay?"

Maya nodded. She stared straight ahead.

"We need to look at this in a whole new way now. The two murders seemed random and unconnected, but now that we know the same gun was used for both . . ."

Maya said nothing.

"When your sister was shot, you were deployed in the Middle East. Is that correct?"

"At Camp Arifjan," she said. "In Kuwait."

"I know."

"What?"

"We checked. Just to make sure."

"Make sure . . . ?" She almost smiled. "Ah. You mean like to make sure I didn't somehow sneak home and shoot my sister and then go back to Kuwait and, what, wait four months and kill my husband?"

Kierce didn't reply. He didn't have to. "It all checked out. Your alibi is rock solid."

"Super," she said.

Maya flashed back again to Joe's call. The tears. The shock. That call. That damn call had been the end of Maya's life as she knew it. Nothing would ever be the same after that. It was remarkable when you thought about it. You travel halfway around the world to some hellhole to fight a crazed enemy. You'd think that was where the danger would originate from, that the real threat to her would be from an armed combatant. You'd think, if your life were about to get blown apart, that it would come from an RPG or an IED or a fanatic carrying an AKM.

But no. The enemy had struck, as enemies often do, where she had least expected it: back home in the good ol' USA.

"Maya?"

"I'm listening."

"The officers investigating your sister's murder believed it was a home invasion. She was . . . Do you know the details?"

"Enough of them."

"I'm sorry."

"I asked you not to patronize me."

"I'm not. I'm just being a human being. What was done to her . . ."

Maya took out her app again. She wanted to see her daughter's face. She needed that anchor. But she stopped herself. No. Not now. Don't bring Lily into this. Not even in the most innocuous way.

"At the time of the murder, the cops also took a good look at Claire's husband, your brother-in-law . . ." He started searching through his papers.

"Eddie."

"Right, Edward Walker."

"He wouldn't do it. He loved her."

"Well, they cleared him," Kierce said. "But now we need to take a closer look at the home life. We need to take a fresh look at everything."

Maya saw it now. She smiled, but there was no humor or warmth. "How long, Detective?"

He kept his head down. "Excuse me?"

"How long have you known about the ballistics report?"

Kierce kept reading the file.

"You've known about it for a while, haven't you? About the same gun killing Joe and Claire?"

"What makes you say that?"

"When you came to my house to check out my Smith and Wesson, I assume it was to make sure that it wasn't the murder weapon—to make sure it didn't match either murder."

"That doesn't mean anything."

"No, but you said you no longer suspected me. Remember?"

He said nothing.

"That's because you already knew I had the perfect alibi. You knew that the same gun had been used to kill my sister. And you knew that I was overseas when Claire was shot. Before then, well, you hadn't found the two guys with the ski masks. I could have made that up. But once you had that ballistics report, you only had to double-check my whereabouts with the military. You did that. I know the procedure. That's not one phone call. So how long have you had the ballistics report?"

His voice was low. "Since the funeral."

"Right. And when did you find Emilio Rodrigo and Fred Katen and get confirmation I was in Kuwait?"

"Late last night."

Maya nodded—just as she had thought.

"Come on, Maya, don't be naïve. Like I said, we looked hard at your brother-in-law when your sister was murdered. Here's one time when there's no sexism. Think about it. You're the spouse. You're alone in a park. If you were me, who would be your number one suspect?"

"Especially," Maya added, "when that spouse served in the military and is, in your eyes, a gun nut?"

He didn't bother defending himself. Then again, he

didn't have to. He was right. You always suspect the spouse.

"So now that we got all that out of the way," Maya said, "what do we do now?"

"We look for connections," Kierce said, "between your sister and your husband."

"The biggest being me."

"Yes. But there are more."

Maya nodded. "They worked together."

"Exactly. Joe hired your sister for his equities firm. Why?"

"Because Claire was smart." Just saying her name stung. "Because Joe knew that she was hardworking and reliable and trustworthy."

"And because Claire was family?"

Maya considered this. "Yes, but not in a nepotistic way."

"What way then?"

"The Burketts are big on family. It's old-world clan-like."

"They don't trust outsiders?"

"They don't *want* to trust outsiders."

"Okay, I get that," Kierce said, "but if I had to work every day with my sister-in-law . . . ugh, shudder. You know what I mean?"

"I do."

"Of course my sister-in-law's a world-class, Olympic-sized pain the ass. I'm sure your sister—" He caught himself now, cleared his throat. "So their working to-gether, Joe and Claire—did it cause any tension?"

"I worried about that," Maya said. "My uncle, he had a business. Very successful. But then other family members wanted in and he let them and it all went to hell. Family and money is never a good mix. Someone is always going to feel resentful."

"But that didn't happen here?"

"Just the opposite. Claire and Joe had this fun new connection. Work. They'd talk business all the time. She would call with ideas. He would remember some-thing that needed to be done the next day and text it to her." She shrugged. "But then again . . ."

"Then again?"

Maya looked up at him. "I wasn't around a whole lot."

"You were deployed overseas."

"Right."

"Still," Kierce said, "none of it adds up. What would make someone kill Claire, hold on to the gun for four months, and then give it to this Katen guy to kill Joe?"

"Yo, Kierce?"

It was another cop in the station. The younger man stood across the room and beckoned for Kierce to come toward him.

"Excuse me a moment."

Kierce headed over to the cop. The young cop leaned in, and the two men started whispering. Maya watched. Her head was still spinning, but her thoughts kept returning to something that didn't seem to concern Kierce in the least.

The nanny cam video.

That was natural, she supposed. He hadn't seen the actual images. He was preoccupied with the facts, and while he didn't completely dismiss what she said as the ravings of a delusional nutbag, he probably figured that it was the work of an overactive imagination or something in that realm. To be fair, even Maya had to consider that possibility.

Kierce finished up the conversation and came toward her.

"What's wrong?"

He grabbed his suit coat and threw it over his shoulder like Sinatra playing the Sands. "I'll drive you home," he said. "We can finish this conversation on the way."

Ten minutes into the ride, Kierce said, "So you saw me talking to that cop before we left, right?"

"Yes."

"That was about your, uh, situation." He kept his eyes on the road. "I mean, what you said about the nanny cam and the pepper spray and all that."

So he hadn't forgotten. "What about it?"

"Well, look, I'm going to ignore for now what you said about the contents, okay? Until I see and we can both analyze the video, there's no reason to discredit or, uh, confirm what may be on that . . . What was it again, a USB drive?"

"An SD card."

"Right, the SD card. There is no reason yet to deal with intangibles. But that doesn't mean there is nothing we can do."

"I'm not following."

"You were assaulted. That's a fact. Check that: You were clearly hit with pepper spray or some agent in that family. Your eyes are still red. I can see that you are still dealing with the residual aftereffects. So whatever else we want to believe, clearly something happened to you."

He made a turn, sneaking a glance at her as he did.

"You said that it was your nanny, Isabella, who assaulted you, right?"

"Right."

"So I sent a man out to her house. You know. To check out your claim."

Her claim. Nice lingo. "So did your man find her?"

Kierce kept his eyes fixed on the road. "Let me ask you a question first."

She didn't like that reply. "Okay."

"During this altercation," he began, speaking with more care now, "did you threaten or choke Isabella Mendez?"

"Is that what she told you?"

"It's a simple question."

"No, I did not."

"You didn't touch her?"

"I may have touched, but—"

"May have?"

"Come on, Detective. I may have touched her to get her attention. The way two women might."

"Two women." He almost smiled. "So now you're playing the woman card with me?"

"I didn't hurt her or anything."

"Did you grab her?"

Maya saw where this was going. "So your man found her?"

"He did."

"And she, what, claimed that she pepper-sprayed me in self-defense?"

"Something like that. She said that you were acting irrationally."

"In what way?"

"She said you were ranting about seeing Joe on a video."

Maya tried to think how to play this. "What else did she say?"

"She said that you scared her. She said that you grabbed her by the shirt, near the throat, in a threatening manner."

"I see."

"Is she telling the truth?"

"Did she mention that I played the video for her?"

"Yes."

"And?"

"She said the screen was blank."

"Wow," Maya said.

"She said that she worried you were delusional. She said that you served in the military and that you often carry a gun. She said when you add all that up—your background, your ranting, your delusions, your assault of her first—"

"Assault?"

"By your own admission, Maya, you touched her."

She frowned but kept still.

"Isabella said that she felt threatened, so she used the pepper spray and ran."

"Did your man ask about the missing SD card?"

"He did."

"Let me guess. She didn't take it and knows nothing about it."

"Bingo," Kierce said. He hit the turn signal. "Do you still want to press charges?"

But Maya could see how this would play out. A gun nut with a controversial past in the military screams about her murdered husband playing with their daughter on a video, grabs the nanny by the lapels—and then accuses the nanny of, what, unjustified use of pepper spray? Oh, and stealing the video of her dead husband.

Yeah, that'll play.

"Not now," Maya said.

Kierce dropped her off at the house. He promised to stay in touch about any new developments. Maya thanked him. She debated picking up Lily at day care, but after one quick look at her new phone app—it was story time, and even from the odd angle of the camera, Maya could see that Lily was riveted—she decided that it could wait.

Dozens of messages and texts were on her phone, all from Joe's family. Oh, damn. She had missed the reading of the will. She didn't much care for her own sake, but Joe's family must have been livid. She picked up the phone and called Joe's mother.

Judith picked up the phone on the first ring. "Maya?"

"I'm sorry about today."

"Are you okay?"

"I'm fine," Maya said.

"And Lily?"

"Fine too. Something came up. I didn't mean to worry you."

"Something came up more important than—"

"The police found the shooters," Maya interrupted. "They needed me to identify them."

Maya heard Judith gasp. "Were you able to?"

"Yes."

"So they're in jail? It's over?"

"It's more complicated than that," Maya said. "Right now, they don't have enough to hold them."

"I don't understand."

"They wore ski masks, so I never saw their faces. Build and clothing isn't enough."

"So . . . so they just let them go? The two men who killed my son are free to walk the streets?"

"They have one on a weapons charge. Like I said, it's complicated."

"Maybe we can talk about it when you come by tomorrow morning? Heather Howell felt it best if we wait until all parties are present before we read the will."

Heather Howell was the family attorney. Maya said her good-byes, hung up, and stared at her kitchen. Everything was sleek and new, and God, she missed that old Formica kitchen table in Brooklyn.

What the hell was she doing in this house? She had never belonged here.

She walked over to the nanny cam picture frame. Maybe the SD card was still inside it. Maya couldn't imagine how that would happen, but she was pretty much open to any interpretation. Had she really seen Joe on that video cam? No. Could he somehow still be alive? No. Had she imagined the whole thing?

No.

Her dad had been a big fan of detective fiction. He used to read Sir Arthur Conan Doyle to Maya and Claire at that Formica kitchen table. How had Sherlock Holmes put it? "When you have eliminated the impossible, whatever remains, however improbable, must be the truth."

Maya picked up the picture frame and looked in the back.

No SD card.

"When you have eliminated the impossible . . ."

The SD card was gone. Ergo, Isabella had taken it. Ergo, Isabella had lied. Isabella had used the pepper spray to incapacitate Maya so she could take the SD card. Isabella was part of this.

Part of what?

One thing at a time.

Maya started to put the frame back on the shelf when something made her stop. She stared at the frame, the digital pictures Eileen had preloaded shuffling by, when the thought hit her anew.

Why had Eileen given her the nanny cam frame in the first place?

Eileen had told her, hadn't she? Maya was alone now. She was leaving Lily with a nanny. Having a nanny cam made sense. Better to be cautious than sorry. That all added up, didn't it?

Maya kept staring at the frame. When she peered hard, she could see the pinhole camera built into the top of the black frame. Odd when you think about it: Sure, the nanny cam was an extra piece of security, but when you let a camera into your house . . .

Were you letting someone else inside too?

Couldn't someone somehow watch you?

Okay, slow down. Let's not get paranoid here.

But now that Maya thought about it, someone had engineered these cameras. Most of these gizmos could be hooked up to direct feeds and watched live in some way. It didn't mean they were, but the potential was there. The manufacturers could have a secret back door in and watch your every move in the same way Maya could flip on her app and take a look at Lily at the day care center.

Holy crap. Why had she let such a thing into her house?

Eileen's voice came back to her.

"So do you trust her?"

And then:

"You trust no one, Maya . . ."

But she did. She trusted Shane. She had trusted Claire. And Eileen?

She had met Eileen through Claire. Maya was still a senior in high school when Claire, a year older, started college at Vassar. She had driven Claire up to school and helped her unpack. Eileen had been assigned as Claire's roommate. Maya remembered how cool she thought Eileen was. She was cute and funny and swore like a sailor. She was loud and bouncy and ferocious. When Claire brought her home to Brooklyn during college breaks, Eileen would debate with Dad for hours, giving better than she took.

Maya had thought she was a balls-to-the-wall hardass. But life changes people. It smothers that kind of larger-than-life woman. Time quiets them down. That firecracker girl you knew in high school—where is she now? It didn't happen to men as much. Those boys often grew up to be masters of the universe. The super successful girls? They seemed to die of slow societal suffocation.

So why had Eileen given Maya the nanny cam?

No point in wondering. Time to confront and figure out what the hell was going on here. Maya headed into the basement. She opened the safe with her index finger. The Beretta M9 was right there, but she took the Glock 26 instead. Smaller. Easier to hide.

She didn't think that she'd need a weapon, but no one ever thinks they do.

Chapter 9

Eileen was in the front yard working on her roses when Maya pulled up. Eileen waved. Maya returned it and put the car in park.

Maya had never had a lot of female friends.

Maya and Claire had grown up on the bottom two floors of a town house in the Greenpoint section of Brooklyn. Her father had been a college professor at NYU. Her mother worked six years as a legal defense attorney but ended up quitting to raise her two children. Her parents weren't pacifists or socialists or anything like that, but they certainly leaned toward the left. They sent their daughters to summer camp at Brandeis University. They made them learn wind instruments and read the classics. They gave their girls formal religious training but stressed their own belief that these were allegories and myths, not facts. They owned no handguns. They didn't hunt or fish or do anything that hinted at outdoorsy.

Maya had been drawn to the idea of flying airplanes at a young age. No one knew how or why. No one in the family flew or had any interest in anything involving flight or mechanics or really anything in the general vicinity. Her parents had assumed that Maya's obsession was a phase. It wasn't. Her parents neither condemned nor condoned her decision to apply for the Army's elite pilot program. They just didn't seem to get it.

During basic training, she had been given a Beretta M9, and as much as people looked for all kinds of complicated psychological reasons why, Maya simply liked firing the gun. Yes, she got that weapons could kill, and understood the destructive nature and could see how many people, mostly men, used them as a dangerous and stupid compensation for their own inadequacies. She got that some people liked guns because of the way the guns made them feel, that some kind of unhealthy transference was going on, and that often it was a very bad thing.

But in her case, Maya simply liked shooting. She was also good at it and drawn to it. Why? Who the hell knows? The same reason people are drawn to basketball or swimming or collecting antiques or skydiving, she guessed.

Eileen stood up and brushed the dirt off her knees. She smiled and started toward Maya. Maya got out of the car.

"Hey, you!" Eileen said.

"Why did you give me that nanny cam?"

Just like that.

Eileen stopped midstride. "Why? What happened?"

Maya looked for that feisty freshman. There were signs of her every once in a while. She was recovering, but time passes and wounds don't fully heal. Eileen had been so smart and tough and resourceful—or so it appeared—and then she met the wrong man. Simple as that.

Robby had been so doting at first. He would flatter Eileen and brag about her. He was proud of her, telling everyone how smart Eileen was; then he became too proud of her, the kind of proud that plays on that line between love and obsession. Claire was concerned, but it was Maya who noticed the bruises first. Eileen had started wearing long sleeves. But neither sister did anything at first because they simply couldn't believe it. Maya had figured that victims of domestic abuse were more . . . victim-y? Weak women get into these situations. Lost or poor or uneducated women, women with no backbone—those are the ones men abuse.

Strong women like Eileen? No way.

"Just answer the question," Maya said. "Why did you give me that nanny cam?"

"Why do you think?" Eileen countered. "You're a widow with a little girl."

"For protection."

"You really don't see that?"

"Where did you buy it?"

"What?"

"The digital frame with the hidden camera. Where did you buy it?"

"Online."

"What store?"

"You're kidding, right?"

Maya just stared at her.

"Sheesh, okay, I bought it on Amazon. What's going on, Maya?"

"Show me."

"Are you serious?"

"If you bought it online, there will be a record of it under past orders. Show me."

"I don't understand any of this. What happened?"

Maya had so admired Eileen. Her sister could be a bit of a goody-goody. Eileen was wilder. Eileen made her feel good. Eileen got her.

But that was a long time ago.

Eileen angrily pulled off her gardening gloves and threw them on the ground. "Fine."

She started for the door. Maya followed behind her. When she caught up, Maya could see Eileen's face was set.

"Eileen . . ."

"You were right before."

"About?"

Tears brimmed in her eyes. "Robby. That's how I got rid of him for good."

"I don't understand."

The house was a split-level built in the 1960s. They stood in the den. One wall was covered with photographs of Kyle and Missy. No pictures of Eileen. No pictures of Robby. But it was the poster on the other wall that drew Maya's eye. Claire had the same one in her den. Using four black-and-white photographs running left to right, the framed print showed the construction stages of the Eiffel Tower. Eileen and Claire had bought them on a backpacking trip the three of them—Eileen, Maya, Claire—took to France during the summer when Eileen and Claire were twenty and Maya was nineteen.

For the first week of their journey, the girls would meet up with different French men every night. They'd make out with them, no more, and giggle the whole night about how cute François or Laurent or Pascal was. A week in, Claire met Jean-Pierre and started the perfect summer romance—intense, passionate, romantic, full of PDA (public displays of affection that made Maya and Eileen gag), and sadly forced to die in six weeks' time.

For a fleeting moment at the end of their stay, Claire actually toyed with the idea of not returning to Vassar for her senior year. She was in love. Jean-Pierre was in love. He begged her to stay. He was a "realistic romantic," he claimed, and so he knew the odds but he also knew that they could beat them. He loved her.

"Please, Claire, I know we can do it."

Claire was simply too practical. She broke his heart

and her own. She came home, cried, and then got on with her regularly scheduled life.

Where, Maya wondered, was Jean-Pierre now? Was he married or happy? Did he have kids? Did he still think about Claire? Did he know, via the web or whatever, that she was dead? How had he reacted to her death? Shock, anger, denial, devastation, sad shrug?

Maya wondered what would have happened if Claire had decided to stay with Jean-Pierre in France. In all likelihood, she would have had a few more weeks, maybe months, of romance before coming back home. She'd have missed a semester at Vassar, maybe, and graduated late.

Big friggin' deal.

Claire should have stayed. She shouldn't have been so damn practical.

"I know you thought that you got rid of Robby for good," Eileen said. "And I thank you for that. You saved my life. You know that."

The midnight text Eileen had sent Maya was simple: **He's going to kill me. Please help.** Maya had driven over with this same weapon in her purse. Robby was drunk and raging, calling Eileen a dirty whore and worse. He'd been spying on Eileen and saw her smile at some guy at the gym. He was throwing things when Maya arrived, searching for his wife, who had found a hiding spot in the basement.

"You scared him that night."

Maya had, perhaps taking it a step too far, but sometimes it was the only way.

"But when he found out you'd redeployed, he started coming around again."

"Why didn't you call the police?"

Eileen just shrugged. "They never believe me. They say the right things. But you know Robby. He can be charming."

And, Maya added to herself, *Eileen never pressed charges.* The vicious cycle of abuse fueled by a mixture of false optimism and fear.

"So what happened?"

"He came back and beat me. Broke two ribs."

Maya closed her eyes. "Eileen."

"I couldn't live with the fear anymore. I thought about getting a gun. You know. It would be self-defense, right?"

Maya said nothing.

"Except then what? The cops would wonder why I suddenly decided to buy a gun. I'd probably still get charged. And even if I didn't, what kind of life is that for Kyle and Missy? Their mom killed their dad. You think they'd ever understand it?"

Yes, Maya thought. But she kept it to herself.

"I couldn't live with the fear. So I set it up to take one more beating. That's all. If I could live through it, maybe I'd be rid of him for good."

Maya saw where this was going. "You taped him with the hidden camera."

She nodded. "I brought the tape to my lawyer. He wanted to take it to the cops, but I just wanted it over.

So he talked to Robby's lawyer. Robby dropped his request for joint custody. He knows the tape is with my lawyer and if he comes back . . . It isn't perfect, but it's better now."

"Why didn't you tell me?"

"Because there was nothing you could do. Because you've always been everyone's protector. I didn't want that for you anymore. I wanted you to be okay too."

"I'm fine."

"No, Maya, you're not."

Eileen bent over the computer. "Do you know how some people want cops to wear cameras all the time? Ninety-two percent of the public. I mean, why not? But I wonder if we all shouldn't wear them all the time. How would we behave? Would we be better to each other? So I started thinking about that. I thought we should record whatever we could. That's why I bought the hidden cameras. Do you get that?"

"Show me the order, please."

"Fine." Eileen didn't protest anymore. "Here."

Maya looked down at the screen. There it was—an order for three digital camera frames with hidden cameras.

"This order is a month old."

"I ordered three for myself. I gave you one of mine."

A month ago. So the idea that Eileen was in on all this—whatever the hell this was—seemed very unlikely. No one could have foreseen all of this a month ago.

And really, what the hell did Maya think Eileen could have done here?

None of it made any sense.

"Maya?"

She turned to Eileen.

"I'm going to skip the part where I'm insulted that you didn't trust me."

"I saw something . . ."

"Yeah, I figured that out. What?"

Maya wasn't in the mood to share that lunacy with Eileen. Eileen might believe, she might not, but either way it would take time to explain and Maya saw no outcome where Eileen could help her down that particular avenue.

"The police learned something strange about Claire's murder."

"A lead?"

"Maybe."

"After all this time?" Eileen shook her head. "Wow."

"Tell me what you remember about it."

"About Claire's murder?"

"Yes."

Eileen shrugged. "It was a home invasion. Drifters, the police thought. That's all I know."

"It wasn't a home invasion. It wasn't drifters."

"What then?"

"The same gun that killed Claire," Maya said, "killed Joe."

Eileen's eyes widened. "But . . . that can't be."

"It can."

"And you learned this on the nanny cam?"

"What? No. The police ran a ballistics test on the bullets they pulled out of Joe's body. They ran the results through a computer to see if the bullet matched any other cases in the system."

"And it was a match for Claire?" Eileen collapsed back. "My God."

"This is where I need your help, Eileen."

Eileen looked up at her as though through a haze. "Anything."

"I need you to think back."

"Okay."

"Was Claire acting any different before her murder? Was anything odd going on? Anything at all?"

"I always thought it was a random thing." Eileen was still stunned. "A home invasion."

"It wasn't. We know that now. I need you to focus, Eileen, okay? Claire is dead. Joe is dead. The same weapon was used to murder both of them. Maybe they were both mixed up in something—"

"Mixed up in something? Claire?"

"Nothing bad. But something was going on. Something that connected the two of them. Think, Eileen. You knew Claire better than anyone."

Eileen lowered her head.

"Eileen?"

"I didn't think it had anything to do with it . . ."

Maya felt that jolt. She tried to stay very still. "Tell me."

"Claire was acting . . . not weirdly or anything but . . . there was one thing."

Maya nodded, trying to encourage her to say more.

"We were having lunch at Baumgart's one day. This was a week, maybe two, before the murder. Her cell phone rang. She turned all white. Now normally she answers the phone in front of me. We don't really have secrets, you know that."

"Go on."

"But this time, Claire grabbed the phone and hurried outside. I looked out the window and I could see she was all animated. She was on for maybe five minutes, then she came back."

"Did she tell you who was on the phone?"

"No."

"Did you ask?"

"Yes. She said it was nothing . . ."

"I hear a 'but.'"

"But it clearly wasn't nothing." Eileen shook her head. "How could I not make her tell me? How could I just . . . ? Anyway, she was distracted the rest of lunch. I tried to raise it a few more times, but she just shut me down. Jesus. I should have done more."

"I don't know what more you could have done." Maya thought about it. "The police would have gone through her phone records anyway. They would have looked into all her calls."

"That's just it."

"What?"

"The phone."

"What about it?"

"It wasn't hers."

Maya leaned forward. "Come again?"

"Her normal phone, the one with the case with the kids' picture on it, was still on the table," Eileen said. "Claire was carrying a second phone."

Chapter 10

The Burkett servants lived in a complex of small homes on the back edge of the Farnwood estate, just left of the delivery entrance. The homes were all one level and reminded Maya of army barracks. The largest belonged to the Mendezes, Isabella's family. Isabella's mother, Rosa, still worked in the main house, though it was hard to say what she did now that all the children were grown.

Maya knocked on Isabella's door. There was no sign of life, but these were hardworking people. Their hours were insane. Maya was far from a socialist, but she found it ironic how much the Burketts complained about staff and workers, really believing that this country was a meritocracy, when everything had been handed to them because, two generations earlier, a grandfather had found a way to exploit real estate laws. She knew most of the Burketts wouldn't last a week working their servants' hours.

Hector's Dodge Ram pickup pulled in behind her. He parked a good distance from her and stepped out.

"Mrs. Burkett?" He looked scared.

"Where's Isabella?"

"I think you better leave."

Maya shook her head. "Not until I talk to Isabella."

"She isn't here."

"Where is she?"

"She went away."

"Away where?"

Hector shook his head.

"I just want to apologize," Maya said. "It was all a misunderstanding."

"I'll tell her you said that." He shuffled his weight from one foot to the other. "I think you better leave now."

"Where is she, Hector?"

"I'm not going to tell you. You really scared her."

"I need to talk to her. You can stay in the room. Make sure she's safe or whatever."

A voice from behind her said, "That's not going to happen."

Maya turned and saw Isabella's mother standing there. She gave Maya a withering glare and said, "Leave."

"No."

Her eyes flicked toward her son. "Come inside, Hector."

Giving wide berth, Hector made his way through the door. With one more glare, Isabella's mother closed it behind both of them, leaving Maya outside.

She should have been prepared for this.

Back off, Maya told herself. *Think it through*.

Her cell phone sounded. She checked and saw that the call was from Shane.

"Hey," she said.

"I looked up that license plate for you," Shane said without preamble. "Your Buick Verano is leased by a company called WTC Limited."

WTC. Didn't ring a bell. "Any idea what that stands for?"

"None. The address is a post office box in Houston, Texas. It looks like some kind of holding company."

"The kind of thing someone uses when they want to stay anonymous?"

"Yep. If we want to learn more, I'll need to get a warrant. And to get that, I'd need a reason for looking into this."

"Just forget it," she said.

"If you say so."

"It's no big deal."

"Don't lie to me, Maya. I hate that."

She didn't reply.

"When you're ready to come clean, call me."

Shane hung up.

*   *   *

Eddie hadn't changed the locks.

Maya hadn't been back to Claire's house—yep, still thinking of it as such—since pulling down Coach Phil's pants. There were no cars in the driveway. Nobody answered her knock. So she took out the key and let herself in. As she entered the foyer, Eddie's words floated back down to her.

"Death follows you, Maya . . ."

Maybe Eddie was right. If that was the case, was it fair to put Daniel and Alexa at risk?

Or, for that matter, Lily?

The boxes with Claire's stuff still hadn't been moved. Maya thought about the mysterious spare phone Eileen had seen. It seemed obvious that the phone was the kind of thing you bought when you didn't want anyone to know who you were calling.

So what had happened to that phone?

If it had been on Claire when she died, the police would have gone through it. Of course, that could very well have happened. They might have recovered it during their investigation and concluded that it was meaningless. But Maya didn't think so. Shane had contacts with the police. He'd looked into the investigation for her. There was nothing there about a spare phone or any unexplained calls.

Which meant the phone had probably not yet been discovered.

The boxes were unlabeled. Eddie seemed to have

done it in a rush, dumping things in a flurry of grief so that clothes were mixed with toiletries, jewelry with papers, shoes with various trinkets. Claire loved cheesy souvenirs. Antiques and true collectibles were deemed too expensive, but Claire always got the snow globe when she visited a new city or tourist attraction. She had a shot glass from Tijuana. She bought a little piggy bank shaped like the Leaning Tower of Pisa. She owned a Princess Di memorial plate, a wiggly Hawaiian hula girl who shook her stuff on a car dashboard, a pair of used Vegas casino dice.

Maya remained stone-faced as she sorted through the goofy tchotchkes that had at one point in their existence made Claire smile. She was in mission mode now. On one level, doing this, sorting through these nothings that her sister had cherished, was intensely painful, and the guilt started seeping in:

Your husband is right. I let death in. I should have been here. I should have protected you . . .

But on another level—a higher, more important level—this guilt and pain helped. They made her mission more discernible. When you can see the stakes, when you realize the true purpose of your mission, it motivates you. It makes you focus. It makes you push away the distractions. You gain clarity of purpose. You gain strength.

But there was no phone in any of the boxes.

After the last box, she collapsed back onto the floor.

Think it through, she told herself. *Get into Claire's head.* Her sister had owned a phone she wanted no one to know about. Where would she hide it . . . ?

A memory came to Maya. Claire had been a junior in high school, Maya a sophomore. Claire, in perhaps her one fit of rebellion, had started smoking cigarettes. Dad had a super sensitive nose. He could smell them on her.

Dad was pretty liberal about most things. Being a college professor, he had seen it all and expected experimentation. But cigarettes struck a nerve. His own mother had died a horrible death from lung cancer. Nana had moved into the small spare room toward the end. Maya remembered the sounds mostly, the haunting, horrible wet sucking-gurgling coming from Nana's room, spending her last few days slowly and agonizingly being choked to death. Maya could barely enter that room after Nana's death. Death lingered. Its smell had seemingly burrowed into the walls. Worse than that, Maya sometimes was sure that she could still hear the sucking-gurgling sound. She had read somewhere that that sound never fully disappears. It just gets fainter and fainter.

Like the sounds of helicopter rotors. Like the sound of gunfire. Like the screams of death.

Maybe, Maya thought now, in that terrible room . . . maybe that was where death first started to follow her.

Maya stayed on the floor and closed her eyes. She

tried to slow down her breathing and keep the sounds at a distance.

The memory nudged her again: Dad hated cigarettes.

Right, okay. Claire started smoking, and Dad would freak out. He started searching Claire's bedroom at night, finding the cigarettes, and throwing small tantrums. The smoking stage didn't last long. But while it did, Claire finally thought of a hiding place their father would never look.

Maya's eyes lit up.

She quickly stood and hurried toward the living room. The old trunk—ironically, Nana's old trunk—was there. Claire had used it as a coffee table. There were family photos on top. Maya started taking them off and putting them on the floor. Most of the photos were of Daniel and Alexa, but there was one of Eddie and Claire from the wedding. Maya stopped and stared at them. Both looked so damned young and hopeful and happy and mostly unsuspecting. These two had no idea what life had in store for them, but then again, no one does, do they?

The inside of the trunk was used to store tablecloths and linens. Maya removed them and started feeling her way along the bottom.

"My father brought the trunk over from Kiev," Nana had told them during a visit when they were little, years before the cancer choked her to death, when Nana was spry and healthy, when she would take them swimming or teach them tennis. "See this?"

The two little girls bent close.

"He built it himself. It's a secret compartment."

"Why was it a secret, Nana?" Claire had asked.

"So he could hide his mother's jewelry and cash. Every stranger is a potential thief. Remember that. You two girls. When you're older. You will always have each other. But never leave your valuables where others can find them."

Maya's finger found the small seam. She dug down, heard the click, and slid back the secret panel. Then, just as she had done as a child, she bent close and looked inside.

The phone was there.

Maya pulled it out with a smile of satisfaction on her face. If she were a more religious person, she would have sworn that her sister and her nana were looking down upon her. But she wasn't religious. The dead always stayed dead. That was the problem.

She tried to flip the phone on, but the battery was completely empty. No surprise. It'd probably been sitting untouched since Claire's murder. Maya turned the phone over and checked the charging socket. It looked somewhat familiar. She'd be able to find a cord and charge it later.

"What are you doing here?"

The voice startled her. Instinctively she rolled away from it and came up prepared to defend herself.

"For chrissake, Eddie."

Eddie's face was red. "I said—"

"I heard you. Give me a second to catch my breath."

So much for clarity and focus, Maya thought. She had been so lost in the brilliance of her discovery that Eddie had been able to enter and sneak up on her without her noticing.

Another mistake.

"I asked you what you—"

"I was going through her boxes," Maya said.

Eddie took a step that had a little too much sway in it. "I told you to stay away."

"So you did."

Eddie wore the same red flannel shirt with the sleeves rolled up to reveal his ropey forearm muscles. He was wiry and tight like a welterweight boxer. Claire had liked that about him, his build. His eyes had the red of drink.

He stuck out his hand, palm up.

"I want your key. Now."

"I don't think so, Eddie."

"I can change the locks."

"You can barely change your clothes."

He looked down at the picture frames and linens strewn on the floor. "What are you doing in that trunk?"

Maya didn't reply.

"I saw you take something. Give it back."

"No."

He eyed her now, his hands forming fists. "I can just take it—"

"No, you can't. Was she having an affair, Eddie?"

That stopped him. His mouth dropped open. Then he said, "Go to hell."

"Did you know about it?"

The welling in Eddie's eyes started up again, and for a moment Maya's eyes found that wedding picture, found Eddie's happy, hopeful face. So maybe it wasn't just the drink that was causing the red. Eddie saw it too, the same photograph, and something in him gave. He collapsed onto the couch. His face fell into his hands.

"Eddie?"

His voice was barely audible. "Who was it?"

"I don't know. Eileen said Claire was getting secret calls. I just found a phone she hid in this trunk."

He kept his face in his hands. "I don't believe it," he said in a voice that had nothing behind it.

"What happened, Eddie?"

"Nothing." He looked up. "I mean, we weren't at our best. But that's marriage. There are cycles. You know all about that, right?"

"We aren't talking about me."

Eddie shook his head and lowered it again. "Maybe, maybe not."

"What's that supposed to mean?"

"Claire worked," he said, too slowly, "for your husband."

Maya didn't like the cadence in his voice. "So?"

"So her excuse, when I asked, was that she was working late."

He met her eyes now. She met his. Maya was not one for talking in circles.

"If you're trying to imply that Claire and Joe . . ."

It was too preposterous to even finish.

"You're the one saying she had an affair," Eddie said, shrugging his way back to his feet. "I'm just telling you where she was."

"So you had some inkling that maybe there was someone else?"

"I didn't say that."

"Yeah, you did. How come you never told the cops about that inkling?"

Now it was his turn not to reply.

"Oh, right," Maya said. "You're the husband. They were already looking at you hard. Imagine if they knew that you suspected her of having an affair."

"Maya?"

She waited. He took a step toward her. She took a step backward.

"Give me that goddamn phone," he said. "And get out of my house."

"I'm taking the phone."

Eddie stood in her path. "You really want to test me?"

Maya thought about the gun in her purse. The truth is, you never forget it. If you carry a weapon, it is always in your thoughts, always weighing you down or pulling at your sleeve. It is always, for better or worse, an option.

Eddie took a step toward her.

There was no way Maya was giving up the phone. Her hand started toward her purse when she heard two more familiar voices.

"Aunt Maya!"

"Yay!"

Daniel and Alexa crashed through the door as only the young can. They gave their aunt a big hug. She hugged them back, making sure neither pressed up against her purse. She kissed them both a little hard, quickly made her excuses, and slipped out the door before Eddie could do anything stupid.

Five minutes later, Eddie called on her mobile.

"Sorry about that," he said. "I loved Claire. God, how I . . . You know all this. And we had troubles, sure, but she loved me too."

Maya was driving the car. "I know, Eddie."

"Do me a favor, Maya."

"What?"

"Whatever you find on that phone, no matter how bad, I need you to tell me. I need to know the truth."

In the rear window Maya spotted the red Buick again.

"Promise me, Maya."

"I promise."

She hung up and took another look in the rearview mirror, but the red Buick was gone. Twenty minutes later, when she got to the Growin' Up Day Care Center, Miss Kitty had her fill out the rest of the paperwork and arrange payment. Lily didn't want to leave, which Maya took as a good sign.

Back at the house, Maya got Lily settled and opened what she referred to as the Drawer of Many Cords. Like most people she knew, Maya never threw out a power cord. The drawer was stuffed past capacity, like a snake-in-a-can, with dozens, maybe hundreds—heck, there was probably a cord that could work a Betamax—for her to go through.

She found an adaptor that fit into the bottom of Claire's phone, plugged it in, and waited for it to have enough juice to work. It took about ten minutes. The phone was rudimentary—just the facts, ma'am—but it did indeed have a call history. She pressed the icon and started to scroll through the calls.

They were all to the same number.

Maya scrolled down and counted sixteen calls. The number was unfamiliar. The area code was 201. That meant northern New Jersey.

Who the hell was Claire calling?

She checked the dates. The calls started three months before her death. The last call came in four days before the murder. So what did that mean? The calling pattern was fairly uneven. There were a lot in the beginning, a lot toward the end, a scattering in the middle.

Was Claire setting up rendezvous?

For a moment Maya flashed back to Jean-Pierre. Her imagination started toying with her then. Suppose Jean-Pierre had gotten in touch with Claire after all these years. You hear about that all the time, especially in the Internet Age. No lover ever completely vanishes when you have Facebook.

But no, it wasn't Jean-Pierre. Claire would have told her.

Really? Was she so sure about that? Claire had been up to something, no question about it, and she hadn't seen fit to tell Maya what it was about. Maya had always thought that she and Claire shared everything, that they had no secrets from each other, but then again, let's be fair here. Maya was on the other side of the world when all this happened, fighting for her country in a forsaken desert instead of being here, home, protecting her sister.

You were keeping secrets, Claire.

So now what?

Do the easiest thing first. Google the phone number. See if she got lucky and something came up. Maya typed the numbers into the search engine and hit the return button.

Bingo. Sort of . . .

The number came up right away, which surprised her. Most times, when you google a number, you get some offer to buy information or background checks on its owner from a third party. The phone number

Claire had been calling was a business of sorts, but like everything else surrounding the swirling insanity of the past few weeks, it led to more questions than answers. The place was indeed in northern New Jersey, near, if the Google map was to be believed, the George Washington Bridge. It was called Leather and Lace—A Gentlemen's Club.

Gentlemen's Club. Euphemism for a strip club.

Maya clicked on the link, just to be sure, and was greeted with a screen full of scantily clad women. Yep. Strip club. Her sister had secured a secret phone and hidden it in their grandmother's old trunk so she could call a strip club.

Did that make sense?

Nope.

Maya tried to throw this new information into the mix. When she added it all up—Claire, Joe, the nanny cam, the phone, the strip club, the rest—Maya considered all the possibilities and came up with bubkes. Nothing made sense. She started grasping at straws. Maybe Claire was having an affair and, what, her boyfriend worked there. Maybe Jean-Pierre was the club manager. The website did offer its "upscale clientele" something called a "French Lapper," though Maya had no idea and did not want to know what that could possibly be. Maybe Claire was leading a secret life and worked there. You read about that sometimes or see it in a bad cable movie. Housewife by day, stripper by night.

Stop.

She picked up the phone and called Eddie.

"You found something?" he said.

"Look, Eddie, if I have to dance around"—she realized the irony the moment the word spilled from her lips—"or worry about filling you in, I'm not going to learn anything, okay?"

"Yeah, sorry, what's up?"

"Do you ever go to strip clubs?"

Silence. Then: "Ever?"

"Yeah."

"Last year, some guys at work had a bachelor party at one."

"And since then?"

"That's it."

"Where was the club?"

"Wait, what does this—"

"Just answer, Eddie."

"Outside of Philadelphia. Cherry Hill area."

"No others?"

"That's it."

"Does a club called Leather and Lace mean anything to you?"

"You're kidding, right?"

"Eddie?"

"No. It means nothing to me."

"Okay, thanks."

"You're not going to tell me what this is about?"

"Not yet. Bye."

Maya sat there and stared at the website. Why would Claire be calling Leather and Lace?

No reason to keep coming up with unfounded theories. She wanted to drive right now and go the club, but she had no sitter for Lily. Growin' Up closed at 8:00 P.M.

Tomorrow, she thought. Tomorrow, she would get to the bottom of Leather and Lace, so to speak.

Chapter 11

Maya had the strangest dream about the reading of Joe's will. The dream was surreal, one of those through-the-shower-stall nocturnal visions where you really can't remember what was said or where exactly you were or any of that. She only remembered one thing.

Joe was there.

He sat in an opulent burgundy leather chair, wearing the same tuxedo he'd worn the night they met. He looked handsome as hell, his eyes fixated on a fuzzy figure reading a document. Maya couldn't hear a word the figure was saying—it was like listening to Charlie Brown's teacher—but she knew somehow that the figure was reading the will. Maya didn't care. Her entire focus was on Joe. She called out to him, tried to get his attention, but Joe would not turn her way.

Maya woke up to the sounds again—the screams, the rotors, the gunfire. She grabbed the pillow and wrapped it around her head, covering her ears, trying to muffle the terrible noise. She knew, of course, that it would do no good, that the sounds were coming from inside her head and, if anything, her efforts would keep them locked there. But she did it anyway. The sounds rarely lasted long. She just had to close her eyes— another bizarre move: closing your eyes when you are trying to drown out sounds—and ride them out.

When the episode subsided, Maya got out of bed and made her way to the bathroom. She looked in the mirror and then wisely decided to open the medicine chest so at the very least she didn't have to look at her gaunt expression. The small brown pill containers were there. She debated taking one or two, but she would need to be sharp today, what with the reading of Joe's will and facing his entire family.

She took a shower and chose a black Chanel pantsuit Joe had picked out for her. Joe had liked to shop for her. She'd tried it on for him, loving the feel and cut, but she'd pretended not to like it because the price was obscene. But she hadn't fooled Joe. The next day, he went back to the store and bought it. It had been lying on the bed, just as it was now, when she came home.

She slipped on the suit and woke up Lily.

Half an hour later, Maya dropped Lily off at Growin'
Up. Miss Kitty wore a Disney princess costume Maya
didn't recognize. "Do you want to dress as a princess
too, Lily?" Lily nodded and went with Princess Miss
Kitty, barely bothering to wave good-bye to her mother.
Maya got back in her car and booted up the Growin'
Up app. She checked the in-room camera. Lily was slip-
ping into an Elsa-from-*Frozen* costume.

"'Let it go,'" Maya sang to herself as she started
driving to her in-laws'.

She flipped on the radio to get her own voice out of
her head and replace it with whatever inanity was on
the morning drive. People who host morning radio
programs cannot believe how funny they are. She
moved it to AM—did anyone listen to AM anymore?—
and put on the all-news channel. There was comfort to
the almost military precision and predictability. Sports
on the quarter hour. Traffic every ten minutes. She was
distracted, half listening at best, when a story caught
her attention:

"Notorious hacker Corey the Whistle has promised
a treasure chest of new leaks this week that he claims
will not only embarrass a leading official in the current
administration but also will definitely lead to resigna-
tion and, most likely, prosecution . . ."

Despite it all, despite what she said about being out
of Corey the Whistle's awful reach, Maya still felt a fresh
shiver surge through her. Shane had wondered why Corey hadn't released it all, if he was just biding his time to

drop the bigger bomb—and yes, the word choice was worthy of a sad ha-ha—on her. She had, of course, wondered that too. Maya Stern was old news now, but the potential was there. Big secrets don't stay secret. They have a way of coming back when you least expect them, rippling and reverberating and causing—again she recognized how often military lingo slips into our regular vocabulary—massive collateral damage.

Farnwood was an old-school rich-people estate. Before Maya met Joe, she had assumed such places were the stuff of history books or fiction. They are not. She drove up to a gate manned by Morris. Morris had been working the gate since the early eighties. He lived in the same workers' compound as Isabella's family.

"Hey, Morris."

He scowled at her, as he always did, reminding her in his own way that she had just married into this family and really wasn't blood. There might have been more to Morris's scowl today, something that could be explained by either lingering sadness at the death of Joe or, more likely, the gossip surrounding Isabella and the pepper spray attack. Morris grudgingly pressed the button, and the gate opened so slowly it was hard to see with the naked eye.

Maya drove up the rolling hill, past a grass tennis court and a full-size soccer field ("It's called a pitch," Joe had told her), neither of which Maya had ever seen used, and arrived at a Tudor mansion that reminded her of Bruce Wayne's on the old Batman TV show. She half expected a bunch of men dressed for a fox hunt to greet her, but instead, her mother-in-law, Judith, stood alone by the door. Maya parked by the stone path.

Judith was a beautiful woman. She was petite with big round eyes and dainty, doll-like features. She looked younger than her years. There had been some work done—Botox, maybe a little something around the eyes—but it was tasteful, and most of her youthful appearance was due either to genetics or her daily yoga routine. Her figure still drew second glances. Men were drawn to her big-time—looks, brains, money—but if she dated, Maya didn't know about it.

"I think she has secret lovers," Joe had told her once.

"Why secret?"

But Joe had just shrugged it off.

She was rumored to have been a West Coast hippie back in the day. Maya believed it. If you looked closely, you could still see a hint of something untamed in the eyes and the smile.

Judith came down the stairs but stopped on the second to last one, making her and Maya about the same height. They exchanged a cheek kiss, Judith looking past her the whole time.

"Where is Lily?"

"In day care."

Maya waited for some surprise to register on her mother-in-law's face. None did. "You need to work it out with Isabella."

"She told you?"

Judith did not bother replying.

"So help me work it out," Maya said. "Where is she?"

"My understanding is Isabella is traveling."

"For how long?"

"I don't know. In the meantime I suggest you use Rosa."

"I don't think so."

"You know that she used to be Joe's nanny."

"I do."

"And?"

"I don't think so."

"So you'll keep her in day care?" Judith shook her head in disapproval. "Years ago, I was involved in day care facilities, professionally speaking." She was a board-certified psychiatrist and still saw clients twice a week at an office on the Upper East Side of Manhattan. "Do you remember all those child-abuse cases in the eighties and nineties?"

"Sure. What, you were called in as an expert?"

"Something like that."

"I thought they were all found to be bogus. Child hysteria or something."

"Yes," Judith said. "The caregivers were exonerated."

"So?"

"The caregivers were exonerated," she repeated, "but maybe the system wasn't."

"I'm not following."

"The children in the day care were so easy to manipulate. Why?"

Maya shrugged.

"Think about it. These kids came up with all these horror stories. I ask myself why. Why were these children so eager to say what they thought their parents wanted to hear? Maybe, just maybe, if their parents had given them more attention . . ."

That, Maya thought, was quite a stretch.

"The point is, I know Isabella. I've known her since she was a little girl. I trust her. I don't know or trust the people at day care—and neither do you."

"I have something better than trust," Maya said.

"Pardon?"

"I can watch them."

"What?"

"Safety in numbers. There are plenty of witnesses, including me." She held up the app, pressed the button, and there was Lily in her Elsa costume. Judith took hold of the phone and smiled at the image. "What is she doing?"

Maya took a look. "Based on the way she's spinning, I'd say she's dancing to *Frozen*."

"Cameras everywhere," Judith said with a shake of her head. "It's a new world." She handed the phone back to Maya. "So what happened with you and Isabella?"

It would not be smart to get into it now, especially

when they were gathering to hear Joe's will. "I wouldn't worry about it."

"May I be blunt?"

"Are you ever not?"

Judith smiled. "In that way, we are the same, you and I. Well, in many ways, we are. We both married into this family. We are both widows. And we both speak our minds."

"I'm listening."

"Are you still seeing your doctor?"

Maya said nothing.

"Your circumstances have changed, Maya. Your husband was murdered. You witnessed it. You could have been killed. You are now raising a child on your own. When you stack all these current stresses on top of your previous diagnosis—"

"What did Isabella tell you?"

"Nothing," Judith said. She put her hand on Maya's shoulder. "I could treat you myself, but—"

"That wouldn't be a good idea."

"Exactly. It would be wrong. I should stick to my roles as doting grandmother and supportive mother-in-law. My point is, I have a colleague. A friend really. She trained with me at Stanford. I'm sure the VA psychiatrists are competent, but this woman is the best in her field."

"Judith?"

"Yes?"

"I'm fine."

A voice said, "Mom?"

Judith turned around. Caroline, her daughter and Joe's sister, was there. The two women looked alike, you could see that they were mother and daughter, and yet where Judith always looked strong and confident, Caroline always seemed to be midcower.

"Hello, Maya."

"Caroline."

More exchanged cheek kisses.

"Heather is waiting for us in the library," Caroline said. "Neil is already there."

Judith's expression turned grim. "Come, let's go then."

Judith stood between Caroline and Maya, letting them both take her by the arms. They walked in silence through the grand foyer and past the ballroom. There was a portrait of Joseph T. Burkett Sr. above the fireplace. Judith stopped and stared at him for a moment.

"Joe looked so much like his father," Judith said.

"He did," Maya agreed.

"Another thing we have in common," Judith said with a hint of a smile. "Same taste in men, I suppose."

"Yep, tall, dark, and handsome," Maya said. "I'm not sure that makes us stand out."

Judith liked that. "So true."

Caroline opened the double doors, and they all entered the library. Maybe it was because Maya had just seen little girls dressing up, or maybe it was because she had recently watched *Beauty and the Beast* with Lily, but the library reminded Maya of the Beast's. The room was two stories high with built-in bookshelves of dark oak from floor to ceiling. The carpets were Oriental and ornate. A chandelier hung from the ceiling. There were two rolling ladders set on cast-iron rails. A large antique globe opened to reveal a crystal decanter of cognac. Neil, Joe's surviving brother, was already having at it.

"Hey, Maya."

More cheek kissing, though sloppier. Everything with Neil was sloppy. He was one of those pear-shaped guys who looked sloppy no matter how meticulously tailored a suit he wore.

"Want one?"

He gestured to the decanter.

"No, thanks," Maya said.

"You sure?"

Judith's lips were pursed. "It's nine in the morning, Neil."

"But five P.M. someplace. Isn't that what they always say?" He laughed. No one joined him. "Besides it's not every day you get to hear the reading of your brother's will."

Judith looked away. Neil was the baby, the youngest of the four Burkett children. Joe was firstborn, followed a year later by Andrew, who had "died at sea"—that was how the family always put it—and then came Caroline and finally Neil. Oddly enough, it was Neil who ran the family empire now. Joseph Sr., never one for senti-mentality when it came to money, had placed him in charge over his older siblings.

Joe had shrugged it off. "Neil is ruthless," he'd told her once. "Dad always liked ruthless."

"Maybe we should all sit," Caroline suggested.

Maya looked at the chairs—the opulent burgundy chairs—and flashed back to her dream. For a moment, she could see Joe in that tuxedo, legs crossed, cuffs creased, looking off, unreachable.

"Where's Heather?" Judith asked.

"I'm right here."

They all turned to the voice in the doorway. Heather Howell had been the family attorney for the past de-cade. Before that, Heather's father, Charles Howell III, worked for the Burketts. Before that, her grandfather Charles Howell II held the post.

No word on the first Charles Howell.

"Fine," Judith said. "Let's get this started."

It was an odd thing with Judith, how easily she slipped from warm maternal figure to professional shrink to, as she was right now, starchy old-world matriarch complete with a British-tinged accent.

They began to take their seats, but Heather Howell stayed standing. Judith looked back at her. "Is there a problem?"

"I'm afraid there is."

Heather was one of those attorneys who exude con-fidence and competence. You wanted her on your side. The first time Maya had met Heather Howell had been immediately after Joe's marriage proposal. Heather had called her into this very room and slapped down a prenup agreement. In a no-nonsense yet not unfriendly tone, she had told Maya, "Signing this document is nonnegotiable."

Now, for the first time, Heather Howell looked a little lost or at least out of her comfort zone.

"Heather?" Judith said.

Heather Howell turned to her.

"What's going on?"

"I'm afraid we will have to postpone the reading of the Last Will and Testament."

Judith looked at Caroline. Nothing. She looked at Maya. Maya just stood there. Judith turned back to Heather. "Do you care to explain why?"

"There are certain protocols we have to follow."

"What kind of protocols?"

"It's nothing to worry about, Judith."

Judith did not like that reply. "Do I look like I'm in the mood to be patronized?"

"No, you don't."

"So why can't we read Joe's will?"

"It isn't that we can't read it," Heather said, weighing each word before allowing it to leave her mouth.

"But?"

"But there has been a delay."

"And again I ask: Why?"

"It's paperwork really," Heather said.

"What do you mean?"

"We, uh, we don't have an official death certificate."

Silence.

"He's been dead almost two weeks," Judith said. "We had a funeral."

Closed casket, Maya suddenly remembered.

It hadn't been Maya's decision. She'd let Joe's family handle that one. It hadn't mattered to her. Death was death. Let them perform whatever ritual eased their pain the most. Closed casket had, of course, made perfect sense. Joe had been shot in the head. Even with the best work a mortician could do, you probably wouldn't want to see that.

Judith's voice again: "Heather?"

"Yes, of course, I know, I mean, I was at the funeral. But this probate requires a death certificate, some kind of proof. It is an unusual case here. I'm having one of my associates check through the case law. Because Joe was, well, murdered, we need verification from official authorities within the police department. I was just informed that it will take a little more time to secure the proofs."

"How long?" Judith asked.

"I really can't say, but I hope it won't be more than a day or two now that we are on it."

Neil spoke for the first time. "What do you mean, proofs? You mean like proof Joe is dead?"

Heather Howell started fiddling with her wedding band. "I really haven't gotten all the facts yet, but before we can enter probate, this . . . Let's call it a snafu, shall we? . . . This snafu just has to be untangled. I have my best people on it. I'll be in touch soon."

With everyone momentarily stunned silent, Heather Howell quickly spun and left the room.

Chapter 12

It's nothing," Judith said, leading Maya back toward the foyer.

Maya did not reply.

"This is how lawyers are. Everything has to be just so, partially for your protection, mostly to up the billable hours." She tried to smile at that, but it wouldn't hold. "My strong belief is that there is just some red tape due to the circumstances . . ." Her voice faded away then, as though she was just realizing that she was talking about Joe, not some legal matter.

"Two sons," Judith said in a hollow voice.

"I'm sorry."

"No mother should have to bury two sons."

Maya took her hand. "No," she said, "no mother should."

"Nor should a young woman have to bury a sister and a husband."

"Death follows you, Maya . . ."

Maybe it followed Judith too.

Judith held on to her hand another moment, then let go. "Please stay in touch, Maya."

"Of course."

They headed outside into the sun. Judith's black limousine was waiting. The chauffeur held the door open.

"Bring Lily around soon."

"I will."

"And please work it out with Isabella."

"The sooner I can see her," Maya said, "the sooner we can put this misunderstanding behind us."

"I'll see what I can do."

Judith slid into the back. The chauffeur closed the door. Maya stood there until the limo was down the drive and out of sight.

When she got to her car, Caroline was waiting.

"Do you have a moment to talk?" Caroline asked.

Not really, Maya thought. She was eager now to be on her way. She had places to go. Two to be exact. First, she wanted to stop in the servants' area again and maybe surprise Rosa. If that didn't work, she had a backup plan to locate Isabella. Second, she needed to go to Leather and Lace and see what connection there could possibly be between this "gentlemen's club" and her late sister.

Caroline put her hand on Maya's arm. "Please?"

"Yeah, okay."

"But not here." Caroline's eyes darted about as she said, "Let's take a walk."

Maya bit back a sigh. Caroline started down the stone driveway. Her little dog, Laszlo, a Havanese, followed. The dog was off leash, but really, when you owned this much land, where could Laszlo go that would be a danger? Maya wondered what it must have been like to grow up here, in a place of such opulence, beauty, and tranquility, where everywhere you looked, the grass, the trees, the edifices, everything belonged to you.

Caroline veered to the right. Laszlo stayed with them.

"My father put that in for Joe and Andrew." Caroline smiled in the direction of the soccer pitch. "The tennis court was my domain. I liked tennis. I practiced a lot. My father saw to it that the best pro from Port Washington came out and gave me private lessons. But I never *loved* it, you know? You can practice all you want, and I had some talent. I was first singles in my prep school. But to reach that next level, you have to be obsessed. You can't fake that."

Maya nodded because she didn't know what else to do. Laszlo walked with his tongue out. Caroline was working up to something. Maya couldn't push it. She would just have to be patient.

"But Joe and Andrew . . . they loved soccer. Loved it. They were both great players. Joe was a striker, as I'm sure you know. Andrew was a goalkeeper. I can't tell you how many hours the two of them would be out there, Joe practicing shots while Andrew practiced stopping them. That net is, what, a quarter mile from the main house, would you say?"

"I guess."

"You could hear their laughter rolling up those hills and right through the windows. My mom would sit in the parlor and just smile."

Caroline smiled now. It was her mother's smile, and yet it was also a facsimile, somehow not nearly as magnetic or powerful as the original.

"Do you know much about my brother Andrew?"

"No," Maya said.

"Joe didn't talk about him?"

He had, of course. Joe had revealed a huge secret about his brother's death that Maya had no intention of sharing with Caroline or anyone else.

"The world thinks my brother fell off that boat . . ."

She and Joe had been at a resort in Turks and Caicos, lying naked in bed. They were both on their backs, staring up at the ceiling. Joe's eyes glistened in the moonlight. The window was open, and the ocean breeze made her skin tingle. Maya had taken his hand then.

"The truth is, Andrew jumped . . ."

Maya said, "He didn't talk about him much."

"Too painful, I suppose. They were so close." Caroline stopped walking. "Please don't misunderstand me, Maya. Joe and Andrew both loved me and, well, Neil was the annoying little brother they tolerated. But really, it was the two of them—Joe and Andrew. They were both at the same prep school when Andrew died, did you know that?"

Maya nodded.

"Franklin Biddle Academy down near Philadelphia. They lived in the same dorm, played on the same soccer team. We have this huge house, but Joe and Andrew still wanted to share a bedroom."

"Andrew killed himself, Maya. He was in that much pain and I never saw it . . ."

"Maya?"

She turned to Caroline.

"What did you make of today? Of this . . . postponement?"

"I don't know."

"No theories?"

"Your attorney made it sound like it was a bureau-cratic snafu."

"And you believe that?"

Maya shrugged. "I was in the military. Bureaucratic snafus are practically the norm."

Caroline looked down.

"What?" Maya said.

"Did you see him?"

"Who?"

"Joe," Caroline said.

Maya felt her entire body stiffen. "What are you talking about?"

"His body," Caroline said softly. "Before the funeral. Did you see Joe's body?"

Maya slowly shook her head. "No."

Caroline raised her head. "Don't you think that's odd?"

"It was a closed casket."

"Was that your choice?"

"No."

"Then whose?"

"I assume your mother's."

Caroline nodded, as if that made sense. "I asked to see him."

Forget peaceful and tranquil—the silence of their surroundings started to feel suffocating. Maya tried to take deep, even breaths. There was always something in the silence, all silences, something she both cherished and feared.

"You've seen your share of dead people, haven't you, Maya?"

"I don't understand what you're getting at."

"When soldiers die, why is it so important that you bring the bodies home?"

Caroline was annoying her now. "Because we don't leave anyone behind."

"Yes, I've heard that. But why? I know you'll say it's to honor the dead and all that, but I think there's something more. The soldier is dead. You can't do anything more for him—or her, I don't mean to be sexist. You bring the body home, not for the dead but for the family, don't you? The loved ones at home, they need to see the deceased. They need the body. They need that closure."

Maya was not in the mood to explore this subject. "What's your point?"

"I didn't just want to see Joe. I *needed* to see him. I needed to make it real. If you don't see a body, you don't quite get it. It's like . . ."

"Like what?"

"Like maybe it didn't happen. Like maybe they're still alive. You dream about them."

"You dream about the dead too."

"Oh, I know. But it's different without closure. When we lost Andrew at sea . . ."

Again that stupid phraseology.

". . . I never saw his body either."

That surprised Maya. "Wait, why not? They recovered it, didn't they?"

"That's what I was told."

"You don't believe it?"

Caroline shrugged. "I was young. They never showed me his body. Closed casket again. I have visions, Maya. Daydreams about him. Still. To this day. I have these dreams where Andrew never died and I wake up and he's standing right there, by that soccer net, and he's smiling and making saves. Oh, I know he's not here. I know he died in an accident, but I also *don't* know. Do you see? I could never accept Andrew's death. Sometimes I think he survived the fall and swam off and he's on an island somewhere, and one day I'll see him and it'll all be okay. But if I could have seen his body . . ."

Maya stood very still.

"So I knew. I knew this time I couldn't make that mistake again. That's why I asked to see Joe's body. I begged really. I didn't care if he looked messed up. That might have even helped me in a way. I needed to do it so I'd accept that he was really gone, you know?"

"And you didn't see him?"

Caroline shook her head. "They wouldn't let me."

"Who wouldn't let you?"

She looked back toward the goalie net. "Two of my brothers. Both dead so young. It could just be bad luck, you know? It happens. But in both cases, I didn't see the body. Did you listen to Heather? No one will officially declare Joe dead. Both my brothers. It's like . . ." She turned and stared straight into Maya's eyes. "Like they could both be alive."

Maya did not move. "But they aren't."

"I know it sounds crazy—"

"It is crazy."

"You had a fight with Isabella, right? She told us. She said you were screaming about seeing Joe. Why did you do that? What did you mean?"

"Caroline, listen to me. Joe is dead."

"How can you be so sure?"

"I was there."

"But you didn't see him die, right? It was dark. You were running away by the third shot."

"Listen to me, Caroline. The police came. They've been investigating. He didn't get up from the two shots I saw and walk away. The cops even arrested two suspects. How do you explain all that?"

Caroline shook her head.

"What?"

"You won't believe me."

"Try me."

"The officer leading the investigation," Caroline said. "His name is Roger Kierce."

"That's right."

Silence.

"Caroline, what is it?"

"I know this is going to sound crazy . . ."

Maya wanted to shake the information out of her.

"We have this private bank account. I won't go into details on it. They aren't important. But let's just say you'd never trace it back to the source. Do you know what I mean?"

"I think so. Wait. Is it called WTC?"

"No."

"It's not out of Houston?"

"No, it's offshore. Why were you asking me about Houston?"

"It doesn't matter. Go on. You have a private overseas account."

Caroline stared at her a beat too long. "So I started going through some recent online transactions."

Maya nodded, tried to look encouraging.

"Most of the transfers went to numbered accounts or offshore holdings, stuff that bounces to various places so it can't be traced back. Again there is no reason to go into details. But there was a name in there too. Several payments made to a Roger Kierce."

Maya took the blow without so much as blinking. "Are you sure?"

"That's what I saw."

"Show me."

"What?"

"You have online access to the account," Maya said. "So show it to me."

Caroline tapped in the password. The same message—"ERROR: UNAUTHORIZED ACCESS"— popped across the screen for the third time.

"I don't understand," Caroline said. She sat in front of the computer in the library. "Maya?"

Maya stood behind her and stared at the screen. *Don't rush,* she told herself. *Think it through.* But this part didn't take much thought. She quickly whittled down the possibilities and realized that one of two things was happening here: Either Caroline was playing her or someone had changed passwords so Caroline could no longer access the online financial records.

"What exactly did you see?" Maya asked.

"I told you. Money transfers to Roger Kierce."

"How many?"

"I don't know. Three maybe?"

"How much were they?"

"Nine thousand dollars each."

Nine thousand. That made sense. Anything below ten grand could go unreported.

"What else?" Maya asked.

"What do you mean?"

"When was the first payment made?"

"I don't know."

"Before or after Joe was murdered?"

Caroline put her finger to her lip and thought about it. "I don't know for absolute sure, but . . ."

Maya waited.

"But I'm almost positive the first one was before."

Two ways for Maya to play it.

One was the obvious. Confront Judith. Confront Neil. Confront them immediately and demand answers. But there were problems with the direct approach. Logistically speaking, neither one of them was home right now, but more than that, what did she hope to find? If they were hiding something, would they admit it? Even if she somehow forced them to log into that account, wouldn't they have gotten rid of the evidence or covered it up somehow by now?

And cover up what?

What did Maya think was happening here? Why would the Burkett family pay off the homicide cop who was investigating Joe's death? Did that make any sense at all? Let's assume that Caroline was on the up-and-up. If the payoffs had started before the murder, well, again, how could they possibly know he'd be the detective who'd catch the case? No, that made no sense. Caroline hadn't been sure about the date of the first payment anyway. It would make more sense—"more sense" was in this case just a hair above "absolutely no sense at all"—if the payments started after the murder.

But to what end?

See several moves ahead. That was the key. And when Maya looked several moves ahead of directly confronting either Neil or Judith, assuming they were the ones behind the alleged payments, she saw nothing substantially beneficial. She'd be revealing herself to them without getting any valuable information in return.

Be patient. Learn what you can first. Then, if need be, confront. They say an attorney should never ask a question unless she already knows the answer. In a similar vein, a good soldier doesn't attack unless she's already calculated and can counter the most likely outcomes.

She'd had a plan before all this: Get hold of Isabella and make her talk. Figure out why Claire was secretly calling Leather and Lace.

Stick to the plan. Start with Isabella's house.

Hector answered the door.

"Isabella is not here."

"Mrs. Burkett thinks she and I should talk."

"She's out of the country," Hector said.

Bullshit. "Until when?"

"She'll call you. Please don't come back."

He shut the door. Maya had expected this. As she headed back toward her car, she circled around Hector's truck and, without breaking stride, slapped a magnetic real-time GPS tracker under his bumper.

Out of the country, my ass.

The tracker was simple: You download the app, you bring up the map, you can see exactly where the vehicle is now and where it has gone. They weren't hard to get. Two stores at the mall sold them. Maya didn't believe for a second that Isabella had left the country.

But Hector, she bet, would eventually lead Maya to his sister.

Chapter 13

Some might figure that Leather and Lace would be closed until the nighttime. They'd be wrong. Located in the shadow of MetLife Stadium, home to both the New York Giants and Jets, Leather and Lace opened at 11:00 a.m. and offered a "deluxe sumptuous lunch buffet." Maya had been to strip clubs before, mostly during leaves. The guys blew off steam there. She'd gone once or twice. They obviously weren't for her, but you'd never guess that from the star treatment female clients received. Every pole dancer hit on her like mad. Maya had theories—less to do with the dancers being gay than being anti-male—but she kept them to herself.

Leather and Lace had the prerequisite meathead at the door. Six four, probably three hundred pounds, no neck, buzz cut, black shirt so tight it worked like a tourniquet on his biceps.

"Well, hello," he said, like someone had offered him a free appetizer. "What can I do for you, little lady?"

Oh boy. "I need to talk to your manager."

He narrowed his eyes and looked her up and down—beef inspection—and nodded. "You got references?"

"I would like to speak to your manager."

Meathead gave her the once-over for at least the third time. "You're a little old for this line of work," he said. Then he nodded again and awarded her with his best smile. "But me, I think you're smoking hot."

"That means a lot," Maya said, "coming from you."

"I'm dead serious. You are hot. Great tight bod."

"It's all I can do not to swoon. Your manager?"

A few minutes later, Maya passed the surprisingly extensive buffet. The crowd was still light. The men kept their heads down. Two women danced onstage with the enthusiasm of middle schoolers waking up for a math test. They couldn't have looked more bored without prescribed sedation. Forget your morals, this was Maya's real problem with clubs like this. They had all the eroticism of a stool sample.

The manager wore yoga shorts and a sleeveless top. He told her to "Call me Billy." Billy was short, spent too much time in the gym, and had thin fingers. His office was painted bright avocado. The computer had monitors watching the dressing room and stages. The camera angles reminded Maya of the ones that shot Lily at Growin' Up.

"First off, let me just say you're hot. Okay? You're hot."

"So I keep hearing," Maya replied.

"And you got that whole toned, athletic thing going on. That's popular nowadays. Like that hot chick in *The Hunger Games*. What is her name?"

"Jennifer Lawrence."

"No, no, not the actress, the character. See, we do the whole fantasy thing here, so we'd want you to be . . ." Billy snapped his thin fingers. "Katniss. That was the lead's name, right? The hot chick in that leather outfit with the bow and arrow and whatever. Katniss Ever-something. But . . ." His eyes widened. "Oh crap, this is sheer genius. Instead of Kat-*niss*, we will call you Kat-*nip*. Get it?"

From behind them a woman's voice said, "She's not here for work, Billy."

Maya turned to see a woman in glasses. She was midthirties and wore a classy tailored suit that stuck out in here like a cigarette in a health club.

"What do you mean?" Billy asked.

"She's not the type."

"Aw, come on, Lulu, that's not fair," Billy said. "You're just being prejudiced."

Lulu half smiled at Maya. "You find tolerance in the strangest places." Then, to Billy: "I'll handle this."

Billy left the office. Lulu moved over and checked

the monitors. She started clicking the mouse, circling through the various surveillance cameras.

"What can I do for you?" Lulu asked.

There was no reason to play around. "My sister used to call here. I'm trying to find out why."

"We accept table reservations. Maybe that was it."

"Yeah, I don't think so."

Lulu shrugged. "I don't know what to tell you. Lots of people call here."

"Her name was Claire Walker. Does that name mean anything to you?"

"Doesn't matter. Even if it did, I wouldn't tell you. You know what kind of business we run here. We pride ourselves on discretion."

"Nice to be proud of something."

"Don't play the judgmental card, Miss . . . ?"

"Maya. Maya Stern. And my sister was murdered."

Silence.

"She had a hidden phone." Maya pulled it out and brought up the history. "The only calls she made or received were from here."

Lulu did not so much as glance down. "I'm sorry for your loss."

"Thank you."

"But there is nothing I can tell you."

"I can turn this phone over to the police. A woman kept this phone a secret. She only called here. Then she ended up murdered. You don't think the cops will be all over this place?"

"No," Lulu said, "I don't. But even if they choose that route, we have nothing to hide. How do you know the phone was even your sister's?"

"What?"

"Where did you find it? In her home? Does she live with someone else? Maybe the phone was theirs, not hers. Was she married? Did she have a boyfriend? Maybe it was his."

"It wasn't."

"You sure? A hundred percent? Because—and this will shock you—men have been known to lie about coming here. Even if you could somehow prove that the phone did indeed belong to your sister, dozens of people use the phone here. Dancers, bartenders, wait-staff, chefs, janitors, dishwashers, even customers. How long ago was your sister killed?"

"Four months ago."

"We delete our video surveillance files every two weeks. Again it's about discretion. We don't want some-one getting a warrant to see if their husband was here or anything. So even if you wanted to look at tape—"

"I get it," Maya said.

Lulu gave her a patronizing smile. "I'm sorry we couldn't be more help."

"Yeah, you seem pretty broken up about it."

"If you'll excuse me."

Maya stepped toward her. "Forget the legal for a second. You know I'm not out to catch an indiscretion. I'm calling on your humanity. My sister was murdered.

The police have all but given up hope of solving the case. The only fresh lead is this phone. So I'm asking you, as a human being, to please help me."

Lulu was already moving toward the door. "I'm terribly sorry about your loss, but I can't help you."

There was an explosion of sunlight when Maya exited the club. It was always nighttime inside places like this, but in the real world, it was barely noon. The sun beat down upon her with both fists. Maya squinted and shaded her eyes with her hand, staggering like Dracula dragged into daylight.

"Didn't get the job?" Meathead asked.

"My loss."

"Shame."

"Yeah."

So now what?

She could indeed do as threatened and bring it to the police. That, of course, meant bringing it to Kierce. Did Maya trust him? Good question. Either he was in some ways taking payoffs or Caroline was lying. Or Caroline was mistaken. Or . . . didn't matter. She didn't trust Caroline. She didn't trust Kierce.

So who did she trust?

Right now it didn't pay to trust anyone, but if there was still one person she believed was telling the truth, it was Shane. Which meant, of course, she would have to be careful. Shane was her friend, but he was also a straight shooter. She had already pushed him to do something that he hadn't liked. She was supposed to see him that night at the gun range. Maybe she would talk to him there, but now that she really thought about it, that seemed unlikely. He was starting to ask too many questions . . .

Wait, hold up.

Maya had been walking through the parking lot, still blinking away the onslaught of the light change, when she spotted it. At first it meant nothing. She was seeing it at a great distance, and there were plenty of them on the road.

Plenty of red Buick Veranos.

This one was parked in the far corner of the lot, half hidden between a fence and a Cadillac Escalade, a big SUV. She looked back toward the door. Meathead was checking out her ass. Big surprise. She waved and started toward the red vehicle.

She needed to see if the license plate matched.

Along the top of the fence, Maya could see surveillance cameras. But so what? Would anyone be watching right now, and if so what would be the harm? She had a plan of sorts. In one of her very rare smart moves recently—not wanting to get caught unprepared again—she'd bought several GPS trackers at the mall. The first was, of course, on Hector's truck.

A second was in her purse, ready to go.

The plan was simple and obvious. First, make sure she had the right car by checking the license plate. Second, walk past the red Buick and slap the GPS tracker under the bumper.

The second part might provide a little bit of a problem. The car was parked in the corner, against a fence, and a casual stroll past it, if spotted, would be awkward at best. Still, the lot was quiet. The few people who pulled in parked on the other side, and while most people might not have any reason to be embarrassed about being here, they weren't exactly puffing out their chests with pride about it either.

The license plate started to come into view, and yes, it was the same car.

WTC Limited. A holding company, maybe for Leather and Lace?

"Wrong way."

It was Meathead. She turned. He moved right next to her. She forced up a smile.

"Sorry?"

"That's the employee parking area."

"Oh," Maya said. "Is it? I'm sorry. I'm so ditzy sometimes." She tried a "tee-hee, aren't I a ditz" laugh. "I parked in the wrong place. Or maybe I wanted the job so badly—"

"No, you didn't."

"Pardon?"

He pointed with his beefy finger back the other way. "You parked over there. On the other side."

"Oh, did I? I'm such an airhead sometimes."

She stood there. He stood there.

"We don't let no one into the employee area," he said. "Company policy. See, some of the guys, they'll come out and they'll wait by a dancer's car. You know what I mean? Or they'll try to get the license plate and call her. We gotta escort the girls out here sometimes so they can avoid the creepy guys. You get my drift?"

"Yes, but I'm not a creepy guy."

"No, ma'am, you certainly are not."

She stood there. He stood there.

"Come on," he said. "I'll escort you to your car."

There was one of those giant warehouse stores across the street and maybe a hundred yards down the road. Maya parked in the lot, positioning her car so she could stake out the employee lot of Leather and Lace. Her hope was that someone would eventually get into the red Buick Verano and then she could follow him.

And then what?

One step at a time.

But what about all that nonsense about looking several steps down the road when you make a plan?

She didn't know. Preparedness was all well and good, but there was also a little something called improvisation. Her next move would be dependent on where that red Buick went. If, say, the car stopped for the night at a residence, then maybe her move would be to figure out who lived at that house.

A strip club gets a fairly varied clientele in dress, if

not gender. There were the blue-collar guys in work boots and jeans. There were business suits. There were guys in cargo shorts and T-shirts. There was even a group of guys in golf clothes, looking like they just came off the links. Hey, maybe the food was good, who knew?

An hour passed. Four people left the employee area of the lot; three entered. None involved the red Buick Verano parked against the fence.

Maya had time to sort through all the recent developments, but time wasn't helping her. She didn't need time. She needed more information.

The red Buick was leased by a company called WTC Limited. Was that something the Burketts held? Caroline had talked about payouts to and from offshore accounts and anonymous companies. Could WTC Limited be something like that? Had Claire known the driver of the red Buick Verano? Had Joe?

Maya and Joe had several joint accounts. She opened them on her phone app and brought up the credit card charges. Had Joe visited Leather and Lace? If so, it wasn't showing up on the statements. Then again, would Joe be that stupid? Didn't places like Leather and Lace know that prying wives might check their husbands' credit card charges and, knowing Lulu's desire for discretion, use another name?

Maybe WTC Limited?

With new hope, she searched for any charge to WTC

Limited. Nothing. The club was in Carlstadt, New Jersey. She searched for any charges made to that city. Again nothing.

Someone parked two spots away from the red Buick. The car door opened, and a pole dancer got out. Yes, Maya knew her occupation. Long blond hair, shorts that barely covered half a cheek, a boob job that lifted them high enough to double as earrings—you didn't need the pole dancing equivalent of gaydar to see that this woman was either a pole dancer or a sixteen-year-old boy's fantasy come to life.

When the shapely pole dancer entered through the employee side door, a man stepped out. The man wore a Yankees baseball cap pulled down low over his sunglass-covered eyes. He kept his head down, his shoulders hunched, the way one does when they want to blend in or hide. Maya sat up. The man sported one of those unruly beards superstitious athletes grow when they're on a playoff run.

She couldn't get a look at him obviously, but still there was something familiar . . .

Maya started up her car. The man kept his head down, hurried his step, and slid into the red Buick Verano.

So this was her man.

Following him would be risky. Maybe her best move was to confront him now. He might spot a tail. She might lose him. So maybe she should stop with the subtlety, pull back into Leather and Lace's parking lot, block his car, demand answers. But there were problems with that scenario too. There was security there, probably a fair amount of it. Meathead would interfere. Others too. Strip clubs were used to handling incidents. Shane's work as an MP backed up what Meathead had said. Men often hung out after the club closed, hoping to approach some dancer they sincerely believed was interested in more than what was in their wallet, though that was never, ever the case. Guys who lack confidence in so many ways still manage to delude themselves into thinking they are irresistible to all women.

In short, there would be security. Better to get him alone, no?

The red Buick backed out of the space and started toward the exit. Maya was on it. She merged onto Paterson Plank Road and immediately felt unsettled. Why? Was it her imagination, or did the red Buick hesitate, as if somehow she had already been spotted? That was hard to fathom. She was a full three cars back.

Two minutes into the ride, Maya realized that tailing him wouldn't work.

She hadn't quite realized it before, but now that her plan was in action, she could see more issues raising their heads. Problem One: He clearly knew her car. He had, in fact, tailed it himself on numerous occasions. One look in the rearview mirror would be all he'd need to put it together.

Problem Two: Lulu or Billy or Meathead or someone else at the club could have warned him about her visit, in fact probably had. So Buick Yankees Cap would be on guard. He might, in fact, have already spotted her.

Problem Three: Depending on how long he had been following Maya, Buick Yankees Cap could have done the same thing Maya did with Hector's truck—put a GPS tracker on it. For all she knew, he had known that she was parked outside the club from the moment she arrived.

This could all be a setup. This could all be a trap.

She could back off, figure out a better way in, and come back to Leather and Lace with a plan. But uh-uh, no way. Enough with the passive approach. She needed answers, and if that meant using a little less caution and erring on the side of boldness, so be it.

They were still in the industrial area, a few miles from the major highway. Once the Buick was there, she'd have no chance. Maya reached into her purse. The handgun was within easy reach. The traffic light turned red. The Buick glided to a stop, first car in line in the right lane. Maya hit the accelerator and veered first left, then back to the right. She knew that she would have to move fast. She passed the Buick on its left, spun the wheel, and angled her car so she blocked him.

She was out of the car, keeping the gun low and out of sight. Yes, this was ridiculously risky, but she had done the calculations. If he tried to back up or make a run for it, she would shoot his tires. Would someone call the police? Probably. But she was willing to take that risk. Worst-case scenario: The police arrest her. She would then tell them about her husband's murder and that this guy had started following her. She might then have to play the hysterical widow a bit, but there was little chance she would be convicted of something serious.

Within seconds, Maya was at the red Buick. The glare on the windshield prevented her from seeing the driver, but that wouldn't last. She considered going to the driver's-side window and threatening him with the gun through the glass, but in the end, she opted for the passenger-side door. It might be unlocked, in which case she could just slip inside. If it wasn't, she could make the same threat through that window.

She reached out, grabbed the door handle, and pulled.

The car door opened.

Maya slipped inside and lifted the gun toward the man in the Yankees cap.

The man turned and smiled at her. "Hey, Maya."

She sat there, stunned.

He took the baseball cap off and said, "Nice to finally meet in person."

She wanted to pull the trigger. She had almost dreamed about this moment—seeing him, pulling the trigger, blowing him away. Her first thought was that simple, instinctive, and primitive: Kill your enemy.

But if she did, forgetting the legal and moral implications for the moment, the answers would probably die with him. And now, more than ever, she had to know the truth. Because the man following her in the red Buick, the man who had secretly communicated with Claire in the weeks before her murder, was none other than Corey the Whistle.

Chapter 14

Why are you following me?"

Corey was still smiling. "Put away the gun, Maya."

In all the photographs, Corey Rudzinski was well-dressed, baby-faced, and clean-shaven. The scruffy beard, the baseball cap, the dad jeans all made for a pretty good disguise. Maya just stared, still pointing the gun at him. Horns started blaring.

"We're blocking up traffic," Corey said. "Move your car and then we can talk."

"I want to know—"

"And you will. But first move your car to the side of the road."

More horns.

Maya reached across and grabbed his car keys. No way she was about to let him slip away. "Don't go anywhere."

"No plans to, Maya."

She pulled her car toward the curb, parked it, and slid back into the Buick's passenger seat. She handed him the keys.

"I bet you're confused," Corey said.

Dr. Understatement. Maya was stunned. Like a boxer on his heels, she needed time to recover, to take the standing eight count, get her head back into the fight. Explanations for how this could be rose into view, but in every case, she was able to shoot them down with too much ease.

Nothing made sense.

She started with an obvious question. "How do you know my sister?"

His smile faded away when she asked that, replaced by what appeared to be genuine sadness, and she realized why. Maya had said, "do you know"—present tense. Corey Rudzinski had indeed known Claire. He had, Maya could see, cared for her.

He faced forward. "Let's take a ride," he said.

"I'd rather you just answer the question."

"I can't stay out here. Too exposed. They won't stand for it either."

"They?"

He didn't reply. He drove her back to Leather and

Lace and parked in the same spot. Two cars pulled in behind them. Had the cars been out on the road with them? Maya thought that maybe they had.

The employee entrance had a keypad. Corey punched in the numbers. Maya memorized the code, just in case. "Don't bother," he said. "Someone still has to buzz you in too."

"You type in a code and a guard checks you out?"

"That's right."

"Sounds like overkill. Or maybe paranoia."

"Yes, I bet it does."

The corridor was dark and stank like dirty socks. They walked through the club. The Disney song "A Whole New World" was blaring. The pole dancer wore a Princess-Jasmine-from-*Aladdin* costume. Maya frowned. Seemed dress-up wasn't just for preschool.

He led her past a beaded curtain and into a private back room. The room was gold and green and looked like a Midwest cheerleader uniform had inspired the décor.

"You knew I came here before," Maya said. "That I talked to that Lulu."

"Yes."

She was putting it together. "So you probably watched me leave. You saw me head over toward your car. So you knew I was following you."

He didn't reply.

"And those two cars that pulled in behind us. They with you?"

"Overkill, Maya. Paranoia. Have a seat."

"On this?" Maya frowned. "How often do they clean the upholstery?"

"Often enough. Sit."

They both did.

"I need you to understand what I do," he began.

"I understand what you do."

"Oh?"

"You think secrets are bad, so you reveal them, damn the repercussions."

"That's not far off, actually."

"So let's skip the rationale. How do you know my sister?"

"She contacted me," Corey said.

"When?"

Corey hesitated. "I'm not a radical. I'm not an anarchist. It's nothing like that."

Maya didn't give a shit what it was like. She wanted to know about Claire and why he was following her. But she didn't want to antagonize him unnecessarily or discourage openness. She stayed silent.

"You're right about secrets. I started out as a hacker. I'd break into places for fun. Then big companies and governments. Like a game. But then I started to see all the secrets. I'd see how the powerful abuse the normal man." He caught himself. "You don't want to hear that speech, do you?"

"Not really."

"Anyway, the point is, we don't hack much anymore.

We give whistle-blowers the freedom to tell the truth. That's all. Because people cannot police themselves when it comes to power and money. It's simple human nature. We twist the truth to suit our self-interest. So the people who work for cigarette companies—they aren't all horrible, evil people. They just can't make themselves do the right thing because it's not in their self-interest. We humans are wonderful at self-justification."

So much for not getting the speech.

A waitress came into the room wearing a top that had the relative width of a headband. "Drink?" she said.

"Maya?" Corey asked.

"I'm fine."

"Get me a club soda with lime, please."

The waitress left. Corey turned toward Maya.

"People think I want to weaken governments or businesses. Actually I want the opposite. I want to strengthen them by forcing them to do the right thing, the just thing. If your government or business is built on lies, then build them on truth instead. So no secrets. No secrets anywhere. If a billionaire is paying off a government official to get that oil field, let the people know. In your case, if your government is killing civilians in a war—"

"That's not what we were doing."

"I know, I know, collateral damage. Great nebulous term, don't you think? Whatever you believe, accident or intentional, we the people should know. We may still want to fight the war. But we should know. Business-men lie and cheat. Sports figures lie and cheat. Governments lie and cheat. We shrug. But imagine a world where that didn't happen. Imagine a world where we have full accountability instead of unjust authority. Imagine a world where there are no abuses or secrets."

"Are there unicorns and pixie dust in this world?" Maya asked.

He smiled. "You think me naïve?"

"Corey—can I call you Corey?"

"Please."

"How do you know my sister?"

"I told you. She contacted me."

"When?"

"A few months before her death. She sent an email to my website. It eventually found its way to me."

"What did it say?"

"Her email? She wanted to talk to me."

"What about?"

"What do you think, Maya? You."

The waitress came back. "Two club sodas with lime." She gave Maya a friendly wink. "I know you didn't order one, hon, but you might get thirsty."

She handed the drinks off, gave Maya a big smile, and then strode away.

"You're not trying to tell me Claire was the one who leaked that combat tape—"

"No."

"—because there is no way she'd even have access—"

"No, Maya, that's not what I'm saying. She contacted me after I released your tape."

That made more sense yet answered nothing. "What did she say?"

"That's why I'm trying to explain our philosophy. About whistle-blowing. About accountability and freedom."

"I'm not following."

"Claire contacted me because she was afraid I was going to reveal the rest of your tape."

Silence.

"You know what I mean, don't you, Maya?"

"Yes."

"You told Claire about it?"

"I told her everything. We told each other everything. At least that's what I thought."

Corey smiled at her. "She wanted to protect you. She asked me not to release the audio."

"And you didn't."

"That's correct."

"Just because Claire asked."

He took a sip of his drink. "I know a man. A group really. They think they're like mine. But they're not. They reveal secrets too, but on an individual scale. Cheating spouses, steroid users, revenge porn, stuff like that. Personal deceptions. If you want to do something unethical anonymously online, this group will out you. Like those hackers of that adultery website did last year."

"And you don't agree with that?"

"I don't."

"Why not? Aren't they ridding the world of secrets?"

"Funny," he said.

"What?"

"Your sister raised that point too. I won't say we are hypocritical, but we do pick and choose our spots, don't we? No way around it. I didn't reveal the audio on your tape for, yes, my own selfish reasons. I had planned to do it later. To maximize the impact of the revelation. More hits on my website. More exposure for my cause."

"So why didn't you?"

"Your sister. She asked me not to."

"Just like that."

"She was convincing. You, Maya, are just a pawn, she explained. You are forced to be what you are by a corrupt system. Part of me wants to reveal that because, again, the truth will indeed set you free. But you'd be irreparably harmed. Claire convinced me that if I did that, I'd be no better than my colleagues who nail small-time cheaters."

Maya was getting tired of the circling. "You were more interested in hurting the war cause than hurting me."

"Yes."

"So you provided the people with your own narrative. Let them hate the government. If they heard the audio, they might blame me instead."

"I guess that's true."

Replacing the truth with his own narrative, Maya thought. Scratch the surface and we are all the same. There was no time or reason to ruminate on that right now.

"So my sister contacted you," Maya said, "to protect me."

"Yes."

Maya nodded. That made sense. Sad, terrible sense. The guilt came rushing back. "So then what happened?"

"She convinced me of the righteousness of her argument." A small smile toyed with his lips. "And I convinced her of the righteousness of mine."

"I don't understand."

"Claire worked for a big corrupt corporation. She had access to the inner sanctum."

It was starting to click. "You convinced her to leak information to you?"

"She saw the righteousness of the cause."

Maya had a thought.

"What?"

"Was it quid pro quo?" Maya asked. "Did Claire agree to help take down Burkett Enterprises in exchange for you not releasing the audio?"

"Nothing so crude."

Or was it just that crude?

"So," Maya said, feeling the answer start to well up, "you got Claire to do your dirty work. And it got her killed."

A shadow crossed his face. "Not just Claire," Corey said.

"What do you mean?"

"She worked with Joe."

Maya let that sink in a moment before she shook her head. "There's no way Joe would turn in his own family."

"Your sister apparently thought otherwise."

Maya closed her eyes.

"Think about it. Claire looks into it. She ends up dead. Then Joe looks into it . . ."

The connection, Maya thought. Everyone was looking for the connection.

Corey thought that he knew what it was.

But he was wrong.

"Joe reached out to me after your sister died."

"What did he say?"

"He wanted to meet."

"And?"

"I couldn't. I had to stay off the grid. I'm sure you read about it. The Danish government was trying to nail me on trumped-up charges. I told him that I could find secure ways to communicate, but he wanted to meet in person. I think he wanted to help. And I think he found a secret that got him killed."

"What were Claire and Joe supposed to be investigating?"

"Financial crimes."

"Can you be more specific?"

"You know the phrase that behind every great fortune is a crime? It's true. Oh, I'm sure you could find exceptions, but scratch the surface behind every major corporation and someone got paid off or someone intimidated the competition."

"And in this case?"

"The Burkett family has a long history of paying off top politicians in this country and abroad. Do you remember the case of the pharmaceutical company Ranbaxy?"

"Vaguely," Maya said. "Fraudulent drugs or something."

"Close enough. The Burketts are doing something similar over in Asia with one of their pharmaceutical holdings called EAC. People are dying because the drugs don't meet specifications, but so far, the Burketts have managed to hide behind claims of local incompetence. In short, they claim that they didn't know anything, that their testing was sound, whatever. It's all lies. They fabricated data, we are sure of it."

"But you couldn't prove it," Maya said.

"Exactly. We needed someone from the inside to get the data."

"So you sent in Claire."

"Nobody forced her, Maya."

"No, you charmed."

"Don't insult your sister's intelligence. She knew the risks. She was brave. I didn't make her. She wanted to do the right thing. You, of all people, should understand that—that she died trying to expose injustice."

"Don't," Maya said.

"What?"

She hated when people made comparisons to soldiers and war. They always managed to be both patronizing and inept. But again, now was not the time.

"So your theory is that someone in Joe's family killed Claire—and then Joe—to hush up exposure?"

"What, you think they're above it?"

Maya thought about that. "They might not be above killing Claire," she said, "but they'd never kill one of their own."

"You may be right." He rubbed his face with his hand and looked off. From the other room, Maya could hear the song "Be Our Guest" from *Beauty and the Beast*, adding new meaning to the line "put our service to the test."

"But," he continued, "I think Claire found something else. Something bigger than manipulating a drug test."

"Like what?"

He shrugged. "I don't know. Lulu told me you found her burner phone."

"Yes."

"I won't go through how the machinations of our communications worked, how the calls here can be rerouted via the dark web and eventually find their way to me. But still. We had agreed on radio silence. We would only communicate when she was ready to give me the final material or if there was an emergency."

Maya leaned forward. "But Claire did reach out."

"Yes. A few days before her death."

"What did she say?"

"That she'd found something."

"Something other than drug tampering?"

He nodded. "Something potentially bigger," he said. "She said she was still putting it together, but she wanted to send me the first piece of evidence." He stopped, stared ahead with his pale blue eyes. "It was the last time we spoke."

"Did she send you that first piece of evidence?"

He nodded. "That's why you're here."

"What?"

But she knew, of course. He had known where she was the entire time—that she had visited the club, that she had talked to Lulu, that she was following him. Corey Rudzinski had not set this up casually. There had been a purpose to all of this.

"You're here," he said, "so I can show you what Claire found."

"The name is Tom Douglass. Two S's."

Corey handed her the printout. They were still in the private back room at the strip club. This was a pretty great spot for a clandestine meeting. No one paid you any attention, and no one wanted you to pay any to them.

"Does the name mean anything to you?" Corey asked.

"Should it?"

Corey shrugged. "Just a general question."

"Never heard of him," Maya said. "So who is he?"

According to the printout, there were monthly payments to "Tom Douglass Security" for nine thousand dollars. Maya noted the obvious: It was the same amount as the purported secret payments to Roger Kierce.

Coincidence?

"Tom Douglass worked as a private investigator in a New Jersey town called Livingston. His business was a small, one-man operation. He mostly did marital work and background checks. He retired three years ago, but the money is still coming."

"So maybe it's legitimate. He's a private eye on retainer. He retired but kept his biggest client."

"I would agree. Except your sister clearly thought that there was more to it."

"Like what?"

Corey shrugged.

"How could you not have asked her?"

"You don't understand how we work."

"Oh, I think I do. So when Claire got murdered over this, did you contact the police?"

"No."

"Or tell them what she was investigating?"

"I told you. I had to stay off the grid when she died."

"Not 'died,'" Maya said. "She was brutalized and murdered."

"I know. Believe me, I get it."

"But not enough to help find her killer."

"Our sources demand confidentiality."

"But your source was murdered."

"That doesn't change our commitment to her."

"Ironic," Maya said.

"How so?"

"You're so big on a world without secrets. But you have no problem creating and keeping your own. What about your everything-out-in-the-open utopia?"

"That's not fair, Maya. We didn't even know her murder was connected to us."

"Sure you did. You kept quiet because you were afraid if it got out that one of your sources was murdered, it would reflect badly on you. You were afraid that someone leaked her name and that got her killed. You were afraid—and probably still are—that maybe that leak came from your organization."

"It didn't," Corey said.

"How do you know?"

"You talked about our paranoia. Our overkill. I'm the only one who knew about Claire. We have safeguards. There is no way her name was leaked by my organization."

"You know the public wouldn't buy that."

He put his hand on his face. "They might misinterpret, that's true."

"They'd blame you."

"Our enemies might use it against us. Our other whistle-blowers might feel threatened."

Maya shook her head. "You really don't see, do you?"

"What?"

"You're justifying keeping secrets. You're doing exactly the same thing as those governments and businesses you condemn."

"That's not true."

"Sure it is. Protect the institution at all cost. You got my sister killed. And you helped her killer go free to shield your organization."

Something ignited behind his eyes. "Maya?"

"What?"

"I don't need lectures on morality from you."

Fair enough. Maya had agitated him, perhaps too much. That was a mistake. She needed him to trust her. "So why are the Burketts paying Tom Douglass?"

"We have no idea. A few months ago, we hacked into Douglass's computer, checked his browsing history, even got a list of his searches. There's no hint. Whatever he was doing, it wasn't just off the books. It was *way* off the books."

"Did you try asking him?"

"Oh, he won't talk to us, and if the police question him, he'll claim attorney-client privilege. All his work product goes through the family law firm, Howell and Lamy."

That was Heather Howell's firm.

"So how do we find out more?" Maya asked.

"We took a run at him and got nowhere," Corey said. "So I was thinking maybe you could give it a try."

Chapter 15

Unlike in the movies, Tom Douglass Investigations didn't have pebbled glass with the name stenciled into it. The office was located in a nondescript brick building on Northfield Avenue in Livingston, New Jersey. The corridor smelled like a dentist's office, which seemed apt based on the number of names listed with a DDS by the entrance. Maya knocked on the solid wood door. No answer. She tried the knob. Locked.

She noticed a man in hospital scrubs standing by the reception desk across the corridor. He was checking her out with the subtlety of a sledgehammer. She returned the smile, pointed at the door, and shrugged.

Scrubs walked toward her. "You have great teeth," he said.

"Gee, wow, thanks." Maya feigned breathless, kept the smile going. "Do you know when Mr. Douglass will be back?"

"You need some investigation help, hon?"

Hon. "Sort of. It's confidential." She bit her lower lip as if to indicate seriousness and yeah, okay, maybe a little coquettishness. "Have you seen him today?"

"I haven't seen Tom in weeks. Must be nice. Just being able to take time off like that."

Maya thanked him and headed toward the exit. Scrubs called after her. She ignored him and picked up her pace. Corey had provided her with Tom Douglass's home address. It was only a five-minute drive. She would try there.

The Douglass house was a much-loved Cape Cod, blue with purple trim. The flower boxes burst with color. The shutters were overly decorative. It was all a bit much, but it worked. Maya parked in the street and started up the walk. A fishing boat on a wheeled rig sat on the side of the garage.

Maya knocked on the door. A woman in her midfifties wearing a black sweat suit opened it.

The woman's eyes narrowed. "May I help you?"

"Hi," Maya said, trying to sound upbeat, "I'm looking for Tom Douglass."

The woman—Maya assumed it was Mrs. Douglass—kept studying Maya's face. "He's not here."

"Do you know when he'll be back?"

"Could be a while."

"My name is Maya Stern."

"Yeah," the woman said. "I recognize you from the news. What do you want with my husband?"

Great question. "Can I come in?"

Mrs. Douglass stepped back to let her enter. Maya really hadn't meant to ask about coming inside. She had just been buying time, trying to figure out the best way to approach it.

Mrs. Douglass led her past the foyer and into the den. The theme there was nautical. Big-time. Stuffed fish hung from the ceiling on wires. The wood-paneled walls were decorated with antique fishing rods and fishing nets and an old captain's wheel and round life preservers. There were family photos involving the seas. Maya spotted two sons, both of whom must have been grown by now. This family of four clearly liked to fish together. Maya had never been much for fishing, but she'd noticed over the years that there were few photographed smiles as bright and authentic as those taken with caught fish.

Mrs. Douglass folded her arms and waited.

The best approach, Maya quickly surmised, would be the direct one.

"Your husband has done work for the Burkett family for a long time."

Blank face.

"I wanted to ask him about what he does."

"I see," Mrs. Douglass said.

"Do you know about his work with the Burketts?"

"You're a Burkett, Maya, aren't you?"

The question rocked Maya back a bit. "I married in, I guess."

"That's what I thought. And I saw that your husband was killed."

"Yes."

"I'm sorry for your loss." Then: "Do you think Tom knows something about the murder?"

Again her bluntness threw Maya. "I don't know."

"But that's why you're here?"

"In part."

Mrs. Douglass nodded. "I'm sorry, but I really don't know anything."

"I'd like to talk to Tom."

"He's not around."

"Where is he?"

"Away."

She started back toward the door.

"My sister was also murdered," Maya said.

Mrs. Douglass slowed her step.

"Her name was Claire Walker. Does that name mean anything to you?"

"Should it?"

"Right before she was killed, she found out about the Burketts' secret payments to your husband."

"Secret payments? I don't know what you're trying to imply here, but I think you better leave."

"What kind of work does Tom do for them?"

"I wouldn't know."

"I have your tax returns for the past five years."

Now it was Mrs. Douglass's turn to show surprise. "You . . . what?"

"More than half your husband's yearly income has come from the Burketts. The payments are substantial."

"So? Tom works hard."

"Doing what?"

"I wouldn't know. And if I did, I certainly wouldn't say."

"Something about those payments troubled my sister, Mrs. Douglass. A few days after Claire found out about them, someone tortured her and shot her in the head."

Her mouth made a perfect O. "And you think, what, Tom had something to do with it?"

"I didn't say that."

"My husband is a good man. He, like you, served in the military." She nodded toward the wall behind her. Beneath a plaque that read "Semper Paratus" were silver crossed anchors, the symbol of the esteemed boatswain's mate. Maya had known a few BMs in the Navy. It was a proud distinction. "Tom worked as a town cop for almost two decades. He took early retirement after getting hurt on the job. He opened up his own firm and he works hard."

"So what did he do for the Burketts?"

"I told you. I wouldn't know."

"Or say?"

"That's right."

"But whatever he did for them was worth nine or ten grand a month going back . . . how long?"

"I wouldn't know."

"You don't know when he started with them?"

"His work was confidential."

"He never talked about the Burketts?"

For the first time, Maya saw a chink in the woman's armor as she said softly, "Never."

"Where is he, Mrs. Douglass?"

"He's away. And I don't know anything." She flung open the door. "I'll let him know you stopped by."

Chapter 16

Most people have a pretty antiquated idea of what a shooting range/gun shop looks like. They picture musty animal taxidermy and bear pelts on the walls, dusty rifles lined up haphazardly, a cantankerous owner behind a counter wearing either early Elmer Fudd hunting gear or a wife-beater T-shirt with a hook for one hand.

That wasn't the case anymore.

Maya, Shane, and their compatriots hung out at a state-of-the-art gun club called RTSP, which stood for Right To Self-Protect or, as some joked, Right To Shoot People. Forget dust—everything in here gleamed like new. The unfailingly solicitous employees all donned black polo shirts neatly tucked into khakis. The weaponry was laid out in glass cases like fine jewelry.

There were twenty shooting ports altogether, ten for the twenty-five-yard-range shooter, ten for the fifteen-yarders. A digital simulator worked pretty much like a life-sized video game. Picture a theater room with some sort of hostile situation—gang attack, hostage taking, Wild West, even zombie infiltration—come to life with fully formed targets coming at you. You "shot" lasers with a real-weight firearm.

For the most part, Maya came to shoot real guns at paper targets and hang with her friends, most of whom had served in the military. This place served that purpose in what their advertisements called "comfort and style." Some people join clubs to golf or play tennis or try their hand at bridge. Maya was a VIP member of the "Guntry Club." Being ex-military, she and her friends had been given a fifty percent discount.

The Guntry Club on Route 10 had dark wood walls and rich carpeting and reminded Maya of either a faux version of the Burkett library or an upscale chain steak house. A pool table sat in the middle of the room. There was lots of leather furniture. Three walls were adorned with flat-screen televisions. The fourth was painted with the words of the Second Amendment, spelled out in enormous cursive letters. There was a cigar room, card tables, and free Wi-Fi.

Rick, the owner, also wore the black polo and khakis and always had a gun on his belt. He greeted her with a sad smile and a fist bump. "Great to have you back, Maya. Me and the boys, when we heard the news . . ."

She nodded. "Thanks for the flowers."

"We just wanted to do something, you know?"

"I appreciate it."

Rick coughed into his fist. "I don't know if this is the right time to raise it, but if you need a job now with more flexible hours . . ."

Rick was constantly offering her a job teaching shooting classes. Women were the fastest-growing demographic for gun buyers and ranges like his. Women also greatly preferred female instructors, of which there were still very few.

"I'll keep it in mind," Maya said.

"Great. The boys are upstairs."

There were five of the gang there that night, including Shane and Maya. The other three headed off to the simulator while Shane and Maya hit the twenty-five-yard range. Maya found Zen in shooting. There was something about the release of breath as you pulled the trigger, the stillness, the quiet before the almost-welcome recoil, that soothed and comforted her.

When they were done, they moved back up to the VIP room. Maya was the only woman. One might think that sexism would rule a place like this, but here, all that mattered was how good you shot. Maya's military notoriety, if not heroism, also made her something of a local celebrity. Some of the guys were awed by her. Some harbored small-time crushes. It didn't bother Maya. Despite what you might read, most soldiers were greatly respectful of women. In her case, they seemed to channel whatever feelings of attraction they possessed into something more chaste or brotherly.

Maya's eyes skimmed over the words of the Second Amendment on the wall.

A well regulated Militia, being necessary to the security of a free State, the right of the people to keep and bear Arms, shall not be infringed.

Awkward grammar, to put it mildly. Maya had learned never to discuss or argue with those on either side. Her father, who had been adamantly anti-gun, used to snap, "You want your big assault rifle? What 'well regulated militia' are you with anyway?" while her pro-gun friends would always counter "What part of 'shall not be infringed' is confusing to you?" It was, of course, amazingly elastic phraseology and proved the adage that everyone always sees what's in their interest. If you loved guns, you found this document to mean one thing. If you hated guns, you thought it meant another.

Shane grabbed Maya a Coke. Alcohol was not allowed there because even the least rational among them realized that guns and alcohol don't mix. The five of them sat around and started shooting the breeze. The conversations always started with the local sports team but quickly moved into deeper terrain. This was the best part for Maya. She was one of them, except she was maybe a bit more. The guys often sought out the female perspective because, news flash, war messes up your relationships at home. It was a cheap cop-out for a soldier to say that nobody at home understood what he was going through, but it was also too damned apt. After you serve in some hellhole, you just see things differently. Sometimes it's in obvious ways, but more often, it's just about textures and hues and scents. Things that used to matter don't and vice versa. Relationships and marriages are hard enough, but you add war into the mix and small fissures become gaping wounds. No one sees what you're seeing—again that clear-eyed, unbiased thing—except your fellow soldiers. It's like one of those movies where only the hero can see the ghosts and everyone else thinks the hero is crazy.

In this room, they all saw the ghosts.

Being single and somewhat emotionally challenged, Shane wasn't good with the confessional stuff. He moved over to the seat in the corner, took out the new novel by Anna Quindlen, and started reading. Shane was a big reader—except, as Maya had seen the other night, out loud to children—and could read anywhere, even on that chopper where the rotors were so loud they seemed to be coming from inside her brain.

Eventually Maya migrated toward him. The TV above their head showed the third quarter of the New York Knicks–Brooklyn Nets game. Shane put down the book as she approached. He swung his long legs up on the leather ottoman and said, "Cool."

"What?"

"I assume you're ready to fill me in now."

She wasn't. She wanted to protect him. Always.

Still Shane wouldn't take that as an answer, and it would be unfair and perhaps detrimental to give him nothing. She debated telling him about meeting Corey Rudzinski in the flesh, but she had no idea how he would react. With anger, probably. Corey had also been very specific in the end:

"No burner phones. We only communicate if there is an emergency. If you need me, call the club and ask for Lulu. If I need you, the club will call your phone and hang up. That'll be your signal to come back here. But, Maya, if I feel slightly uneasy, I'm gone. Probably for good. So say nothing."

Say nothing—that felt like the right play for now. If she blew that relationship, Corey would likely disappear. She couldn't risk that.

But there was another avenue she could take.

Shane stared at her and waited. He could do that all night.

"What do you know about Kierce?" Maya asked him.

"The homicide cop working Joe's case?"

Maya nodded.

"Not much. He's got a solid reputation, but it's not like we hang out with the NYPD. Why?"

"You remember Joe's sister, Caroline?"

"Right."

"She told me that the family has been giving Kierce money."

Shane made a face. "What do you mean, giving him money?"

"Just under ten grand three times."

"For what?"

Maya shrugged. "She doesn't know."

She filled him in on what Caroline had told her about the payoffs, about her password not working, about Maya's decision to wait before she confronted Neil or Judith.

"It makes no sense," Shane said. "Why the hell would Joe's family want to bribe Kierce?"

"You tell me," Maya said.

He considered that for a moment. "We both know the rich are weird."

"We do."

"But are they paying Kierce in hopes he'll, what, do a better job? Make Joe's case a priority? It already is. Do the Burketts think they should tip a cop or something?"

"I don't know," Maya said. "But there's something more."

"What?"

"Caroline claims that the family started paying Kierce *before* Joe died."

"Bullshit."

"That's what she thinks."

"She's wrong. It doesn't even make sense. Why would they give Kierce money before the murder?"

Again Maya said: "I don't know."

"It's not like, what, they predicted Joe would get

murdered and which detective would work the case?"
Shane shook his head. "You know what the most likely
answer is, don't you?"

"No."

"Caroline is playing you."

Maya had considered that.

"Come on, that whole part with her going online in
front of you and suddenly, gasp, the password has
changed? That seems awfully convenient, doesn't it?"

"It does," Maya agreed.

"So she's lying. Wait, strike that."

"What?"

Shane turned toward her. "Caroline is a first-class
flake, right?"

"Of the highest order."

"So maybe she's not lying," Shane said, warming up
to his new theory. "Maybe she just imagined the whole
thing. Put the pieces together. You have this first-class
flake. Her brother is murdered. You all meet to discuss
the will. Then that gets canceled because of, what,
some paperwork snafu?"

"Not just a snafu," Maya said. "There's something
wrong with his death certificate."

"Even better. So she's under stress."

Maya frowned. "So she imagined seeing payments to
a homicide cop?"

"It's as likely as any other scenario right now." Shane
sat back. "Maya?"

She knew what was coming.

"Can you stop it, please?" he said.

"Stop what?"

He frowned. "It makes my tummy hurt when you lie to me."

"I'm not lying to you."

"Semantics. What aren't you telling me?"

Too much probably. Again she debated telling him more, but again she had the knee-jerk reaction of protecting him. She considered telling him about Claire's secret phone, but that would just lead to Corey. She didn't want to go there yet. She hadn't told him about what she had seen on the nanny cam either, but that could wait too. Always better to be cautious. Things can always be said later, but things can never be unheard.

Shane leaned close, made sure nobody could hear, and then whispered, "Where did you get that bullet?"

"You need to leave that alone."

"I did you a huge favor."

"And your favors come with strings, Shane?"

That stung him into silence, as she had known it would. She moved the topic back to Caroline.

"You said something interesting about Caroline being under stress," Maya said.

Shane waited.

"She didn't just talk about Joe. She talked about her other brother."

"Neil?"

Maya shook her head. "Andrew."

Shane made a face. "Wait, the one who fell off the boat?"

"He didn't fall."

"What do you mean?"

Finally. Something she felt safe confiding in him. "Joe was there. On the boat with him."

"Right, so?"

"So Joe told me it wasn't an accident. He said Andrew committed suicide."

Shane fell back in the chair. "Yowza."

"Yeah."

"Does the family know?"

Maya shrugged. "I don't think so. They all claim it was an accident."

"And Caroline raised this yesterday?"

"Yep."

"Why?" Shane asked. "Andrew Burkett died, what, nearly twenty years ago, right?"

"In a way I think it was natural," Maya said.

"How so?"

"Two brothers. Supposedly very close. Both dying young and tragically."

Shane nodded, seeing it now. "More reason why her imagination might get the better of her."

"And she never saw Joe's body."

"Come again?"

"Caroline. She never saw Joe's body. Or Andrew's. She wanted that. For closure. So Andrew dies at sea.

She never sees his corpse. Joe gets murdered. She never sees his either."

"I don't get it," Shane said. "Why didn't she see Joe's?"

"The family wouldn't let her or something, I don't know. But look at it from her viewpoint. Two dead brothers. And no dead bodies. Caroline never saw either one of them in a casket."

They fell into silence, but Shane saw it now. Caroline had hit a nerve when she talked to Maya about the need for a body. Maya and Shane had seen it time and time again during their time overseas. When a soldier died in battle, his family often couldn't accept the death until they saw definitive proof.

The dead body.

Maybe Caroline was right. Maybe that was the real origin of why soldiers make sure to bring everyone, even the dead, home.

Shane broke the silence. "So Caroline is having trouble accepting Joe's death."

"She's having trouble accepting *both* deaths," Maya said.

"And she thinks the man who is investigating Joe's murder is being paid off by her family."

That was when it hit Maya so hard she almost fell over. "Oh no . . ."

"What?"

Maya swallowed. She tried to think it through, tried

to organize her thoughts. The boat. The captain's wheel. The fishing trophies . . .

"Semper paratus," she said.

"What?"

Maya met Shane's eye. "Semper paratus."

"It's Latin," Shane said. "It means 'Always ready.'"

"You know it?"

The boat. The fishing trophies. The captain's wheel and life preservers. But mostly the crossed anchors. Maya had assumed the crossed anchors meant the Navy. They often do. But someone else used crossed anchors to award their boatswain's mates.

Shane nodded. "It's the motto of the Coast Guard."

The Coast Guard.

The branch of the Armed Forces with jurisdiction in both international and domestic waters. The Coast Guard could claim jurisdiction in any death on the high seas . . .

"Maya?"

She turned to him. "I need another favor, Shane."

He said nothing.

"I need you to find out who the lead investigator was in the maritime death of Andrew Burkett," she said. "I need you to see if it was a Coast Guard officer named Tom Douglass."

Chapter 17

Putting Lily to sleep was usually a routine task. Maya had heard all the horror stories about little kids who made bedtime a nightmare. Not Lily. It was as though she'd had enough of the day and was ready to just put it behind her. Her head hit the pillow without argument and, poof, sleep. But tonight, after Maya tucked her into bed, Lily said, "Story."

Maya was exhausted, but wasn't this one of the joys of motherhood? "Sure, sweetie, what would you like to read?"

Lily pointed to a Debi Gliori book. Maya read it to her, hoping it would work like hypnosis or a boring coworker and Lily's eyes would get droopy before closing for the night. But the book was having the opposite of the intended effect—Maya was the one drifting off while Lily poked her to stay awake. Maya managed to finish the story. She closed the book, started to rise, and Lily said, "Again, again."

"I think it's time to go to sleep, sweetie."

Lily started crying. "Scared."

Maya knew that you weren't supposed to let your child stay in your room during moments like this, but what those parental instructional manuals forget is that all human beings, even parents, will take the easier way out when exhausted. This little girl had lost her father. She was too young to get that, of course, but there still had to be something there, some subconscious pang, some primitive knowledge that all was not right.

Maya scooped Lily up. "Come on. You can sleep with me."

She carried Lily and gently set her down on Joe's side of the bed. She laid out pillows along the edge of the bed in a makeshift rail and then, to be on the safe side, threw a bunch more on the floor in case Lily somehow rolled through this tenuous barricade. Maya pulled the covers up and tucked them under Lily's chin, and as she did, Maya had one of those sudden "pow" moments sneak up on her, the ones all parents experience, when you are simply overwhelmed by your love for your child, when you are awestruck and you can feel something rising inside of you and you just want to hold on to it and yet, at the same time, that caring, that fear of losing this person, scares you into near paralysis. How, you wonder, will you ever relax again, knowing how unsafe the world is?

Lily closed her eyes and fell asleep. Maya stayed there, unmoving, watching her daughter's little face, making sure the breaths were deep and even. She stayed that way until mercifully her mobile phone rang and broke the spell.

She hoped that it might be Shane with an answer on Tom Douglass, though he'd told her that he wouldn't be able to look into the man's military records until the morning. She grabbed the phone and saw her niece Alexa's name pop up. In a small panic—here too was another person she could never lose—Maya quickly hit the green button.

"Everything okay?"

"Umm, yeah," Alexa said. "Why wouldn't it be?"

"No reason." Man, Maya needed to calm the hell down. "What's up, kiddo? You need help with your homework?"

"Right, and if I did, you think I'd call you?"

Maya laughed. "Good point."

"Tomorrow is Soccer Day."

"Excuse me?"

"It's the lame thing we do in our town where all the grades have a game and they sell booster stuff and there's a moon bounce and a carnival and all that. I mean, it's fun for the little kids."

"Okay."

"I know you said you were busy, but I was hoping you and Lily could come."

"Oh."

"Dad and Daniel will be there too. His game is at ten, mine's at eleven. We can take Lily around, get her a balloon animal—Mr. Ronkowitz, my English teacher, makes them for all the little kids—take her on the rides. I thought it might be fun. We miss her."

Maya looked over at Lily sleeping next to her. The overwhelmed feeling returned in force.

"Aunt Maya?"

Alexa and Daniel were Lily's cousins. Lily adored them. Maya wanted them—needed them—to be a big part of Lily's life. "I'm glad Lily's already asleep," Maya said to Alexa.

"Huh?"

"Because if I told her she was going to see her cousins tomorrow, she would be too excited to go anywhere near her bed."

Alexa laughed. "Great, see you in the morning? It's at the town circle."

"Right."

"Oh, and just FYI. My stupid coach will be there."

"No worries. I think the two of us get each other now."

"Good night, Aunt Maya."

"Good night, Alexa."

*   *   *

The night was bad.

The sounds began their assault when Maya was in that gentle cusp between consciousness and sleep. The clamoring, the screams, the rotors, and the gunfire were relentless. They would not pause. They would not let up. They grew louder and stayed. Maya wasn't in her bed. She wasn't back there either. She was in this in-between world, suspended, lost. All was darkness and noise, unceasing, endless noise, the type of noise that seemed to come from within her, as though some small creature had climbed inside her head and started screeching and scratching from within.

There was no escape, no rational thought. There was no here or now, no yesterday or tomorrow. That would all come later. Right now there was nothing but the agony of the sounds shredding through her brain like a reaper's scythe. Maya put her hands on either side of her head and pushed hard as though trying to crush her own skull.

It was that bad.

It was the type of bad that made you want to do anything to please—

—oh God please—

—make it stop. It made you think about picking up a gun and silencing the sounds, if you knew where you were, if you knew that you were so close to your bedside table where you kept a gun in that small safe . . .

Maya didn't know if it lasted minutes or hours. It seemed endless. Time had no meaning when the sounds suffocated you. You just rode it out and tried to stay afloat.

But at some point, a new sound, a more "regular" sound, penetrated her auditory hell. The sound seemed to come from a great distance. The sound seemed to take a long time to reach her and register. It had to fight through the other deafening sounds—one of which, Maya realized as she started to float up toward consciousness, was her own self screaming.

A doorbell. Then a voice:

"Maya? Maya?"

Shane. He started banging against the door.

"Maya?"

She opened her eyes. The sounds didn't flee so much as mockingly fade away, reminding her that they might grow quiet but they were always there, always with her. Maya again thought about that theory that no sound dies, that if you scream in the woods and you hear an echo, that echo just grows fainter and fainter but never completely goes away. Her sounds did the same.

They never fully left her.

Maya looked to her right, to where Lily had been sleeping.

But she wasn't there.

Maya's heart leapt into her throat. "Lily?"

The knocking and doorbell had stopped. Maya bolted upright. She swung her legs out of bed. When she tried to stand, the head rush knocked her back into a seating position.

"Lily?" she called again.

From downstairs, Maya heard the door open.

"Maya?"

It was Shane, inside the house now. She'd given him a key for emergencies.

"Up here." Maya tried again, making it to a standing position this time. "Lily? I can't find Lily!"

The house shook as Shane ran up the stairs two at a time.

"Lily!"

"I got her," Shane said.

He appeared at her door, carrying Lily with his right arm. Relief flooded Maya's veins.

"She was at the top of the stairs," Shane said.

There were tears on Lily's face. Maya hurried over to her. Lily cringed for a moment, and Maya realized that her daughter had probably woken up to her mother's screams.

Maya slowed down and made herself smile. "It's okay, sweetie."

The little girl buried her face into Shane's shoulder.

"I'm sorry, Lily. Mommy had a nightmare."

Lily wrapped her arms around Shane's neck. Shane looked toward Maya, not even trying to hide the pity and concern on his face. Maya's heart crumbled into a million pieces.

"I tried to call," he said. "When you didn't answer . . ."

Maya nodded.

"Hey," Shane said too cheerfully. He wasn't good with cheerful. Even Lily could sense that his tone was off. "Let's all go downstairs and have breakfast, what do you say?"

Lily looked wary, but she was also recovering quickly. That was the thing about kids. They are ridiculously resilient. They have, Maya thought, the coping skills of the best soldiers.

"Oh, guess what?" Maya said.

Lily looked at her mother warily.

"Today we're going to a carnival with Daniel and Alexa!"

That made the little girl's eyes widen.

"There'll be rides and balloons . . ."

Maya kept talking about the wonders of Soccer Day, and in a matter of minutes, the storm of last night dissipated in the glow of a new day. For Lily at least. But for Maya, the grip of fear, especially because it had obviously touched her daughter, held on to her for far too long.

What had she done?

Shane didn't ask her if she was okay. He knew. Once they had Lily settled in front of her breakfast and moved out of her earshot, Shane said, "How bad?"

"I'm fine."

Shane just turned away.

"What?"

"Lying to me gets easier and easier for you."

He was right.

"Very bad," she said. "Happy now?"

Shane turned back to her. He wanted to hug her—she could see that—but they didn't do that. Too bad. She could have used it.

"You need to talk to someone," Shane said. "What about Wu?"

Wu was the shrink from the VA. "I'll call him."

"When?"

"When this is over."

"When what is over?"

She didn't answer.

"It's not just about you anymore, Maya."

"Meaning?"

He looked over at Lily.

"Low blow, Shane."

"Too bad. You have a daughter you're raising on your own now."

"I'll take care of it."

Maya checked the time. Nine fifteen. She tried to remember the last time that had happened, when she had slept past 4:58 A.M., but she couldn't. She also wondered about Lily. So what had gone on? Had her daughter woken up and listened to her mother scream? Had Lily tried to wake her, or did she just cower in fear?

What kind of mother was she?

"Death follows you, Maya . . ."

"I'll take care of it," she said again. "I just need to see this through."

"And by 'see this through,' you mean 'find out who killed Joe'?"

She didn't reply.

"You were right, by the way," Shane said.

"About?"

"That's why I'm here. You asked me to look into Tom Douglass's time in the Coast Guard."

"And?"

"He served fourteen years. That's where he got his first taste of law enforcement. And yes, he was the officer in charge of the investigation into the death of Andrew Burkett."

Boom. It made sense. It made no sense.

"Do you know what his findings were?"

"Accidental death. According to his report, Andrew Burkett fell overboard at night and drowned. Alcohol was probably involved."

They just stood there for a few moments and let it sink in.

"What the hell is going on, Maya?"

"I don't know, but I plan to find out."

"How?"

Maya quickly took out her mobile phone and called the Douglass home. There was no answer. Maya left a message: "I know why the Burketts were paying you. Call me."

She left her cell phone number and hung up.

"How did you find out about Douglass?" Shane asked.

"It isn't important."

"Really?"

Shane stood up and started pacing. You didn't have to know him as well as Maya did to realize that this wasn't good.

"What?" she said.

"I called Detective Kierce this morning."

Maya closed her eyes. "Why would you do that?"

"Oh, I don't know. Maybe because you threw out a pretty big accusation last night."

"It was Caroline's accusation."

"Whatever. I wanted to size him up a little."

"And?"

"I like him. I think he's a straight shooter. I think Caroline is full of crap."

"Okay, just forget it."

Shane made an annoying buzzing sound like a game show effect when you give the wrong answer.

"What?"

"Sorry, Maya, wrong answer."

"What are you talking about?"

"Kierce wouldn't share any information on the actual investigation with me," Shane continued. "Which is what a good cop, a cop who plays by the rules and doesn't take bribes, would do."

Maya didn't like where this was going.

"But," Shane said, raising a finger in the air, "he felt that it would be okay to let me know about a certain incident that happened in your home recently."

Maya glanced over at Lily. "He told you about the nanny cam."

"Bingo."

Shane waited for her to explain. She didn't. They both stood there and stared at each other for too long. Shane broke the silence.

"Why wouldn't you tell me something like that?" he asked.

"I was going to."

"But?"

"But you already think I'm unstable."

Shane made the annoying buzzing noise again. "Wrong. I may think you need help—"

"Exactly. You're all over me to call Wu. And what would you have thought if I told you I thought I saw my murdered husband on a nanny cam?"

"I would have listened," Shane said. "I would have listened and tried to help you get to the bottom of it."

She knew that he meant it. Shane grabbed a chair, moved it close to her, sat down.

"Tell me what happened. Exactly."

No point in hiding it anymore. She told Shane about the nanny cam, about Isabella using pepper spray, about Joe's missing clothes and her visit to the Burkett workers' compound where Isabella lived. When she was finished, Shane said, "I remember that shirt. If you imagined it all, why would it be missing?"

"Who knows?"

Shane rose and started for the stairs.

"Where are you going?"

"I'm going to check his closet, see if it's there."

She was going to protest, but this was how Shane was. He had to play it all the way through. She waited. He came back five minutes later.

"Gone," he said.

"Which doesn't mean anything," Maya added. "A million reasons a shirt wouldn't be in his closet."

Shane sat back across from her and plucked his lower lip. Five seconds passed. Then ten. "Let's talk it out for a bit."

Maya just waited.

"You remember what General Dempsey said when he visited camp?" Shane asked. "About predictability in the theater?"

She nodded. General Martin Dempsey, chairman of the Joint Chiefs of Staff, had said that, of all human endeavors, the one that is most unpredictable is warfare. The only cardinal rule about what happens in battle is that you never know what will happen in battle. You have to be ready for what seems impossible.

"So let's play it through," Shane said. "Let's say that you really did see Joe on that nanny cam."

"He's dead, Shane."

"I get that. But just . . . let's go step by step. Just as an exercise."

She rolled her eyes for him to get on with it.

"Okay, so you look at this nanny cam on, what, your TV?"

"Laptop. You plug in an SD card."

"Right, sorry. The SD card. That's the one Isabella took after she sprayed you?"

"Yes."

"Okay, so you put this SD card into your laptop. You see Joe playing with Lily on the couch. Let's eliminate the obvious. It wasn't, like, an old recording, right?"

"Right."

"Are you sure? You said Eileen gave the nanny cam to you after the funeral. But could someone have put in an old recording or something? A tape someone made of the two of them before Joe was killed?"

"No. Lily was wearing exactly what she was wearing that day. It was filmed at the exact right angle, taken from that very spot on the shelf and aimed at the couch. There was a trick to it, sure. Had to be. Joe was, I don't know, photoshopped or something. But it wasn't an old piece of film."

"Okay, so we've eliminated that possibility."

This was getting ridiculous. "What possibility?"

"That it was an old tape. So let's try something else." Shane started plucking his lip again. "Let's pretend— just for the sake of argument—that it really was Joe. That he's still alive." Shane held up his hands, even though she hadn't said anything. "I know, I know, but just bear with me, okay?"

Maya bit back the sigh and shrugged a "suit your-self."

"How would you do it?" he asked. "If you were Joe and you wanted to fake your death."

"Fake my death and then, what, sneak into my house and play with my kid? I don't know, Shane. Why don't you tell me? You obviously have a theory."

"Not a theory exactly, but . . ."

"Does it involve zombies?"

"Maya?"

"Yes?"

"You use sarcasm when you're being defensive."

She frowned. "Those psych courses," she said. "They are really paying off."

"I don't know what you're so afraid of here."

"I'm afraid of wasting my time. But okay, Shane. Forget zombies. Give me your theory. How would you fake your death, if you were Joe?"

Shane kept plucking at his lip. Maya was afraid he might draw blood.

"Here is how I *might* do it," he said. "I *might* hire two street punks. I *might* give them guns with blanks."

"Wow," Maya said.

"Just let me finish, but I'll skip the mights if you don't mind. I, Joe, would set it up. I would have blood capsules or something like that. So it looks real. Joe was the one who liked that spot in the park, right? He knew the lighting situation. He knew it would be dark enough so you wouldn't see exactly what was going on. Think about it. Do you really believe those two punks just happened to be there? Wasn't that odd to you?"

"Wait, that's the part you find odd?"

"That whole robbery angle . . ." Shane shook his head. "It always felt like nonsense to me."

Maya sat there. Kierce had already proven that the robbery angle was nonsense when the ballistics test told him that the same gun had killed both Joe and Claire. Obviously Shane didn't know that.

"Suppose it was all a setup," Shane said, warming up to his outlandish conspiracy theory. "Suppose these two punks were hired to fire blanks and make it look like Joe was dead."

"Shane?"

"Yes."

"You realize how crazy that sounds, right?"

He kept plucking that lower lip.

"The cops were there too, Shane, remember? People saw the body."

"Okay, let's take that one at a time. First off, the people who saw the body. Sure. If you were the only witness, it wouldn't be enough. So Joe lies there with the fake blood or whatever. In the dark. A few people see him. It's not like they took his pulse or anything."

Maya shook her head. "Are you kidding?"

"Do you see a problem with my theory?"

"Where to begin?" Maya countered. "What about the cops?"

He spread his hands. "Didn't you yourself tell me that a payoff had been made?"

"To Kierce, you mean? Your new buddy who you liked and seemed to follow the rules?"

"I could be wrong about him. Wouldn't be the first time. And maybe Kierce made sure he was on duty when the murder happened. If it was a setup, Joe would know the when and where. So Kierce made sure his name came up in the rotation. Or maybe, I don't know, the Burketts also paid off the chief or captain or whatever so Kierce's name came up and he was first on the scene."

"You should make one of those YouTube conspiracy tapes, Shane. Was 9/11 an inside job too?"

"I'm giving you possibilities, Maya."

"So let me get this straight," she said. "They were all in on it. The punk kids who Kierce arrested. The cops at the scene. The medical examiner. I mean, if Joe is carted off as dead, there's an autopsy, right?"

"Hold up," Shane said.

"What?"

"Didn't you say that there was some kind of issue with the death certificate?"

"A bureaucratic snafu. And stop plucking at your lip, please."

Shane almost smiled. "There are holes in what I'm saying. I admit that. I could ask Kierce to see the autopsy photos—"

"Which he won't give you."

"I can be pretty resourceful."

"Don't be. Oh, and if they went to this much trouble, who's to say they couldn't doctor up some autopsy photos too?"

"Good point."

"I was being sarcastic." Maya shook her head. "He's dead, Shane. Joe is dead."

"Or he's messing with you."

Maya mulled that over for a few moments. "Or," she said, "someone is."

Chapter 18

occer Day was like something out of a nostalgic American movie that was just a little too perfect, too Norman Rockwell, to be authentic. There were tents and booths and games and rides. There were laughs and cheers and referee whistles and music. Food trucks offered up burgers and sausages and ice cream and tacos. You could buy pretty much anything in the town's green-and-white colors—T-shirts, caps, hoodies, polos, decals, water bottles, coffee mugs, key chains, fold-out chairs. Even the bounce house and inflatable slides were green and white.

Every grade had set up their own activity booth. The seventh grade girls applied temporary tattoos. The eighth grade boys had a radar gun and goalie net so you

could see the speed of your kicks. The girls' sixth grade
had set up a face-painting booth.

That was where Maya and Lily found Alexa.

When Alexa spotted them, she dropped her paint-
brush and ran toward them yelling, "Lily! Hey!"

Lily, who had been holding her mother's hand, let
go now. She giggled and covered her mouth with her
tiny hands and quivered with that level of anticipation
and joy that only little children can reach. The quiver-
ing and giggles grew as Lily's cousin barreled toward
them. The giggles grew into shrieking laughs when
Alexa scooped Lily off the ground.

Maya stood there, a definite spectator in this greet-
ing, and smiled.

"Lily! Aunt Maya!"

It was Daniel now hurrying toward them. Eddie
trailed behind his son, a smile on his face too. The scene
felt so unreal to Maya, almost obscene in the middle of
the personal chaos, but that was okay. The world has
lines and fences. More than anything, Maya wanted to
keep these three children on the right side of them.

Daniel gave his aunt a quick kiss on the cheek on his
way to Lily. He took her from his sister and hoisted her
high in the air. The sound of Lily's laugh, a sound of
pure undiluted innocence, made Maya pull up. When,
she wondered, was the last time she had heard her
daughter make a sound like that?

"Can we take her on the rides, Aunt Maya?" Alexa
asked.

"We'll be careful," Daniel added.

Eddie moved up next to Maya.

"Sure," Maya said. "You need some money?"

"We got it," Daniel said, and they were off.

Maya gave Eddie a quick smile. Her former brother-in-law looked better today, clean-shaven and clear-eyed. He kissed her cheek. No smell of booze. Maya turned her gaze back on the three kids walking away. Daniel had put Lily down between Alexa and himself. Lily held on to Daniel with her right hand, Alexa with her left.

"Beautiful day," Eddie said.

Maya nodded. It was indeed. The sun was shining as though on a director's cue. Here was the American dream, spread out before Maya like a warm blanket, and the overwhelming feeling for her was that she didn't belong here, that her very presence was a dark cloud blocking that glowing light.

"Eddie?"

His hand cupped his eyes to keep the sun out. He turned toward her.

"Claire wasn't cheating on you."

His eyes welled up so fast he had to look away. He hunched over, and for a second, Maya worried that he might be crying. She reached out, wanting to put a hand on his shoulder, but she stopped short and let the hand fall to her side.

"You're sure?" he said.

"Yes."

"And that phone?"

"Do you remember my, uh, troubles with that combat tape that got released?"

"Yes, of course."

"There was more to them."

"What do you mean?"

"The guy who leaked it—"

"Corey the Whistle," Eddie said.

"Right. He didn't release the audio."

Eddie looked confused.

"I think Claire talked him out of it."

"That audio," Eddie said. "It would have made it worse for you?"

"Yes."

Eddie nodded, but he didn't ask what was on it. "Claire was so upset when that scandal broke. We all were. We were worried about you."

"Claire took it a step further."

"How?"

"She contacted Corey. She hooked up with his organization."

There was no reason to go into Claire's possible motives with Eddie. Maybe Claire worked with Corey as quid pro quo for leaving Maya alone. Maybe Corey, who could be persuasive and charming, had convinced her that helping him take down the Burkett family was the moral and just thing to do. Didn't matter in the end.

"Claire started to gather dirt on the Burketts," she said. "To help Corey's organization take them down."

"Do you think that's what got her killed?"

Maya looked over at her daughter. Alexa's whole team had gathered around Lily to ooh and aah. They were taking turns putting green-and-white face paint on her, and even at this distance, Maya could feel her daughter's joy.

"Yes."

"I don't understand," Eddie said. "Why didn't Claire tell me?"

Maya kept her eyes on the children, playing her part as the silent sentinel. She could feel Eddie's gaze, but she kept silent. Claire hadn't told him because she wanted to keep him safe. In doing so, in keeping Eddie completely ignorant, Claire had in all likelihood saved his life. She had loved her husband. She had loved him very much. Jean-Pierre was a stupid fantasy that would have curdled in the light of reality like turned milk. Claire, the loving pragmatist, had seen that, even if Maya, so impetuous with her own love life, couldn't. Claire had loved Eddie. She had loved Daniel and Alexa. She had loved this life with its Soccer Days and face painting under the bright sun.

"Do you remember anything unusual, Eddie? Anything that might fit into this?"

"Like I told you before, she started working later. She was distracted. I would ask her what was wrong, but she didn't want to tell me." His voice grew soft. "She told me not to worry."

The kids finished the face painting and started toward the carousel.

"Did she ever mention a man named Tom Douglass?"

Eddie thought about it. "No. Who is he?"

"He's a private detective."

"Why would she go to him?"

"Because the Burketts have been paying him off. Did you ever hear her talk about Andrew Burkett?"

He frowned. "Joe's brother who drowned?"

"Yes."

"No. What does he have to do with it?"

"I don't know yet. But I need you to do something."

"Name it."

"Look at everything again with fresh eyes. Her travel records, her personal files, anyplace she may have hid things. Whatever. She was trying to take down the Burketts. She found out that they were paying off this Tom Douglass, and I think that was the catalyst for something bigger."

Eddie nodded. "I will."

They both stood there and watched Daniel hoist Lily onto a carousel horse. Daniel stayed on one side, Alexa on the other. Lily beamed.

"Look at them," Eddie said. "Just . . ."

Maya nodded, afraid to speak. Eddie had said that death followed her, but it probably wasn't that simple. All around her, children and families played and laughed and reveled in the glory of this seemingly ordinary day. They did so without fear or care because they didn't get it. They all played and they all laughed and they felt so damn safe. They didn't see how fragile it all was. War was far away from them, they thought. Not just another continent but another realm. It couldn't touch them.

But they were wrong about that.

It had touched one of them already, more specifically Claire, and Maya was to blame. What she had done in a combat helicopter over Al Qa'im, like those sounds that wouldn't ever leave her, started an echo, a reverberation, and eventually that echo found its way to her sister.

The truth was so obvious and so deeply painful. If Maya hadn't made those mistakes in that chopper, Claire would still be alive. She would be standing here, overwhelmed by the beauty and laughter of her children. It was Maya's fault that she wasn't. Claire was not here, and somewhere, behind the happy smiles of Daniel and Alexa, was a sadness that would always haunt them.

Lily started to spin her head, looking around. She spotted her mother and waved. Maya swallowed and waved back. Daniel and Alexa waved too and beckoned for Maya to join them.

"Maya?" Eddie said.

She said nothing.

"Go to them."

Maya shook her head.

"You're not on guard duty right now," he said, a little too in her thoughts. "Go and enjoy your daughter."

But he didn't get it. She didn't belong here. She was an outsider, out of her element—even though, ironically, this was the way of life she had fought and risked everything to protect. Yes, this. Right here. This very moment. Yet she couldn't cross that line and be a part of it, could she? Maybe that was the deal you made. You can participate or you can protect, but you really can't do both. Her fellow soldiers would understand. Some might force themselves to cross over. They'd smile and go on the carousel and buy the T-shirts, but there would be something behind the eyes, something that couldn't quite let go, something that kept them scanning the perimeter for approaching danger.

Did that ever go away?

Maybe. But not yet. So Maya stood there, watching, a silent sentinel.

"You go," Maya said.

Eddie thought about it. "No, I'm good here with you."

They stayed there and watched.

"Maya?"

She said nothing.

"When you find out who killed Claire, you'll need to tell me."

Eddie wanted to be the one to avenge his wife. That wouldn't happen. "Okay," she said.

"Promise?"

What was one more lie? "Promise."

Her mobile phone buzzed. She checked the number. Tom Douglass's home line. She stepped to the side and brought the phone to her ear.

"Hello?"

"I got your message," Mrs. Douglass said. "Come by as soon as you can."

"Let me take Lily home with us," Eddie said. "The kids will be thrilled."

It would indeed make things easier. If Maya were to try to pull Lily away from the festivities, she would understandably throw a tantrum worthy of, well, a two-year-old.

"It's about that Tom Douglass," she said, even though he hadn't asked. "He lives in Livingston. It shouldn't take more than a couple of hours."

Eddie made a face.

"What?"

"Livingston. That's Exit 15W on the Turnpike, right?"

"Right, why?"

"The week before Claire was killed," he said, "her E-Z Pass showed a couple of hits through that toll booth."

"Was that unusual for her?"

"I never really checked her E-Z Pass before, but yeah, I mean, we don't go down that far."

"What do you make of it?"

"There's some fancy mall down there. I figured maybe that's where she went."

Or he didn't want to look too closely, which was understandable. No matter. Maya hurried back to her car. Her sister had been murdered because she was getting too close to a secret. Maya was sure of it. That secret had to do with Tom Douglass and, by extension, Joe's brother Andrew Burkett. How Andrew Burkett, who'd been dead almost fifteen years when Maya and Joe met, could possibly have led to Claire's murder was still a mystery.

She started toward the highway, flipping stations, finding nothing she liked. It wouldn't do to overanalyze right now. Her daughter was safe with Claire's family.

She hooked up the playlist on her phone via the Bluetooth and tried to clear her mind. Lykke Li came on singing "No Rest for the Wicked." Lykke sang that she let her "good one" down and then the killer line: "I let my true love die." Maya sang along, lost in that small bliss, and when the song was over, she hit the back arrow, played it again, sang it all the way through to the also-killer end stanza: "I had his heart, but I broke it every time."

Joe had given her this song. Their relationship had been a mad whirlwind, but that had been Maya's disastrous romantic history. Forty-eight hours after meeting at that charity function, Joe had suggested flying down to Turks and Caicos on the Burketts' private plane. Maya had swooned and acquiesced. They spent the weekend at a villa at the Amanyara resort.

She had expected this new relationship to follow her normal impetuous pattern: intense, sizzling, over-the-top, maniacal romantic connection—followed in short order by a quick cut to black. Sizzle to fizzle. Love to good-bye. For Maya, everyone she fell for became her Jean-Pierre. For maybe three weeks.

So after week one, when she woke up to find that Joe had made her an online playlist, she listened hard to every song, ciphering out hidden meanings in the lyrics, while lying on her back like a teenager and staring at the ceiling. She loved his taste in music. The songs had done more than speak to her. They had penetrated her defenses, weakened her, left her ripe for, sexist as it might sound, education.

Still, Maya knew it took two to tango. She had relished whirling helplessly in Joe's vortex—drink, song, travel, sex—but from the start, like with every one of her romantic entanglements, she could see the end in sight. That was okay for her. She had a life in the military. Marriage, kids, Soccer Days—they were not part of the plan. By all rights, Joe should have ended up being another good memory.

Her relationships eventually turned bad. But the memories didn't.

Except Maya ended up getting pregnant, and in her ensuing confusion about what to do, Joe stepped up big-time. There was the proposal on one knee while violins played. He promised her happiness. He promised her love. He told her that he was proud of her military service and swore to do all he could so that she could achieve her career goals. They would be different, he said, living by their own set of rules. Joe's passion was a force unto itself. It swept her along, and before she knew it, Captain Maya Stern was a Burkett.

Lykke Li faded away and Oh Wonder's "White Blood" came on. Why on earth, she asked herself, was she listening to Joe's heartbreakers? Simple answer: because she liked the songs. In a vacuum, forgetting where it had all gone, these songs still reached inside her and touched her, even this one, even with the gut-wrenching opening lines:

> *"I'm ready to go, I'm ready to go,*
> *"Can't do it alone . . ."*

Beautiful but bullshit, Maya thought as she spotted Tom Douglass's boat by the garage. She was ready to do it alone.

Before Maya could ring the bell, the front door opened. Mrs. Douglass was there. Her face was drawn, the skin pulled tight. She looked left and right, opened the screen door, and said, "Get in."

Maya stepped inside. Mrs. Douglass closed the door behind her.

"Is someone watching us?" Maya asked.

"I don't know."

"Is your husband home?"

"No."

Maya kept silent. The woman had called her back because she wanted something. Let her say what it was.

"I got your phone message," Mrs. Douglass said.

Maya barely nodded.

"You said you knew what work my husband was doing for the Burketts."

This time Mrs. Douglass waited her out. Maya kept it brief.

"That's not what I said."

"Oh?"

"I said I knew why the Burketts were paying your husband."

"I don't see the difference."

"I don't think he did work for them," Maya said. "Unless accepting a bribe is work."

"What are you talking about?"

"Mrs. Douglass, stop jerking me around, please."

Her eyes went wide. "I'm not. Please tell me what you learned."

Maya could hear the desperation in the woman's voice. If she was lying, she was pretty good at it.

"What did you think your husband was doing for the Burketts?" Maya asked.

"Tom's a private eye," she said. "I assumed that he

was doing confidential private investigation work for a powerful family."

"But he never told you what the work specifically entailed?"

"I told you. His work was confidential."

"Come on, Mrs. Douglass. Are you telling me that your husband would come home from work every day and never tell you anything that went on at the office?"

A tear escaped and ran down her cheek. "What was Tom doing?" she asked, her voice a whisper. "Please tell me."

Again Maya debated which road to take and settled on the most direct route. "Your husband was in the Coast Guard. When he was serving, he investigated the death of a young man named Andrew Burkett."

"Yes, I know. That's how Tom met the family. They liked the work he did on that case. So when he opened up his own place, they hired him to do more."

"I don't think so," Maya said. "I think they wanted him to report the death as an accident."

"Why?"

"That's what I need to ask your husband."

Mrs. Douglass sat on the couch as though her knees had given way. "They paid him for so many years, so much money . . ."

"Money isn't a problem for the Burketts."

"But that much? That long?" She put a trembling hand to her mouth. "If what you're claiming is true— and I'm not saying it is—then it had to be big."

Maya knelt down. "Where is your husband, Mrs. Douglass?"

"I don't know."

Maya waited.

"That's why I called you back. Tom's been missing for three weeks."

Chapter 19

Mrs. Douglass had reported her husband missing to the police, but really, when a fifty-seven-year-old man goes off without suspicion of foul play, there is little the police can do.

"Tom loves to fish," she said. "He goes away for weeks at a time. The police saw that. I told them he wouldn't do that without telling me but . . ." She gave a helpless shrug. "They put his name in the system, whatever that means. One of the detectives said that they could open a full investigation, but they wouldn't be able to look at his work files without a court order."

Maya left a few minutes later. Enough waiting. She called her former mother-in-law. Three rings later, Judith said in a low voice, "I'm in with a patient. Is everything okay?"

"We need to talk."

There was a strange pause, and Maya wondered whether Judith was making her excuses and leaving the room. "Meet me at my office. Five o'clock okay?"

"Done."

Maya hung up and called Eddie about picking up Lily.

"Let her stay," he said. "She's having a blast with Alexa."

"You sure?"

"Either you're going to have to let Lily visit a lot more or I'm going to have to hire an adorable two-year-old to come by."

Maya smiled. "Thanks."

"You okay?"

"I'm good, thanks."

"Don't do what she did, Maya."

"What's that?"

"Don't lie to protect me."

He had a point, but then again, where would they be right now if Claire had confided in him?

There was a car parked in her driveway. A familiar figure sat on a bench by her back door, taking notes on a yellow legal pad. Maya wondered how long he had been sitting there. More than that, she wondered why he was there now.

Was it Shane—or another coincidence?

She pulled up and put the car in park. Ricky Wu didn't look up until Maya was all the way out of the car.

He closed his pen with a click and smiled at her. Maya did not smile back.

"Hello, Maya."

"Hello, Dr. Wu."

He didn't like to be called Doctor. He was one of those shrinks who really wanted to be on a first-name basis. Maya's father used to play a Steely Dan song from the seventies called "Doctor Wu." She always wondered if that was the reason he winced a bit whenever she called him that.

"I called and left you messages," Wu said.

"Yes, I know."

"I thought it might just be better if I stopped by."

"Did you now?" Maya unlocked the door with her key. She entered. Wu followed her inside.

"I thought I might pay my respects," he said.

She made a tsk-tsk noise. "I'm surprised."

"Pardon?"

"I didn't think you'd try to renew our patient-shrink relationship with a lie."

If Wu was offended, his smile didn't show it. "Can we sit down for a minute?"

"I'd rather stand."

"How are you feeling, Maya?"

"I'm okay."

He nodded. "No recent episodes?"

Shane, she thought.

He would never buy it if she insisted that they had gone away completely. "Some," Maya said.

"Want to tell me about them?"

"I got them under control."

"I'm surprised."

"What?"

Wu arched an eyebrow. "I didn't think you'd try to renew our patient-shrink relationship with a lie."

Touché, Maya thought.

Wu tried the gentle smile. Maya was about to put him off when, without warning, she flashed back to Lily's scared face from that morning. Tears surprised her, stinging her eyes. She turned her back to him and fought them off.

"Maya?"

She swallowed hard. "I need them to stop."

Wu moved a little closer. "What happened?"

"I scared my kid."

She told him about the previous night. Wu listened without interrupting. When she finished, he said, "I might want to switch your medication. For patients suffering with similar symptoms, I've been having good success lately with Serzone."

Maya no longer trusted her voice. She nodded.

"I have some in the car, if you'd like."

"Thank you."

"No problem." He moved closer. "May I make an observation?"

She frowned. "So I can't just get the meds and be left alone?"

"Sorry, Maya, there's always a catch."

"Figured that. Okay, what's your observation?"

"You never admitted you needed help before."

"Okay, good observation."

"That's not the observation."

"Oh."

"You finally admitted it," he said, "to protect your child. You wouldn't do it for yourself. It had to be for Lily."

"Yep, another good observation," she said.

"You're not trying to make yourself better. You're trying to protect your child." He tilted his head in that shrink way of his. "When do you stop thinking that way?"

"When do I stop thinking about protecting my child?" Maya shrugged. "When does any parent?"

"Touché," Wu said, putting both palms on the counter. "Glib answer, but touché. But you need to listen to me. The *D* in 'PTSD' stands for 'disorder.' You can't just tough this out. You want to keep your child safe? Then you need to work through this."

"I agree," she said.

Wu smiled. "Well, that was easy."

"I'll make an appointment."

"Why don't we start right now?"

"I don't have much time."

"Oh, this first session won't last long."

She thought about it and again figured why not. "It's similar to what I've experienced in the past."

"More intense?"

"Yes."

"How often are the episodes coming?"

"You keep calling them that. 'Episodes.' Except that's a polite word for what they are, isn't it? They are hallucinations."

"I don't like that term. I don't like the connotations—"

She interrupted him. "Can I ask you something?"

"Of course, Maya."

Spur-of-the-moment decision, but she decided to go with it. Might as well make him useful. "I had something else happen to me. Something connected to all this."

Wu looked at her and nodded. "Tell me."

"My friend bought me a nanny cam," she began.

Again Wu listened without interrupting. She told him the story about seeing Joe on the laptop. Wu managed to keep his face from revealing too much.

"Interesting," he said when she was done. "This happened during the day, am I correct?"

"Yes."

"So not at night," he said more to himself than her. Then again: "Interesting."

Enough with the interesting. "My question is," Maya said, "did I hallucinate it, or is it a hoax or something?"

"Good question." Ricky Wu sat back down, crossed his leg, even stroked his chin. "The brain is a tricky thing, of course. And in your situation—PTSD, a sister murdered, a husband murdered in front of your eyes, the pressure of being a single parent, ignoring most therapies—the most logical conclusion is that . . . Well, again I don't like the connotations. But I think most experts would conclude that you imagined or, yes, hallucinated seeing Joe on that computer screen. The simple diagnosis, which is often the best, is that you wanted to see him so badly, you did."

"Most experts," Maya said.

"Pardon?"

"You said, 'Most experts would conclude.' I'm not really interested in most. I'm interested in what you think."

Wu smiled. "I'm almost flattered."

She said nothing.

"You'd think that I would agree with that diagnosis. You've been ducking me. It would serve you right. You left treatment earlier than I wanted. You then faced added pressures. You miss him. You not only lost the career that defined you, but now you are forced into the role of a single mother."

"Ricky?"

"Yes?"

"Get to the 'but,' please."

"But you don't suffer from hallucinations. You have vivid flashbacks. That's common with PTSD. Some believe that those vivid flashbacks can be similar or even the same as hallucinations. The danger then is that those hallucinations can lead to psychosis. But what you have, be they vivid flashbacks or hallucinations, has always been auditory. At night, when you have your episodes, you never see the dead, do you?"

"No."

"You're not haunted by those faces. The three men. The mother." He swallowed. "The child."

She said nothing.

"You hear the screams. You don't see the faces."

"So?"

"So that's not uncommon. Thirty to forty percent of combat veterans with PTSD report auditory hallucinations. In your case, it has been exclusively auditory. I'm not saying you didn't"—he made quote marks with his fingers—"'see' Joe. You may have. But what I am saying is that it isn't consistent with your diagnosis or even the disorder. I can't validate a hypothesis that because of your PTSD you imagined seeing your husband on a silent video tape."

"In short," she said, "you don't think I imagined it."

"What you call hallucinations, Maya, are flashbacks. They are of things that actually occurred. You don't see or hear things that never happened."

She sat back.

"How do you feel right now?" he asked.

"Relief, I guess."

"I can't be certain, of course. At night, are you still on that helicopter?"

"Yes."

"Tell me what you remember."

"It's the same, Ricky."

"You get the distress call. The soldiers are cornered."

"I fly in. I fire." She wanted to move it along. "We've been through this."

"We have. What happens next?"

"What do you want me to say?"

"You always stop here. Five people were killed. Non-combatants. One was a mother of two—"

"I hate that."

"What?"

"They always say that. 'One was a woman. A mother.' It's such sexist crap, isn't it? A civilian is a civilian. The men were fathers. No one ever says that. 'A mother and a woman.' Like that makes it worse than a father and a man."

"Semantics," he said.

"What?"

"You get angry at the semantics because you don't want to face the truth."

"God, I hate when you talk like this. What truth don't I want to face?"

He gave her the sympathetic eyes. She hated the sympathetic eyes. "It was a mistake, Maya. That's all. You need to forgive yourself. That guilt haunts you and sometimes, yes, it manifests itself into those auditory flashbacks."

She crossed her arms. "You disappoint me, Dr. Wu."

"How so?"

"It's trite, that's all. I feel guilt about dead civilians; ergo, once I stop blaming myself, I'll be all better."

"No," he said. "It's not a cure. But it might make your nights a little easier."

He didn't get it, but then again, he had never heard the audiotape from that day. Would it change things for him? Maybe, maybe not.

Her cell phone buzzed. One ring on her phone. She checked the number.

"Ricky?"

"Yes."

"I have to pick up my kid now," she lied. "Can I get those new meds?"

Chapter 20

The caller ID had read "Leather and Lace."

Corey had made it clear. If he called and hung up, that meant he wanted to meet.

When she pulled into the lot, the bouncer leaned into her window and said, "Glad you got the job."

Man, she hoped that the bouncer was in on it and that her being a stripper wasn't viewed as a realistic cover.

"Park in the employee lot and use the employee entrance."

Maya did as he asked. When she got out of the car, two of her "colleagues" smiled and waved. Keeping in character, Maya smiled and waved back. The employee door was locked, so Maya looked up into the camera and waited. She heard the telltale buzz and opened it. Another man was standing there, giving her the cold eye.

"You're armed?" he asked.

"Yes."

"Let me have it."

"No," Maya said.

He didn't like that answer, but a voice from behind him said, "It's okay."

Lulu.

"Same room as before," Lulu said to her. "He's waiting for you."

"Right to work then," Maya said in a bad attempt at a half joke.

Lulu smiled and shrugged.

She could smell the cannabis before she turned the corner and saw Corey lighting up. He took a deep inhale, stood, and offered her a hit.

"I'm good," she said. "You wanted to see me?"

Corey held the smoke in a bit and nodded. When he released it, he said, "Take a seat."

Again she frowned at the upholstery.

"No one uses this room," he said, "but me."

"That supposed to make me feel better?"

She expected a small smile at the very least, but suddenly he was up and pacing, clearly on edge. Maya sat, hoping that might calm him down a bit.

"Did you visit Tom Douglass?" he asked.

"Sort of."

"What do you mean?"

"I visited his wife. Tom Douglass has been missing for three weeks."

That stopped the pacing. "Where is he?"

"What part of 'missing' is confusing you, Corey?"

"Jesus." He took another hit. "Did you figure out why the Burketts were paying him?"

"In part." She still didn't know if she trusted him, but then again, what other choice did she have right now? "Tom Douglass served in the Coast Guard."

"So?"

"So he investigated the accidental death of Andrew Burkett."

"What the hell are you talking about?"

She filled him in on what she had learned and what she had already known via Joe about Andrew's death being a suicide. Corey kept nodding, a little too hyped up, and she started to wonder when the mellow would kick in.

"So let's put this together," Corey said, still pacing. "Your sister starts investigating. She stumbles across these Burkett payments to Tom Douglass. Boom, she's tortured and killed. Boom, your husband's killed. Boom, Tom Douglass goes missing. That about right?"

His timeline was slightly off. It wasn't Claire, Joe, Tom. It was Claire, Tom, Joe. But she didn't bother to correct him.

"But there's something else to consider," Maya said.

"How's that?"

"You don't murder someone to hide a son's suicide. You might pay them off. But you don't kill them."

Corey nodded. "And assuming it was the Burketts who were making the payments," he added, still nodding with too much vigor, "you certainly don't kill your own son."

His eyes were red, she could see now. From cannabis or tears, she didn't know which.

"Corey?"

"Yeah."

"You guys have sources. Good sources. I need you to hack into Tom Douglass's life."

"Did that already."

"You did it weeks ago looking for clues on his work. But we need everything now. His credit card statements, ATM payments, when he last made a transaction, what his habits are, where he could go. We need to find him. Can you do that?"

"Yeah," Corey said. "We can do that."

He started pacing again.

"What else is wrong?" Maya asked.

"I think I have to disappear again. Maybe for a very long time."

"Why?"

Corey lowered his voice to a near whisper. "Something you said last time you were here."

"About?"

He looked left, then right. "I got ways out of here," he said. "Secret ways."

Maya wasn't sure what to make of that. "Okay."

"There's even a hidden door in that wall over there.

I can hide, or there's a tunnel to the river. If the cops ever try to surround this place, even quietly or whatever, I can get out. You wouldn't believe the measures I have in place here."

"I can see that. But I don't see why that means you have to disappear."

"A leak!" Corey shouted, spitting out the word as if it truly disgusted him, which, she assumed, it did. "You were the one to first raise that, right? You said one possibility was that someone inside my organization leaked Claire's name. I've been thinking hard about it. Suppose my operation . . . I mean, suppose we're not as airtight as I thought. Do you realize how many people could be exposed? Do you know how many of them would suffer huge, possibly even fatal, consequences?"

Whoa, Maya needed to calm him down. "I don't think it was a leak, Corey."

"Why not?"

"Because of Joe."

"I'm not following."

"Claire was killed. Joe was killed. You said that before—that Joe may have been helping her. So there's your leak. Claire told Joe. She may have also told someone else, or Joe might have, or they might have just screwed up when they were investigating."

She didn't care if it was true or not. She just needed him not to disappear on her.

"I don't know," Corey said. "I don't feel safe."

She stood and put her hands on his shoulders. "I need your help, Corey."

He wouldn't meet her eye. "Maybe you were right. Maybe we should go to the police. Like you said. I give them all the information I have. Anonymously. Let them do the rest."

"No," Maya said.

"I thought that's what you wanted."

"Not anymore."

"Why not?"

"There's no way to do that without exposing yourself and your organization."

He frowned and turned back toward her. "You care about my organization?"

"Not even a little bit," Maya said. "But you'll blow our chances if you do that. You'll run. I need you, Corey. We can do this better than the cops."

She stopped.

"There's something else," he said. "What is it?"

"I don't trust them."

"The cops?"

She nodded.

"But you trust me?"

"My sister did."

"And it got her killed," Corey said.

"Yeah, it did. But you can't keep going back like that. If you don't get her to become a whistle-blower, yep, she's probably still alive. But if I don't kill civilians on that copter, then you don't release that tape, and Claire never even meets you. For that matter, if I chose another career, Claire is probably at home right now, playing with her two kids instead of rotting in the ground. Lots of sliding doors, Corey. Waste of time to play it that way."

Corey stepped back and took another deep toke. When he could speak again, he said, "I don't know what to do."

"Stay. Look into Tom Douglass. Help me finish this."

"And I guess I should just trust you."

"You don't have to just trust me," she said. "Remember?"

He saw it now. "Because I still have something on you."

Maya didn't bother replying. Corey looked at her. She knew that he wanted to ask her about the audio portion of that tape. But she wanted to ask him something about it too.

"Why didn't you release the audio?" she asked.

"I told you."

"You said my sister talked you out of it."

"That's right."

"But I'm not completely buying that. It took time for her message to reach you. The story made a splash, but it was starting to die down by then. You'd have been back in the headlines."

"You think that's all I care about?"

Again Maya didn't bother replying.

"Without headlines, the truth never gets out. Without headlines, we can't recruit more truth tellers."

She didn't need the speech again. "All the more reason to release the audio, Corey. So why didn't you?"

He moved toward the couch and sat down. "Because I'm also a human being."

Maya sat down.

Corey lowered his head into his hands for a moment and took a few deep breaths. When he looked up, he was more clear-eyed, calmer, less panicked. "Because I figured that you'd have to live with yourself, Maya. With what you'd done. And sometimes that's punishment enough."

She said nothing.

"So how do you live with it, Maya?"

If Corey expected a truthful answer to that question, he would have to get in a very long line.

For a few moments, they just sat there in silence, the din of the club seemingly miles away. Nothing more to learn here, Maya thought. It was time to go to Judith's office anyway.

Maya rose and headed for the door. "See what you can find on Tom Douglass."

Chapter 21

Judith's office was located on the ground floor of an apartment building on the Upper East Side of Manhattan, one block from Central Park. Maya had no idea what sort of patients Judith saw nowadays. She was a Stanford University–trained MD and now a clinical professor on staff at Weill Cornell Medicine, though she didn't teach any classes. That someone who worked part-time could hold these positions was only a surprise to those who didn't recognize the power of the Burkett name and big donations.

Shock alert: Money means power and gets you stuff.

Judith went professionally by her maiden name, Velle. If this was to semihide the conflict of the Burkett name or because that was what many women did was anyone's guess. Maya headed past the doorman and found Judith's office door. Judith shared her space with two other part-time physicians. All three names—Judith Velle, Angela Warner, and Mary McLeod—were on the door with a long list of letters after them.

Maya turned the knob and pushed open the door. The waiting room was empty and small—one love seat, one couch. The artwork was generic enough to work in a roadside chain motel. The walls and carpeting were beige. A sign on the far door read: "IN SESSION. PLEASE HAVE A SEAT."

There was no receptionist. Maya guessed that the patients were often high profile, and so the fewer people who saw them, the better. One patient would be in session. When finished, that patient would exit into the corridor via a door located in the doctor's office. The waiting patient—or, in this case, Maya—would then be shown in. Neither patient would see the other.

The desire for privacy and discretion was understandable, of course—Maya didn't want anybody knowing about her "disorder" either—but it was probably harmful too. Doctors kept stressing that mental disease was the same as physical disease. Telling someone who was clinically depressed, for example, to shake it off and get out of the house was tantamount to telling a man with two broken legs to sprint across the room. That was all well and good in theory, but in practice, the stigma continued.

Maybe, to be more charitable, it was because you could hide a mental disease. Maybe if Maya could hide two broken legs and still somehow walk, she would. Who knew anymore? Right now, she had to get through this and then worry about treatment. The answers were out there, tantalizingly close. No one would be safe until she got to the truth and punished the guilty.

She might not be able to do that with broken legs. But she sure as hell could do it with PTSD.

Maya checked her watch. Five minutes until the hour was up. She tried to read whatever inane magazines were there, but the words swam by her. She played with her mobile phone, some game with making words out of four letters, but her concentration was shot. She moved close to the door. She didn't put her ear against it and listen in, but she stood close enough to hear the low murmur of two female voices. Time passed slowly, but eventually Maya could hear the inner door open. The patient was probably exiting.

Maya hurried back to her seat, picked up a magazine, crossed her legs. Ms. Casual. The door opened, and a woman Maya guessed was a well-kept sixty smiled at her.

"Maya Stern?"

"Yes."

"This way, please."

So there was a receptionist, Maya thought. She just worked from inside the office. Maya followed the woman inside, assuming she would find Judith sitting at a desk or maybe on a chair next to a couch or some such shrink-like environment. But Judith wasn't there.

Maya turned to the receptionist. The receptionist stuck out her hand.

"I'm Mary."

Maya got it now. She glanced at the diplomas on the wall. "As in Mary McLeod?"

"That's right. I'm a colleague of Judith's. She hoped that maybe we could have a chat."

According to the diploma, both women had gone to medical school at Stanford. Maya spotted an under-graduate one for Judith at USC. Mary had gotten her BS from Rice University and did her residency at UCLA.

"Where is Judith?"

"I don't know. We both only work part-time. We share this office."

Maya did not bother hiding her annoyance. "Yes, I read your name on the door."

"Why don't you sit for a moment, Maya?"

"Why don't you pound sand, Mary?"

If Mary McLeod was flustered by Maya's belliger-ence, her face didn't show it. "I think I can help you."

"You can help me by telling me where Judith is."

"I already told you. I don't know."

"Bye now."

"My son served two tours. One in Iraq, one in Af-ghanistan."

Maya couldn't help herself. She hesitated.

"Jack misses it. That's the part they never talk about, isn't it? It changed him. He hated it. And yet he wants to go back over. Part of it is guilt. He feels like he left friends over there. Part of it is something else. Something he has trouble articulating."

"Mary?"

"What?"

"Are you lying about having a son in the military?"

"I wouldn't do that."

"Sure you would. You're manipulative. You and Judith manipulated me into coming into this office. You manipulated me into this room. You're trying various manipulations to get me to talk to you."

Mary McLeod stood ramrod straight. "I'm not lying about my son."

"Maybe not," Maya said. "But either way, you and Judith should both know that without trust, you can't have a doctor-patient relationship. This whole little sham to get me here broke that trust."

"That's nonsense."

"What's nonsense?"

"That without trust, you can't have a doctor-patient relationship."

"Are you serious?"

"Suppose a loved one—maybe your sister—had shown all the signs of having cancer—"

"Oh, don't go there."

"Why, Maya, what are you afraid of? Suppose that cancer could be cured if you just could get your loved one to a physician. If you and that physician conspired to get her into his office—"

"It's not the same thing."

"Yes, Maya. It is. It is exactly the same thing. You're not getting that, but it is. You need help, just like that cancer patient."

This was a waste of time. Maya wondered whether Mary McLeod was part of all this or if she was being sincere—if Judith had, in fact, manipulated and lied to her old colleague. It didn't matter.

"I need to see Judith," Maya said.

"I'm sorry, Maya. I can't help you there."

Maya headed for the door. "You can't help me at all."

Screw it.

Maya dialed the number as she headed back to her car. Judith answered on the second ring.

"I hear it didn't go so well with my colleague."

"Where are you, Judith?"

"Farnwood."

"Don't go anywhere," Maya said.

"I'll be waiting."

She drove in through the service entrance again, hoping maybe to catch Isabella wandering outside or something, but the entire compound appeared empty. Maybe she should break in and poke around, see if she could find a clue as to where Isabella might be hiding, but that was risky and she didn't have the time. Judith would know how long a ride from New York City to Farnwood would be.

The butler answered the door. Maya could never remember his name. It wasn't something like Jeeves or Carson. It was something ordinary like Bobby or Tim. Still, as befitted his servant station, Bobby/Tim looked down his nose at her.

Without preamble, Maya said, "I'm here to see Judith."

"Madam is expecting you," he said in some faux British prep school accent, "in the parlor."

"The parlor" was what rich people called a living room. Judith wore a black pantsuit and a strand of pearls that came down almost to her waist. Her earrings were silver hoops, her hair stylishly slicked back. She held a crystal glass in her hand, posed as though she were shooting a magazine cover.

"Hello, Maya."

No need for pleasantries. "Tell me about Tom Douglass."

Her eyes narrowed. "Who?"

"Tom Douglass."

"I don't know that name."

"Think hard."

She did. Or pretended to. After a few seconds passed, Judith shrugged theatrically.

"He worked in the Coast Guard. He investigated your son's drowning."

The glass dropped from Judith's hand, shattering on the floor. Maya did not jump back. Neither did Judith.

They just stood there a moment, the glass shards rolling to a stop.

There was a hiss in Judith's voice when she asked, "What the hell are you talking about?"

If this was an act . . .

"Tom Douglass is a private investigator now," Maya said. "Your family has been paying him almost ten thousand dollars a month for years. I would like to know why."

Judith wobbled a bit, like a fighter who was trying to take advantage of the eight count. The question had staggered her, no question about it. If the stagger came from the fact that she hadn't known about the payoff or hadn't expected Maya to find out about it was still anyone's guess.

"Why would I pay off this Tom . . . What did you say his last name was?"

"Douglass. Two *s*'s. And you tell me."

"I have no idea. Andrew died in a tragic accident."

"No," Maya said. "That's not how he died. But you know that already, don't you?"

Judith's face lost all color. The pain was so clear now, so obvious, that Maya almost looked away. Attack mode was all well and good, but whatever the final truth was, they were talking about the death of this woman's child. Her pain was real and whole and consuming.

"I have no idea what you're talking about," Judith said.

"How did it happen then?"

"What?"

"How exactly did Andrew fall off the boat?"

"Are you serious? Why would you be bringing that up now, all these years later? You never even knew him."

"It's important." Maya took a step toward her former mother-in-law. "How did he die, Judith?"

She tried to hold her head up, but the fault lines wouldn't let her. "Andrew was so young," she said, trying her best to hold on. "There was a party on the yacht. He had too much to drink. The sea was rough. He was up on deck alone and fell off."

"No."

Judith's voice was a snap. "What?"

For a split second, Maya thought that Judith was going to leap across the room and attack her. But the moment passed. Judith looked down, and when she spoke again her voice was soft, almost pleading.

"Maya?"

"Yes."

"Tell me what you know about Andrew's death."

Was Maya being played here? It was hard to tell. Judith looked completely worn out, devastated. Did she really not know about any of this?

"Andrew committed suicide," Maya said.

Judith tried very hard not to wince. She shook her head stiffly, just once. "That's not true."

Maya just gave it time, let her move past the rote denial.

When Judith did, she asked, "Who told you that?"

"Joe."

Judith shook her head again.

"Why are you paying off Tom Douglass?" Maya asked again.

In war, they call it the thousand-yard stare, that blank, empty, unfocused gaze when a soldier has simply seen too much. Judith had something like that going on now.

"He was only a boy," Judith muttered, and while Maya was the only one in the room, Judith wasn't speaking to her. "He wasn't even eighteen yet . . ."

Maya took a step toward her. "You really didn't know?"

Judith looked up, startled. "I don't understand what you're after here."

"The truth."

"What truth? What does this have to do with you anyway? I don't understand why you'd start digging this all up."

"I didn't dig it up. Joe told me."

"Joe told you that Andrew committed suicide?"

"Yes."

"He confided that to you?"

"Yes."

"Yet all these years later, you felt compelled to defy his wishes and tell me." Judith closed her eyes.

"I don't mean to be bringing you pain."

"Right," Judith said with a sad chuckle, "I can see that."

"But I need to know why you'd be paying off the Coast Guard officer who was investigating Andrew's death."

"Why would you need to know that?"

"It's a long story."

Judith's chuckle was more pained than any sob. "Oh, I think I have time, Maya."

"My sister found out about it."

Judith frowned. "She found out about this supposed payoff?"

"Yes."

Silence.

"And then Claire was murdered," Maya said. "And then Joe was murdered."

Judith arched an eyebrow. "You're saying they're connected? Claire and Joe?"

So Kierce hadn't told her. "The same gun killed them both."

Maya's words landed like another blow, staggering her back. "That can't be."

"Why can't it be?"

Judith closed her eyes again, summoned some inner strength, opened them. "I need you to slow down and tell me what's going on here, Maya."

"It's simple. You're paying off Tom Douglass. I want to know why."

"Seems to me," she said, "you already figured that out."

Judith's sudden change in demeanor threw her. "The suicide?"

Judith managed a smile.

"You wanted to cover up a suicide?"

Judith stayed still.

"Why?" Maya asked.

"Burketts don't commit suicide, Maya."

Did that make sense? No, of course not. What was she missing? Time to change direction, get Judith back off her footing. "So why did you pay off Roger Kierce?"

"Who?" Judith made a face. "Wait. The police officer?"

"Yes."

"Why on earth would we pay him?"

We. "You tell me."

"I assure you I have no idea. Is this something else your sister supposedly uncovered?"

"No," Maya said. "Caroline told me."

Another small smile came to Judith's lips. "And you believed her?"

"Why would she lie?"

"Caroline wouldn't lie. But . . . she gets confused."

"Interesting, Judith."

"What?"

"You paid off two men. Both were investigating the deaths of your sons."

Judith shook her head. "This is all a lot of nonsense."

"Luckily, we can solve this easily," Maya said. "Let's ask Caroline."

"Caroline isn't around right now."

"So call her. This is the twenty-first century. Everyone has a mobile phone. Here"—Maya held up her phone—"I have her number right here."

"That won't do any good."

"Why not?"

"Let's just say," Judith continued, her words coming slower now, "Caroline can't be disturbed."

Maya lowered the phone to her side.

"She's . . . Caroline isn't well. This happens to her. She needs rest."

"You put her in a loony bin?"

Maya had intentionally used the derogatory term to draw blood. It worked. Judith visibly cringed.

"That's a horrible way to put it," Judith said. "You of all people should be sympathetic."

"Why 'of all people' . . . ? Oh, you mean because of my own issues with PTSD?"

Judith did not bother replying.

"So what trauma has Caroline faced?"

"Not all trauma occurs on the battlefield, Maya."

"I know. Some might occur by having two brothers die young and tragically."

"Precisely. Those traumas have caused issues to arise."

"Issues to arise," Maya repeated. "You mean, for example, Caroline thinking her brothers are still alive?"

Maya had expected that her words would be another blow, but Judith seemed ready this time. "The mind wants," Judith said. "The mind can want so, so badly that it manifests delusions. Conspiracy theories, paranoia, visions—the more desperate you are, the more susceptible. Caroline is immature. That's her father's fault. He sheltered her and overprotected her. He never let her deal with adversity or stand on her own. So when the strong men in her life started to die—her support system—Caroline could not accept that."

"So why wouldn't you let her see Joe's body?"

"She told you that?" Judith shook her head. "None of us saw Joe."

"Why not?"

"You of all people should know why. My son was murdered. He was shot in the face, wasn't he? Who would want to look at that?"

Maya considered that and decided once again it didn't fully add up. "How about when Andrew was pulled out of the water?"

"What about that?"

"Did you see his body?"

"Why would you ask that? My God, you can't possibly believe . . ."

"Just tell me if you saw him."

Judith swallowed hard. "Andrew's body had been at sea for more than twenty-four hours. My husband identified him, but . . . it wasn't easy. The fish had gotten to him. Why would I want to . . ." She stopped and narrowed her eyes. Her voice was a whisper now. "What are you trying to do here, Maya?"

Maya just looked at her. "Why are you paying off Tom Douglass?"

She took her time. "Let's say what Joe told you about Andrew's death was true."

Maya waited.

"Let's say that Andrew did commit suicide. I was his mother. And I couldn't see it. I couldn't save Andrew in real life. But maybe I can protect him now. Do you understand?"

Maya studied her face. "Sure," she said.

But she didn't.

"Whatever happened to Andrew—whatever he suffered all those years ago—it has nothing to do with today. It has nothing to do with Joe or your sister."

Maya didn't believe that for a moment. "And the payoffs to Roger Kierce?"

"I told you. That simply isn't true. Caroline made it up."

There was nothing more to mine here. Not yet anyway. Maya had to dig more, get more information. She was still missing too many pieces of the puzzle.

"I better go."

"Maya?"

She waited.

"Caroline isn't the only one who may need rest. She isn't the only one who wants so badly she may start seeing things that aren't there."

Maya nodded. "Subtle, Judith."

"I wish you'd let Mary or me help you."

"I'm fine."

"No, you're not. We both know that. We both know the truth, don't we?"

"What truth is that, Judith?"

"My boys have been hurt enough," Judith said with an edge in her voice. "Don't make the mistake of hurting them more."

Chapter 22

Lily was out in the front yard playing some kind of tag game with her uncle Eddie when Maya turned the corner. Maya slowed the car down and pulled to the curb. For a few moments, she just sat and watched. Alexa came out the front door and joined the festivities, both she and her father faking as though they couldn't quite tag Lily, dramatically falling to the ground when they reached out and missed, and even from that distance, even with Maya's window closed, she could hear Lily's shrieks of laughter.

Mawkish to think of it so plainly, but was there any sound as joyful as the undiluted laughter of a child? The irony between the sounds—this one that rang far too rarely in Maya's ears versus the ones that haunted her nights without mercy—did not escape her, but then again, there was no point in dwelling. She put the car back in drive, forced a smile onto her face, and cruised to the front of Claire and Eddie's house.

Maya gave the horn a little honk and waved. Eddie turned, his face flushed from happy exertion, and raised his hand in return. Maya got out of the car. Alexa stood upright too. Lily didn't like that—Eddie and Alexa ending the game—so she kept tapping them on the leg, daring them to start the chase anew.

Alexa came over and gave her aunt a hug. Eddie kissed her on the cheek. Lily crossed her arms and pouted.

"I stay!" Lily demanded.

"We can play tag when we get home," Maya told her.

Not surprisingly, this did nothing to appease Lily.

Eddie put his hand on Maya's arm. "Do you have a second? I wanted to show you something." He turned to his daughter. "Alexa, do you mind watching Lily for a few more minutes?"

"Sure."

That made Lily smile. Maya could hear the laughter start up again as she headed inside with Eddie.

"I checked Claire's E-Z Pass records," he said. "From what I could see, she visited that Douglass guy twice within a week."

"That doesn't surprise me," Maya said.

"I didn't think it would. But where she went after the second time might." He had printed out the records. He handed her a sheet and pointed to the first highlighted section.

"So a week before the murder," Eddie continued, "Claire travels down to Livingston. See the time stamp?"

Maya nodded: 8:46 A.M.

"Now if you follow it, she got on the Parkway at nine thirty-three instead of the Turnpike. See the next few lines?"

"Yes."

"She didn't head back home," Eddie said. "She traveled south instead. At Exit 129 she moved from the Parkway back to the New Jersey Turnpike and got off at Exit 6."

It was on the bottom of the page. Exit 6, Maya knew, was the Pennsylvania Turnpike.

"Anything after that?" Maya asked.

"Right over here. She took Interstate 476 south."

"Toward Philadelphia," Maya said.

"Or the Philadelphia area at least," Eddie said.

Maya handed him back the sheets. "Any reason Claire would be down there that day?"

"None."

Maya didn't bother asking him about friends Claire could have visited or shopping she might have done or even if she might have suddenly fancied a trip to Independence Hall. Claire hadn't gone there for any of that. Claire had spoken to Tom Douglass. She had learned something from him. And that something had taken her to Philadelphia.

Maya closed her eyes.

"Not to make a stupid Liberty Bell joke," Eddie said, "but is any of this ringing any bells?"

Maya had no choice, so she told Eddie yet another lie. "No," she said. "No bells at all."

It rang bells, albeit distant ones.

As Caroline had reminded her, when Andrew died, he and Joe had both still been in high school. A boarding school, to be more exact. An upper-crust, old-money prep school called Franklin Biddle Academy.

Located right outside Philadelphia.

Eileen called her on the drive home. "Remember how we used to do Chinese takeout on Wednesday nights?"

"Of course."

"I'm starting up the tradition again. You home?"

"Just about."

"Great," Eileen said with too much enthusiasm. "I'll get our favorites."

"Something wrong?"

"I'll be there in twenty minutes."

There were too many possibilities spinning through Maya's head. For the first time she tried to let it go. For just a few moments. Get back to the basics. Know what you know. Most people oversimplify Occam's razor to mean the simplest answer is usually correct. But the real meaning, what the Franciscan friar William of Ockham really wanted to emphasize, is that you shouldn't complicate, that you shouldn't "stack" a theory if a simpler explanation was at the ready. Pare it down. Prune the excess.

Andrew was dead. Claire was dead. Joe was dead.

But at the same time, she couldn't just dismiss everything else she had learned, could she? Could she just dismiss what her own eyes had seen, or again should she accept the simplest answer? And what *was* the simplest answer?

Well, it wasn't pleasant.

But for the sake of exercise, strip it down. Be as objective as you can. Then ask yourself: Was the person who had seen the video on that nanny cam reliable—or had she undergone enough stress, strain, and outright trauma to be someone of questionable judgment?

Be objective, Maya.

It was easy to trust your own eyes, wasn't it? We all did. We weren't crazy. The other guy was. That was part of the human condition. We understand our own perspective too well.

So step outside it.

The war. No one understood. No one could see her truth. They all thought that Maya was weighed down and guilt-ridden over the death of those civilians. That would make sense. They see it from their perspective. You feel guilty, the theory went, and that manifests itself in the painful flashbacks. You try therapy. You take drugs. Death surrounds you. No, check that. Death does more than that.

"Death follows you, Maya . . ."

Was a person like this—a person surrounded by death, a person who had fooled even those closest to her into believing that her condition was based, in part, on feeling guilty—someone whose judgment you trusted? Stripping away the excess and the complications: Could such a person be trusted to look at the facts rationally and learn the truth?

Objectively, no.

But then again, screw objectivity, right?

Conclusion: Someone was messing with her bigtime.

Judith had been awfully cagey when it came to the whereabouts of Caroline. Maya took out her phone and called her sister-in-law. It went to voicemail. Hardly a surprise. When the message beeped, Maya said, "Caroline, I want to make sure you're okay. Please call me the moment you get this."

Eileen was parked in the driveway when Maya got home. Maya pulled the car to a stop. Lily had fallen asleep in the backseat. She got out of the car and started to open her back door when Eileen said, "Let her sleep for a second. We need to talk."

Maya turned and faced her friend. Eileen had been crying.

"What's wrong?"

"I may have messed up," she said. "With that nanny cam."

Eileen started shaking.

"It's okay," Maya said. "Let me get Lily in the house and we can—"

"No," Eileen said. "We need to talk about it out here."

Maya looked a question at her.

"It may not be safe to talk inside," Eileen said, lowering her voice. "Someone might be listening."

Maya glanced through the car window at Lily. She was still asleep.

"What happened?" Maya asked.

"Robby." The abusive ex.

"What about him?"

"You wouldn't tell me what happened with your nanny cam, remember?"

"Right, so?"

"You came to my house. You were angry, upset. You were even suspicious of me. You wanted me to prove that I bought it."

"I remember," Maya said. "What does this have to do with Robby?"

"He's back," she said with tears starting to pour down. "He's been watching me."

"Whoa, slow down, Eileen."

"I got these by email." She reached into her purse and shoved a bunch of photographs toward Maya.

"They came from an anonymous email address, of course. Untraceable. But I know. It's Robby."

Maya started looking through them. The photos had been taken inside Eileen's house. The first three were in her den. Two had her kids, Kyle and Missy, playing on the couch. The last was just of Eileen, sweaty, a glass of ice water in her hand, wearing a sports bra.

"I'd just come home after working out," Eileen said in way of explanation. "No one was there. So I took off my shirt and threw it in the downstairs hamper."

Maya could feel the panic welling inside of her, but she kept her voice even. "The angle," Maya said, riffling through the photographs of Eileen and her children. "These photos—they were taken by your nanny cams?"

"Yes."

Maya felt her stomach plummet.

"Look at this last one."

It was a photograph of Eileen on a couch with a man Maya had never seen. They were kissing.

"That's Benjamin Barouche. We met on Match.com. It was our third date. I had him back to my place. The kids were upstairs asleep. I didn't even think twice about it. This afternoon, I get these pictures in my email."

Why hadn't Maya thought of this before?

"So someone hacked into—"

"Not someone. Robby. It had to be Robby."

"Okay, so Robby hacked into your nanny cams?"

Eileen started to cry. "I thought the cams weren't connected to the web, you know? I mean, they use an SD card. I didn't realize. It's not even that uncommon. Hacking into cameras, I mean. People do it with those FaceTime and Skype cameras and . . . I should have put security measures up. But I didn't know." She stopped and wiped the tears from her face.

"I'm so sorry, Maya," she said.

"It's okay."

"I don't know what happened with your nanny cam," Eileen said. "And it's okay if you don't want to tell me. But I thought that maybe this would explain it. That maybe someone hacked in and could see you and Lily."

Maya tried to digest this new information. Right now, she couldn't figure out exactly what this news meant or if it related to her situation. Could someone have made a video of Joe in another place and uploaded it to her nanny cam? And if that was the case, so what? It had still been filmed in that room, still recorded on that couch.

But was she being watched?

"Maya?"

"I didn't get any emails like this," Maya said. "No one sent me photographs."

Eileen looked at her. "What then? What happened with your nanny cam?"

"I saw Joe," Maya said.

Chapter 23

Maya carried Lily upstairs and tucked her into the bed. She debated checking the back of the nanny cam to see if the Wi-Fi was on, but right now, she didn't want to tip off whoever might be watching her.

Watching her. Wow. Talk about sounding paranoid.

She and Eileen set up the Chinese in the formal dining room, far away from the possibly prying eye of the nanny cam. Maya filled her in on what she'd seen on the nanny cam, on Isabella . . . and then she stopped with the confessional because she was being stupid.

Fact: Eileen had brought that nanny cam into her house.

Maya tried to let that go, but the suspicion buzzed

in her ear. She could quiet it, but it wouldn't go away, not completely.

"What are you going to do," Maya asked, "about Robby?"

"I gave copies of the photographs to my attorney. He said without proof there's nothing I can do. I made sure the Wi-Fi setting was completely off. There's a company that's going to come in and make sure my network is secure."

That sounded like a pretty good plan.

Half an hour later, after she had walked Eileen to her car, Maya called Shane. "I need another favor."

"You can't see," Shane said, "but I'm sighing theatrically."

"I need someone we trust to come in and sweep my place for bugs."

She explained about Eileen and the hacked nanny cam.

"Do you know if yours was hacked?" he asked.

"No. Do you have someone who can help me?"

"I do. But I have to be honest. This is all sounding a little . . ."

"Paranoid?" she finished for him.

"Yeah, maybe."

"Were you the one who called Dr. Wu?"

"Maya?"

"What?"

"You're not okay."

She said nothing.

"Maya?"

"I know," she said.

"Nothing wrong with needing help."

"I need to get through this first."

"Get through what exactly?"

"Please, Shane."

There was a brief pause. Then: "I'm sighing again."

"Theatrically?"

"Is there any other way? I'll come by with some guys and sweep your place in the morning." He cleared his throat. "You armed, Maya?"

"What do you think?"

"Rhetorical question," he said. "I'll see you in the morning."

Shane ended the call. Maya wasn't quite ready yet for another horror-filled night of flashbacks. Instead, she turned her attention toward Claire's trip to Philadelphia.

Lily was still asleep. Maya knew that she should wake her daughter and change her out of the clothes she'd worn all day and give her a bath and put her in clean pajamas. The "good" moms would insist on that, of course, and for a moment, Maya could also see their disapproving gazes. But those other moms weren't carrying a gun and dealing with murder, were they? They didn't even get that blood-soaked worlds like hers lived side by side with theirs, neighbor to neighbor; that while they worried about arts and crafts and after-school activities and karate classes and enrichment programs, the family next door was dealing with death and terror.

Was someone watching her?

There was not much she could do about that right now. There were other things, important things, that had to be dealt with right away, so she put the paranoia in a box and broke out her laptop. If her house was indeed bugged—and that still seemed like overkill to her—they could also have tapped into her Wi-Fi. To be on the ridiculously safe side, she changed her home network's name and password and used a VPN—virtual private network—to browse.

That would probably be enough, but who knew?

She got back online and started searching for the name "Andrew Burkett." Not unexpectedly, there were several—a college professor, a car salesman, a graduate student. She tried adding in other key words and searching back in time. A few articles on Andrew's death began to pop up. A large local newspaper covered it thusly:

YOUNG BURKETT SCION
DROWNS OFF YACHT

Buzzwords. "Yacht," not "boat." And, of course, "scion." They had used the same term with Joe. "Scion"—the rich even get their own name for a descendant. She scrolled through the articles. No one knew exactly where in the Atlantic Ocean Andrew had fallen off, but that night, the family yacht, *Lucky Girl*, had sailed across the midway point between the port of embarkation, Savannah, Georgia, and the destination port of Hamilton, on the island of Bermuda. That covered a lot of ocean.

According to the news reports, Andrew Burkett was last seen going out on the upper deck of the *Lucky Girl* at 1:00 A.M. on October 24 after a long night of partying with "family members and classmates." He was reported missing at 6:00 A.M. Joe had mentioned that three of their soccer teammates from Franklin Biddle had been on board, along with his sister, Caroline. Neither Burkett parent had been on board. Judith and Joseph, along with young Neil, had been waiting for them at a deluxe hotel in Bermuda. Their caretakers on the trip had been the fairly extensive cruise staff—and, whoa, one name listed in the article was Rosa Mendez, Isabella's mother, who was mostly "in charge of young Caroline."

Maya reread the relevant sections. She mulled them over for a few moments before continuing.

Andrew's body was discovered the day after he was reported missing. The cause of death in later pieces was listed as drowning. Neither foul play nor suicide was ever mentioned.

Okay, now what?

Maya typed in Andrew's name with the words "Franklin Biddle Academy." The school's website popped up with a link to their online community for alumni. Maya clicked it and saw a drop-down menu for various class pages. She did the math in her head, figured out what year Andrew should have graduated, and clicked it. There were listings for homecoming events and an upcoming reunion and, of course, a link to donate money to the academy's capital campaign.

On the bottom of the page was a button that read: "In Memoriam."

When Maya clicked it, two headshots of students appeared. They both looked so damned young, but of course, so did the kids she served with in the military. Maya again thought about those picket fences, those thin lines, those different worlds existing side by side. The young man in the photograph on the right was Andrew Burkett. Maya had never really taken the time to study her almost-brother-in-law's face before. Joe wasn't one to keep old family photographs around the house, and while the Burketts had a portrait of Andrew in one of the distant parlors, Maya had always managed to avoid paying much attention to it. In this photograph, Andrew did not look very much like his far more handsome brother Joe. Andrew favored his mother. Maya kept looking at the young face, as though there might be a clue in it, as though Andrew Burkett might even now rise from this old-school portrait and demand the truth be told.

That didn't happen.

I'll figure it out, Andrew. I'll avenge you too.

Maya turned her gaze to the photograph of the other deceased young man. The name under the pic-

ture was Theo Mora. Theo looked to be Latino or
maybe just had darker coloring. In the photograph, he
had the awkward, forced smile of, well, a high school
boy posing for his school portrait. His hair looked as if
it had been slicked down but had stubbornly started to
regain control. Like Andrew, he wore a jacket and
school tie, though where Andrew's tie was a perfect
Windsor, this boy's looked like that of a middle manager taking the late train home.

The caption on top of the page read: "Gone Too
Soon But Always In Our Hearts." There was no other
information. Maya started googling Theo Mora. It
took some time, but she finally found an obituary in a
Philadelphia newspaper. No articles. Nothing else. Just
a simple obituary. It listed the date of death as Septem-
ber 12, which was maybe six weeks *before* Andrew toppled off that yacht. Theo Mora had been seventeen
when he died, the same age as Andrew.

Coincidence?

Maya read it again. No cause of death was listed. She
tried putting the names "Andrew Burkett" and "Theo
Mora" in the same search. Two Franklin Biddle Academy pages came up. One was the link to the "In Memoriam" listing she'd already visited. She clicked the
other link and landed on the school's "Varsity Sports
Booster" page. She found an archive of all the team
rosters. Maya headed to the soccer page for that year.

Lo and behold, Andrew and Theo Mora had been
teammates.

Could two seniors in the same high school on the same soccer team dying less than two months apart be a coincidence?

Sure.

But when you add in the Tom Douglass payoffs, when you add in Claire driving to Philadelphia, when you add in that Tom Douglass was now missing and Claire had been tortured and murdered . . .

No coincidence.

She checked the rest of the roster. Joe, a post-grad that year, had been on the team too. No surprise—he was a co-captain. But, man, that was a lot of death for one high school soccer team.

She clicked another link and found a photograph of the team. Half the team was standing, half kneeling in front of them. They all looked proud and young and healthy. Maya's eyes quickly found Joe standing—again no surprise—in the dead center. The rakish smile had been there, even then. She looked at him for a moment, so damn handsome and confident, so ready to take on the world and knowing that he would always whip it, and she couldn't help but think about his ultimate fate.

In the team picture, Andrew stood next to his brother, almost literally in Joe's shadow. Theo Mora was in the front row on one knee, second from the right. He still had the awkward, forced smile. Maya scanned the other faces, hoping one might be familiar. None were. Three of these other boys had been on the yacht that night. Had she ever met any of them before? She didn't think so.

She moved back to the roster and printed out the names. In the morning, she could look them up and . . .

And what?

Call or email them, she guessed. Ask if they'd been on that yacht. See if they knew anything about what happened to Andrew or, perhaps more relevantly, how Theo Mora had died.

She kept searching online, but nothing new came up. Maya couldn't help but wonder whether Claire had done something similar. Unlikely. Odds were that she had learned something from Tom Douglass, something about this damn school, and with Claire's go-right-to-the-top philosophy, she had driven down to Franklin Biddle Academy and started asking questions.

Had that been what got her killed?

One way to find out. The next day Maya would take a road trip to Philadelphia.

Chapter 24

Another horrible, flashback-filled night.

Even in the midst of it, even while the sounds ricocheted through her skull like hot shrapnel, Maya tried to slow it down and see whether Wu was right, whether she was just having flashbacks or if she was hearing things that she had never heard before. Hallucinations. But every time she got close, as in any sort of nocturnal voyage, the answer became smoke, elusive. The pain from the sounds grew, and so, in the end, Maya just held on until morning.

She woke up exhausted. She realized it was Sunday. No one would be at the Franklin Biddle Academy to answer her questions on a Sunday. Growin' Up Day Care was closed on Sundays. Maybe that was for the best. A soldier takes advantage of downtime. If you have a chance to rest, you do so. You let the body and mind heal whenever you can.

All of this horror could wait a day, couldn't it?

Maya would take the day off from death and destruction, thank you very much, and just spend a normal day with her daughter.

Bliss, right?

But Shane showed up at 8:00 A.M. with two guys who gave her a quick nod and got to work sweeping for possible listening devices or cameras. As they started up the stairs, Shane picked up the nanny cam in the den and checked the back of it.

"Wi-Fi is switched off," Shane said.

"Meaning?"

"Meaning there's no way anyone could spy on you with this, even if the technology somehow exists."

"Okay."

"Unless, of course, there's some kind of back way in. Which I doubt. Or someone came in and switched it off because they knew we'd be checking."

"That sounds unlikely," Maya said.

Shane shrugged. "You're the one having your house swept for bugs. So let's be thorough, shall we?"

"Okay."

"First question: Besides you, who has a key to this house?"

"You do."

"Right. But I've questioned me and I'm innocent."

"Funny."

"Thanks. So who else?"

"No one." Then she remembered. "Damn."

"What?"

She looked up at him. "Isabella has one."

"And we don't trust her anymore, do we?"

"Not even a little."

"Do you think she'd really show up again and play around with that picture frame?" Shane asked.

"I would say it's unlikely."

"Maybe you should get some cameras and security," he said. "At the very least, change the locks."

"Okay."

"So you have a key, I have a key, Isabella has a key." Shane put his hands on his hips and let loose a long sigh. "Don't bite my head off," he said.

"But?"

"But what happened to Joe's?"

"Joe's key?"

"Yes."

"I don't know."

"Did he have it with him when, he, uh—"

"Was murdered?" Maya finished for him. "Yes, he had his key on him. At least I assume he did. He usually carried a house key. Like everyone else in the free world."

"Did you get back his belongings?"

"No. The police must still have them."

Shane nodded. "Okay then."

"Okay what?"

"Okay whatever. I don't know what else to say,

Maya. It's so goddamn bizarre. I don't get any of this, so I'm asking questions until maybe something becomes clear. You trust me, right?"

"With my life."

"Yet," Shane said, "you won't tell me what's going on."

"I *am* telling you what's going on."

Shane turned, looked at himself in the mirror, and narrowed his eyes.

"What are you doing?" she asked.

"Seeing if I really look that dumb." Shane turned back to her. "Why were you asking me about that Coast Guard guy? What the hell does Andrew Burkett, who died in high school, have to do with any of this?"

She hesitated.

"Maya?"

"I don't know yet," she said. "But there could be a connection."

"Between what? Are you saying that Andrew's death on the boat has something to do with Joe's murder in Central Park?"

"I'm saying I don't know yet."

"So what's your next step?" Shane asked.

"Today?"

"Yes."

Tears almost came to her eyes, but she kept them in check. "Nothing, Shane. Okay? Nothing. It's Sunday. I'm grateful you guys came over, but here's what I want to happen: I want you guys to finish sweeping this place. Then I want you all to leave so on this gorgeous autumn Sunday I can take my daughter out for a classic, cliché-ridden mommy-daughter day."

"For real?"

"Yes, Shane, for real."

Shane smiled. "That's so cool."

"Yeah."

"Where are you two going to go?"

"To Chester."

"Apple picking?"

Maya nodded.

"My parents used to take me there," Shane said with a lilt in his voice.

"You want to come?"

"No," he said in the gentlest voice she had ever heard. "And you're right. It's Sunday. We'll speed this up and get out of here. You get Lily ready."

They finished up, found no bugs, and with a kiss on the cheek, Shane was gone. Maya packed Lily into her car seat and started the day. Mother and daughter did it all. They took a hayride. They hit the petting zoo and fed the goats. They picked apples and ate ice cream and found a clown who dazzled Lily with balloon animals. All around them, hardworking people spent their valuable day off laughing and touching and complaining and arguing and smiling. Maya studied them. She tried to stay in the moment, tried to just disappear into the joy of an autumn day with her daughter, but again it all felt so elusive, distant, as though she were just observing and not really experiencing it for herself. Her comfort zone was protecting these moments, not participating in them. The hours passed, the day ended, and Maya wasn't sure how she felt about any of it.

Sunday night was no better. She tried the new pills, but they did nothing to quiet her ghosts. If anything, the sounds seemed to feed off whatever she was taking, the volume amplified.

When she woke up with a sharp gasp, Maya quickly reached for the phone to call Wu. She stopped herself before hitting send. For a moment she even considered calling Mary McLeod, Judith's colleague, but there was no way she would do that either.

Deal with it, Maya. It won't be much longer now.

She got dressed, dropped off Lily at Growin' Up, and called into work to say that she wouldn't be able to make it.

"You can't do this to me, Maya," Karena Simpson, her boss and fellow former Army pilot, told her. "I'm running a business here. You can't cancel out a lesson at the last minute."

"Sorry."

"Look, I know you're going through some stuff—"

"Yeah, Karena, I am," she said, interrupting her. "And I think I may have rushed coming back. I'm sorry to leave you high and dry like this, but maybe I just need more time."

It was part lie, part truth. She hated looking weak, but this was also necessary. Maya knew now that she wouldn't be coming back to that job. Not ever.

Two hours later, she entered Bryn Mawr, Pennsylvania, and drove past the trimmed hedges and stone sign reading "Franklin Biddle Academy." The sign was small and tasteful, and in the lushness of this fall afternoon, it could easily be missed. That was, of course, the point. As she pulled past the green quad and into the visitors' lot, everything around her screamed pampered, patrician, privileged, powerful. All the *P*s. Even the campus had a sense of entitlement about it. You could smell the crisp dollar bills more than the fallen leaves there.

Money buys seclusion. Money buys fences. Money buys various degrees of insulation. Some money buys the urban world. Some money buys suburban neighborhoods. Some money—big, big money—buys a place like this. We are all just trying to get deeper and deeper into a protective cocoon.

The main office was housed in a Main Line stone mansion called Windsor House. Maya had decided not to call ahead. She had looked up the headmaster online and figured that she would just surprise him. If he wasn't in, so be it. She would find someone else to talk to about the subject. If he was in, she was sure that he would see her. He was a prep school headmaster, not a head of state. Plus, there was a Burkett Dormitory still on campus. Her last name was sure to open most closed doors.

The woman at the reception desk spoke in a hushed voice. "May I help you?"

"Maya Burkett here to see the headmaster. I'm sorry, I don't have an appointment."

"Please have a seat."

But it didn't take long. Maya had learned online that the headmaster for the past twenty-three years was a former graduate and then teacher named Neville Lockwood IV. With a name and pedigree like that, she expected a certain look—ruddy face, aristocratic features, receding blond hairline—and she got not only that from the man who greeted her now, but also wrap-around-the-ears wire-rimmed glasses, a tweed jacket, and, yes, an argyle bow tie.

He took both her hands in both of his.

"Oh, Mrs. Burkett," Neville Lockwood said with that accent that again said more about class than geographical location, "all of us here at Franklin Biddle are so sorry about your loss."

"Thank you."

He started to show her toward his office. "Your husband was one of our most beloved students."

"That's kind of you to say."

There was a large fireplace stacked with gray logs. To the side was a grandfather clock. Lockwood sat behind his cherrywood desk, offering her the plush chair in front of it. Her chair was set slightly lower than his, and Maya figured that was no accident.

"Half the trophies in the Windsor Sports Hall we owe to Joe. He still has the career scoring record in soccer. We were thinking . . . Well, we were thinking of doing something in memoriam to him in the field house. He loved it so there."

Neville Lockwood gave her a somewhat patronizing smile. Maya returned it. These sports reminiscences could be an entry to an ask for money—Maya wasn't good at picking up on such things—but either way, she decided to push ahead.

"Do you know my sister, by any chance?"

The question surprised him. "Your sister?"

"Yes. Claire Walker."

He considered it for a moment. "The name does ring a bell . . ."

Maya was going to say that Claire had visited here approximately four or five months ago and was then murdered not long after, but something that serious would stun him and probably close him down. "Never mind, it's not important. I wanted to ask you some questions about my husband's time here."

He folded his hands and waited.

She had to tread gently. "As you know, Headmaster Lockwood—"

"Please call me Neville."

"Neville." She smiled. "As you know, this academy is a source of both great pride . . . and tragedy for the Burkett family."

He looked appropriately solemn. "You're talking about your husband's brother, I assume?"

"I am."

Neville shook his head. "Such a terrible thing. I know the father passed away a few years back, but poor Judith. Losing another son."

"Yes," Maya said, taking her time. "And I don't know how to raise this exactly, but with Joe dead, well, in terms of this school, that's three members of the same soccer team."

The color in Neville Lockwood's face started to drain away.

"I'm talking now about the death of Theo Mora," Maya said. "Do you recall that incident?"

Neville Lockwood found his voice. "Your sister."

"What about her?"

"She came to campus asking about Theo. That's why the name was familiar. I was off campus at the time, but I heard about it later on."

Confirmation. Maya was on the right track.

"How did Theo die?" she asked.

Neville Lockwood looked off. "I could send you away right now, Mrs. Burkett. I could tell you that the school has strict privacy laws and that it would be against school policies to reveal any details."

Maya shook her head. "That would be unwise."

"Why would you say that?"

"Because if you don't answer my questions," Maya said, "I may have to involve less discreet authorities."

"Really?" A small smile toyed with his lips. "And that's supposed to frighten me? Tell me, is this the part where the evil headmaster lies to protect the reputation of his elite institution?"

Maya waited.

"Well, not me, Captain Stern. Yes, I know your real

name. I know all about you. And not unlike the military, this academy has a sacred honor code. I'm surprised Joe didn't tell you about it. Our Quaker roots call for consensus and openness. We don't hide things. The more one knows, we believe, the more one is protected by the truth."

"Good," Maya said. "So how did Theo die?"

"I will ask, however, that you respect the family's privacy."

"I will."

He sighed. "Theo Mora died of alcohol poisoning."

"He drank himself to death?"

"It happens, sadly. Not often. In fact, it was the only time in the history of this campus. But one night, Theo binge-drank. He was not known as a partier or anything like that. But that's often how it happens. You don't know what you're doing and you overdo it. Theo probably would have been found and saved in time, except he ended up stumbling into a basement. A custodian found him the next morning. He was already dead."

Maya wasn't sure what to make of that.

Neville Lockwood put his hands on his desk and leaned forward. "Could you tell me why you and your sister are asking about this now?"

Maya ignored the question. "Did you ever wonder," she began, "about having two students from the same school and on the same soccer team dying so close together?"

"Yes," Neville Lockwood said. "I wondered about it a great deal."

"Did you ever consider the possibility," Maya continued, "that there could be a connection between Theo's death and Andrew's?"

He leaned back in his chair and steepled his fingers. "To the contrary," he said, "I don't see how there could not be a connection."

That was not the answer Maya had been expecting.

"Could you elaborate?" she asked.

"I was a math teacher. I taught all kinds of courses in statistics and probabilities. Bivariate data, linear regression, standard deviation, all that stuff. So I look at things as equations and formulas. That's how my mind works. The odds that two students from the same small, elite all-boys prep school die within months of each other are very slim. The odds that those two boys were in the same grade make the odds slimmer still. The odds that both played on the same soccer team, well, again, you can start to rule out coincidence." He almost smiled now, raising one finger in the air, lost as though back in the classroom. "But when you add the final factor into the equation, the possibility of coincidence is lowered to almost zero."

"What final factor?" Maya asked.

"Theo and Andrew were roommates."

The room fell silent.

"The odds that two seventeen-year-old roommates at a small prep school would both die young and not in some way be related . . . I confess that I don't believe in odds that long."

In the distance Maya could hear a church-like bell sound. Doors began to open. Young boys began to laugh.

"When Andrew Burkett drowned," Neville Lockwood continued, "an investigator came by. Someone from the Coast Guard who dealt with any sort of deaths at sea."

"Was his name Tom Douglass?"

"Could have been. I don't remember anymore. But he came to this very office. He sat right where you are now sitting. And he too wanted to know about the possibility of a connection."

Maya swallowed. "You told him you saw one."

"Yes."

"Could you tell me what it is?"

"Theo's death was a tremendous shock to our community. How it happened was never reported in the papers. The family wanted it that way. But as much as we were all shocked by what happened, Andrew Burkett was Theo's best friend. He was devastated. I assume that you met Joe well after Andrew died, so you didn't know Andrew, did you?"

"No."

"They were very different, the two brothers. Andrew was a far more sensitive boy. He was a sweet child. His coach used to say that was the quality that held Andrew back on the soccer pitch. He didn't have to be victorious in battle, like Joe. He lacked the aggression, that competitive edge, that killer instinct that you need in the trenches."

Again, Maya thought, with the inane war metaphors to describe athletics.

"There may have been more issues with Andrew," Neville Lockwood added. "I really can't say or reveal more, but all that matters for the sake of this discussion was that Andrew took Theo's death very hard. We closed campus for a week after the death. We had counselors at the ready, but most of the boys headed home to, I don't know, recuperate."

"How about Andrew and Joe?" Maya asked.

"They went home too. I remember your mother-in-law rushing down with Andrew's old nanny to pick them up. Anyway, all the boys, including your husband, returned to campus. All the boys—except one."

"Andrew."

"Yes."

"When did he come back?"

Neville Lockwood shook his head. "Andrew Burkett never came back. His mother felt it best if he took the semester off. Campus life returned to normal. That's how these things are. Joe led the soccer team to a great season. They won their league and were prep school state champions. And after the season ended, Joe took a few of his teammates to celebrate on the family yacht . . ."

"Do you know which boys?"

"I'm not sure. Christopher Swain for certain. He

was co-captain with Joe. I don't remember who else. Anyway, you wanted to know about the connection. I think it's obvious now, but here is my hypothesis. We have a sensitive boy whose best friend tragically dies. The boy is forced to leave school and perhaps, theoretically, has to deal with depression issues. Perhaps, again theoretically, the boy has to take antidepressants or other mood-altering drugs. He is then sailing on a yacht with people who remind him of both this tragedy and what he missed and loved about campus life. There is a raucous party on board. The boy has too much to drink, which mixes badly with whatever medications he might be taking. He's on the boat in the middle of the water. He goes up to the top deck and looks out at the ocean. He's in tremendous pain."

Neville Lockwood stopped there.

"You think Andrew committed suicide," Maya said.

"Perhaps. It's a theory. Or perhaps the mix of alcohol and medications caused a loss of equilibrium and he fell over. Either way, the proof, if you will, is the same: Theo's death directly led to Andrew's. The most likely hypothesis is that the two deaths are thus connected."

Maya just sat there.

"So now," he said, "that I've told you my theory, perhaps you can tell me why this is relevant today."

"One more question if I may."

He nodded for her to go ahead.

"If two deaths from the same team are that unlikely, how do you explain three?"

"Three? I'm not following."

"I'm talking about Joe."

He frowned. "He died, what, seventeen years later?"

"Still. You're the probability guy. What are the odds that his death isn't somehow connected?"

"Are you saying that your husband's murder is somehow related to Theo and Andrew?"

"Seems to me," Maya said, "like you already said it."

Chapter 25

There was nothing more to learn.

Neville Lockwood walked her out a few minutes later. Maya sat in her car for a moment. Up ahead was the storied landmark of Franklin Biddle, an eight-story Anglican bell tower. The four notes of the Westminster chimes sounded again. Maya checked her watch. They went on the quarter hour, she assumed.

She took out her phone and started googling again. Theo Mora's parents were named Javier and Raisa. She started searching "white pages" sites to see if they lived in the area. She found a Raisa Mora within the Philadelphia city limits. It was worth a try.

Her cell phone rang. The caller ID for Leather and Lace popped up. She lifted the phone to her ear, but of course, whoever was on the other end had already hung up. The signal that Corey needed to see her. Well, she was a solid two hours away, and she had other places to be. Corey would just have to wait.

Raisa Mora's street was packed with seen-better-days row houses. Maya found the right address and headed up steps of cracked concrete. She pressed the buzzer, listened for footsteps, heard nothing. Smashed bottles lined the walk. Two doors down a man in an open flannel shirt over a wifebeater tee gave her a toothless smile.

They were a long way from those Westminster chimes.

Maya pulled open the screen door. It opened with a rusty groan. She knocked hard.

"Who is it?" a woman from inside called out.

"My name is Maya Stern."

"What do you want?"

"Are you Raisa Mora?"

"What do you want?"

"I want to ask you about your son Theo."

The door flung open. Raisa Mora wore a diner-waitress uniform of faded mustard. Her mascara was smeared. There was more gray than black in the hair bun. She wore socks, and Maya could imagine that she had just come from some too-long work shift and kicked her shoes into a corner.

"Who are you?"

"My name is Maya Stern"—then, thinking better of it, she added, "Burkett."

That last name got her attention. "You're Joe's wife."

"Yes."

"You're a soldier, right?"

"Former," Maya said. "Do you mind if I come in?"

Raisa crossed her arms and leaned against the door frame. "What do you want?"

"I want to ask about your son Theo's death."

"Why would you want to know about that?"

"Please, Mrs. Mora, you have every reason to ask me, but I really don't have time to explain it all. Let me just say this. I'm not sure we know all there is to know about your son's death."

Raisa stared at her for several seconds. "Your husband was murdered recently. I saw that in the paper."

"Yes."

"They picked up two suspects. Saw that too."

"They're innocent," Maya said.

"I don't understand." The facade didn't so much crack as give way just enough for a tear to appear. "You think, what, Joe's murder has something to do with my Theo?"

"I don't know," Maya said as gently as she could. "But is there any harm in just answering my questions?"

Raisa kept her arms crossed. "What do you want to know?"

"Everything."

"Come on in then. I'm going to need to sit down."

The two women sat together on a threadbare couch that had clearly seen better days, but then again, so had the rest of the room. Raisa handed Maya a framed family photograph. The hues had been faded by age or too much sun or, more likely, both. Five people were in the picture. Maya recognized Theo with two smaller boys who she assumed were his brothers. Behind the three children stood Raisa, looking not all that much younger though a hell of a lot happier, and a stocky man with a big mustache and wide smile.

"That's Javier," Raisa said, pointing to the man. "Theo's father. He passed away two years after Theo died. Cancer. That's what they say. But . . ."

Javier had a good smile, the kind you could feel even in a photograph, the kind that made you wonder what his laugh sounded like. Raisa took the photograph back from Maya and gingerly placed it back on the shelf.

"Javier came here from Mexico. I was a poor girl living in San Antonio. We met and . . . you don't need to hear this."

"No, go ahead."

"Doesn't matter," Raisa said. "We ended up in Philadelphia because Javier had a cousin who got him a job doing landscaping. You know. Mowing lawns for rich people. That kind of thing. But Javier—" She stopped, smiled at some memory. "He was smart, ambitious. Really personable too. Everybody liked Javier. He had that way about him. You know what I mean? Some people—they're just kind of magic. They draw people to them. My Javier was one of them."

Maya nodded toward the photograph. "I can see that."

"You can, right?" Her smile faded away. "Anyway, Javier did a lot of work for the families on the Main Line, including the Lockwood family."

"As in the headmaster?"

"His cousin, actually. Super rich financial guy. He mostly lived in New York, but he kept an estate out here too. Snootiest-looking man you ever met with his blond hair and jutted jaw and all that, but he was kind too. He liked Javier. The men started talking a lot. One day, Javier told him about Theo." The pain came back to her face all at once. "He was such a special boy, my Theo. So smart. Great athlete. Really had it all, as they say. Like all parents, we wanted a better life for him. Javier, he wanted to get Theo into a better school. Turns out Franklin Biddle Academy was looking to get a few scholarship kids in, you know, financial aid so they could say that the school was"—she made quote marks with her hands—"'diverse.' So this Lockwood guy wanted to help. He talked to his cousin the headmaster, and next thing you know . . . Have you been to the school?"

"Yes."

"Ridiculous, right?"

"I guess."

"But Javier was so happy when Theo got in. Me, I was worried for Theo. How do you fit in at a place like that when you come from a place like this? It's almost like, I don't know, what do they call it when scuba divers come up too fast? The bends. It felt like that to me. I didn't say anything though. I'm not stupid. I could see what an opportunity this could be for Theo. You know what I mean?"

"Yes, of course."

"So one morning, Javier goes off to work." Raisa Mora clasped her hands as though in desperate prayer, and Maya figured that they were getting close. "Me, I got the late shift at work. So I was home. The doorbell rings." Her gaze traveled in that direction. "They don't call. They ring the doorbell, you know, like Theo was in the army or something. It's Headmaster Lockwood and some other school official, I don't remember his name. They're just standing there and I see their faces and you'd think I would know, right? You'd think I would see them standing there with their eyes down and looking all sad and that I'd get it right away and then I'd collapse onto the ground screaming, 'No, no!' But it wasn't that way at all. I smiled at them. Said, 'Well, this is a nice surprise.' Showed them in. Asked them if I could get them some coffee and then . . ." She almost smiled. "You want to hear something awful?"

Maya thought that she already had—what could be more awful?—but she nodded.

"I found out later that they actually taped everything they said to me. Lawyer's advice or something. They actually had a tape recorder going the whole time they're telling me how my boy's body was found by some custodian in the basement. I didn't get it. 'Custodian?' I said. They said his name, like that would matter. Theo had too much to drink, they told me. Like an overdose with alcohol. I said, 'Theo doesn't drink,' and they nodded like that made perfect sense, that it's always the boys who don't know what they're doing who end up drinking too much and dying. They said normally a kid can be saved when this happens, but Theo stumbled around and ended up in a corner of the basement. No one saw him until the next day. By then, it was too late."

Same thing, almost word for word, that Neville Lockwood had told her.

It was starting to sound practiced, rehearsed.

"Was an autopsy done?" Maya asked.

"Yes. Javier and me, we met with the coroner ourselves. Nice woman. We sat in her office, and she told us it was alcohol poisoning. I guess a lot of boys got drunk that night. Some kind of party that got out of control. But Javier, he didn't believe it."

"What did he think happened?"

"He didn't know. He thought maybe someone pressured Theo, you know. New kid in school, poor kid, so the rich kids pressured him and he drank too much. He wanted to make a big stink about it."

"And you?"

"I didn't see the point," she said with an exhausted shrug. "Even if that was true, it wouldn't bring Theo back, would it? And that's what happens everywhere, doesn't it? Kids in this neighborhood get pressured too.

So what was the point? And then . . . I know it's wrong, but then there's the money to consider."

Maya got what she meant. "The school made a financial offer?"

"You see these other two boys in the picture?" She wiped the tears from her eyes and stuck out her chest. "That's Melvin. He's now a professor at Stanford. A professor and he's barely thirty years old. And Johnny is in medical school at Johns Hopkins. The academy made sure that our boys never had to pay for their education. Gave Javier and me some money too. But we just put it in accounts for the children."

"Mrs. Mora, do you remember Theo's roommate at Franklin Biddle?"

"You mean Andrew Burkett?"

"Yes."

"He would have been, what, your brother-in-law. The poor boy."

"You remember him then?"

"Of course. They all came to Theo's funeral. All these handsome, rich-looking boys with their blue blazers and school ties and wavy hair. All dressed exactly the same, all lining up to say 'My condolences' like rich-boy robots. But Andrew, he was different."

"How so?"

"He was sad. Really, really sad. He wasn't just, I don't know, going through the motions."

"Were they close? Andrew and Theo?"

"I think so, yes. Theo said Andrew was his best friend. When Andrew fell off that boat not long after, I mean, I read it was an accident. But that didn't make sense to me. The poor boy loses his best friend—and then he falls off a boat?" She looked up at Maya with an arched eyebrow. "It wasn't an accident, was it?"

Maya said, "I don't think so, no."

"Javier suspected that. We went to Andrew's funeral, did you know that?"

"No, I didn't."

"I remembered saying to Javier, 'Andrew seemed so sad about Theo.' I wondered if grief killed him, you know what I mean? Like he was so sad that he ended up maybe jumping off that boat?"

Maya nodded.

"But Javier didn't believe that."

"What did he believe?"

Raisa looked down at her clasped hands. "Javier said to me, 'Grief don't do that to a man. Guilt does.'"

There was silence.

"See, Javier, he couldn't handle what happened. The settlement, he said it was blood money. I didn't see that. Like I said, maybe those rich boys had pushed Theo a bit, but in the end, I mean, I'd always thought the reason Javier went so crazy was because he blamed himself. He was the one who pushed Theo to go to a school where he didn't belong. And, God help me, I blamed him too. I tried to hide it, but I think Javier could always see it on my face. Even when he got sick.

Even when I nursed him. Even when he lay in his bed and held my hand and died. Javier saw that look on my face—maybe it was even the last thing he ever saw."

She lifted her head, wiped a tear with her index finger.

"So maybe Javier was right. Maybe it wasn't grief that killed Andrew Burkett. Maybe it was guilt."

They sat there for a few moments. Maya reached out and took Raisa's hand. It wasn't like her. It wasn't a gesture Maya often made. But it felt right.

After some time had passed, Raisa said, "Your husband was murdered a few weeks ago."

"Yes."

"And now you're here."

Maya nodded.

"That's not a coincidence, is it?"

"No," Maya said, "it's not."

"Who killed my boy, Mrs. Burkett? Who murdered my Theo?"

Maya told Raisa Mora that she didn't know the answer.

But she was starting to think that maybe she did.

Chapter 26

When Maya got back in her car, she just stared out the front windshield for a little while. She wanted so much to lower her head and cry. But there was no time. She checked her phone. Two more hang-ups from Leather and Lace. They must be getting desperate. Maya decided to break protocol. She called the number back and asked for Lulu.

"May I help you?" Lulu asked.

"Enough with the cloak-and-dagger. I'm in Philadelphia."

"One of our best girls got sick, so we have an opening for you to dance tonight. If you want the job, it's urgent that you come in."

Maya held back the eye roll. "I'll be there."

Using her smartphone, she googled Christopher Swain, the soccer team co-captain, who had been on that yacht that night. He worked in Manhattan for the aptly named Swain Real Estate. The family had tons of holdings in all five boroughs of New York City. Great. More super wealth to navigate. She found an email address for him on the Franklin Biddle alumni page and sent him a short message:

My name is Maya Burkett. My husband was Joe. It is urgent that we speak. Please contact me as soon as you can.

She included all her contact information.

Two hours later, Maya pulled into Leather and Lace and parked in the employee lot. She started to get out of her car when the passenger door opened and Corey slipped inside and ducked down.

"Drive," he whispered.

Maya didn't hesitate. She put the car in reverse and was out of the lot in a matter of seconds.

"What's wrong?" she asked when they reached the road.

"We need to take a ride."

"Where?"

He gave her an address in Livingston, off Route 10.

"Livingston," Maya said. "I assume this has something to do with Tom Douglass?"

Corey kept looking behind him.

"We aren't being tailed," she said.

"You're sure?"

"Yes."

"I needed to get out of there. I don't want them to know."

Maya didn't ask why. It wasn't her concern. "So where are we going?"

"I've been tracking Tom Douglass's emails."

"You personally?"

In the corner of her eye she saw him smile. "You probably think I have a big staff."

"I know you have a lot of . . . 'Followers' seems too weak a word. More like they worship you."

"Until they don't. I can't trust them. I'm just the new cause célèbre. People get distracted easily. Remember 'Kony 2012'? So yes, I do most of it myself."

Maya tried to get him back on track. "And you were following Tom Douglass's emails?"

"Right. He still uses AOL, if you can believe it. The guy is four steps behind old-school. He does very little by email. Not one has been read or sent in almost a month."

Maya veered to the right and got on the highway. "Which is when his wife says he vanished."

"Exactly. So earlier today Douglass got an email from a guy named Julian Rubinstein for an unpaid bill. From what I gather from the email, Rubinstein rents Douglass his storage shed behind a body shop in Livingston."

"A car body shop?"

"I guess so, yeah."

"Weird spot for a storage shed," she said.

"There's no automatic payment by credit card, no paperwork, nothing like that. He pays the guy in cash."

Trying to keep it all off the books, Maya thought.

"So I guess Douglass missed his last payment," Corey said. "That's why Julian Rubinstein emailed him a reminder. It was all friendly, like, 'Hey, Tom, long time, no see, you're behind,' that kinda thing."

Maya's hands tightened on the wheel. This sounded like something. "You have a plan?"

Corey lifted a gym bag into view. "Ski masks, two flashlights, a chain cutter."

"We could just ask his wife for access."

"If she has the right to give it to us," he said. "And what if she says no?"

He had a point.

"There's something else, Maya."

She didn't like the tone.

"I didn't lie, but you need to understand. I had to test your loyalty."

"Uh-huh," Maya said.

They stopped at a red light. Maya turned to him and waited.

"I didn't tell you everything."

"So tell me now," she said.

"Your sister."

"What about her?"

"She sent me more material on EAC Pharmaceuticals than I told you about."

Maya nodded. "Yeah, I figured that."

"How?"

There was no reason to tell him everything either. "You knew the Burketts were up to something illegal, but you didn't have anything specific. That's what you said at first. Then you pointed out about EAC Pharmaceuticals. I figured that she had to have given you more."

"Right. But see, what she gave us still wasn't enough. We could leak what we had, but if we did, well, there would be time to sweep it under the rug. It was too early in the investigation to tip our hands. We needed more."

"So Claire kept digging."

"Yes."

"And she found Tom Douglass."

"Right. Except Claire said that he had nothing to do with EAC Pharmaceuticals. It was something else, something bigger."

The light turned green. Maya eased on the accelerator. "Once Claire was killed, why didn't you at least release what she gave you?"

"Like I said, it wasn't really enough. But more than that, I wanted to figure out the Tom Douglass connection. Claire seemed more concerned with that than the fake drugs, frankly. So if we revealed what I knew, I worried that they would just cover it all up. I wanted to find out more."

"So with Claire dead," Maya said, "you got me to start digging."

He didn't argue the point.

"You're something, Corey."

"I'm manipulative, I admit."

"That's a polite word for what you are."

"It's for a just cause."

"Right. So why are you telling me now?"

"Because someone died from the fake drugs. A three-year-old boy in India. He had a fever from an infection. They started treating him with EAC's version of amoxicillin. It didn't do anything. By the time the doctor switched antibiotics, it was too late. The boy went into a coma and died."

"Horrible," Maya said. "How did you find out about it?"

"Someone at the hospital. An anonymous physician wants to turn whistle-blower. He kept detailed charts, made audio and visual recordings, even saved some tissue samples. That, along with what Claire told me . . . It's still not enough, Maya. The Burketts will blame the Indians running the pharmaceutical companies. They'll hide behind expensive lawyers who know how to muddy the waters. It may wound them a little. It may cost them millions, maybe hundreds of millions. But . . ."

"You think Tom Douglass is their kryptonite."

"I do, yeah." There was a lilt in his voice now. "Claire thought so too."

"You're enjoying this," Maya said.

"Didn't you sometimes enjoy combat?"

She didn't answer.

"It doesn't mean I don't take it seriously. But yeah, I get excited."

Maya signaled right and made the turn. "Was that how you felt when you got my helicopter video? Excited?"

"Truth? Yes."

They fell into silence. Maya drove. Corey fiddled with the radio. After about half an hour, they took the exit off Eisenhower Parkway. The GPS said they were less than a mile away.

"Maya?"

"Yes."

"You're still friends with a lot of your military pals. Shane Tessier for one."

"You keeping tabs on me?"

"Some."

"What's your point, Corey?"

"Do any of them know what's on the audio of that helicopter? I mean—"

"I know what you mean," she snapped. Then: "No."

He was about to ask a follow-up, but Maya stopped him with "We're here."

When she made the left turn onto a dirt road, her eyes started scanning the area for surveillance cameras. None present. She pulled the car to a stop a block away from JR's Body Shop.

Corey handed her the ski mask. She shook her head. "We'll be less obvious without them. It's dark. We are a couple looking for our car after hours or something."

"I need to be extra careful," he said.

"I know."

"I can't be spotted."

"You got the facial growth, you got the baseball cap. You'll be fine. Grab the chain cutter and keep your head down."

He looked doubtful.

"Or wait here and I'll do it."

She opened the car door and got out. Corey didn't like it, but he grabbed the chain cutter and followed. They walked in silence. It was dark now, but Maya didn't turn on the flashlight. She kept scanning her surroundings. No cameras. No security. No houses.

"Interesting," Maya said.

"What?"

"Tom Douglass chose here to rent a storage unit."

"What do you mean?"

"There's a CubeSmart storage right down the street. A Public Storage too. They have security cameras and easy access and all that. But Tom Douglass didn't choose there."

"Because he's old-school."

"Could be," Maya said. "Or it could be that he really didn't want anyone to know about this. Think about it. You hacked into his credit cards. If he was paying by check or credit card at a normal storage facility center, you'd probably have found some record of it. He clearly didn't want that."

JR's Body Shop was made of concrete painted the yellow of a Ticonderoga pencil. The two garage bay doors were shut. Maya could see the padlocks, even at a distance. The grass hadn't been mowed in a long while, if ever. There were rusted car parts scattered across the property. Maya and Corey circled toward the back. A vehicle graveyard blocked their path. Maya spotted a beaten-down once-white Oldsmobile Cutlass Ciera from the midnineties, the same car her dad had once owned, and for a moment, she flashed back to that day: Dad turning the corner, all of them waiting, Dad honking his horn, that crooked smile on this face, Mom hopping in the front, Claire and Maya sliding into the back. It wasn't a flashy car, far from it, but Dad loved it, and Maya couldn't help, stupid as it felt, looking at this Oldsmobile and wondering whether it was the exact one that had made her dad so happy on that day, how every vehicle in this pile of junk had one day been driven off the lot new and shiny, with excitement and hope and expectation, and now they lay in tatters, dying piece by piece in the back lot of an old body shop off Route 10.

"You okay?" Corey asked.

She moved ahead without replying. She flicked on her flashlight. The yard had to be two, maybe three acres, and in the back right-hand corner, almost hidden from view by an old Chevy van, Maya spotted two outdoor sheds, the kind people buy at Home Depot or Lowe's to store their shovels and rakes and gardening stuff.

She pointed at them with the flashlight beam. Corey squinted and then nodded. They started to move closer in silence, high-stepping it over the hubcaps and engine parts and car doors that littered their path.

The sheds were small, maybe four feet high and four feet wide. Maya guessed that they were made from resin or some other sort of heavy-duty, all-weather plastic. These were the kind of units you assembled yourself in about an hour. Both units were padlocked closed.

They kept moving, but when they were about ten yards away, both Maya and Corey pulled up from the smell at the exact same moment.

With mounting horror on his face, Corey looked at Maya. Maya just nodded.

"Oh no," Corey said.

Corey wanted to turn and run right then and there.

"Don't," Maya said.

Corey stopped.

"It'll be worse if we run," she said.

"We don't even know what that smell is. It could be an animal."

"Could be."

"So we just leave now."

"You leave, Corey."

"What?"

"I'm staying. I'm opening it. I can handle the blow-back. You can't. I get that. You're already a wanted man. So go. I won't tell anyone you've been here."

"What will you tell them?"

"Don't worry about it. Go."

"I'll want to know what you found."

Maya had had enough with the indecision. "Then hang around another minute."

The chain cutter sliced through the padlock like a hot knife through butter. When the door flew open, a human arm popped out.

"Oh God," Corey said.

The smell made him gag, step back, and start to dry heave. Maya stayed where she was.

The rest of the body started to slip out. Maya could see that the corpse was in pretty bad shape. The face was starting to rot, but based on the pictures she'd seen, plus the size and gray hair, it was Tom Douglass. She stepped toward the body.

"What are you doing?"

She didn't bother answering. It wasn't that dead bodies had stopped bothering her after she'd seen too many. It was just that they didn't shock her anymore. She peered into the shed behind the body. Empty.

Corey started dry heaving again.

"Go," she said.

"What?"

"If you throw up here, the cops will see it. Get out of here. Now. Get back to the highway and find a food place. Call Lulu or someone to pick you up."

"I don't feel comfortable leaving you here alone."

"I'm not in danger. You are."

He looked left. He looked right. "Are you sure?"

"Go."

She moved to the other shed, snipped the lock, looked inside.

Also empty.

When she glanced behind her, Corey was in the distance, staggering past the car parts toward the exit. She waited until he was out of sight. Maya checked her watch. She wiped her prints off the chain cutters and hid them inside the Oldsmobile. Even if found, they'd prove nothing. She waited another twenty minutes to be on the safe side.

Then she called 9-1-1.

Chapter 27

Maya had a story and she stuck to it:

"I got a tip to come here. When I arrived, the lock was broken. An arm was sticking out. So I opened the door some more. And that's when I called nine-one-one."

The police asked what kind of "tip." She said it was anonymous. They asked what her interest was in this. She went for the truth here because they would learn it from Tom Douglass's widow anyway: Her sister, Claire, who had been murdered, had conversed with Tom Douglass not long before her death, and Maya wanted to know why.

The questions kept coming in various forms. She said that she needed to arrange pickup for her daughter at day care. The cops let her do so. She called Eddie and quickly explained the situation.

"You okay?" Eddie asked.

"Fine."

"This has to be connected to Claire's murder, right?"

"No doubt."

"I'll get Lily now."

Maya reached the Growin' Up Day Care via Skype and, surrounded by police presence, explained that Lily's uncle Eddie would be picking her up today. Miss Kitty did not readily accept that. She made Maya jump through all the hoops and then insisted on phone-call backups to make sure it was all on the up-and-up. Maya welcomed the security overkill.

Hours later, Maya finally had had enough. "Are you arresting me?"

The lead cop, an Essex County detective with the most glorious helmet of curly hair and bold eyelashes, hemmed and hawed. "We can arrest you for trespassing."

"Then do that," she said, putting her hands out, wrists together. "I really need to go home to my daughter."

"You are a suspect here."

"For what exactly?"

"What do you think? Murder."

"Based on?"

"How did you end up here tonight?"

"I told you already."

"You'd learned that the victim was missing from his wife, correct?"

"Correct."

"Then you got a tip from a mystery source to check this storage shed."

"Right."

"Who was the mystery source?"

"It was anonymous."

"By phone?" Curly asked.

"Yes."

"Home phone or mobile?"

"Home."

"We're going to check your call records."

"You do that. But for now, it's late." She started to stand. "So if that's all for tonight—"

"Hold up."

Maya recognized the voice and cursed under her breath.

NYPD detective Roger Kierce walked toward them with his caveman swagger, his arms jutting out from his squat body.

"Who are you?" Curly asked.

Kierce flashed his badge and gave his name. "I'm investigating the shooting death of Joe Burkett, Ms. Stern's husband. Do you guys have a cause of death here?"

Curly looked warily at Maya for a moment. "Maybe we should talk alone?"

"Looked like a slit throat," Maya said. They both

looked at her. "Hey, I really have to go. I'm trying to save us all time."

Kierce made a face and looked back toward Curly.

"There is what appears to be a knife wound at the throat," Curly said, "but we don't know more than that yet. The county medical examiner will give us her findings in the morning."

Kierce pulled up the chair next to Maya, twirled it so the back was in the front, and then made a big production of sitting/straddling it. Maya watched him, wondering about what Caroline had said about Kierce taking payoffs from the Burketts. Was it true? She doubted it, but true or false, raising it at this juncture seemed an unwise move.

"I could call my attorney right now," Maya said. "We both know you guys don't have enough to hold me."

"We appreciate your cooperation in this matter," Kierce said without an iota of sincerity, "but before you go . . . Well, I think we've been looking at this all wrong."

He was waiting for her to bite.

"What have *we*"—she emphasized the word—"been looking at wrong, Detective?"

Kierce put his hands on the top of the chair back. "You keep stumbling over dead bodies, don't you?"

Eddie's words: *"Death follows you, Maya . . ."*

"First your husband. Now this private investigator."

He gave her a smile.

"Are you trying to make a point, Detective Kierce?"

"I'm just saying. First, you're with your husband in the park. He ends up dead. Then you come searching for God knows what. Tom Douglass ends up dead. What's the common denominator in all this?"

"Let me guess," Maya said. "Me?"

Kierce shrugged. "You can't help but notice that."

"No, you can't. So what's your theory, Detective? Did I kill them both?"

Kierce shrugged again. "You tell me."

Maya put up her hands in mock surrender. "Yeah, you got me. I guess I, what, killed Tom Douglass weeks ago judging by the condition of the body. Then I jammed his corpse into that storage bin, got clean away with it apparently, still went to his wife looking for him for some odd reason, and then—help me here, Kierce—I came back to reveal the body and implicate myself?"

He just sat there.

"And yes, I see the obvious connection between this and my husband. I guess I'm stupid enough to stick around murder scenes because that's a great way to get away with it, right? Oh, and in the case of Joe, I even—wow, I'm good—somehow tracked down the gun someone used to kill my sister, even though I wasn't even in the country when she was murdered, and used it on him. That about right, Detective Kierce? Did I leave anything out?"

Kierce said nothing.

"And while you're trying to prove I committed

two . . . Or, wait, did I kill my sister too? No, you told me already I couldn't have done that one because you know I was serving our country overseas . . . But while you're proving all of this, maybe we could also take a look at your relationship to the Burkett family."

That got Kierce's attention. "What are you talking about?"

"Never mind." Maya rose and started toward the exit. "Look, you guys waste time any way you want. I'm going to pick up my daughter."

They'd impounded her car.

"You got a warrant already?" Maya asked.

Curly handed it to her.

"Fast," she said.

Curly shrugged.

Kierce said, "I'll give you a ride."

"No, thanks."

Maya paged a taxi from her smartphone. It arrived in ten minutes. When she got back to her house, she grabbed the other car—Joe's car—and headed to Claire and Eddie's house.

Eddie was at the front door before she reached it. "So?"

She stayed in the doorway and told him about the night. Behind Eddie, she could see Alexa playing with Lily. She thought about Alexa and Daniel. Such good kids. Maya was result-oriented. You have good kids, you were probably good parents. Did Claire deserve all the credit for that? Who, in the end, would Maya trust most to raise her daughter?

"Eddie?"

"What?"

"I kept something from you."

He looked at her.

"Philadelphia did mean something to me. It was where Andrew Burkett went to school." She filled Eddie in on that connection as well. She debated taking it one more step and telling him about seeing Joe on that nanny cam, but right now she simply couldn't see what that would add.

"So," Eddie said, when she finished, "we have three murders." He meant Claire, Joe, and newly discovered Tom Douglass. "And the only connection, as far as I can see, is Andrew Burkett."

"Yes," Maya said.

"It's obvious, isn't it, Maya? Something happened on that boat. Something so bad that, all these years later, it's still killing people."

Maya nodded.

"So who else was there that night?" Eddie asked. "Who else was on that boat?"

She thought about her email to Christopher Swain. So far, no answer. "Just some family and friends."

"Which Burketts were on board?" Eddie asked.

"Andrew, Joe, and Caroline."

Eddie rubbed his chin. "Two of them are dead."

"Yes."

"So that leaves . . . ?"

"Caroline was only a kid. What could she have done?" Maya peered behind him. Lily looked sleepy. "It's getting late, Eddie."

"Yeah, okay."

"And I need to put you on the pickup list at Lily's school," Maya said. "They won't let you take her out again unless we do that in person."

"Yeah, that Miss Kitty told me. We have to go in together and take an ID picture and all that."

"Maybe we could do that tomorrow, if you're free."

Eddie looked at Lily sleepily playing some sort of patty-cake game with Alexa. "That should work."

"Thank you, Eddie."

All three of them—Eddie, Alexa, and now Daniel—walked Maya and Lily out to the car. Lily again tried to protest their departure, but she was too tired to do it with any sort of two-year-old-tantrum effectiveness. Her eyes were closed by the time Maya snapped the car seat buckle into place.

On the ride home, Maya tried to shake off the dead but of course that was easier said than done. Eddie was right. Whatever was happening now had a direct link to whatever happened on that yacht seventeen years ago. It made no sense, of course, but there it was. She longed for the simplicity of Occam's razor again, but perhaps the more apropos philosophy once again came from Sir Arthur Conan Doyle via his creation Sherlock

Holmes: "When you eliminate the impossible what remains, however improbable, must be the truth."

They say you can't bury the past. That was probably true, but what they really meant was that trauma ripples and echoes and somehow stays alive. It wasn't so different from what Maya was still experiencing. The trauma from that helicopter assault rippled and echoed and stayed alive, if only within her.

So go back. What was the initial trauma that started it all?

Some would say the night on the yacht, but that wasn't where it started.

What was?

Go back as far as you can. That was where the answer usually lay. And in this case, Maya could trace it back to the campus of Franklin Biddle Academy and the death of Theo Mora.

The house felt surprisingly lonely when Maya got back. She usually longed for that solace. Not tonight. Lily stayed groggy, far closer to asleep than awake, as Maya bathed and changed her. Maya secretly hoped that Lily would wake up now, that they could spend some time together, but that wasn't happening. Lily's eyes stayed closed. Maya carried her back to bed and tucked her in.

"Hey, sweetie, how about a story?"

Maya could hear the neediness in her voice, but Lily did not stir.

She stood over the bed and watched her daughter.

For a moment, she felt wonderfully normal. She wanted to stay here, in this room, with her daughter. Whether that desire came from being a brave sentinel or a scared-to-be-alone mom, Maya couldn't say right now. Did it matter? She pulled up a chair and sat by the dresser near the door. For a long time, she just stared at Lily. Various emotions rose and crashed like waves at the beach. Maya didn't stop them or judge them. She just let them roll through with as little interference as possible.

She felt oddly at peace.

There was no reason to sleep. The sounds would come alive if she did. Maya knew that. Let them stay quiet a little while longer. Just sit here and watch Lily. Wouldn't that be far more restful and peaceful than hopping on that nightmarish nocturnal gerbil wheel in her head?

Maya wasn't sure how much time passed. An hour maybe. Could have been two. She hated to leave the room, even for a second, but she needed to grab her notebook and a pen. She did so quickly, suddenly afraid to have her daughter out of her sight for even a few minutes. When she came back into Lily's room, she took the same seat by the door and started to write the letters. The pen felt odd in her hand. She rarely wrote anymore. Who did? You typed your missives on a laptop and then you clicked the send button.

But not tonight. Not for this.

She was finishing up when her mobile phone vibrated. It was almost morning. She checked the caller

ID and hurried to answer when she saw it was Joe's sister, Caroline.

"Caroline?"

The voice on the other end was a whisper. "I saw him, Maya."

Maya felt her blood go cold.

"He's back. I don't know how. He said he'd see you soon."

"Caroline, where are you?"

"I can't tell you. Don't tell anyone I called. Please."

"Caroline—"

The phone clicked off. Maya called the number. It went to voicemail. She didn't bother leaving a message.

Deep breaths. In and out. Flex, release . . .

She wouldn't panic. That would simply not do. She sat back down, tried to dissect the call rationally, and for maybe the first time in a very long time, things started to clear.

But that clarity didn't last long.

Maya heard a car pull into her driveway.

Caroline's voice came back to her: *"He said he'd see you soon . . ."*

She hurried to the window, expecting to see . . .

What exactly?

Two cars pulled up the driveway and stopped. Roger Kierce got out of his unmarked police vehicle. Curly got out of his Essex County police cruiser.

Maya turned away from the window. She took one more look at her daughter before she headed down the stairs. Fatigue was starting to fray her edges, but Maya fought through it. The end was in sight. It might be in the distance. But it was finally in view.

She didn't want them ringing the bell and waking Lily, so she opened the door as they made their approach.

"What is it?" she asked with more impatience than she intended.

"We found something," Kierce replied.

"What?"

"You're going to have to come with us."

Chapter 28

Miss Kitty managed to keep the bright smile plastered on, even though she had recognized the unmarked police car from Maya's first visit. Before Maya could say anything, Miss Kitty raised her hand in a stop gesture.

"No need to explain."

"Thank you."

As had quickly become customary, Lily went to Miss Kitty with no reservations. Miss Kitty opened the door to that sun-bright yellow room. The happy laughter seemed to swallow her daughter whole. Lily disappeared without so much as a backward glance at her mother.

"She's a wonderful girl," Miss Kitty said.

"Thank you."

Maya left her car in the Growin' Up lot and got into Kierce's. He tried to start a conversation during the ride, but Maya was having none of it. They drove to Newark in silence. Half an hour later, Maya was ensconced in a classic interrogation room in the county police station. There was a video camera set up on a small tripod on the table. Curly made sure that it was facing her and then switched it on. He asked her if she was willing to answer questions. She said yes. He asked her to sign a sheet indicating that. She did.

Kierce had big hands with hairy knuckles. He placed them on the table and tried to give her a "relax, it's all good" smile. Maya did not return it.

"Do you mind if we start at the beginning?" he asked.

"Yes."

"Pardon?"

"You said you have some new information," Maya said.

"That's correct."

"So why don't you start there?"

"Bear with me a second first, okay?"

Maya said nothing.

"When your husband was shot, you identified two men who you claimed tried to rob you and your husband?"

"Claimed?"

"It's just terminology, Mrs. Burkett. Do you mind if I call you Mrs. Burkett?"

"Nope. What's your question?"

"We found two men who fit those descriptions. Emilio Rodrigo and Fred Katen. We asked you to identify them, which you did to the best of your ability, but according to your testimony, they wore ski masks. As you know, we couldn't hold them, though we are prosecuting Rodrigo on a weapons charge."

"Okay."

"Before your husband's murder, did you know either Emilio Rodrigo or Fred Katen?"

Whoa. Where was he going with that? "No."

"You've never met either one of them before?"

She looked at Curly. He was a stone. Then she turned back toward Kierce. "Never."

"You're sure?"

"Yes."

"Because one theory is that it wasn't a robbery, Mrs. Burkett. One possible theory is that you hired them to kill your husband."

Maya again looked at Curly, then again back at Kierce.

"You know that's not true, Detective Kierce."

"Oh? How do I know that?"

"Two ways. One, if I had hired Emilio Rodrigo and Fred Katen, I wouldn't have identified them to the police, would I have?"

"Maybe you wanted to double-cross them."

"Sounds risky on my part, don't you think? From what I understand, the only tie you had to these two men was my testimony. If I don't say anything, you never go after them. So why would I identify them? Wouldn't it be in my best interest to keep mum?"

He had no answer to that.

"And if for some odd reason," she continued, "you do think I, what, hired them and then set them up, why would I say they wore ski masks? Wouldn't I just positively ID them so you could make the arrest?"

Kierce opened his mouth, but Maya, taking a page from Miss Kitty, stopped him with a hand gesture.

"And before you give some bullshit excuse, we both know that's not why I'm here. And before you ask how I know that, we are in Newark, not New York City. We are in the jurisdiction of Curly here—sorry, I don't remember your name."

"Essex County detective Demetrius Mavrogenous."

"Great, do you mind if I stick with Curly? But let's stop wasting all of our time, shall we? If this was about Joe's murder, we would be in your Central Park Precinct, Detective Kierce. Instead, we find ourselves in Newark, which is Essex County, the jurisdiction for Livingston, New Jersey, which was where the body of Tom Douglass was located last night."

"Not located," Kierce said, trying to regain any kind of momentum, "but found. By you."

"Yes, well, that's not new information, is it?"

She stopped and waited.

"No," Kierce finally said. "It isn't."

"Great. And I'm not under arrest, am I?"

"No, you're not."

"So stop with the games, Detective. Tell me what you found that led to my being here this morning."

Kierce looked at Curly. Curly nodded.

"Please look at the screen to your right."

There was a flat-screen television hung on the wall. Curly picked up a remote, turned it on, and a video came to life. It was from a CCTV security camera at a gas station. You could see one gas pump and, in the background, the street and a traffic light. Maya couldn't say where this gas station was located exactly, but she had a pretty good idea of where this was going. She sneaked a glance at Kierce. Kierce was watching her for a reaction.

"Hold up," Curly said, "right here."

He hit the pause button. He started to zoom in, and Maya could see her car at the red light facing right. The camera focused in toward the back of her car. "We can only make out the first two letters, but they match your license plate. Is that your car, Mrs. Burkett?"

She could argue and say that there were probably other BMWs with license plates that started with those two letters, but what was the point? "It appears to be."

Kierce nodded at Curly. Curly lifted the remote and pressed the button. The camera moved toward the passenger-door window. All eyes fell to her.

"Who is that man in the passenger seat?" Kierce asked.

There was too much glare on the window to see more than a baseball cap and a smudge that was unmistakably a person.

Maya did not reply.

"Mrs. Burkett."

She stayed silent.

"You told us last night that you were alone when you found Mr. Douglass's body, isn't that correct?"

Maya looked at the screen. "I don't see anything here that contradicts that."

"You're clearly not alone."

"And I'm clearly not at the body shop where the body was found."

"Are you telling us that this man—"

"You sure it's a man?"

"Pardon?"

"I see a smudge and a baseball cap. Women wear baseball caps."

"Who is this, Mrs. Burkett?"

She was not about to tell them about Corey Rudzinski. She had agreed to come here with them because she wanted to know what they had. Now she knew. So again she asked, "Am I under arrest?"

"No."

"Then I think it's time I left."

Kierce grinned at her. She didn't like the grin. "Maya?"

No more Mrs. Burkett.

"That's not why we brought you in."

Maya stayed where she was.

"We spoke to Mrs. Douglass, the widow. She told us about your visit."

"No secret there. I told you that last night."

"And so you did. Mrs. Douglass told us that you came because you believe that your sister, Claire, had questioned her husband. Isn't that correct?"

Maya saw no reason not to admit this. "As I already told you."

Kierce gave her the head tilt. "How did you know your sister visited Tom Douglass?"

That she didn't want to answer. Kierce had clearly expected that.

"Did you get another anonymous tip from a mystery source?"

Maya didn't answer.

"So, if I have this right, you got a tip from a mysterious source about Claire reaching out to Tom Douglass. And then you got a tip from a mysterious source about Tom Douglass's storage unit. Tell me, Maya: Did you back up either of those tips on your own?"

"What do you mean?"

"Did you have any proof your mystery source was telling the truth?"

She made a face. "Well, I know that Claire did visit Tom Douglass."

"Did she?"

Maya started to feel a niggling at the back of her neck.

"And while I agree Tom Douglass was indeed at the storage shed—that was certainly a good tip—your mystery source kind of left you holding the bag, wouldn't you say?"

Kierce rose and walked toward the television screen. "And I assume," Kierce said, pointing at the baseball cap smudge, "that this is your mystery source?"

Maya said nothing.

"I assume that this man—just for the fun of it, let's say it's a man; I think I see facial hair—was the one who led you to the storage shed?"

Maya folded her hands and put them on the table. "And if he did?"

"He was clearly in your car, correct?"

"So?"

"So"—Kierce came back over, placed his fists on the table, and leaned toward her—"we found blood in the trunk of your car, Mrs. Burkett."

Maya stayed perfectly still.

"Type AB-positive. The same blood type as Tom Douglass. Do you mind telling us how it got there?"

Chapter 29

They had a blood type, but the DNA test confirming that the blood in the trunk of her car belonged to Tom Douglass was still pending. There wasn't enough to hold her.

But they were getting close. Time was running out.

Kierce volunteered to drive her home. She accepted this time. For the first ten minutes of the ride, they both sat in silence. Kierce finally broke it.

"Maya?"

She stared out the window. She had been thinking about Corey Rudzinski, the man who, in a sense, started this all. Corey had been the one who released the copter combat video that started her tailspin. Again she could go back even further in time, to her actions on that very mission, to her decision to join the mili-

tary, all of that. But really, what started her world un-
raveling, what had directly led to the deaths of Claire
and Joe, was releasing that cursed tape.

Had Corey the Whistle played her?

Maya had been so anxious to get him to trust her
that she had forgotten that maybe it wouldn't be wise
to trust a man who had done so much to destroy her.
She replayed his words in her head. Corey had said
Claire had come to him, that she had reached out via
his website. Maya had accepted that. But was it true?
Think about it for a second. It did in some ways
make sense that Claire would contact Corey and try
to stop him from releasing that audio. But it also
made sense, just as much sense, maybe even *more*
sense, that Corey would reach out to Claire, that he
could use the audio to either manipulate or straight-
out blackmail her into gathering information on the
Burketts and EAC Pharmaceuticals.

Had Corey manipulated Maya too?

Had he gone so far as to manipulate her into taking
the fall for Tom Douglass's murder?

"Maya?" Kierce said again.

"What?"

"You've been lying to me from day one."

Enough, Maya thought. It was time to turn the tables on him. "Caroline Burkett tells me that you've
been taking bribes from the Burkett family."

Kierce might have smiled. "That's a lie."

"Is it?"

"Yes. I just don't know if Caroline Burkett lied to you"—he gave her a quick glance and then had his eyes on the road again—"or if you're lying now to distract me."

"Not a lot of trust in this car, is there?"

"No," Kierce agreed. "But you're running out of time, Maya. Lies never die. You can try to smother them, but lies will always find a way to show themselves again."

Maya nodded. "That's deep, Kierce."

He chuckled at that. "Yeah, that was a bit much, wasn't it?"

They pulled into her driveway. Maya reached for the door handle, but the door was locked. She looked at Kierce.

"I'm going to find the answer," he said. "I just hope that it doesn't lead back to you. But if it does . . ."

She waited for the click of the door unlocking. When the sound came, she opened the door and left without bothering with a good-bye or thanks. When she got inside, Maya made sure that the doors were locked before she headed down the dark stairwell.

The basement had started life as a rather upscale "man cave"—three flat screens, an oak bar, a wine cooler, a pool table, two pinball machines—but Joe had been slowly converting it over into a playroom for Lily. The dark wood paneling had been stripped off, and the walls painted bright white. Joe had found life-sized decals of various characters from Winnie the Pooh and

Madeline and plastered them everywhere. His oak bar was still there, though he'd promised to remove that too. Maya hadn't cared if it stayed. In the far corner of the basement was one of those Step 2 indoor play-houses Joe had bought at Toys "R" Us on Route 17. It was fort-themed ("manly," Joe had claimed) with a kitchenette ("womanly," he almost claimed, but his survival instinct took over), a working doorbell, and a window with shutters.

Maya headed for the gun safe. She bent down, checked the basement steps even though she knew she was alone, and then placed her fingertip on the glass. The safe came with the ability to store thirty-two sepa-rate fingerprints, but only she and Joe had ever worked it. She had debated adding Shane's fingerprints in case he ever needed to get one of her weapons or if she needed him to get one out for whatever reason, but she just hadn't had the chance.

Two clicks signaled that her fingerprint was recog-nized and the safe unlocked. Maya turned the knob and opened the metal door.

She took out the Glock 26, and then, because it was better to put her mind completely at ease, she made sure all the other guns were still in place—that no one had come here, opened the safe, and taken one.

No, she didn't believe Joe was alive, but at this stage, she would have to be stubbornly crazy to completely dismiss the notion.

She took the guns out one by one, and even though

she had done it recently, she once again opened them up and gave them a thorough cleaning. She always did that. Every single time she touched a gun, she re-checked it and cleaned it. Doing so, being so anal about her weaponry, had probably saved her life.

Or ruined it.

She closed her eyes for a second. So many crazy what-ifs in all this, so many sliding-door moments. Had it all started on the campus of Franklin Biddle Academy or on that yacht? Could it have simply ended there, in the past, or did her combat mission over Al Qa'im somehow bring it back to life? Was Corey to blame for awakening those ghosts? Was Claire? Was having that leaked tape released to the world the cause? Was it go-ing to Tom Douglass?

Or was it opening this damn safe?

Maya didn't know anymore. She wasn't sure she cared either.

The guns in plain sight, the guns she had shown to Roger Kierce, were the ones that had all been legally registered in New Jersey. They were present and ac-counted for. Maya reached her hand toward the back, found the spot, pressed against it.

A secret compartment.

She couldn't help but think of Nana's trunk in Claire's house, how the idea of the fake wall and secret compartment started generations ago in Kiev, and now here she was, carrying on the family tradition.

Maya still kept two guns back here, both bought out

of state and thus untraceable to her. Nothing illegal about that. They were both there, but what had she expected? That Ghost Joe had come and stolen one of them? Heck, ghosts don't have fingerprints, do they? Ghost Joe couldn't open the safe, even if he wanted to.

Oh boy, she was feeling punchy.

The buzz of her mobile phone startled her. She checked the number but didn't recognize it. She hit the answer button and said, "Hello?"

"Is this Maya Burkett?"

It was a man's voice, smooth like one of those guys on NPR radio, but there was an unmistakable quiver in it.

"Yes, it is. Who is this?"

"My name is Christopher Swain. You sent me an email."

Joe's high school soccer co-captain. "Yes, thank you for calling me back."

Silence. For a moment she thought that perhaps he had hung up.

"I wanted to ask you some questions," she said.

"About?"

"About my husband. About his brother Andrew."

Silence.

"Mr. Swain?"

"Joe is dead now. Is that correct?"

"Yes."

"Who else knows you've contacted me?"

"No one."

"Is that the truth?"

Maya felt her grip on the phone tighten. "Yes."

"I'll talk to you, then. But not on the phone."

"Tell me where to go."

He gave her an address in Connecticut.

"I can be there within two hours," she said.

"Don't tell anyone you're coming. If you're with someone, they won't let you in."

Swain hung up.

They?

She made sure the Glock was loaded and closed the safe. She strapped on a leather IWB (inside waistband) holster, which would keep the Glock concealed, especially when she wore certain flex-fabric jeans and a dark blazer. She liked the feel of carrying. On some alternate planet, you weren't supposed to like it—it was wrong, it showed you were violent, whatever—but there was something both primitive and comforting in the weight of the weapon. That could, of course, be a danger too. You get overconfident. You tend to let yourself get into situations that you shouldn't because, hey, you could always shoot your way out of them. You start to feel a little indestructible, a little full of yourself, a little too brave, a little too macho.

Carrying guns gave you options. That was not always a good thing.

Maya stuck the nanny cam frame in the back of the car. She didn't want it in the house anymore.

She put the address Christopher Swain had given her into her map app, which informed her the ride with current traffic conditions would take one hour, thirty-six minutes. She blasted Joe's playlist on the ride. Again she couldn't say why. The first song was Rhye's "Open," which starts hot and heavy with the line "I'm a fool for that shake in your thighs," but a few lines later, in the afterglow of the moment, you can feel a gap growing between the lovers: "I know you're faded, mmm, but stay, don't close your eyes."

In the next song, Lapsley gorgeously sang a warning: "It's been a long time coming, but I'm falling short." Boy, did that feel apropos.

Maya got lost in the music, singing out loud, drumming on the steering wheel. In real life, in the helicopter, in the Middle East, at her home, everywhere, she cut it all off and kept it down. But not here. Not alone in a goddamn car. Alone in goddamn cars, Maya blared the music and shouted every lyric.

Damn right.

The final song, as she hit the Darien town line, was a haunting beauty from Cocoon called, weirdly enough, "Sushi," and once again the opening line smacked her like a two-by-four: "In the morning, I'll go down the graveyard, to make sure you're gone for good . . ."

That sobered her up.

Some days, every song seems to be talking directly to you, don't they?

And some days, a lyric may hit too close to home.

She drove down a narrow, quiet street. Thick woods lined both sides of it. The phone map showed that the address was at the end of a dead end. If that was the case, and she had no reason to doubt it, the residence was in a secluded spot. There was a guard booth at the top of the driveway. The gate was lowered. Maya pulled up to it as the guard approached her.

"May I help you?"

"I'm here to see Christopher Swain."

The guard vanished back into his hut and picked up the phone. A moment later, he hung up and came back over to her. "Drive up to the guest lot. It'll be on the right. Someone will meet you there."

Guest lot?

As she drove up the driveway, she realized that this was not a residence. So what was it? There were security cameras on trees. Buildings of rain-gray stone started popping up. The overall feel, what with the seclusion and stone and layout, was very similar to Franklin Biddle Academy.

There were probably ten cars in the guest lot. When Maya parked, another security guard drove toward her in a golf cart. She quickly took out her gun—no doubt in her mind there would be some kind of wanding or metal detector here—and jammed it into her glove compartment.

The security driver took a cursory look at the car and invited her to get into the passenger seat of the golf cart. Maya did.

"May I see your ID, please?"

She handed him her driver's license. He snapped a photograph of it with his camera phone and gave it back to her. "Mr. Swain is in Brocklehurst Hall. I'll take you there."

As they began to drive, Maya spotted various people—mostly in their twenties, men and women, all white—huddled oddly in groups or walking fast in pairs. Many, too many of them, were smoking. Most wore jeans, sneakers, and an assortment of sweatshirts or heavy sweaters. There was what looked like a college quad, except there was a fountain statue of what might have been the Virgin Mary dead center.

Maya asked out loud what she'd been asking herself. "What is this place?"

The security guard pointed at the Virgin Mary. "Until the late seventies, it was a convent, believe it or not."

She believed it.

"Full of nuns back then."

"No kidding," Maya said, trying not to sound too sarcastic. Like what else would a convent be full of? "And what is it now?"

He frowned. "You don't know?"

"No."

"Who are you visiting?"

"Christopher Swain."

"It isn't my place to say anything."

"Please." She said it in a voice that made him suck in his gut. "I just need to know where I am."

He sighed, just to give the impression of thinking it over, and said, "This is the Solemani Recovery Center."

"Recovery." A euphemism for a rehab center. That explained it. The irony—the rich taking over a beautiful secluded spot that used to house nuns who probably vowed to live a life of poverty. Then again, look at this place. Some vow of poverty. Maybe it wasn't irony exactly, but it was something.

The golf cart pulled up to what looked like a dormitory.

"Here we are. Just go through the doors there."

She was buzzed in by yet another security guard, and sure enough, she had to walk through a metal detector. A woman met her on the other side with a smile and a handshake.

"Hello, my name is Melissa Lee. I'm a facilitator here at the Solemani."

"Facilitator." Another all-purpose euphemism.

"Christopher asked me to take you to the solarium. I'll show you the way."

Melissa Lee's heels clacked and echoed in the empty corridor. The place was convent silent except for those heels. If you knew that—and you had to if you worked here every day—why would you choose to disrupt the solace with your shoes? Was it part of a uniform? Was it intentional? Why not just wear sneakers or something?

And why was she thinking of something so banal anyway?

Christopher Swain stood to greet her like a nervous date. He wore a well-tailored black suit, white shirt, thin black tie. He had the kind of facial growth that took some planning to look unplanned. His hair was skater boy with blond highlights. He was good-looking, albeit trying too hard. Whatever had brought him to this place had etched lines on his face. He probably didn't like that. He'd probably add Botox or fillers, but Maya thought it gave the otherwise privileged look some character.

"Can I get you anything?" Melissa Lee asked.

Maya shook her head.

Melissa gave half a smile and looked at Swain. With touching concern in her voice, she said, "Are you sure you want me to leave, Christopher?"

"Yes, please." His tone was tentative. "I think this is an important step for me."

Melissa nodded. "I do too."

"So we will need some privacy."

"I understand. I'll be nearby just in case. Just holler."

Melissa gave Maya another half smile and left. She closed the doors behind her.

"Wow," Swain said when they were alone. "You're really beautiful."

Maya didn't know what to say to that, so she kept her mouth closed.

He smiled and openly looked her up and down. "You're stunning *and* you give off that air of unattainability. Like you're above it all." He shook his head. "I bet Joe couldn't resist you the moment he saw you, am I right?"

Now was not the time to play a feminist card or get offended. She needed him to keep talking. "Pretty much, yeah."

"Let me guess. Joe gave you some cheesy pickup line, something funny but maybe self-deprecating and vulnerable. I'm right, aren't I?"

"You are."

"Swept you off your feet, didn't he?"

"Yes."

"Oh man, that Joe. The dude was three steps above charismatic when he wanted to be." Swain shook his head again as the smile started to fall away. "So is he really dead? Joe, I mean."

"Yes."

"I didn't know. No news in here. One of the rules. No social media, no Internet, no outside world. We get to check our email once a day. That's how I saw your message. Once I did . . . Well, my doctor said it would be okay to read the news report. I have to say, I was shocked to hear about Joe. Would you like to sit down?"

The solarium was clearly a more recent addition that was trying to fit in with the old and not totally succeeding. There was a snapped-together vibe about it. The roof was a dome with faux stained glass. There were plants, sure, but fewer than one might imagine in a room dubbed a solarium. Two leather chairs sat in the middle of the room facing each other. Maya took one, Swain the other.

"I can't believe he's dead."

Yeah, Maya thought, she was getting that a lot.

"You were there, right? When he was shot?"

"Yes," Maya said.

"The news reports said you escaped unharmed."

"Yes."

"How?"

"I ran away."

Swain looked at her as though he didn't entirely believe that. "It must have been scary for you."

She said nothing.

"The news outlets described it as a robbery gone wrong."

"Yes."

"But we both know that's not true, don't we, Maya?" He put his hand through his hair. "You wouldn't be here if it were just a robbery."

His manner was starting to unnerve her. "Right now," Maya said, "I'm just trying to put together what happened."

"It's incredible," he said. "I still can't believe it."

There was an odd smile on his face.

"Believe what?"

"That Joe is dead. Sorry for harping on that. It's just that he was . . . I don't know if it would be right to say he was 'so full of life.' That's so hackneyed, isn't it? But let's say Joe was a life force. You know? He seemed so strong, so powerful, like a fire that raged so out of control you could never put it out. There was almost something—I know this is silly—immortal about him . . ."

Maya shifted in her seat. "Christopher?"

He was gazing out a window.

"You were on the yacht the night Andrew went overboard."

He didn't move.

"What really happened to his brother Andrew?"

Swain swallowed hard. A tear escaped from his eye and slid down his cheek.

"Christopher?"

"I didn't see it, Maya. I stayed on the lower deck."

There was a chill in his voice.

"But you know something."

Another tear.

"Please tell me," Maya said. "Did Andrew really fall?"

His voice was like a stone dropping down a well. "I don't know. But I don't think so."

"So what happened to him?"

"I think . . . ," Christopher Swain said before taking a deep breath, summoning some inner resolve, and starting again. "I think Joe pushed him off the boat."

Chapter 30

Swain sat with both hands gripping the chair arms.

"It started when Theo Mora came to Franklin Biddle Academy. Or maybe that was when I started to see it."

They had pushed their chairs closer together, almost knee-to-knee, somehow needing to be physically closer in this room that seemed to be growing ever colder.

"You probably think it was the old cliché about the rich not wanting the poor sullying their elite institutions. You can almost picture it, can't you? We rich kids all ganged up on Theo or picked on him. But that wasn't how it was."

"How was it?" Maya asked.

"Theo was funny and outgoing. He didn't make the

mistake of backing off or kowtowing to us. He fit right in. We all liked him. He didn't seem all that different in many ways. I know people want to paint the rich one way and the poor another, but when you're kids—and that's what we were, or what I thought we were, just kids—you just want to hang out and belong."

He wiped his eyes.

"And it didn't hurt that Theo was a great soccer player. Not good. Great. I was thrilled. We had a chance to win it all that year. Not just the state as a prep school, which we did, but win the entire state tournament outright, including all the big public and parochial schools. Theo was that good. He could score from anywhere. And maybe that was the problem."

"How so?"

"He wasn't a threat to me. I was a midfielder. He wasn't a threat to his roommate and best friend, Andrew. Andrew was a goalie."

Swain stopped and looked at Maya.

"But Joe was a striker too," she said.

Swain nodded. "I'm not saying he was openly hostile to Theo, but . . . I've known Joe since we were in first grade. We grew up together. We were always captains of the soccer team. And when you spend that much time with a person, you get a chance to see the facade slip away sometimes. The anger that would come out. His flashes of rage. When we were in eighth grade, Joe put a kid in the hospital with a baseball bat. I don't remember what it was even about anymore. I just remember three of us pulling him off the poor kid. Cracked his skull. A year later, this girl Joe liked, Marian Barford, was going to go to the dance with Tom Mendiburu. Two days before, there's a fire in the science lab and Tom barely gets out alive."

Maya swallowed away the bile. "No one reported any of this?"

"You didn't know Joe's dad, did you?"

"No."

"He was an intimidating man. There were rumors he was in with some rough customers. Whatever, payoffs were made. The family's more, shall we say, unsavory friends would stop by and request your silence. Plus, well, Joe was good at it. He didn't leave a lot of evidence. We talked about his charm before. He could fake contrition like nobody's business. He would apologize. He would cajole. He was rich and powerful, and those moments, that darker side, he could really keep it hidden when he had to. Again, I remind you, I knew him my whole life. And even I saw it only a handful of times. But when I did . . ."

The tears started coming again.

"You're probably wondering what I'm doing in a place like this."

She hadn't been. She had figured that he was an addict of some kind and was here for help. What else could it be? She wanted him to keep telling the story, but if he needed this sidetrack, it would probably be a mistake to stop him.

"I'm here," he said, "because of Joe."

She tried not to make a face.

"I know, I know, I'm supposed to take responsibility for myself. That's what they always say. And yeah, I keep trading one addiction for another. I've been in here for booze, for pills, for coke . . . you name it. But I wasn't always like this. In school I used to get teased because I wouldn't have more than a beer. Didn't like the taste. I tried pot once my senior year. It made me nauseated."

"Christopher?"

"Yes."

"What happened to Theo?"

"It was supposed to be a prank. That was what Joe told us. I don't know if I believed him or not, but . . . I was so weak. Check that. I'm still weak. Joe was the leader. I was the follower. Andrew was a follower too. And really, what was going to be the harm? A little hazing. It happens all the time at schools like Franklin Biddle. So that night, we jumped Theo. You know what I mean? We came to his room—me, Joe, Andrew was already there—and we jumped on him and we carried him downstairs."

He was looking off now, the thousand-yard stare, and a funny smile came to his face. "You know something?"

"What?"

"Theo went along with it. Like he got it. He was getting hazed. This was part of it. He was that cool a kid. I remember that he was smiling, you know, like this was all good. And then we get down to that room and we throw him in the chair. Joe started tying him up. We helped out. We're all laughing, and Theo is pretending to call for help, that kind of thing. I remember I left this one knot loose. Joe came by and tightened it. Then, when Theo was all tied down, Joe took out a funnel. You know the kind. For drinking? He stuck it into Theo's mouth, and I remember Theo's eyes changed then. Like, I don't know, like maybe he was starting to get it. Two other guys were there. Larry Raia and Neil Kornfeld. We were all laughing, and Andrew started to pour beer down the funnel. Guys were chanting, 'Chug chug.' And then, the rest is like a dream. A nightmare. Like I still can't believe it all happened, but at some point, Joe replaced the beer with grain alcohol. I remember Andrew saying, 'Wait, Joe, stop . . .'"

His voice faded away.

"What happened?" Maya asked, but it seemed obvious now.

"Suddenly Theo's leg started thrashing, like he was having a seizure or something."

Christopher Swain started to cry. Maya wanted to reach out her hand and put it on his shoulder. At the same time, she also wanted to punch him in the face. So instead she just sat there and waited.

"I've never told that story before yesterday. Not to anyone. But after your email . . . my doctor, she knows some of it now. That's why she thought it would be good to talk to you. But that night, I mean, that's when

I went off the rails. I was so scared. I knew that if I said something, Joe would kill me. Not just back then. Now. Even now. I still feel . . ."

Maya tried to keep him talking. "So you, what, stuck the body in the basement?"

"Joe did."

"But you were there, right?"

Swain nodded.

"So I doubt Joe lifted him alone, did he?"

He shook his head.

"Who helped Joe?"

"Andrew." He looked up. "Joe made Andrew help him."

"Is that what made Andrew crack?"

"I don't know. Maybe Andrew would have cracked anyway. Andrew, me . . . we were never the same after that."

Javier Mora had been right. It wasn't grief. It was guilt.

"So then what happened?"

"What could I do?"

There were plenty of things he could have done, but Maya wasn't there to prosecute or to give him absolution. She wanted information. That was all.

"I had to keep the secret, didn't I? So I smothered it away. I tried to go on with my regular life, but nothing was the same. My grades tumbled. I couldn't concentrate. That's when I started drinking. Yes, I know it sounds like a convenient excuse—"

"Christopher?"

"What?"

"You all ended up on that yacht six weeks later."

He closed his eyes.

"What happened?"

"What do you think happened, Maya? Come on. You know now. So you tell me. You put it together."

Maya leaned forward. "So you're all on that boat heading for Bermuda. You all start drinking. Probably you especially. It's the first time all of you have been together since Theo's death. Andrew is there. He's been in therapy, but it hasn't done him any good. The guilt is destroying him. So he makes a decision. I don't know exactly how it worked, Christopher, so maybe you can tell me. Did Andrew threaten you guys?"

"Not threaten," Christopher said. "Not really. He just . . . He started pleading with us. He couldn't sleep. He couldn't eat. God, he looked horrible. He just said that we had to come forward because he didn't know how long he could keep this bottled up inside. I was so drunk I could barely understand what he was saying."

"And then?"

"And then Andrew went outside to the upper deck. To get away from us. A few minutes later, Joe followed him." Swain shrugged. "The end."

"You never told anyone?"

"Never."

"The other two guys, Larry Raia and Neil Kornfeld . . ."

"Neil was going to Yale. He ended up changing his mind and headed to Stanford. Larry went to school overseas, I think. Paris maybe. We finished up our senior year in a daze and never saw each other again."

"And you've kept this secret for all these years."

Swain nodded.

"So why now?" Maya asked. "Why are you willing to tell the truth now?"

"You know why."

"No, I'm not sure I do."

"Because Joe is dead," he said. "Because I finally feel safe."

Chapter 31

Christopher Swain's words echoed in her ears as she walked back to the guest lot. *"Because Joe is dead . . ."*

In the end, it all came back to that nanny cam, didn't it?

Time to get analytical here. There were three possibilities that explained what she had seen on that nanny cam:

One, the most likely, was that someone had set it up using some kind of Photoshop program. The technology existed. She had only seen the video for a brief time. It could be done easily enough.

Two, almost tied for most likely, Maya had imagined or hallucinated Joe, or in some other way, her mind had played tricks on her and thus conjured up the image of Joe being alive. Eileen Finn liked to send her those optical illusion videos, where you think you're seeing something and then the camera moves just a little and you realize that your eye has preconceived a certain image. Add in Maya's PTSD, her meds, her sister's murder, her guilt about that, the night in Central Park, all the rest . . . how could Maya really dismiss that as a real possibility?

Three, least likely, Joe was somehow still alive.

If the answer was Two—it was all in her head—there was little to be done about it. She still needed to go through all this because the truth, while it won't set you free, will help right the world in some way. But if the answer was either One (Photoshop) or Three (Joe was alive), then it meant one thing without question:

Someone was screwing with her big-time.

And if it was either One or Three, it almost certainly meant something else: Isabella had lied. She had seen Joe on that nanny cam video. The only reason Isabella would have pretended not to see Joe, pepper-sprayed Maya, grabbed the SD card, and then gone into hiding was fairly simple: She was in on it.

Maya got back into her car, turned on the engine, and hit her playlist. Imagine Dragons came on telling her not to get too close, it's dark inside, it's where her demons hide.

They didn't know the half of it.

She clicked on the app for the GPS she'd attached to Hector's car. First off, assuming Isabella was in on it, she wasn't the kind to act alone. Her mother, Rosa, who had been on the yacht that night, would be in on it. Her brother, Hector, too. Second—man, she was thinking arithmetically today—there was a chance, of course, Isabella had gone someplace far away, but Maya doubted it. She was around. It was just a question of finding her.

She retrieved the gun from her glove box, checked the GPS, and saw that Hector's truck was currently parked in the servants' complex at Farnwood. Maya clicked the history button, seeing all the places the truck had traveled over the past few days. The only place that didn't seem to fit the work pattern of a landscaper was an address he constantly visited in a Paterson, New Jersey, housing project. He could, of course, have friends or a girlfriend there. But something about it didn't feel right.

So now what?

Even if Isabella was hiding there, it wasn't as though she could just go to the address and start knocking on doors. She needed to be more proactive. It was coming down to it now. She had most of the answers. She needed to find out the rest and put an end to it once and for all.

Her mobile rang. She saw on the caller ID that it was Shane.

"Hello?"

"What have you done?"

His tone chilled her blood.

"What are you talking about?"

"Detective Kierce."

"What about him?"

"He knows, Maya."

She said nothing. The walls were starting to close in on her now.

"He knows I tested that bullet for you."

"Shane . . ."

"The same gun killed Claire and Joe, Maya. How the hell can that be?"

"Shane, listen to me. You have to trust me, okay?"

"You keep saying that. 'Trust me.' Like it's some kind of mantra."

"I shouldn't need to say it." Pointless, she thought. There was no way she could explain it to him right now. "I gotta run."

"Maya?"

She hung up the phone and closed her eyes.

Let it go, she told herself.

She started down the quiet road, distracted by Shane's call, by what Christopher Swain had told her, by all the emotions and thoughts swirling through her head.

Maybe that explained what happened next.

A van started coming toward her from the opposite direction. The tree-lined road was narrow, so she slowly shifted her vehicle a little to the right to give the van room to pass her. But as the van got close, it suddenly swung to its left, cutting in front of her.

Maya slammed on the brakes to avoid hitting the van. Her body jutted forward, restrained by the straps, even as the lizard-instinct part of the brain came to a realization:

She was being attacked.

The van had cut off any forward motion, so she was reaching for the gear to put the car in reverse when she heard the knocking on her window. She looked and saw the gun facing her head. In her peripheral vision, she saw someone else at the window on the passenger side.

"It's okay." The man's voice was hard to hear through the window. "We aren't here to hurt you."

How had the man gotten to the side of her car so fast? He couldn't have gotten out of the van. There wasn't that kind of time. This had been carefully orchestrated. Someone had realized that she would be at the Solemani Recovery Center. The road was quiet. Very little traffic. So these two men had probably been hiding behind a tree. The van cuts her off. They step out.

Maya just sat very still and considered her options.

"Please step out of the car and come with us."

Option One: Reach for the gear and shift the car in reverse.

Option Two: Go for the gun in the hip holster.

The problem with both options was simple. The man had his gun at her head. Maybe his friend by the other window did too. She wasn't Wyatt Earp and this wasn't the O.K. Corral. If the man wanted to shoot her, she would have no chance of reaching either the gun or the gearshift in time.

Which left Option Three: Get out of the car—

That was when the man with the gun said, "Come on. Joe is waiting."

The side door of the van began to slide open. Sitting in her car, both hands on the wheel, Maya could feel her heart pounding against her rib cage. The van door stopped halfway. Maya squinted, but she couldn't see inside. She turned to the man with the gun.

"Joe . . . ?" she said.

"Yeah," the man said, his voice suddenly tender. "Come on. You want to see him, right?"

She looked at the man's face for the first time. Then she looked at the other man. He didn't have a gun in his hand.

Option Three . . .

Maya started to cry.

"Mrs. Burkett?"

Through the tears, she said, "Joe . . ."

"Yes." The man's voice grew insistent. "Unlock the door, Mrs. Burkett."

Still crying, Maya weakly fumbled for the unlock button. She pressed it and pulled the door handle. The man stepped back to let the door swing. He still had the gun on her. Maya half fell out of the car. The gunman started to reach for her arm, but Maya, still with the tears, shook her head and said, "No need."

She straightened up and then stumbled toward the van. The gunman let her go. And that told Maya everything.

The van door slid open a little more.

Four men, Maya calculated. The driver, the vandoor opener, the passenger-side guy, the gunman.

As she got closer to the van, all her training, all those

hours in the simulator and at the shoot house, started to kick in. She felt an odd calm now, a moment of near Zen, that feeling when you are in the eye of the hurricane. It was all about to happen now, and one way or the other, if she came out of it alive or dead, she was being proactive. She wasn't controlling her own destiny—that sort of thinking was nonsense—but when you've trained and when you're prepared, you can act with a sort of comforting confidence.

Still stumbling, Maya turned her head just a little, just the slightest bit, because what she saw now would decide everything. The gunman had not grabbed hold of her when she got out of the car. That was the reason she had poured on the fake tears and semihysterics. To see how he would react. He had fallen for it. He had let her go.

He hadn't frisked her.

That meant three things . . .

She glanced behind her. The man had indeed lowered his gun to his side. He had relaxed. He felt she was no longer an active threat.

One, no one had warned the man that she'd be armed . . .

Maya had been planning the sequence from the moment she started with the tears. The tears were designed to act as a weapon—to make the kidnappers relax; to make them underestimate her; to give her time, before getting out of the car, to plan exactly what she would do.

Two, Joe would know that she'd be armed . . .

Her hand was already near her hip as she started to run. Here's a fun fact most people don't know. Shooting a handgun with accuracy is difficult. Shooting a handgun at a moving target is very difficult. Seventy-six percent of the time, trained police officers miss the shot between three and nine feet. The percentage is north of ninety percent for civilians.

So you always moved.

Maya looked toward the back of the van. Then, without so much as a misstep or warning or even hesitation, she tucked into a roll, hit the pavement as she pulled her Glock out of its holster, and came up aiming directly at the man with the gun. The man had noticed the move, had started to react, but it was too late.

Maya aimed for the center of his chest.

In real life, you never shoot to wound. You point the weapon at the center of the chest, the largest target, the best chance of hitting at least something should your aim be off, and you just keep firing.

Which is what Maya did.

The man went down.

Three, the conclusion: Joe had not sent them.

Several things happened at once.

Maya kept rolling, kept moving, so she wasn't a stationary target. She turned to where the other man was, the one who had been at her passenger side. She swung her gun up, ready to fire, but the man ducked away behind her car.

Keep moving, Maya . . .

The van door slammed shut. The engine roared to life. Maya was behind it now, using it as a shield in case the other guy came up firing. She obviously couldn't stay. The van was about to move, probably in reverse, probably trying to crush her.

Maya made the instinctive decision.

Flee.

The man with the gun was down. The guys in the van were panicking. The final man was hidden behind her.

When in doubt, do the simple thing.

Still using the van as something of a shield, Maya ran into the woods. The van shot backward, almost hitting her. Maya stayed to its side, and then, fully blocked off from the guy by her passenger door, she turned and ran the last few feet.

Don't stop . . .

The woods were too thick for her to look behind her while she was running, but at some point, she ducked behind a tree and risked a quick look. The man who had been hiding behind the passenger seat was not following her. He sprinted straight for the van and dove in while the van was still moving. The van completed the K-turn and, with tires peeling the pavement, shot back down the road.

They had left the gunman she had shot by the side of the road.

The entire episode, from the moment Maya tucked and rolled until now, had probably taken fewer than ten seconds.

Now what?

The decision took almost no time. She had no choice really. If she called it in or waited for the authorities, she would certainly be arrested. Being in the park when Joe was shot, finding Tom Douglass, the ballistics tests, now another man shot with her own gun—there would be no quick explanation.

She hurried back to the road. The gunman was flat on his back, legs splayed.

He could be faking it, but Maya doubted it. Still she kept her gun at the ready.

No need. He was dead.

She had killed the man.

No time to dwell on that. A car would be coming any second. She quickly went through his pockets and grabbed his wallet. No time to check his ID now. She debated grabbing his phone—she wouldn't be able to use hers anymore—but that seemed too risky for obvious reasons. Finally, she considered taking his gun, which was still clutched in his hand, but that was really the only evidence, if everything else went south, that she had acted in self-defense.

Plus, she still had her Glock.

She had already done the calculations in her head. The gunman's body was near the side of the road. It wouldn't take much to push it two or three feet and then let it roll down the embankment.

With one quick glance to make sure no cars were approaching, that was exactly what Maya did.

The gunman rolled more easily than she would have thought, or maybe adrenaline had made her stronger. He slid straight down, his limp body smacking into a tree.

He was, at least temporarily, out of sight.

The body would be found, of course. Maybe in an hour. Maybe in a day. But in the meantime, it would buy Maya enough time.

She rushed back to her car and slid into the driver's seat. Her phone was going crazy now. Shane calling her back. Probably Kierce starting to wonder what the hell was going on too. In the distance, a car started coming toward her. Maya kept her calm. She started up her car and gently hit the accelerator. She was just another visitor departing the Solemani Recovery Center. If there were CCTV cameras anywhere nearby, they would show a van speeding off and then, a minute or two later, a normal-driving BMW that had an excuse to be in the area driving by.

Deep breaths, Maya. In and out. Flex, relax . . .

Five minutes later, she was back on the highway.

Maya put some distance between herself and the dead body.

She turned off her phone, and then, because she wasn't sure if the phone could still be tracked, she smashed it against the steering wheel. Thirty miles later, she stopped in a CVS parking lot. She checked the gunman's wallet. No ID, but he did have four hundred dollars in cash. Perfect. Maya was low and didn't want to use an ATM.

She bought three disposable cell phones and a baseball cap with the cash. She checked her face in the store's bathroom mirror. A disaster. She washed up as best she could and threw her hair into a ponytail. She put the cap on and came out looking presentable.

Where would the kidnappers go?

They were probably no longer a threat. There was an outside chance that they'd go to her house and wait for her, but that seemed very risky. The van was likely stolen or a rental or had fake plates, something, so they would probably just call it a day.

Still she had no intention of going to her house.

She called Eddie. He answered on the second ring. She told him where to meet her. He said that he was on his way and mercifully didn't ask any follow-up questions. This too was a risk, but it was minimal. Still, when she got closer to the Growin' Up Day Care, she gave the surroundings a serious examination. Interestingly enough, Growin' Up was almost set up the way you might an army base. You really couldn't approach it without being seen. There were layers of security. Sure, someone could shoot their way in, but really, with the buzz-locked doors by the entranceway and into each room, you'd be able to contact authorities—the police station was a block away—in no time.

She circled one more time. Nothing suspicious.

When she saw Eddie's car enter the lot, she pulled in behind him. The Glock was back in her waistband. Eddie parked. Maya parked next to him and got out of the car. She slid into the passenger seat next to him.

"What's going on, Maya?"

"I need to sign you up so you're able to pick up Lily."

"And that weird phone number you called me from?"

"Let's just do this, okay?"

Eddie looked at her. "Do you know who killed Claire and Joe?"

"Yes."

He waited. Then he said, "But you won't tell me."

"Not right now, no."

"Because . . . ?"

"Because I don't have time. Because Claire wanted to protect you."

"Maybe I don't want to be protected."

"It doesn't work like that."

"Like hell it doesn't. Maybe it's time I helped."

"Right now," she said, "you can help by coming inside with me." She reached for the knob and pulled it. With a heavy sigh, Eddie did the same thing. When he turned his back, when he started to step out of the car, Maya jammed an envelope into the bottom of his laptop bag. Then she got out too.

Miss Kitty buzzed them in and helped them fill out the paperwork. As they took the ID photograph of Eddie, Maya looked into the sun-bright yellow room and spotted her daughter. Seeing Lily made her heart feel suddenly light. Lily wore a smock, one of Maya's old shirts, and her hands were covered in paint. There was a big smile on the little girl's face. Maya stood there and felt a hand reach inside her chest and squeeze.

Miss Kitty came up behind her. "Do you want to go inside and say hello?"

Maya shook her head. "Are we done here?"

"We are. Your brother-in-law can now pick her up at any point."

"I don't have to call to give him permission?"

"That was what you requested, right?"

"It is."

"And that's what we've done."

Maya nodded, her eyes still on Lily. She took one more look at her daughter and started to turn away. She faced Miss Kitty. "Thank you."

"Are you all right?"

"I'm fine." She looked past her at Eddie. "We better go."

When they were both out in the parking lot, Maya asked to borrow Eddie's phone. He handed it to her without objection. She signed into her GPS tracking app via the website.

Hector's truck was back at that Paterson location.

Good. Time to stay proactive. She debated asking Eddie if she could keep his phone, but someone might eventually figure that out and track it. She handed it back to him.

"Thank you."

"Are you going to tell me what's going on?"

When they reached their cars, Maya said, "Wait a second." She opened the back of her car, found the toolbox, took out a screwdriver.

"What are you doing?" Eddie asked.

"I'm switching our license plates."

She didn't think Kierce would put an APB out on her yet, but there was no harm in being overcautious. Maya started on the front bumper. Eddie took out a dime, used it as screwdriver, and started on the back. Two minutes later, they were done.

She started to get back into her car. Eddie just stood there and watched her.

Maya stopped for a second. There were a million things she wanted to tell him—about Claire, about Joe, about everything. She opened her mouth, but she of all people should know that nothing good would come out of it. Not today. Not now.

"I love you, Eddie."

He used his hand to shade the sunset from his eyes. "I love you too, Maya."

She got into the car and started for Paterson.

Chapter 32

She found Hector's Dodge Ram in a parking lot of a high-rise on Fulton Street in Paterson.

Maya parked on the street and walked past the gate. She checked the Dodge Ram's doors, hoping one might be unlocked. No luck. She debated what to do. There was no way to find out where Hector was in the building. She also didn't know if he was with Isabella or not. It was too late to care about that. Her goal now was simple.

She would make Hector tell her where Isabella was.

So Maya got back in her car and waited. She kept her eyes on the high-rise entrance, shifting her gaze every once in a while to Hector's pickup in case he came toward it from another direction. Half an hour passed. She wished that she had some kind of Internet access—she wanted to see if Corey, as she expected, had started to post some details about EAC Pharmaceuticals—but her cell phone was smashed and the throwaways only had phone and texting service. She bet that he had. It would explain the attempted kidnapping. Corey had posted parts of the story, and now someone, probably a Burkett, was trying to clean up any loose ends.

Hector appeared at the door.

Maya already had the gun out of her holster. Hector lifted his key fob and pressed the button. The truck lights blinked, unlocking the door. Hector looked troubled, but then again, this was not a man who often looked relaxed or happy.

Maya's plan was pretty simple. Follow Hector to his car. Sneak up on him. Stick the gun in his face. Make him take her to Isabella.

It wasn't exactly a subtle plan, but there was no time for that.

But as Maya started toward him, coming toward him from the truck's rear, she realized that that might not be necessary.

Isabella walked out of the entrance too.

Bingo.

Maya ducked behind a car. So now what? Did she wait for Hector to leave before making her move? If she stuck a gun in Isabella's face with Hector still there, how would he react? Not well, she imagined. He had a mobile phone. He could call for help or shout or . . . mess it up somehow.

No, Maya would have to wait for him to leave.

Hector slid into his truck. Staying low, Maya moved a car closer. She kept the gun out of sight. She hoped that nobody would see her skulking about, but if they did, it would only arouse suspicion, not confirm it. She doubted that they would call the cops, but that was a chance she'd have to take.

Isabella veered to her left.

Wait, hold up.

Maya had thought Isabella had come out to wave good-bye or maybe have a last word with her brother through his truck window. But that wasn't the case.

Isabella was getting in on the passenger side of the truck.

Maya had two choices here. One, go back to her car and follow them. She would seriously consider doing just that, following the truck, but she was afraid that she'd lose them, and without her cell phone, she could no longer track them.

Two . . .

Enough.

She hurried to the truck, flung open the back door, slid in, and placed the muzzle of the gun at the back of Hector's head.

"Hands on the wheel." Then, pointing the gun at

Isabella before returning it to Hector's skull: "You too, Isabella. Hands on the dashboard."

Both stared at her in shock for a moment.

"Now."

They slowly moved their hands to where she wanted. Remembering how she had underestimated Isabella the last time they tangoed, Maya reached forward and grabbed Isabella's pocketbook. She peered inside.

Yep, there was pepper spray as well as her mobile phone.

Hector's mobile was in the cup holder. Maya grabbed it and threw it in Isabella's bag. She wondered whether Hector was carrying. Keeping the gun on him, she quickly patted him down in the obvious places. Nothing. She grabbed the truck's key and put it in the same bag too. She dropped the bag on the floor in front of her, and that was when she saw something that made her pull up.

It was a color that caught her eye . . .

"What do you want?" Isabella asked.

There was a pile of clothes on the floor behind the driver's seat.

"You can't just put a gun—"

"Shut up," Maya said. "If you so much as breathe, I'll blow Hector's head off."

There was a gray sweatshirt on the top of the pile. She pushed it away with her foot. And there, coming into view so clear she almost pulled the trigger in rage, was a too-familiar forest green button-down shirt.

"Talk," Maya said.

Isabella glared at her.

"Last chance."

"I have nothing to say."

Maya started talking instead. "Hector's about Joe's height and build. So I assume he played the part of Joe in your video? You let him into the house. He acted out the scene. Lily knew Hector. She would go to him willingly. Then you just got a videotape of Joe's face from . . ." That smile. The one he flashed on the video. "My God, was that from our wedding video?"

"We have nothing to say to you," Isabella said. "You won't kill us."

Enough. Gripping the gun harder, Maya brought the metal butt down hard on Hector's nose. The break was audible. Hector howled. Blood seeped through his fingers.

"Maybe I won't kill you," Maya said, "but the first bullet goes into his shoulder. Then his elbow. Then his knee. So start talking."

Isabella hesitated.

Maya reared back the gun and smacked Hector again, this time on the side of the ear. He groaned and fell to the side. Instinctively, Isabella took her hands off the dashboard, trying to reach her brother. Maya pistol-whipped her across the face, pulling up on the power enough so that it hurt but didn't cause any serious damage.

Still, Isabella was bleeding now too.

Then Maya pressed the muzzle of the gun on Hector's shoulder and started to squeeze the trigger.

"Wait!" Isabella shouted.

Maya didn't move.

"We did it because you killed Joe!"

Maya kept the muzzle in place. "Who told you that?"

"What difference does it make?"

"You think I killed my own husband," Maya said, nodding at the gun in her hand. "So why would you think I won't just shoot your brother?"

"It was our mother."

Hector was talking now.

"She said you killed Joe. She said we had to help prove it."

"Help how?"

Hector sat up. "You didn't kill him?"

"Help how, Hector?"

"Like you said. I dressed up as Joe. We let your nanny cam tape it. I took the SD card back to Farnwood. The family had hired a CGI Photoshop guy. An hour later, I came back to the house with it. Isabella put it in the frame."

"Wait," Maya said, "how did you know I had a nanny cam?"

Isabella made a scoffing noise. "Suddenly the day after the funeral you have a new digital frame already loaded up with pictures of your family? Please. You're the only mother I know that doesn't keep any pictures of her daughter around. You don't even hang up her artwork. So when I saw that frame—how stupid do you think I am?"

Maya remembered now how good Isabella had been on those videos, always smiling and engaged. "So you, what, told your mother about it?"

Isabella didn't bother answering.

"And I assume it was her idea for you to hit me with the pepper spray."

"I didn't know what you'd be like after you saw it. I was just supposed to get the SD card from you. So you couldn't show it to other people."

They wanted her isolated.

"If you showed it to me," Isabella continued, "I was supposed to pretend I didn't see it."

"Why?"

"Why do you think?"

But it was obvious. "I was supposed to slip up, start questioning my sanity . . ."

Maya's voice drifted off. She stared straight past them now, straight through the truck's windshield. Isabella and Hector looked at her, then turned to see what had captured her attention.

Standing there, directly in front of Hector's truck, was Shane.

*   *   *

"If you move," Maya said to Hector and Isabella, "I'll shoot you dead."

She opened the back door, got out, and reached back to take Isabella's pocketbook with her. Shane just stood there and waited for her. His eyes looked red.

"What are you doing?" Shane asked.

"They set me up," Maya said.

"What?"

"Hector wore Joe's clothes. Then someone Photoshopped his face from a video."

"So Joe is . . . ?"

"Dead. Yes. How did you find me, Shane?"

"GPS."

"I don't have my phone with me."

"I put trackers on both your cars," Shane said.

"Why did you do that?"

"Because you haven't been acting rationally," he said. "Even before that nanny cam thing. You have to see that."

Maya said nothing.

"So yeah, I was the one who called Dr. Wu. I thought maybe he could get you back into therapy. And yeah, I put the trackers on your car in case you needed help. Then when Kierce contacted me about those ballistics tests and you wouldn't answer my calls . . ."

She looked back at the pickup truck. No movement.

Deep breaths . . .

"There's something I need to tell you, Shane."

"About the ballistics test."

She shook her head.

Flex, relax . . .

"About that day over Al Qa'im."

Shane looked confused. "What about it?"

She opened her mouth, closed it.

"Maya?"

"We had already lost men. Good men. I wasn't going to let us lose any more."

Her eyes starting welling up.

"I know," Shane said. "That was our mission."

"And then we spotted that SUV. And I'm listening to our guys pleading for help, and that SUV is bearing down on them. We set the target. We called it in. But they wouldn't let us engage."

"Right," Shane said, "they wanted to make sure they weren't civilians."

Maya nodded.

"So we waited," Shane said.

"While those boys pleaded for their lives."

The side of Shane's mouth twitched. "It was tough listening to that. I know. But we did what was right. We waited. We followed protocol. It wasn't our fault that those civilians died. When we got confirmation—"

Maya shook her head. "We never got confirmation."

Shane stopped and looked at her.

"I turned your signal off."

"What . . . what are you . . . ?"

"JOC radioed back for us to hold off."

He shook his head. "What are you talking about?"

"They didn't give us the go-ahead. They believed that at least one of the people in the SUV was a civilian, possibly underage. They radioed that it was only about fifty-fifty that the people in the SUV were the enemy."

Shane's breathing had grown ragtag. "But I heard—"

"No, you didn't, Shane. I relayed it to you, remember?"

He just stood there.

"You think what's on the audiotape would be bad for us because we sounded celebratory after we destroyed the target. But that wasn't what Corey had on me. He had the radio call telling me that there could be civilians in that SUV."

"And you shot anyway," Shane said.

"Yes."

"Why?"

"Because I didn't care about the civilians," Maya said. "I cared about our boys."

"Jesus, Maya."

"I made a choice. I wasn't going to lose another one of ours. Not on my watch. Not if I could help it. And if civilians died, if there was collateral damage, so be it. I didn't care anymore. That's the truth. You think I have these horrible flashbacks because I feel guilty about those dead civilians. It's just the opposite, Shane. I have them because I *don't* feel guilty. Those deaths don't haunt me. What haunts me, Shane, what lingers inside me, is the knowledge that if I was up there again, I would do the exact same thing."

Now Shane had tears in his eyes.

"So you don't have to be a shrink to figure it out. I'm forced to relive what happened every night—but I can never change the outcome. That's why those flashbacks won't ever leave me, Shane. Every night, I'm back on that chopper. Every night, I try to find a way to save those soldiers."

"And every night, you kill those civilians again," Shane said. "Oh Christ . . ."

He stepped toward her, arms open, but she shook him off. There was no way she could handle that. She quickly turned around and looked behind her. Isabella and Hector still hadn't moved.

It was time to get going.

"What did Kierce tell you, Shane?"

"Joe and Claire were killed by the same gun," Shane said. "You knew that already, right? Kierce told you."

Maya nodded.

"But you didn't tell me, Maya."

She didn't bother replying.

"You told me everything except the results of that ballistics test."

"Shane . . ."

"I figured that you were working on your own to find Claire's killer. The cops were useless. I figured that you came up with something."

Maya kept her eyes on the pickup truck. It wasn't so she could keep an eye on Hector and Isabella so much as that she couldn't face Shane.

"You gave me that bullet *before* Joe was shot," Shane said. "You asked me to see if it came from the same weapon that murdered Claire. It matched. You wouldn't tell me how you got it. And now I know the same weapon killed Joe too. How can that be?"

"Only one way," Maya said.

Shane shook his head, but he already knew. She met his eye and held it.

"I killed him," Maya said. "I killed Joe."

Chapter 33

Maya wore the baseball cap and drove Hector's pickup truck. She headed to Farnwood via the back gate and made her way to the main house. Darkness had fallen. Security was still around, but it was pretty lax. No one questioned or bothered to stop the familiar Dodge Ram.

Shane was holding Hector and Isabella to make sure that they didn't warn anyone of her arrival at the mansion. Using the throwaway cell phone, Maya called Leather and Lace and asked for Lulu.

"I can't help you anymore," Lulu said.

"I think you can."

After she hung up, Maya parked to the side of the main house. The grounds were dark. She crept to the back and tried the kitchen door. It was unlocked. The house was empty and still. No lights had been kept on. Maya moved toward the fireplace and paused. Then she sat alone in the front parlor and waited. Time passed. Her eyes adjusted to the dark.

She saw the past all in snap flashes, but it was the first one, the opening of the gun safe, that changed everything. She had been overseas and home for the first time since Claire's death. She visited the gravesite. Joe had driven her. He had been acting odd, but that really hadn't set her off much. She was starting to wonder about him though, about how little time they had actually spent together, what with the whirlwind romance, her service, his work, but again that wouldn't have meant anything to her.

Was she thinking that she really didn't know the man very well? No. She only thought that now, in hindsight.

It was opening the gun safe that changed everything.

Maya was meticulous when it came to her guns. She kept them sparkling clean, and so the moment she took out her Smith and Wesson 686s, she knew something for certain.

One of them—the one she kept in the hidden compartment—had been used.

Joe had reiterated when she'd come home how he hated guns, that he had no interest in going with her to the range, that he really wished that she didn't keep them in the house.

In short, he doth protest too much.

It was odd, looking back on it, why a man who had

no interest in guns would still want to have his fingerprint in the safe database. "Just in case," Joe had said.
"You never know."

There are moments in life when everything changes.
It was again like one of those optical illusions. You see
only one thing, and then you shift something just a little, and everything changes. That was how she felt,
holding this gun that someone who clearly didn't know
what they were doing had tried to clean.

It was a gut punch. It was a betrayal of the worst kind.
Sleeping with the enemy—she felt a fool and worse. And
yet it also made terrible, horrible sense somehow.

She knew.

Even as she went into denial, she knew that this gun,
her own gun, had killed her sister. She knew it even
before she went to the range and shot it and brought
the bullet to Shane. She knew even before she talked
Shane into secretly testing it against the .38 found in
Claire's skull.

Joe had killed Claire.

Still there was a chance she was wrong. There was a
chance a clever hit man had broken into the safe, used
her gun, put it back. There was a chance it wasn't Joe at
all. That was why she switched the two Smith and Wesson 686s, putting the one Joe had taken from the safe's
hidden compartment for out-of-state purchases and
switching it with the one registered in New Jersey that
she kept in plain view. She made sure none of her other
guns were loaded or had ammunition . . .

Only the Smith and Wesson in the hidden compartment.

She started digging through Joe's stuff and intentionally left clues that she had done so. Maya wanted him to know that she was onto him. To see if he would react. To get enough information to make him tell her why he had killed Claire.

Yes, Kierce was right. It was Maya who called Joe that night, not the other way around.

"I know what you did," she had said.

"What are you talking about?"

"I have proof."

She told Joe to meet her in that spot in Central Park. She arrived early and cased the area. She spotted two street punks—she would later learn their names were Emilio Rodrigo and Fred Katen—walking past Bethesda Fountain. She could see from the way Rodrigo moved that he was carrying a weapon.

Perfect. Fall guys who could never be convicted.

When they met up, she gave Joe every chance.

"Why did you kill Claire?"

"I thought you said you have proof, Maya. You have nothing."

"I will find proof. I won't rest. I will make your life hell."

It was then that Joe pulled out the loaded Smith and Wesson 686 he'd found in the safe's hidden compartment. He was smiling at her. That was what she thought anyway. It was probably too dark to see that and her eyes were drawn to the gun. But right now, as she relived what had happened, she could swear Joe was smiling.

He aimed the gun at the center of her chest.

Whatever she had thought before—all that talk about what she knew—it fled out the window at the sight of the man she'd pledged to love forever pointing a loaded gun at her. She had known, and yet she hadn't believed it, accepted it, not really, it was all a mistake, and somehow, forcing his hand like this would show her what she had missed, how she got it wrong.

Joe, the father of her child, wasn't a murderer. She hadn't shared her bed and her heart with a killer who tortured and murdered her sister. There was still a chance that somehow it could all be explained away.

Until he pulled the trigger.

Now, sitting in that foyer in the dark, Maya closed her eyes.

She could still remember the look on Joe's face when the gun didn't go off. He pulled the trigger again. Then again.

"I removed the firing pin."

"What?"

"I took the pin off the hammer so it couldn't fire."

"It doesn't matter, Maya. You'll never prove I killed her."

"You're right."

That was when Maya took out her other Smith and Wesson, the same one Joe had used to kill Claire, and shot him three times. She intentionally missed killing him with the first two. She was an expert markswoman.

Most street-punk robbers were not. So death from a single shot would be too obvious.

Kierce: *"The first bullet hit your husband's left shoulder. The second hit landed in the right tangent of his clavicle."*

She'd worn a trench coat and gloves she'd bought for cash at a Salvation Army store. That was where any powder residue would end up. She ripped them off and threw them in a bin over the wall and onto Fifth Avenue. They wouldn't be found, but if they were and someone decided to test them for powder residue, big deal—they couldn't be traced to her. She bent down now and hugged Joe as he died, making sure to get plenty of his blood on her shirt. She put both guns in her handbag. Then she stumbled back toward Bethesda Fountain.

"Help . . . please . . . someone . . . my husband's . . ."

No one searched her. Why would they? She was a victim. At first, everyone was concerned with her possible injuries and finding the killers. The confusion paid off. She had been prepared to dump the handbag somewhere—there was nothing in it but the weapons—but in the end, there had been no need. She just held on to them and eventually took them home. She dumped the murder weapon in a river. She put the firing pin back on the hammer of the registered Smith and Wesson and put it back in the safe. That was the one Kierce took and tested.

Maya knew that the ballistics test would confirm her "innocence" and confuse the police. The same gun had killed Joe and Claire. Maya had a rock-solid alibi for Claire's death—she was serving overseas—ergo there was no way she could be the killer of either. She didn't like the idea of putting two innocents—Emilio Rodrigo and Fred Katen—through the police rigmarole, but one of them had indeed been carrying. She also knew that, with her own testimony about them wearing ski masks, the charges would never stick. They would never go down for the crime.

Compared to what she had done in the past, the collateral damage to those two was negligible.

The case was all an unsolvable mess, which is what she wanted. Claire had been murdered, and her murderer had been punished. The end. It was justice of sorts. Maya didn't know everything, but she knew enough. She and her daughter would be safe.

And then that nanny cam video changed everything yet again.

From her seat in the foyer, Maya heard the car pull up. She stayed in the chair. The front door opened. She could hear Judith talking about how boring the event had been. Neil was with her. So was Caroline. The three walked in together.

Judith flipped on the lights and gasped out loud.

Maya just sat there.

"My God," Judith said, "you scared me half to death. What are you doing here, Maya?"

"Occam's razor," Maya said.

"Pardon me?"

"'Among competing hypotheses, the one with the fewest assumptions should be selected.'" Maya smiled. "In short, the simplest answer is usually the most likely. Joe didn't survive the shooting. You just wanted me to believe that."

Judith looked at her two children and then turned back to Maya.

"You set up that nanny cam stunt, Judith. You told Rosa's family that I killed Joe, but there was no way to prove it. So you wanted to shake the tree a little."

Judith didn't bother denying it. "And what if I did?" Her voice was pure ice. "There's no law against trying to capture a killer, is there?"

"None that I'm aware of," Maya agreed. "I had an idea right from the start, of course. You're manipulative. You spent your career doing mind tricks."

"They were psychological experiments."

"Semantics. But I saw Joe die. I knew that he couldn't be alive."

"Ah, but it was dark," Judith said. "You could have been mistaken. You tricked Joe in some way. Got him to go to that spot in the park. He could have tricked you back. Replaced your bullets with blanks. Something like that."

"But he didn't."

Neil cleared his throat. "What do you want, Maya?"

Maya ignored him, kept her eyes on Judith. "Even if I didn't buy that he was alive, even if I didn't crack under the pressure and confess, you knew I'd react."

"Yes."

"I'd figure that someone was screwing with me. I'd start looking into it. Maybe I'd misstep and you could nail me for the murder. I'd trip up somehow. Plus, you all needed to find out what I knew. And you all played your parts for Mommy's little psychological experiment. Caroline fed me those lies about thinking her brothers were alive and that Kierce was on the family payroll. Complete fabrications. But it was a lot of things coming at me. The nanny cam, the missing clothes, the phone calls. Anyone would start to question their sanity. So I did. I would have to have been insane to not at least entertain the idea that I was losing my mind."

Judith smiled at her. "Why are you here, Maya?"

"I have a question for you, Judith."

She waited.

"How did you know I killed Joe?"

"So you admit it."

"Sure. But how did you know it?" Maya looked over at Neil, then at Caroline. "Did she tell you how, Caroline?"

Caroline frowned and turned to her mother.

"I just knew," Judith said. "A mother knows."

"No, Judith. You knew I killed him because you knew I had a motive."

Caroline said, "What is she talking about?"

"Joe murdered my sister."

"That's not true," Caroline said, her voice that of a petulant child.

"Joe killed Claire," Maya said. "And your mother knew."

"Mom?"

Judith's eyes were blazing. "Claire stole from us," she said.

Caroline: "Mom . . ."

"More than that, Claire tried to destroy us all—the entire Burkett name and fortune. All Joe did was try to stop her. He tried to reason with her."

"He tortured her," Maya said.

"He panicked. That I will admit. She wouldn't tell him what she'd done. She wouldn't give him back the information. I'm not condoning his behavior, but your sister started this. She tried to destroy this family. You, Maya, should understand. She was the enemy. You attack the enemy with full force. You fight back with whatever you have. You never show mercy."

Maya felt the rage, but she wouldn't let it consume her. "You stupid, evil woman."

"Hey." It was Neil, coming to his mother's defense. "That's enough."

"You don't get it, do you, Neil? You think Joe was protecting the family fortune? That it was about the EAC Pharmaceuticals stuff?"

Neil looked at his mother in a way that confirmed that Maya was right. Maya almost burst out laughing. She turned to Judith.

"That's what Joe told you, right? Claire had gotten the goods on your pharmaceutical scam. And with everything coming down now around you, you, Neil, no longer trusted Mommy's plan. You panicked and sent those kidnappers after me. You wanted to see what I knew. And you told the guys about my mental state. You told them that if they said Joe was waiting for me, I would, what, crumble?"

Neil stared at her with undisguised hatred. "You'd weaken at least."

Judith closed her eyes. "Stupid," she muttered.

"'Joe is waiting.' That's what the guy said. And that was your mistake, Neil. You see, if Joe was behind it, if Joe had sent guys after me, he would have made sure they knew that I was armed. Those guys didn't."

"Maya?"

It was Judith.

"You killed my son."

"He killed my sister."

"He's dead. He can't be prosecuted. But three witnesses heard your confession. We'll make a case."

"You don't understand," Maya said. "Joe didn't just kill my sister. He killed Theo Mora—"

"That was a hazing incident gone wrong."

"He killed Tom Douglass."

"You have no proof of that."

"And he killed his own brother."

Everyone stopped then. For a few seconds, there was dead silence, that kind of heavy silence like even the furniture was holding its breath.

"Mom?" It was Caroline. "That's not true, is it?"

"Of course it's not," Judith said.

"It's true," Maya said. "Joe killed Andrew."

Caroline turned to Judith. "Mom?"

"Don't listen to her. It's a lie."

But there was a quake in Judith's voice now.

"I visited Christopher Swain today, Judith. He told me that Andrew was cracking, that on that boat, Andrew told Joe that he was going to turn them all in for what they did to Theo. Then Andrew went up alone to the top deck. And Joe followed him."

Silence.

Caroline started crying. Neil looked at his mother as though pleading for help.

"That doesn't mean Joe killed him," Judith said. "You may believe it does in some horrible fantasy in your diseased head, but you yourself told me what happened. You told me the truth."

Maya nodded. "Andrew jumped. He committed suicide."

"Yes."

"And Joe saw it. That was what he told me."

"Yes, of course."

"Except that's not what happened. Joe and Andrew went up on that deck at one A.M."

"That's right."

"But nobody reported Andrew missing until the next morning." Maya tilted her head. "If Joe had seen his brother jump, wouldn't he have sounded the alarm right then and there?"

Judith's eyes went wide as though she'd taken a punch to the gut. Maya saw it now. Judith had been in denial too. She knew, yet she hadn't known. It was amazing how much we can blind ourselves to such obvious truths.

Judith dropped to her knees.

"Mom?" Neil asked.

Judith started to cry like a wounded animal. "It can't be true."

"It is true," Maya said, standing up now. "Joe killed Theo Mora. He killed Andrew. He killed Claire. He killed Tom Douglass. How many more did he kill, Judith? He took a baseball bat to some kid's head in the eighth grade. He tried to burn a kid alive in high school over a girl. Joseph Sr. saw it. That's why he gave control of the company to Neil."

Judith just kept shaking her head.

"You raised and protected and nurtured a killer."

"And you married him."

Maya nodded. "I did."

"You really think he could have fooled you?"

"I don't think. I know it."

Judith, still on her knees, looked up at her. "You executed him."

Maya said nothing.

"It wasn't self-defense. You could have brought him in."

"Yes."

"But you chose to murder him instead."

"You would have tried to protect him again, Judith. I couldn't have that." Maya took a step toward the front door. Neil and Caroline moved backward. "But it will all come out now."

"If it does," Judith said, "you'll go to jail for life."

"Yeah, maybe. But the EAC Pharmaceuticals thing will come out now too. It's all over now. There's nothing left."

"Wait," Judith said. She stood.

Maya stopped.

"Maybe we can make a deal."

Neil said, "Mom, what are you talking about?"

"Hush." She looked up at Maya. "You wanted justice for your sister. You got it. Now we all come together."

"Mom?"

"Just listen to me." She put her hands on Maya's shoulders. "We blame the EAC Pharmaceuticals scandal on Joe. We suggest that maybe that was what led to his murder. Do you see? Nobody has to know the truth. Justice has been served. And maybe . . . maybe you were right, Maya. I . . . I'm Eve. I raised Cain to kill Abel. I should have known. I don't know if I can live with myself or if I can ever make amends, but maybe, if we all just keep our heads, I can still save my other two children. And I can save you too, Maya."

"It's too late for deals, Judith," Maya said.

"She's right, Mom."

It was Neil. Maya turned to him and saw that he was pointing a gun in her direction. "But I have a better idea," he said to Maya. "You stole Hector's truck. You broke into our house. You are, I'm sure, armed. You admitted killing Joe and now you are going to kill us. Only, I shoot you in time and save us. We still pin the EAC scandal on Joe, but now we don't spend our lives looking over our shoulders."

Neil glanced at his mother. Judith smiled. Then Caroline nodded. The whole family had come together.

Neil fired the gun three times.

Poetic, Maya thought. That was how many times she'd shot Joe.

Maya collapsed to the ground, arms and legs spread. She was on her back. She couldn't move. She expected to feel cold, but that wasn't the case. The voices came to her in quick snatches:

"No one will ever know . . ."

"Check her pockets . . ."

"She doesn't have a gun . . ."

Maya smiled and looked toward the fireplace.

"What's she smiling about . . . ?"

"What's that above the fireplace? It looks like . . ."

"Oh no . . ."

Maya's eyes blinked and then closed. She waited for the sounds—the copters, the gunfire, the screaming—to begin their assault. But they didn't come. Not this time. Not ever again.

There was darkness and silence and then, finally, peace.

Chapter 34

The elevator doors are about to close when I hear a woman call out my name.

"Shane?"

I stick my hand out to hold the elevator. "Hello, Eileen."

She rushes in, smiling, and kisses me on the cheek. "Been a long time."

"Too long."

"You look good, Shane."

"So do you, Eileen."

"I heard you had a knee replacement. Are you okay?"

I wave off her concern. We both smile.

It's a good day.

"How are your kids?" I ask.

"Great. Did I tell you Missy is teaching at Vassar?"

"She was always a smart one. Like her mother."

Eileen puts her hand on my arm and leaves it there. We are both still single, though we'd had our moment way back when. Enough said there. We ride the rest of the way in silence.

By now you've all seen the video from that nanny cam Maya put above the Farnwood fireplace—they used to call it "going viral" when something got that big—so I'll tell you the rest of what I know.

That night, after Maya convinced me to keep an eye on Hector and Isabella, she called someone who worked with Corey the Whistle. I never learned the person's name. No one did. They set up a live feed using the nanny cam. In short, the world was able to watch everything that went on in the Burkett house that night. They watched it live. Corey the Whistle was a pretty big deal already—this was in the days when that kind of transparency was in its infancy—but after that night, his site became one of the biggest on the web. I obviously had a personal beef against it for putting our mission up. But in the end, Corey Rudzinski used the publicity Maya got him that night to do a lot of good. Scared, wounded, powerless people who'd been afraid to tell the truth suddenly had the courage to come forward. Corrupt governments and businesses toppled.

So in the end, that had been Maya's idea: expose the truth for the world to see in live time. It was just that nobody expected that ending.

A murder right before your eyes.

The elevator doors open.

"After you," I say to Eileen.

"Thank you, Shane."

As I follow her down the corridor, still limping with the new knee, I can feel my heart swelling in my chest. I admit that as I get older, I get more emotional. I'm more prone to cry at life's good moments.

When I turn the corner and enter the hospital room, the first person I see is Daniel Walker. He's thirty-nine years old now and stands six four. He works three floors up as a radiologist. Next to him is his sister, Alexa. She's thirty-seven with a little one of her own. Alexa does digital design, though I don't really know exactly what that is.

They both greet me with hugs and kisses.

Eddie is there too, and his wife, Selina. Eddie was widowed nearly ten years before he remarried. Selina is a wonderful woman, and I'm happy that Eddie found happiness after Claire. Eddie and I shake hands and do that guy thing where we half hug.

Then I look at the bed where Lily is holding her new baby girl.

Ka-pow. My heart explodes in my chest.

I don't know if Maya went to the Burketts that night knowing that she was going to die. She left her gun in the car. Some theorize she did that so the Burketts wouldn't be able to claim self-defense. Maybe. Maya left me a letter that she wrote the night before her death. She left Eddie one too. She wanted Eddie to raise Lily if anything happened to her. Eddie did that in spectacular fashion. She wrote that she hoped Daniel and Alexa would be good older siblings to her daughter. They were that and then some. I was to be Lily's godfather, Eileen the godmother. Maya wanted us to stay in her life. Eileen and I did that, but with Eddie, Daniel, Alexa, and then Selina, I don't think Lily needed us.

I stayed—I still stay—because I love Lily with a ferocity a man usually saves only for his own child. And maybe I stay for something else. Lily is like her mother. She looks like her mother. She acts like her mother. Being around her, doing things for her—stay with me here—is the only way I get to keep Maya with me. That may be selfish, I don't know. But I miss Maya. Sometimes, like when I used to drop Lily off after a baseball game or movie, I would almost feel like I was rushing somewhere to tell Maya all about the day and assure her that Lily was doing well.

Silly, right?

From her bed, Lily looks up and smiles at me. It is her mother's smile, though I rarely saw it beam like this.

"Look, Shane!"

Lily doesn't remember her mother. That kills me.

"You done good, kid," I say.

People talk about Maya's crimes, of course. She did kill civilians. She did, whatever justification you might give, execute a man. Had she survived, she would have gone to prison. No question about it. So maybe she chose death over life in prison. Maybe she chose to make sure the Burketts went down and couldn't be in her child's life over rotting in a cell and taking the risk. I don't know anymore.

But Maya claimed to me that she never felt guilty about what she did overseas. I don't know about that either. Those horrible flashbacks tore through her every night. People who feel no remorse aren't haunted by their actions, are they?

She was a good person. I don't care what they say.

Eddie told me once that he sometimes felt as though death was a part of Maya, that death followed her. It's an odd way of putting it. But I think I get it. After what happened in Iraq, Maya couldn't silence the voices. Death had stayed with her. She tried to rush forward, but Death would tap her on the shoulder. It wouldn't leave. I think maybe Maya saw that. I think, more than anything else, she wanted to make sure death didn't follow Lily.

Maya didn't leave a letter for Lily to open at a certain age or anything like that. She hadn't told Eddie how to raise her or why she had chosen him. She just knew. She knew that he would be the right choice. And he was. Years ago, Eddie asked me for my take on what to tell Lily about her biological parents and when. Neither of us had a clue. Maya often said that kids didn't come with instruction manuals. She had left it up to us. She trusted that we would do what was best for Lily when the time came.

Eventually, when Lily was old enough to understand, we told her.

The ugly truth, we decided, was better than the fanciful lie.

Dean Vanech, Lily's husband, bounces into the room and kisses his wife.

"Hey, Shane."

"Congrats, Dean."

"Thanks."

Dean is military. I bet Maya would like that. The happy couple sit on the bed and marvel at their child the way new parents are supposed to. I look back at Eddie. He has tears in his eyes. I nod.

"Grandpa," I say to him.

Eddie can't answer. He deserves this moment. He gave Lily a good childhood, and I'm grateful. I will always be there for him. I will always be there for Daniel and Alexa. I will always be there for Lily.

Maya knew that, of course.

"Shane?"

"Yes, Lily."

"Would you like to hold her?"

"I don't know. I'm kind of clumsy."

Lily won't have any of that. "You'll do just fine."

Bossing me around. Like her mother.

I come to the bed and she hands me the baby, making sure to put the tiny head in the crook of my arm. I stare down at her in something approaching awe.

"We named her Maya," Lily says.

I nod now because I can't speak.

Maya—my Maya, the old Maya—and I saw a lot of people die. We used to talk about how dead was dead. That was it, Maya used to say. You die. It's over. But right now, I'm not sure. Right now, I look down and I think maybe Maya and I got that one wrong.

She's here. I know it.

ACKNOWLEDGMENTS

The author (that would be me) wishes to thank the following: Rick Friedman, Linda Fairstein, Kevin Marcy, Pete Miscia, Air Force Lieutenant Colonel T. Mark McCurley, Diane Discepolo, Rick Kronberg, Ben Sevier, Christine Ball, Jamie Knapp, Carrie Swetonic, Stephanie Kelly, Selina Walker, Lisa Erbach Vance, Eliane Benisti, and Françoise Triffaux. I'm sure they made mistakes, but let's go easy on them.

The author (still me) also wants to acknowledge Marian Barford, Tom Douglass, Eileen Finn, Heather Howell, Fred Katen, Roger Kierce, Neil Kornfeld, Melissa Lee, Mary McLeod, Julian Rubinstein, Corey Rudzinski, Kitty Shum, and Dr. Christopher Swain. These people (or their loved ones) made generous contributions to charities of my choosing in return for having their names appear in the novel. If you'd like to participate in the future, visit HarlanCoben.com or email giving@harlancoben.com for details.

Finally, I am ridiculously proud to be a USO tour

veteran. Several humble servicemen and servicewomen spoke freely on the condition that I not list their names here, but they did ask me to acknowledge their many brave fellow vets (and their families) who still suffer psychological injuries from volunteering to be part of a military that's been at war for more than a decade.